SOJOURNER OF
WARREN'S CAMP

Sojourner of Warren's Camp

Joseph Dorris

iUniverse, Inc.
Bloomington

Sojourner of Warren's Camp

iUniverse books may be ordered through booksellers or by contacting:

iUniverse
1663 Liberty Drive
Bloomington, IN 47403
www.iuniverse.com
1-800-Authors (1-800-288-4677)

ISBN: 978-1-4620-6347-5 (sc)
ISBN: 978-1-4620-6349-9 (hc)
ISBN: 978-1-4620-6348-2 (e)

Printed in the United States of America

iUniverse rev. date: 11/16/2011

In Memory of Kippy

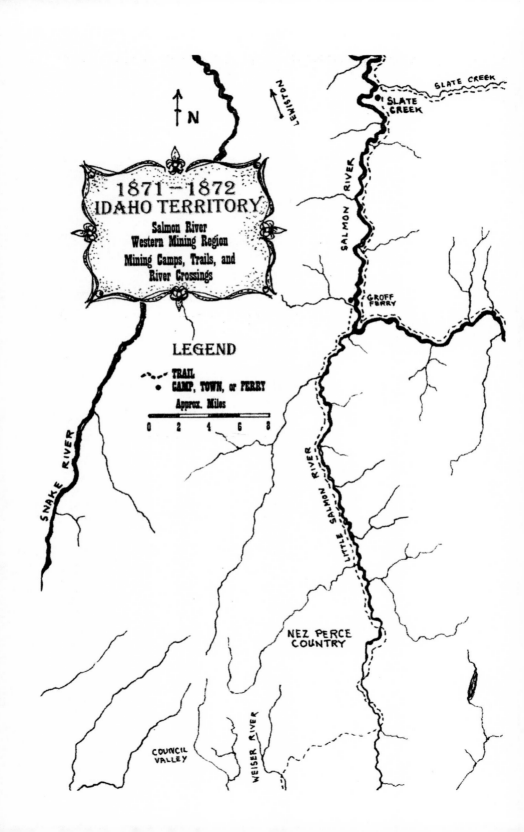

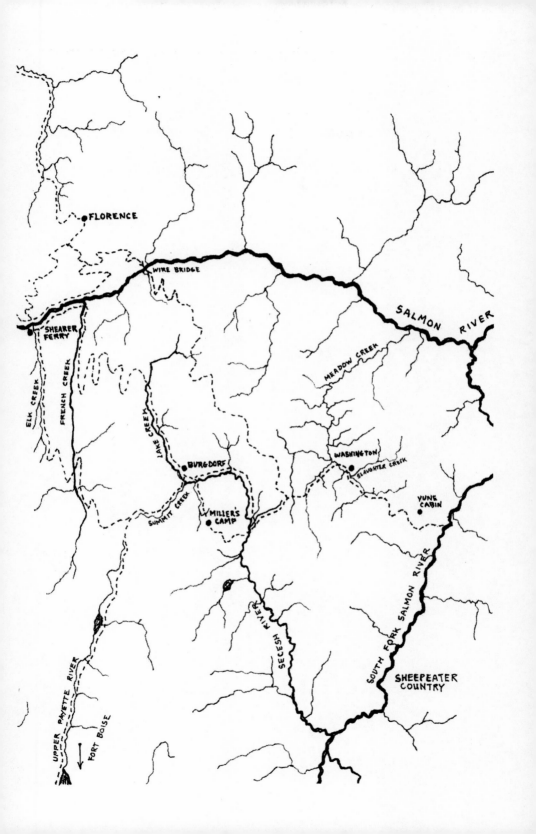

THE TRAIL IN

CHAPTER 1

Charles Chambers sat his horse, pausing a moment for his son and the mule he led to catch up. Below him, fingers of green meadows crisscrossed by ribbons of silvery water reached out from between stands of conifers. A small herd of elk with a bull, its new antlers shrouded in velvet, browsed near dark spruce. Geese and ducks spotted the ponds and quiet streams. Tree-covered slopes with lingering snowbanks rose beyond, catching the last rays of sunlight in the gathering shadows.

"That's the Mulpah down below. Least that's what the Nez Perce Indians call it—the Little Salmon River. It runs straight north to the main Salmon." Charles adjusted his hat and pushed back his sandy hair.

"It's hard to believe, Pa," replied Samuel. He had brought his horse and the mule up.

A small river meandered through the meadows below. Snow lay scattered beneath the trees, and here, where they had crossed over the divide from Council Valley, it lay in deep, rotten drifts.

"We've gone far enough for the day." Charles swung his lanky frame down. "If we get an early start tomorrow, we can make it to the main Salmon. Within the week, we should be in Warren's camp."

Charles watched as his son dismounted and began loosening the cinch to his saddle. Samuel was slightly built with blond hair and striking blue eyes. He was still fourteen, but in many ways already a man. Charles had doubted his decision to bring the boy, but he had realized that even if Samuel sometimes lacked the strength, he had the heart to do a man's job. The boy never complained. He looked for what needed to be done and did it.

Charles recalled his own youth. He had had to grow up fast on the frontier. He had lost his own parents early. A brother had been killed during the Indian Wars. He thought he had left it all behind when he had met and married Mary Travis. They built themselves a small farm in central Iowa, and soon after, Samuel was born and then Emma and Jeremiah. Those were magical days until the Southern Uprising. He went to war when Samuel was not quite four. He often regretted those years—not for fighting in the war but for not being able to see his family grow. He felt a wash of emptiness. Both Emma and Jeremiah had died from the flu. He yet had a young daughter, Elizabeth, born after the war.

He watched as his son struggled to remove the saddle from the black gelding. Spooky—Samuel had named him. The boy heaved the saddle to the ground, catching his look.

"It ain't gettin' any lighter, Pa." He cracked a grin.

Charles smiled. Samuel's high spirits during their journey had been uplifting.

He pulled his own saddle from the mahogany bay he had brought home from the war—not much more than a colt back then. Black mane and tail, black socks melding into a red, well-muscled body, the gelding had been destined to be a cavalry horse; however, the war ended, and he took him back to Iowa. Buster—Jeremiah had named him.

He felt unease, reflecting on the families back home. Mary had not been able to keep up their farm when he had left for the war. She found it easier to take the children and return to her parents' farm. And she should have. Her brother, Jake, had also heeded the call to war. Together, it was safer for the two families. But after the war, life had become strained. Charles had always felt like the outsider. Although Jake and his wife and children had the original cabin, he and Mary were but awkward visitors crammed into her parents' home. To make matters worse, Jake came home missing a leg, a victim to a Minié ball. They struggled to get the farm to produce enough to feed the two families.

"We could go farther," Samuel said. He had begun loosening the mule's packs.

"Good spot here for a camp," Charles replied. "Farther down we might be inviting trouble. This is Nez Perce country."

He helped Samuel lift the packs to the ground. They had done well. None of their gear had been lost, and they had recently purchased staples at Fort Boise—sugar, salt, flour. Packing them in would conserve the meager grubstake he had put together from what little cash he had saved and from what he had borrowed from Jake. He expected prices to be at least triple in Warren's camp.

They picketed the horses and mule. If the Nez Perce found the animals wandering, they would consider them their own. A few days past, they had come across an Indian family fishing along the Weiser River, but the family had fled into the brush when they spotted them. They seemed rather poor, although they were dressed in heavy skins, an indication they were skilled hunters. Their lodges appeared to be not much more than brush piles with a few skins stretched over them. Charles assumed they were a band of Weisers and assured Samuel they were harmless. Otherwise, since leaving Iowa, they had seen only a few Indians camped around the settlements. But now he realized they were in the heart of a Nez Perce hunting ground, and it was likely some bands roamed the river below.

He ran a line between trees for a tarpaulin. The weather looked good, but experience told him they could be in rain or snow by morning, especially at this elevation. They had camped just below the divide between Council Valley and the Little Salmon River drainage. The sun had dropped below the horizon, now catching only the highest peaks and throwing the snow and greening meadows into purple shadows.

Unlike the Snake River plain, dark green conifers mixed with bright green aspens covered the hillsides. The trail that crossed the plain had been hot and dry, running through sagebrush and barren and broken basalt. Water had been scarce, and they had been forced to work their way to the river each evening. Only after they turned up the Weiser and had followed it for a couple of days did they finally come back into timber.

The odors from burning wood and sizzling venison mingled in the evening air. Two days ago, Samuel had killed a young doe. Charles joined him at the fire. "Smells good."

"Here, Pa, have some." Samuel handed him a plate with a thick piece. He then cut a piece for himself.

Charles chewed a sliver, enjoying the rich flavor. "Tastes mighty fine, son."

Samuel nodded but did not reply, his mouth full. Charles noticed. He could not help but realize that his son was still a skinny boy, no matter what he ate, much like himself before he began shooting up in his own teenage years and began putting on muscle and weight. He could not help but wonder how Samuel kept going all day without an ounce of fat on his body.

Charles paused. Now that they neared their destination, he could not withold his thoughts. "I guess we'll know in a few days, if I'm not making the biggest mistake of my life."

Samuel flashed a look.

"All this could be nothing but a wild-goose chase, son. We could end up no better off than when we left Iowa."

"But the way you tell of what O'Riley said, all we got to do is scoop up the gold and put it in sacks, remember?"

"Not quite." He managed a laugh. Samuel stretched what he had said, but since telling the story, the boy had been completely caught up with the quest. "Even if we find the ledge and it isn't dug up, it won't be that easy. It's lode gold."

"You said O'Riley marked it. We'll find it."

"He also said you had to pert near be standin' on it to see it." Charles waved toward the hills. "I've been studying this country. All the ridges look the same, and the heavy timber and brush make it near impossible to see a thing."

Samuel quit chewing. "Hey, Pa, you're the one who's supposed to be sure about this."

Charles tried to lessen his doubts. "I 'spect you're right. I keep second-guessing myself. O'Riley wouldn't have left it to get his brother if it hadn't been good." He shook his head. "I can't begin to feel how he must have felt when he got home and found his brother had been killed at war." He sliced off another piece of venison. "He wouldn't talk when I first met him. He didn't seem to care if he lived or died, just so long as he could kill Rebs. It was only after a few scrapes together that he opened up. Then he told me about the ledge, but by then he just wanted the war to be over so he could return to look for it. He wanted me with him when he did. He had decided his brother would have wanted as much. So I got to believe it's still there."

He had told Samuel the story before. The man he fought alongside, Kevin O'Riley, had been grubstaked by his brother. O'Riley had agreed to return for his brother if he struck pay dirt. He had first tried the Clearwater and then Florence, two new strikes in Idaho Territory. When news reached him that James Warren had discovered gold south of the Salmon River, he headed there. He and others eventually located a good placer and began working it. At some point, while O'Riley had been hunting, he struck a rich ledge, and as he had promised, he left camp to return for his brother.

"Maybe it was lucky you and O'Riley got to be friends."

"For sure. We wouldn't be sitting here otherwise," Charles said. "Funny how things work out. I always figured after O'Riley got wounded, he had healed up and headed back on his own to find the gold. I didn't blame him. Surprised me to blazes last winter when I found out he had died."

Samuel nodded. "In a way, O'Riley and his brother are kind of like you and Uncle Jake. Uncle Jake helped grubstake us, and now he's counting on us to find that ledge. And we're gonna do it," Samuel proclaimed.

"*If* it's still there." Charles tried to temper Samuel's enthusiasm, but he felt the excitement as well. *This* would be the answer to getting a place of their own and to helping out Jake. He owed Mary's brother.

"It's there, Pa," Samuel replied. "I can feel it in my bones."

"Then it's in our hands to finish what O'Riley started." Charles reached over to the boiling coffeepot. "How about some coffee?"

He filled Samuel's cup and took a sip from his own, feeling its warmth in the evening chill.

"So you think we're still doin' the right thing, Pa?"

"For sure," Charles quickly replied. "I only regret leaving your ma and sister for so long."

"So do I," Samuel said quietly.

"We can't worry, son. They're going to be just fine. Even on one leg, your uncle Jake is pretty capable. And your cousin Daniel, he's getting to be big enough to be of some help. What is he ... nine?"

"I reckon."

He eyed Samuel. "How about you? *You* still glad you came?"

"You bet," Samuel said, but then as if he had misgivings, he asked, "But what if we don't find it?"

"We'll take up some placer mining. Or if worse comes to worst, I can take a job at one of the mines. Either way, we should make something by season's end to get a start on our own place again."

Samuel pushed his hands across his knees and quietly questioned, "But what if I can't hold my own? I mean, I'll try my best, Pa, but what if I can't do it?"

"You'll do fine. This country don't care how old you are or who you are. But it seems to me it does care what kind of spirit you got. And from my judging, son, you got that down just fine."

*   *   *

Moonlight across his face woke Charles. His breath hung in the chilly air. Frost had formed on their bedding despite the tarpaulin. He glanced to where Samuel slept, his body pulled up into a small mound. Samuel's hat as well as his canvas trousers and tattered dobby shirt, which lay crumpled across his saddle, were covered in frost. He smiled to himself. His own clothing was stored at the foot of his bed. The boy would be in for a surprise come morning.

He pulled his hat down to block the bright moonlight and turned to catch some more sleep. He thought of Samuel's concerns. He prayed to God he would not let the boy down. He did not know the likelihood of finding gold, nor a thing about prospecting for that matter. He did not fear hard work. If it was work that it took, he could do that. He knew Samuel would as well, but Samuel was right. He was still a boy.

CHAPTER 2

Samuel woke early to a morning chill, the coldest night yet. Wood smoke drifted to him from the campfire his father already tended. He stood to dress and immediately felt the stinging cold of frost raining down onto his neck and bare back as his head hit the tarpaulin. He grabbed his clothes and danced toward the fire, trousers half-pulled up.

Charles eyed him, grinning.

"Blasted cold, Pa," Samuel said. He pulled on his shirt, tucked it in, and fixed his suspenders. "I didn't expect frost last night."

"That I can see," Charles said and chuckled.

Samuel gave him a look and then ran his hand through his hair, spraying his father with icy particles. "Not funny."

Charles ducked. "Careful, it's still a long ways to Washington."

Samuel sat and began pulling on his boots, stiff from the cold. "Thanks for the fire. Can't believe it's so cold."

"We're at high elevation. By the time we drop down into the main Salmon today, it will seem like summer."

Samuel rubbed his hands over the fire. It felt good. Frequently, he was the one to start and tend the cook fire. He guessed his father had been worrying about things and had risen early. He guessed it was about their family and Uncle Jake. His father had seemed almost relieved to begin the trip, like he now had a chance to make things right about something.

He watched his father work the coffeepot down into the coals. There were deep creases around his eyes, which Samuel had always figured came from squinting in the sun, but now he realized that maybe they were from worry.

Charles nodded at his shirtsleeve. "Soon as we strike it rich, we need to get you a new shirt, or maybe you might need to do a bit of sewing."

Samuel examined the tear. "Caught it on a branch yesterday." His trousers were becoming tattered as well.

Charles nodded. "How about you work up breakfast? I've just about got us some coffee."

Samuel gathered the cups and utensils as well as his coat, a short tan frock, which was similar to his father's. He pulled it tight, feeling the cold until it gathered some warmth. He could not understand how it could be so cold. Everything around them was greening up. His breath frosted. He guessed the air moving over the scattered snowbanks caused the chill.

"Thought it was almost summer," he said, squatting again, rubbing his hands, shivering.

Charles laughed. "Here, this will warm you up some." He poured the coffee.

Samuel took a sip, feeling the warmth spread as he swallowed. "Thanks." He cut a piece of salt pork and tossed it into the pan to add some grease before he added the thin strips of venison.

After breakfast, they took apart the tarpaulin and beat the frost from their gear. Samuel strapped his day pack and bedroll behind Spooky's cantle. He patted the horse and stroked its white blaze. Otherwise Spooky was entirely black. "You've done good, boy." Spooky's ears flicked, and he rolled his eyes. Samuel figured he understood.

By the time they reached the valley floor, the sun had burned away the frost. Steam rose from the waterways, and dew glittered from the grass and brush.

The river, a myriad of small, braided streams, was high with snowmelt and rain from the late spring. It had backed up into the low areas, forming expanses of flooded meadows. They pushed their horses through the water and crossed to the east side, trying to find drier ground along the valley flanks.

Toward the north end of Salmon Meadows, they spotted an Indian encampment across the valley.

"Nez Perce from the looks of the horses," Charles said. "Best we try and avoid them." He left the trail and headed eastward toward the timber on the hillsides.

"Doubt it will do any good, Samuel. If we spotted them, they're sure to have seen us. Keep watch."

Samuel felt a tenseness in his chest and nervously scanned the landscape, wondering what they would do if they did spot the Nez Perce. Would they fight them? Would they try to run? There was nowhere to run.

Salmon Meadows and Council Valley were gathering places for numerous tribes, including the Nez Perce, Weiser, and Sheepeater Indians. Seasonally, they came to dig the camas bulbs as well as to hunt and fish. They were at peace during those times—trading, socializing, and holding contests—however, the festivities never precluded a young man from taking a pony that was not closely watched.

Samuel figured the Indians were fishing. They had seen a couple of salmon in the upper reaches of the Weiser, and here, they had already spotted several long, silvery shapes drift upstream away from their horses.

Spooky's ears pricked forward about the same time three mounted Nez Perce broke into view from a line of timber. Samuel felt his throat tighten. Despite his intense watch, he had failed to see them. It was as if they had formed out of the air. Rapidly, they closed the gap until they were within a few paces. The man in the lead greeted them and signed for peace.

"Guess we aren't going to avoid them, son." Charles returned the sign and pulled up Buster.

Samuel felt his heart quicken and checked for his knife. *Useless against three rifles,* he thought. Despite his fear, the Nez Perce struck Samuel as handsome people. A boy who was not much older than he was rode slightly behind the other two men.

The Nez Perce rode forward, fanning out as they looked over the Chambers' horses and mule. Their features were sharp and clean, and the sun gleamed from their bronze chests. Feathers and ermine skins hung from charcoal hair. Wearing just leggings and breechcloths, they were dressed for hunting.

Their horses, magnificent, stamping and bobbing their heads impatiently as their riders drew near, impressed Samuel. The man in front rode a white mount with scattered dark gray spots across its rump. The second horse was chestnut brown with a white rump and socks. The boy rode a similar horse but with a gray-spotted rump.

They gestured and talked among themselves a moment before the lead man pointed to the packs on the mule and signed to Chambers, speaking unknown words.

Charles shook his head. He pointed toward the mountains and then to the packs, bringing his hand toward his heart. The gesture was clear to the Nez Perce, and they shook their heads. They had seen enough prospectors in the country to know Chambers was not interested in trading. He would also pose no threat.

Charles clucked to Buster and pushed past. Samuel followed, leading the mule. Then impulsively, he pointed to the boy and nodded. He gestured to the boy's horse, touched his chest, and grinned. The youth understood his gestures and smiled; he gestured in return. *Yes, he had a good horse.*

After they had traveled a moment, Samuel spoke, "I've never seen such fine horses."

"Nor are you likely to again, unless you run into more Nez Perce," Charles replied. "Those were appaloosa. One of the characteristics is the spots you saw."

"They look powerful fast. I don't think we could have outrun them if they had wanted our gear. Do you, Pa?"

"Not even close, and they know it."

"I'm glad they were friendly. Do you suppose they were trying to trade?"

"That's what I understood. I don't know what we'd trade for though."

"One of their horses."

Charles laughed. "I doubt that. Our entire outfit ain't worth one of those horses."

"I 'spect not," Samuel said. "They sure looked fancy with those saddles and blankets, but I don't think I'd ever want to fight them. They all had rifles."

"And they're outstanding marksmen." Charles clucked to Buster, encouraging him up and over a downed log. "It won't be good if the United States ever picks a fight with them."

"Our army could lick them."

"I wouldn't be so sure. With fast horses and rifles in country they know, they would be a match for any cavalry soldier," Charles said. "Remember, I've been to war."

*   *   *

The trail continued, a faint trace along the river. The meadows shrank as the walls of the gorge pinched inward. In places, standing water formed wide expanses, making it difficult to discern the trail from the river. Another stream entered from the east, also high and frothy white. It merged with the Little Salmon directly above the canyon.

They recrossed to the west bank near where the river slowed and pooled before it plunged into the gorge. At last, they were out of the marshes and flooded areas along the streams. The horses had spent a good part of the day slogging through water.

The rock changed from gentle granite to sharp, fractured basalt. Eons in the past, lava had filled the gorge and solidified, damming the river and forming a lake where Salmon Meadows now spread. Water forced its way through fractures until it eventually cut the channel through which the river now surged.

They reached a series of steep falls, water thundering over them, booming in exploding spray through the narrow clefts. Samuel studied the snow-white water, glad to be on solid rock. A large salmon leaped from the spray, its rosy sides glinting in the sun. It slipped back into the churning foam, and another rocketed out of the spray past it.

"Would you look at that, Pa!"

"I see," Charles replied. "They're trying to get over the falls to get upstream to spawn."

"I can't believe how huge they are. That one must have been three feet long."

They watched for a moment, as first one salmon and then another hurled itself upward. Samuel noticed some eagles perched in a nearby snag. He figured they were waiting for them to leave and that their presence had disturbed their fishing.

By midday, the air had warmed to where it was almost uncomfortable. The river broadened, and the gorge widened. In many places, it overflowed its banks and crept up into the shrubs and trees. The canyon walls rose steeply, thickly carpeted with dark timber and bright green brush. They had dropped considerably in elevation, and Samuel strained his neck to see the canyon rim.

Areas along the river opened into grassy benches amid towering pines. Syringa, a medium-height shrub, grew along the craggy draws. Thickly covered with yellow-centered white blossoms, its sweet fragrance mingled with the pungent fragrance of pine and fir.

Ridges of black basalt spilled downward from the peaks above, ending in jagged cliffs where the river slammed into them. The trail crossed above these areas where the river broadened and ran more shallow. But for Samuel, each crossing became more worrisome.

When they circled above one cliff, they found that the trail apparently ended. It did not appear to have crossed the river, for there was no visible route on the far side. They continued following a faint trace along the east side until it also disappeared up a draw.

"Game trail," Charles spat. "Somewhere we missed a crossing." He headed downward toward the river.

Samuel said nothing. He did not like it one bit. The high water appeared swift and deep, and he could see farther downstream to where it broke into a seething torrent of thundering white water as it squeezed between the cliffs.

"Can't figure this out," Charles muttered when they reached the river. "Didn't think people had to swim their animals, but it appears the only way. Water's too deep right now. Doesn't help that it's near flood stage."

"For sure, Pa," Samuel breathed. He did not think this was where the trail crossed. "Maybe we should scout back upstream and look for another spot." He broke and tossed a branch into the dark green water and watched as it was snatched up and carried quickly downstream into the rapids. The water gurgled at Spooky's hooves, racing incredibly fast past them. The shadowy form of a salmon scooted past. Samuel shivered, scared. He could swim, but in water this fast and high and with rapids below, no man would survive.

"Worth a try, son," replied Charles. "Can't see how this is a crossing. Maybe in lower water this is okay, but for sure, it ain't okay now." He turned Buster back up the steep trail. "I'm guessing the trail is underwater. We'll just have to find another way."

Charles shielded his eyes, scanning. Finally, he pointed across. "I think we can do it."

"I don't, Pa." Samuel did not often disagree with his father, but he felt a numbing fear. If they tried crossing here, they would certainly be swept into the rapids.

"There's a break in the rocks where those shrubs are growing. It should be wide enough to lead the horses through," Charles continued. "If we can find a place upstream to cross, we can work our way along the far side."

They scouted a short distance before they came to a riffle at the head of a deep hole. Rocks had partially filled the river, causing it to spread and run shallow before gathering into a deep trough below.

Charles eased Buster into the water. It quickly rose to the animal's brisket. Any deeper and the horse would be swimming. The horse staggered downstream.

Heart hammering, Samuel followed, leading the mule. He angled Spooky farther upstream into the bottom of the rapids. They struggled a few yards and then came up short. The mule refused to follow. Irritated, Samuel turned and tugged on the lead. "Mule don't want to follow," he hollered. "Come on, Molly," he urged, jerking the rope.

The mule brayed and then splashed into the water. Almost immediately, it slipped. It lunged forward but slid into deeper water, tightening the lead against Spooky, pulling him downstream.

Water rose, gushing over Samuel's boots. He felt a clammy helplessness as he tried to steady Spooky and pull the mule back upstream. The horse stumbled.

"Cut the rope!"

Frantically, Samuel fumbled for his skinning knife. The mule went down, and Spooky struggled to keep his feet. Water briefly surged over Samuel's legs into his lap. Spooky scrambled upward, partially freeing himself from the sucking current. Samuel finally freed his knife and brought the blade against the rope. Snapping loudly, it hissed and snaked away. Spooky scrambled onto his feet, surged through the water, and lunged upward out of the river onto the bank. Desperately, Samuel clung to the shaking horse.

Molly rolled over in the current, pulled her head up, eyes frantic, and began swimming for the bank. Swept into the chute between the vertical rock faces, the mule bumped against the cliff. Surging her body against it, a hoof came out and pawed at it. A sickening feeling flooded Samuel as he helplessly watched. Molly's head, eyes wide, disappeared downstream. A horribly emptiness filled Samuel. They had lost their mule … and gear. *Poor Molly.*

"Come on, Samuel," Charles hollered. He turned up through the brush and rocks, leading Buster. "We got a mule to catch."

Samuel scrambled upward, leading Spooky through the faint rocky chute. He remounted and made his way downstream as quickly as possible.

"I'll be a son of a gun," muttered Charles. "She made it through, Samuel!"

Molly, packs still intact, stood on the bank, dripping water.

"Thank the Lord, Pa." Samuel cheered, reaching the mule and catching her up.

Charles examined her. "Seems okay from what I can tell. Best get these packs off and see what the damage is."

Samuel took hold of a pack. "Pretty dang heavy now it's soaked up all the water."

Charles tested it. "Reminds me of a story I once heard." He helped undo the pack hitches. "Some miner was using a mule string to pack rock salt into town. To get there, they had to cross a river. Didn't take long for the mules to figure out if they rolled in the water, their loads got lighter. He couldn't figure out how to keep the mules from rolling. Then he got an idea and borrowed some cotton bales. The mules rolled in the water, soaked it up, and after carrying four hundred pounds of water just once, they quit rolling."

Samuel grinned.

"Don't know if it's a true story or not, but from the looks of things right now, it sure could be." He handed a bundle of their clothes to Samuel. "Here, we best wring these out."

Samuel twisted each piece, watching the water pour out and run in rivulets across the dirt. He spread the items across shrubs in the sun to dry.

Charles sorted through their supplies. "Speaking of salt, looks like we lost some of ours … and the flour, some of that's ruined … and the sugar." He began tossing the wet portions and repacking what remained dry. "There goes the savings we had from buying at Fort Boise. Guess we'll have to resupply in Washington. Only it'll cost triple what it should. Guess that means you go hunting."

That suited Samuel just fine. He enjoyed that far more than the fixing and cleaning.

They continued downstream and crossed several more tributaries that cascaded through the narrow valleys and emptied themselves into the Little Salmon.

Charles paused at one of streams. "I don't mind saying it. You'd almost have enough ground to plow along this stream, and the grass on the hills looks rich."

"Pretty rocky, I'd say," Samuel observed.

"Certainly not like Iowa." Charles nudged Buster onward.

*   *   *

They had lost several hours drying and repacking their gear, and shadows now grew long in the canyon. Swallows dipped low, skimming the river, catching up water for their mud nests. Orange light bathed the edges of the highest peaks.

"Guess we'd best find a dry bench where we can pitch camp before it gets too dark," Charles offered. "We'll have to wait till morning to make the main Salmon."

The trail crossed another small creek, turbulent with water filling to its banks. Charles turned up it through the brush and rocks.

Buster suddenly shied and bucked sideways, almost unseating Charles. "Whoa! Whoa, fella!" Charles pulled his horse back. "Rattlesnake, Samuel. Watch it."

Samuel had already paused.

"Can't tell where it's at. Brush is too thick. Can hear it though." He leaned from his saddle, trying to see. "Sounds mad." Charles dismounted. "Hold Buster." He gave the reins to Samuel and waded into the brush, thrashing it with a long stick. "That should do it." He remounted and carefully picked his way upward.

Samuel strained to see more snakes. He hated them. He did not like the idea of bedding down with them as company. "Maybe we should find another spot."

"We'll be okay. By dark, they'll skedaddle."

Samuel was not so sure.

They moved beyond a rock outcrop to where the ground leveled and opened up. The area was trampled and barren, evidently used by others before them. Samuel was relieved. At least he stood a chance of seeing any snakes. A couple of fire pits remained, and a trail led down toward the creek. While his father took care of their gear, Samuel led the horses and mule to the water. Thick brush grew along the creek, and he grew nervous. He grabbed a stick and thrashed the brush as he had seen his father do. Cold chills raced down his back as he half-expected to see a snake. Where there was one rattler, there were others. He hoped the stock could find enough grass and wondered how they avoided getting snake-bitten. He put the bell on Molly for the night.

His father had started a fire and was frying venison and mixing cornmeal.

"I'll be glad when we get to a place we can stay and fix something besides mush," complained Samuel.

"As will I," exclaimed Charles as he set the skillet on the fire to simmer. He tossed some dried apple slices into a small kettle of water to soften. "Tomorrow, we need to keep our eyes peeled for some grouse or rabbits for some fresh meat. This is the last of the venison."

"For sure, Pa."

"Also some greens of some type. Should be some watercress along the main river." Charles sliced off a piece of venison for him.

Starved, Samuel chewed it while the hasty pudding cooked. A funny name, he reflected, because there was nothing hasty about it.

"Couple more days, we'll be hunting gold, Samuel. I'm ready."

"I'm glad. This is the worst trail we've been on."

"Not many come this way. When we hit the main Salmon, we'll intersect the main trail." Charles threw some coffee grounds into the now boiling water and stirred the corn pudding.

"This water's high, Pa. If it's high on the Salmon, can we get to Washington?"

"I'm sure people are getting through."

Samuel was not sure. He ate in silence, worrying, watching the light fade from the canyon walls, but he was glad for his father's company.

CHAPTER 3

Samuel woke to a gray sky. He stumbled to the cook fire where his father was frying some salt pork with last night's mush that he had cut into cakes.

"Ready to roll?" Charles asked, flipping a cake. "I'm hoping to make it to Shearer's ferry. Unless we run into flooded trails today, we should make it by evening."

"As long as we get rolling before the sun comes up and the rattlers wake." Samuel pulled on his boots and laced them.

After a quick meal, they headed downstream. The timber gave way to open hillsides and sagebrush. Black basalt formed ledges from which creeks spilled in white tendrils. The gorge broadened, and the Little Salmon meandered farther to the east behind stands of cottonwood and willow.

Samuel kept careful watch on Molly, but she seemed fine. Now that her swim was past, Samuel recalled the sight, laughing to himself. He wondered if old Molly had not enjoyed the plunge. Remembering her head bobbing through the rapids, it sure looked that way.

To the north, a sunlit notch in the mountains rising on either side of the river began to broaden. Rounded hills steeply climbed upward from the canyon. Dark conifers crowned their summits and spilled down the ravines between the barren, fingerlike ridges. They had dropped down from the forested meadows and had broken into sight of a broad, treeless canyon.

"Would you look at that, Pa," Samuel breathed. Now visible, the Salmon River came in from the east and swung north, a broad, dancing, sparkling ribbon. The Little Salmon, spilling over its banks, raced downward to meet it, a torrent of white water until it merged with the larger river.

Samuel gazed east, the direction they needed to travel. "No way we can cross it, Pa." Samuel shuddered. He reflected on their recent brush with disaster.

"We don't. We follow the main Salmon north for several miles and cross on the new ferry. The trail we need is on the other side." Charles jutted his chin in the direction.

Samuel strained to see but could not. The river was at least two hundred yards wide and a clump of cottonwoods masked the shore. "Seems like a roundabout way of getting to Washington," he said."

"Nigh on everyone else comes by way of Lewiston from the northwest. This is the only route from the east. They say Warren's camp is at the end of the world. I'm beginning to believe it."

The faint trace they followed eventually swung west and then north along a bench, shouldering the Salmon a hundred feet below.

Samuel studied a section of rapids, huge rolling waves like liquid hills racing downward. The green water slid over cabin-sized boulders, piled itself into huge swells, and then dropped into a series of holes. This river was anything but flat. *That* was the difference between it and the Snake, he decided. The Salmon had as much *up and down* to it as it had *across*.

"Looks mighty powerful, Pa," he said quietly, throat dry, "and the water's awful high." He wondered how even a ferryboat could cross. "Some of the other rivers we crossed were wider, but this one's all moving, and you know it's gotta be deep."

"Some call it the River of No Return. You might get a boat down it, but you ain't going to be bringing it back up." His father's comment did nothing to calm Samuel's concern.

About four miles north, they reached John Groff's place at the mouth of Race Creek. A ferryboat bobbed in the water, moored on their side of the river. It differed from those Samuel had seen on the Snake. Not just a flat-bottomed floating bridge, it was a deck built across two smaller boats.

"Hello!" Charles called toward the cabin.

A young man came forth, squinting in the bright sun. He was the first white man they had seen since they had turned north out of Fort Boise two weeks ago.

"Howdy, travelers," he greeted. "Heading north? You want to rest a bit? Can I take care of your stock?"

Father and son swung down. The men shook hands and introduced themselves. Jesse Fischer had come to the region to try his luck at gold mining but had struck out. He did odd jobs, just now getting the caretaker job from the ferry owner, John Groff.

"We won't be staying," explained Charles.

"Shucks. Want a hot meal then?" Fischer asked. "I can rustle up some beans and pork chops. Might have some apple pie as well. Just a buck a plate."

Samuel's mouth began to water. He had not had a home-cooked meal in weeks, but the price stunned him. In Iowa, a dollar could buy five meals.

"Sounds mighty good, but we'll pass," replied Charles. "Just need for you to take us across. We're headin' to Washington."

"You're lucky," continued Fischer. "Just opened the ferry. The water's been high. Otherwise, you'd have had to camp awhile until it dropped some."

"Isn't there another ferry downriver at Slate Creek?"

"There is, but you'd be swimming the river long before that. No trail this side of the river after a couple more miles." Fischer grinned. "Mr. Groff put this ferry in for folks like yourselves coming by way of the Little Salmon. They had to have a way to get across. 'Course they could of swum it here like they used to, if they didn't mind gettin' their gear wet."

"And if they didn't mind waiting for the water to drop." Charles eyed the engorged river.

"And that," Fischer said and laughed.

"How much you need?" Charles reached for his purse.

Fischer scratched his head. "Cost is a buck for each horse and rider and heavy-packed mule." He glanced at Molly. "But I reckon I can call her light-packed and make her four bits. That makes it two dollars and four bits."

Charles's mouth tightened as he counted out the coins. "Last ferry we used was on the Snake. It cost eight bits." He handed over the coins.

Samuel guessed their grubstake was running low. They needed cash to live on in Washington until they found gold, and it would be tighter now that they had lost some of their staples.

"Everyone comes this way, says the same thing." Fischer hefted the coins and then pocketed them. "Why you headin' to Washington, if you don't mind my askin'? Not much going on there anymore." He grabbed a coiled rope and headed toward the ferry.

"We're plannin' on trying some placering."

Samuel knew that was their story while they searched for the ledge.

Jesse Fischer ran his hand through his dark hair and studied Charles. "Not my business, mister, but don't 'spect you'll find much. The placers have been pretty much worked out for a number of years, especially the easy ones. A few bigger companies are still having a go of it in deeper gravels but not much else. Besides, a lot of Chinamen are movin' in."

Charles looked up. "Chinamen?"

"Yep, they're stormin' the country. Once Warren's camp voted to allow them in, they been flooding in. Pert near every day I see them across from me walking along, headin' up the trail with their belongings tied onto them poles they carry across their shoulders."

Fischer tossed the rope into the ferry and began undoing the planking about midships. He gestured to Charles. "Help me undo the pins on that end so we can get this ramp down."

Samuel studied the boat with concern. It was nothing more than some decking about twenty-five feet long by fifteen feet wide with a railing that spanned two canoelike boats. The lumber was rough-hewn yellow wood and smelled strongly of freshly sawn pine. He hoped the contraption would float.

Cautiously, Samuel walked the horses up the planking, feeling the boat sink as he did so. Water rose to almost over the gunwales of the smaller boats, gurgling more loudly. The heaving motion of the river seemed a living thing. Fischer took the reins from him and looped them about a rail, facing the horses upstream.

Samuel returned for Molly. She would not budge. He slapped her rump and tugged hard, convincing her to begrudgingly step aboard. She was the only bright one among the bunch, including himself, he thought.

He looped her lead about the rail next to Spooky, patting her. "Easy, ol' gal." She quivered and stepped to the side. He stroked Spooky's muzzle as well, staring at the swift black water, bracing himself. The river ran deep and fast, making a loud sucking noise as it shouldered past.

A couple of lines ran from each corner of the bow of the decking to a yoke that held two pulleys that ran along a single, thin wire strung across the river. Samuel hoped it would not snap.

Fischer pulled out a pipe, lit it, and drew a couple of puffs. He took up slack on one of the wires, which tilted the bow of the ferry into the current, and then took hold of a tall wheel.

The boat shuddered and began sliding across. Samuel wondered how Fischer made it work. The operators on the Snake either rowed or pulled on ropes to bring the boat across. Instead, Fischer stood quietly, gently manipulating the wheel and smoking his pipe. Samuel wondered why the current did not snatch the boat and carry it downstream.

"You got a mighty fine lookin' outfit," Fischer said, eyeing Molly and their packs. "Come far?"

Charles shrugged. "A far enough piece, you might say." He offered nothing further.

Fischer turned to Samuel. "Hey, bud, we get to shore, take this rope and tie us off until I can get the bow angled back. There's a bit of a squirrely current next to the ramp, especially in this high water."

Gulping, Samuel took the rope. He felt the power of the river. The noise of the gurgling water all but drowned out their talking. The ferryboat bucked and rocked underneath. Samuel gazed anxiously toward the far shore slowly creeping closer. Deep black water raced through the channel ahead.

More separated them from the shore where they had launched. Nervously, he patted Spooky. He felt he was in the middle of a flood, prevented from being swallowed up only by a thin wire that he felt certain would soon snap.

"At least you'll find the trail here better than down the Little Salmon," Fischer continued. "Lot of folks come this way over the past several years. Some are even taking up homesteads. Mostly downriver." He pointed with his pipe. "Maybe if the gold don't work out, you and your boy can find a piece of land before it's all claimed up."

Charles glanced downriver. "The thought crossed my mind. Especially when we came through Salmon Meadows. That looked like mighty good soil."

"*Except* that country, mister. I wouldn't look at homesteading there just yet. That's Indian country—Nez Perce." Fischer turned the wheel, taking up slack on the wire, adjusting the bow. "That's where they like to rendezvous— do some huntin' and tradin'."

"Yes, we ran into a few."

"Ran into some?" Jesse Fischer looked up, frowning. He addressed Samuel. "Get ready, bud."

Samuel climbed over the railing and held on, the water near to licking his boots, surging past. He shivered. He imagined himself being yanked off the landing back into the river before he could tie them off. The ferry bumped the ramp, and he jumped. He quickly ran the line around the post and snubbed it off.

"Thanks, bud," Fischer said. He turned back to Charles. "You may be getting' rich after all. Anyone who rides through a Nez Perce encampment and ain't walkin' when he comes out the other side is plumb lucky. Them Nez Perce like horses better than anything in the world."

"They probably looked at how poor ours were and decided otherwise."

They led the stock off and mounted up. "Thanks for the assist." Charles waved.

"Anytime," Fischer replied. "Good luck mining."

After they were out of earshot, Samuel turned to his father. "Think the Chinamen have found O'Riley's spot?"

"Don't know, Samuel. I can't believe there's all that many going in, and I doubt all the ground's been dug like he says. Besides, they likely won't be looking for lode gold."

*　　　*　　　*

The day had warmed. Samuel kept his eyes peeled for rattlesnakes, although most of the trail was clear. He thought he heard one buzz, but because the horses did not shy, he figured it was the wind rattling some dry brush. Nevertheless, he intently studied every movement.

The trail turned eastward and followed above the Salmon's churning waters. The river averaged 150 yards wide. Where it narrowed, it ran swift and deep against the canyon walls. Samuel became nervous in those places. If Spooky slipped, nothing below would prevent them from rolling into the river. He worried about meeting other riders coming down the trail. Custom dictated whoever was fully packed would have right of way, but two fully packed outfits would need to work it out. He shivered at the thought of having Spooky step off the trail. There was no room.

Samuel gazed upward toward the canyon rim. Steep, barren hills climbed for hundreds of feet. He wondered how anyone could climb such steep country. He wondered if there was any way up and out of this gorge. There had to be. Warren's camp was up there somewhere to the east.

As they rounded a bend, they spotted a cabin on a grassy bar above the river and caught the smell of wood smoke. A fenced garden showed rows of green. A couple of men worked a rocker below the trail near the confluence of a small creek and the river.

"We'll see a lot of that in a few days," Charles said.

Samuel thought of the goldfields to where they headed and felt his heart quicken. "Can we take a look?"

"I don't see why not." Charles turned and shouted, "Ho, the camp! May we come in?"

Both men turned abruptly. One stepped toward a rifle leaning against a tree, but when he saw that Charles and Samuel posed no danger, he straightened and hailed back, waving. "Yo, come on down—but only if you're packin' wimin and whiskey."

"Sorry," Charles yelled back, "just me and my boy."

Samuel turned Spooky off the trail and followed his father, picking his way down between the boulders toward the creek.

"Watch for snakes," Charles advised.

"Yes, sir." His father had no need to remind him.

When they reached the miners, Charles explained, "Thought my boy should see what we're after, if you don't mind."

"Not at all. Always good to have some company." The smaller man squinted through pale eyes and reached out a hand. "I'm Pete, and this here's Hallelujah." He pointed toward his partner, a taller, lanky man. "This place is Berg's Bar. August Berg homesteaded here in '64. He's out to Slate Creek getting supplies. We just winter here."

Charles shook Pete's hand. "I'm Charles Chambers, and this here's my son, Samuel."

"You brung your kid to this country?" asked Pete, running his hand through a graying beard.

"He can do a man's work, and we've got work for two families. Had to bring him."

The men nodded, and Samuel shook their hands. He could tell from the manner in which they shook that they recognized him as an equal and not as a boy, and he warmed.

"Don't want to disappoint you. It's gonna take four men at least to do any good. 'Course, you can still get lucky," said Pete. "Where you headin'? Florence by any chance? That's where we got diggins."

"Warren's camp," Charles replied. "Knew a guy once that mined there. Said if you can dig deep enough, you can still do well."

"Maybe so. Maybe so." Hallelujah eyed them. He was a tall man with a narrow face and ears that stuck out, accentuated by a thick, dark beard. "We dug around there a bit but never found much. Oh, some of the quartz mines are openin' up, but I was never in it for just a workingman's wage. I was always in it for the chance of gettin' lucky rich."

Charles shook his head. "We aren't in it for a wage either. So I guess we're figuring on getting lucky rich as well."

Hallelujah laughed and helped them picket the horses and mule where they could reach water. "You come well outfitted—mighty fine bay you got." He raised an eye. "Must not have come too far?"

"The horse is courtesy of the Union Army. Otherwise, I'd be pretty skimpy myself."

"Hear! Hear!" Hallelujah thumped Pete and exclaimed. "To the Union." He gave a smart salute. "Careful, though. You'll find most folks in this country were Southern sympathizers."

Pete interjected, "We didn't heed the call. We was already in California. Figured it'd be over with before we got there. Sure didn't expect Mister Lincoln's war to last four damn years."

Samuel eyed his father. He knew his father did not need to hear excuses. He often told him that many people who headed west did so to avoid the war. "Many were scallywags and ne'er-do-wells," he had often said.

Charles nodded. "You can thank men like Samuel's uncle. At least I came home with a horse. He came home missin' a leg."

The smile faded from Hallelujah's face. "Hell of a thing. Hell of a thing."

"That's part why we're here," explained Charles. "I had a good place, but with the call to war, I managed to lose it. Got home to nothing."

"Sorry to hear that."

"Now we're trying to go home with some money to put down on some land for farming."

Pete shrugged. "We've seen a lot of folks come through, tryin' to make things better. I wish I could say you'll do well at Warren's camp, but fact is most of the placers have been worked out, and the Chinamen are goin' in and takin' up what's left."

"That's what I've been hearing," said Charles quietly. He pushed on the rocker. "So how does one of these contraptions work?"

"First, you can see how it's built on rockers," replied Pete, "so you can rock it side to side.

"Now you notice the hopper up here." He jiggled a wooden box with a perforated metal plate in its bottom. "That's where you load it. You work the gravel through this riddle sheet and rake out the big rocks. The small stuff with the gold drops down and is caught in the riffles." He turned. "Come on, Hallelujah. Get me some gravel we can throw in for these folks."

Hallelujah dropped down into a pit dug into the bank, grabbed up a pick, and knocked down some earth and cobbles. He filled a bucket with gravel and handed it up for Pete to grab.

"Shore is a heavy one, Hallelujah. Must have a couple one-pound nuggets in it!"

"One-pound nuggets—" Samuel caught himself as he realized Pete had to be joking.

"Well, hell yes, kid!" Pete continued, squinting at him. "How'd you think Hallelujah got his name? First one-pounder he ever saw, he shouted 'hallelujah' so loud miners from a mile around came a runnin'." He dumped the gravel into the hopper.

"You both can fetch me some water." He gestured toward a couple of buckets and began picking out rocks.

As Samuel filled a bucket in the creek and then lugged it back up, he began to realize the amount of work it took.

"You're kidding about that one-pounder." Samuel was not entirely sure.

"Hell no, kid," Pete replied. "It was a one-pounder all right. A pound nugget of *hematite*." Pete laughed.

"Hematite?" The name was unfamiliar to Samuel.

"Iron ore. In rich placers, you'll find it mixed in with the gold because it's heavy," Pete explained.

"Well, truth be told, several people did come a runnin' and, after seeing the hematite, took up to yelling 'hallelujah' whenever they found a chunk in their boxes. That lasted about a day afore they sort of lost interest, but Hallelujah's name stuck, and that's a fact."

"For sure," replied Hallelujah. "But I'm still fixin' to turn up a big nugget one of these days. Won't be a pounder—that's pure dreamin'—but it might be an ounce. They found a couple that weighed an ounce downriver at Lucile Bar."

Charles raised his eyes. "I guess if we don't do any good at Warren's camp, we can always try Lucile."

"I wouldn't bother," said Pete. "Like most of the river below here, it's all claimed up—at least all the good spots. Some of it by homesteaders like Mr. Berg here. Besides ranching and growing a few crops, they do some placer mining.

"Then there's others that have claims here on the river and also up at Warren's camp or Florence. They work the mountain camps while there's water and then come down here and work the bars in the winter."

Pete raked around the gravel he had dumped into the hopper and tossed out the larger rocks.

"Hallelujah and I'll be headin' up to our diggins in Florence in a few days, but there's still snow on the trails going in. Besides, we're near to bedrock here."

He poured water over the remaining material, gently rocking the cradle as he did so.

"Water washes out the dirt and gravel," Pete explained. "The gold is so heavy that by rockin' back and forth, it quickly settles to the bottom. There's a canvas under the hopper that helps even out the flow of water and spread the gravel over the riffles. The riffles catch most of the gold, if'n there is any."

With one hand, he ladled water through the hopper while he rocked with the other.

"Here, kid, you can pour. I'll rock. Now not too much. We want an even flow."

Samuel poured water from the bucket, but it appeared that he just washed out all the gravel they had put into the box.

"That's it," Pete said. "The trick is to have the right amount of flow—enough to tumble the gravel through but not much more. Most of the gold down here's flour gold. It's come so far from the mountains it's been ground to tiny specks and can easily be washed back out."

He quit the gentle rocking motion. "Let's take a look."

Pete pulled the hopper off the rocker, revealing the sloped canvas beneath. Water glistened in the sun off black sand that had caught behind the cleats.

Samuel saw nothing. He was looking for pea-sized nuggets.

Pete pointed. "See that stringer of yellow? That's all gold, my friend."

Samuel stared. What first appeared to be a light band of sand edging the black was a line of bright yellow gold dust caught behind the uppermost cleat.

Samuel felt a surge. "That's a bunch. How much is it worth, do you reckon?"

"'Bout four bits," replied Pete. "Looks like a lot, but it really ain't."

"But if you do that much on each bucket, you'll have a lot by the end of the day."

Pete laughed. "That's already a bunch of buckets."

Samuel felt disappointed. That meant a lot of work. "But you do find more than this sometimes?"

"Yep, sometimes we get small flakes, and those add up fast. The closer we get to bedrock, the more we find—that's why Hallelujah's down so deep and why we're stayin' awhile. We'll keep running buckets most of the day, and then we'll wash the fines with quicksilver. We should get about half an ounce."

"That's ten dollars!" Samuel said excitedly. Five dollars a day was a decent wage.

"No, about seven," replied Pete, "and some of it's Mr. Berg's."

Samuel frowned, puzzled. "An ounce is worth twenty dollars."

"Gold combines with silver. This gold here runs about fourteen dollars an ounce."

Samuel's frown deepened.

"Actually, that's not bad. Most of the gold up at Warren's camp only goes for twelve dollars an ounce."

Samuel looked up at his father, concerned and now doubtful.

"We'll just have to find more is all," Charles replied quietly.

Samuel's neck prickled with anticipation. He was anxious to be finding his own gold. "How'd you know there was gold here?"

"We didn't for sure, but most of the bars along the river have pretty good flour gold. I had to check around with my pan before I decided this was a good spot." Pete squinted at him. "You ever use a gold pan?"

Samuel shook his head. Neither he nor his father had. They figured they would learn somehow.

"You got one, don't you? Go get it."

Samuel opened one of Molly's packs and pulled out the bright silver pan.

"Put it back." Pete laughed. "You'll need to season that one. Still has oil sticking to it. You'll lose all the flour gold."

Samuel frowned.

"Throw it on the fire tonight and then throw it in the water after it gets cherry red. That usually does the trick. It'll darken it up some as well. Helps you see the gold better."

Samuel flushed with embarrassment.

"Use one of mine." He handed him a blackened pan. "See that bank up there? Go get a pan of dirt."

Samuel obtained some dirt and took it to Pete.

"I'll just demonstrate. You can figure it out for yourself later."

He plunged the pan into the water and began breaking up the dirt clods with his hands and tossing out pebbles. "The gold will settle to the bottom, but you got to mix it good with water and shake it down."

He began swirling the pan, washing the top layer off back into the stream. He dunked the pan again, stirred it some, and repeated the process. Quickly, he worked the gravel down, washing off some, shaking the pan, washing it again. Eventually, only a small amount of black sand remained.

"Here." He handed the pan to Samuel. "Wash the water across the black sand. Tell me if you see anything."

Samuel took the pan, surprised at its weight. He rocked the water gently across the sand. Several tiny specks of gold winked up.

"That's gold." Samuel laughed. "Real gold."

"Now that's how you prospect. You check all the creeks by washing some samples down. When you find a good spot, you get serious and build something like this rocker."

"I'm mighty obliged, Pete," Samuel managed.

They shook hands and said farewell.

"Good luck to ya both. Hope ya find that one-pounder, lad," Hallelujah hollered.

Samuel could not help but think about it.

CHAPTER 4

Pinched between steep, rugged slopes ascending on both sides, the river became a churning line of white water. The trail climbed upward until it had a toehold on the slope above a steep slide area. Two hundred feet below, the river exploded angrily against the face.

"Sure looks mighty rough down there," Samuel said. "Sure hope ol' Spooky keeps his feet. I wouldn't want to take a wrong step here." He felt his heart hammering, and he clung more tightly to Spooky.

"Nope."

"How's Buster doing?" Samuel felt dizzy, looking down at the churning river, and found he had to focus on the trail in front of him to keep himself steady. "Should I cut Molly loose and let her between us?"

Charles was glancing back when Buster slipped. "Easy, boy. Easy." He pulled the horse to a stop and dismounted. "Best we walk." A section of trail had been washed out, leaving an open cut descending to the river below. "Go ahead. Put Molly between us. She'll follow me."

Samuel dismounted and tugged Molly past Buster. The mule plodded forward, seemingly without a care. Samuel's heart raced.

The trail was a thin thread across the wash, and beyond, which was not much wider, it clung scantily to the steep wall. Below, the river seethed white at the foot of the washout, eating at it. Huge swells had formed where the water dropped over rock ledges and had cut into the wall making it slide. Other travelers had crossed the face, but no trail had been reestablished.

Samuel edged his way across, leaving plenty of slack for Spooky. If the horse slid, he decided he could do nothing to stop the animal.

Gradually, the slope lessened, and the trail broadened. They remounted and descended toward the river and emerged onto a gentle bench.

"See the steam rising across the river, Samuel?"

Samuel had already been studying the steam snaking upward between the trees, trying to see its source.

"That's the Indian hot springs. I understand it's mostly hot mud. They say it's good for arthritis and such that ails you."

The thought of a warm bath appealed to Samuel but without mud. "Be kinda hard to cross to it."

"I guess when the water's not as high, you could swim the river. I think the Nez Perce just come over the mountains."

On the far side of the bench, they reached a turbulent stream and paused to water the stock. When Samuel returned to the shade of a lone pine, he broke out some dried peaches and beef from the lunch pouch he kept handy on Molly. He handed some dried beef to his father.

After their visit with Pete and Hallelujah, Samuel had been thinking about their chances. "Pa, what if we don't find O'Riley's spot? You think we'll find enough gold to placer if we don't? A half an ounce a day isn't enough, is it?"

"No, it's not, son, even if we didn't need some of it to live on," Charles admitted. "But I'm still figuring on finding O'Riley's ledge."

"But what if we don't find it?" Samuel pressed.

"I think we can find a placer that does better than half an ounce. The good placers in Warren's camp yield at least an ounce a day. But it's not for you to worry. We have plenty of options."

But Samuel did worry. Two families back in Iowa were relying on them.

"Here, son, I'll take a few of those peaches." Charles reached into the bag. "And quit thinking about finding enough gold." He gently punched Samuel. "I can tell you're thinking about it."

"I can't help it, Pa. We gotta do well. If we don't ... well, how they gonna make it back at home?"

"Now you know everyone back home is fixed for the season. You and I made sure of that before we left," Charles said quietly. "If we go bust here, we can head home early."

"And if we do head back ... so much for ever getting a place of our own."

"No, someday we will, even if not from gold mining." Charles took some of the beef. "But I'm countin' on finding O'Riley's spot and making the richest strike yet."

"Sure, Pa." Samuel studied the river rolling past. He felt less certain.

*   *   *

The trail they followed curved northeastwardly around a massive black knob.

Across the river, jagged cliffs cut by narrow chutes descended from the skyline for hundreds of feet into the water. A few scraggly shrubs clung to the sides of some of the chutes, but nothing—not even grass—grew within them. Rock avalanches tearing loose during each rainstorm had scoured the ravines. There was no beach, no shore, just a jumble of broken rocks partially damming the flow of the river, creating exploding haystacks of white water.

Samuel pointed. "Guess that explains why there's no trail that side of the river."

Charles glanced up. "If so, it'd have to climb over the top."

Riding quietly, spellbound, Samuel had been studying the tortured, black mountains. The farther upstream they rode, the more Samuel felt he was descending into the bowels of hell. Nothing could climb out of this canyon. He wondered how they would climb out of it to reach Warren's camp.

The trail bent east and then ran due south, broadening slightly. Swinging due east again, descending cliffs appeared to block the trail. The ridgeline directly above split into several heavily fractured spines that plummeted steeply into the river. On both sides, sheer cliffs rose from the river depths. The river appeared to have carved a channel through a wall of solid rock. On faith alone, Samuel figured the trail had to go through somewhere, somehow.

Three riders emerged from a cleft onto the trail.

"Maybe they'll turn out for us, Pa," Samuel said. "We're the ones fully packed."

Charles had already begun moving to the side and off the trail. "Take it easy, son." He reached back, pulled out his rifle, and placed it across his pommel. "This might not be good."

Samuel wondered what his father had seen or sensed. He touched his knife, wishing for a rifle. He felt his heart begin to race, and his mouth grew dry.

"Howdy," Charles greeted. "Can you make it past?"

The lead man on a black horse stopped in front of Charles, keenly eyeing him and Samuel. His eyes appeared yellowed, unhealthy. The second man, who had a pockmarked face and pale eyes, crowded forward beside him.

"You fellas must be newcomers." The first man turned his head and spat before he returned his gaze to Charles. A stubble beard showed a gap where a ragged scar crossed his left cheek.

"You'd be correct," Charles replied. "We've just come into this country. I take it you guys are ranch hands?"

The man did not reply. He jerked his head at the second man and nodded down trail.

The man hesitated. "Not the right trail, boss."

The first man's eyes narrowed. "Shut it. I'll decide." He cussed.

Samuel's heart raced. He urged Spooky up closer to his father.

The younger man moved past him, turned his bay across trail, and blocked it.

The first man pushed a greasy hand across his vest and shirt to his shoulder, revealing a holstered pistol. "Now we can talk."

"Name's Chambers." Charles held out his hand. "Charles Chambers. And this is my son, Samuel."

The man spat again but did not reach out to shake. "I don't cotton to strangers, especially ones who uncover their weapons."

"If that's your feeling, I understand," replied Charles evenly. "I suggest you explain that to him." He jerked his head toward the third man.

The man, scraggly black hair and beard, had edged up on his gray. A rifle jutted from under his long, black frock coat.

The first man glanced at him. "Damn it, Ramey."

Ramey pushed the rifle fully into view, twisting his hand on the rifle stock, revealing two missing fingers. "Didn't want trouble," he spat. His dark eyes, which were sunken behind a sharp nose and shaded by his battered black hat, flashed as they deliberately moved from Charles to Samuel. A chill swept over Samuel.

He turned back to Charles. "Point taken." Still, he did not offer his hand. "Quentin Dudgin's my name." He nodded toward the younger man down the trail and then back at the third man. "Clay Bender and Ramey Smith."

"Gentlemen." Charles nodded.

"I take it you're headin' to Warren's camp," Dudgin continued. "Goin' to do some minin', or are you resupplyin' someone?" He eyed Molly's packs.

"Aim to do some placer mining if we can find some decent ground," Charles replied. "Plan to go straight through to the freight landing tonight. Want to make Washington by tomorrow if we can. What about you?"

"Work wherever we can get it. Some ranching like you said. Might hang it up now it's turnin' to minin' season. Might take up a gold pan ourselves." Dudgin glanced toward Bender. "Tain't that so, Clay?" He spat again and spurred the black. "Well, good luck to you, Chambers. Might see you in Washington someday."

Charles and Samuel kept to the side as the two men passed. Ramey Smith keenly studied them, his dark eyes piercing, revealing what Samuel took to be cruelty. Charles waited until the three were well out of sight before he returned his rifle to its scabbard.

"They're lying through their teeth, Samuel."

"I know. If they were working for any kind of a ranch, their horses would be in better shape, and they wouldn't smell like they hadn't bathed in months—the rancher's wife would see to that."

"You're right," Charles said and laughed. "I noticed something else. I could see fresh tracks before the cleft. You'll notice there aren't any now. They ducked into that cleft, probably intending to dry-gulch us."

Samuel felt a chill wash over him. "Then what made them decide not to?"

"I don't rightly know. Probably because they wanted to know what we were packing," Charles said and then paused. "Maybe because of you. They wouldn't jump a kid. But maybe now they're planning on catching us after dark. You noticed they asked our intentions?"

"Yes." Samuel shivered. "So what do we do, Pa?" His hands twisted on the reins.

"Well, for starters, we make it to the Shearers and tell them what's up. Tomorrow, we keep our eyes open for their tracks. I'll know if they're in front of us again."

"What can we do if they *do* get in front of us?" Samuel's voice cracked.

"I've got a few tricks, but let's see what tomorrow brings. Trust me, okay?"

"Okay, Pa," Samuel said quietly. He *did* trust his father. When things seemed darkest, his father always had an answer.

"I wish I had a rifle," Samuel added. His father did not reply.

They entered the crevice, the river running black and angry below them bound on both sides. A wide grassy ledge ran along the top of the cliff about a hundred feet above the river. Across the river, the opposite bank had formed similarly. It was as if a knife had slit a passage for the river. Had there been no ledge, the canyon would have been impassable.

Another mile, the canyon broadened, and the river's silvery waters spread and quieted. A partially submerged island stood a few yards from the far shore. A cabin and some outbuildings appeared beyond on a tree-covered bench. They had reached Shearer's ferry.

CHAPTER 5

They sat their horses overlooking the river crossing. The ferryboat bobbed against a dock on the far bank, but no one appeared to be around.

"What do we do now, Pa?"

Charles pulled his rifle and fired a round into the air, the explosion reverberating from the canyon walls.

A man emerged from the cabin, striding toward the ferry, waving his arms, and saying something they could not make out.

"What if the ferry operator hadn't been home?"

"No problem," Charles replied.

"Huh?"

"See that wire the ferry runs on," he said, pointing. "I'd have had you shinny up that and crawl your way over and row the ferry back."

It took a moment for Samuel to realize his father's joke.

"My luck, I'd fall off halfway across and drown."

The operator drifted the ferry toward them, dipping a sweep, correcting the bow as the boat crossed the rough water. Although similarly built, Shearer's boat appeared older and more heavily used than Groff's.

"Tie me off, will you?" The operator threw a line toward Samuel.

Samuel caught it and immediately snubbed it to the post. The man eased down a ramp and came ashore.

"Howdy, folks," he said, offering his hand. "I'm George Shearer. My father and I operate this ferry."

Charles introduced himself and Samuel.

"Fee is two dollars, same as Slate Creek."

"Actually, we came down the Little Salmon and used Groff's ferry."

"Ah, that one. Lucky you got here." George grinned.

"Not a lot of choice," Charles replied.

"Not this time of year. Pretty good runoff we got." He pointed at the water high up into the brush along the banks. "I surmise you're heading to Warren's camp. Not many folks but Chinamen going in there now."

"That's what we keep hearing."

"They're all headed over the new China trail." George led Buster up the ramp.

"China trail?"

"Everyone used to go up Elk Creek here behind our place, but the Chinese started going over French Creek. There's a good hot springs up on the other side, what makes a nice stopping place before heading on to Washington. Staked by a German fellow by the name of Fred Burgdorf."

"The folks at Fort Boise only mentioned French Creek. I didn't know about Elk Creek."

"No reason to go over Elk Creek anymore. It has to drop down onto French Creek anyway, and it's steep as hell. French Creek is shorter."

They secured the horses and mule and hoisted the ramp back into place.

"You ferry across three sorry-looking riders earlier?" Charles asked.

"Nope. Last people I ferried across were six Chinamen loaded to the hilt with mining gear yesterday morning."

"What I figured," Charles replied. "You'd remember these men—one, a scar on his cheek, wearing a vest; one in a black frock coat, missing a couple fingers; the third, younger."

George shook his head. "Why do you ask?"

"We ran into them an hour ago on the trail just before that narrow section. One pulled his rifle, and I thought we were about to get dry-gulched."

"Could have been their intentions. We've had a few folks get their gear stolen, including a couple of horses." George adjusted the rudder and straightened the bow to cut across the choppy water. "Usually, it's the expressmen that have the trouble. Besides the mail, they carry most of the gold dust out. They're prime targets. One of them, Warren Hunt, been here since day one. Was jumped a while back by a couple road agents. He rode all night with them on his tail and made it here a day early. We were on business downstream so the boat was on the other side. He couldn't swim his horse on account of the mail and the gold. And he sure as hell wasn't about to head back from where he had come, so he hitched his leg over the wire and crawled across and brought the boat back on his own."

Charles eyed Samuel. "I told Samuel that's what he'd have to do if you hadn't been here. He didn't believe me."

"Well, I surmise it's been done more than once, but that wire'll cut you to pieces if you don't have gloves. Me, I would have swum across to get the boat, but I guess Warren wasn't much of a swimmer."

They drifted softly into the far bank. Without prompting, Samuel jumped off to tie off the ferryboat.

"Good boy you got there, Mr. Chambers. Got a head on his shoulders."

"I believe so, but don't let him hear you say so."

They led the stock down the ramp.

Charles continued, "I'm not so sure those three won't be back tagging after us."

"Pretty late in the day now. You could camp here."

"I had planned to push on a ways and camp near the freight landing."

"We'd be happy to put you up. You could buy yourselves a good hot meal and some grain for your stock. Grain will cost considerably more in Washington." He patted Buster. "From the looks of your stock, I'm guessing you've been on the trail a while."

Charles turned to Samuel. "What do you think, son?"

Samuel could not hold back his grin. "We've been on the trail for over sixteen hundred miles, and you want to know what I think about a home-cooked meal?"

"Now wait a minute. You're not implying anything bad about my cooking?"

"Let's see … corn mush, corn mush, a little salt pork, corn mush, corn mush. What do *you* think, Pa?"

They brushed their stock down, fed and watered them, and turned them out to graze with other livestock that were scattered on the lower hills near the cabin.

They headed to the river to wash up, Charles taking his razor and shaving mug.

"You're shaving?" Most of the time, his father shaved on Sundays when they both took time to clean up.

"It's been a long time since we've been in the company of a woman, Samuel. Appears to me to be the right thing to do." Carefully, he cut away a week's whiskers.

Samuel slicked his hair and checked his fingernails.

*　　*　　*

Dinner was served in a large, well-furnished room lit by a couple of kerosene lamps. The furniture was sturdy and well built, not rustic stumps as Samuel had expected. A cloth-covered table was set with plates, glasses, and eating silver. Wonderful odors wafted in from the adjoining room. Samuel felt as if he had returned to civilization.

Both Frederick and Susan Shearer brought in the dishes of food and set them on the table—sweet potatoes with a sorghum sauce, roast pork, cornbread with butter, new green peas, and beet greens.

"Well, gentlemen," Mrs. Shearer said. "The meal is served. Please help yourselves to all you want. Save some room for apple pie and coffee."

Platters of food made their way around the table, and Samuel loaded his plate. He took a bite of the sweet potatoes, savoring the taste, feeling ecstatic. It was his first since he had left Iowa.

Presently, George addressed Charles. "Noticed your bay has a US Army brand on it."

"Yes, I always tell folks he's the only good thing I got from the war. When I got back to Iowa, I had lost my farm, so I decided to keep the colt."

"Better than what I got from the war," George spoke evenly.

"You fought in the war? Who's unit? Where you from?" Charles asked.

"Born and raised in Virginia."

The silence was thick.

Charles started to rise up. "Sorry, George. I didn't think— Guess Samuel and I will turn in now."

"Sit down, Charles. I don't mind. Fact is I spent most of the war in Yankee prisons. The last bout was at Fort Delaware, courtesy of a Union soldier whom I had a disagreement with."

Charles sat heavily. "I'm darn sorry to hear that, George. Delaware was a cesspool."

"They all were, Charles. North or South, it didn't matter. I watched a lot of men die in prison. I stayed alive by catching and eating the rats the guards dumped from gunnysacks off the wall for their amusement." He stared into his water glass and swirled it before he took another drink. "Not memories I care to recollect." He leaned back, a slight smile. "But I did get out early on my own initiative, and according to Union records, I'm still an escapee. Told my commanding officer, General Bradley Johnson, that I had to go and reconnoiter for Yankees. Got here and found the war was over. Now don't *that* beat all." He smiled. "Sure was good to find my folks out here and get a new start. Guess I'll have to go back one day and find the good general and tell him I found the Yankees."

The men laughed.

Mrs. Shearer rose. "Who's ready for apple pie?"

Heads nodded. Impulsively, Samuel rose to help.

"Thank you, young man, but you just have a seat. I can handle this."

Shortly, Mrs. Shearer returned and set out large slabs of apple pie in front of each of them. She also poured everyone a steaming cup of coffee.

"Now tell me what you think of this pie," she said, putting the coffeepot down. "Got our first real crop of apples a few years back. Mr. Shearer is mighty proud of them."

Pie already in his mouth, Samuel looked up. "Mighty good, ma'am."

"Real fine." George tipped his cup toward his parents as Charles saluted with his own.

"And what's your story?" George turned to Charles.

"Like I said, the only good that came out of the war for me was Buster." Charles was silent. "I lost too many friends to recollect, and Samuel's uncle came home missing a leg."

"Sorry to hear that." George frowned.

"That's partly why we're out here." Charles spread his hands. "When I lost our place, I moved in with my wife's folks and her brother and his family. We now got a lot of mouths to feed from a poor piece of ground. I'm out here trying to get some gold for new land."

"Guess we all got ghosts to bury from the war," George muttered.

"It's okay. I made it. When I heeded the calling, I thought it was the right thing."

George set his cup down. "As did I. To me, I was fighting for Virginnie. Didn't matter what the war was really about. To me, it was about serving Virginnie. That's how I was brought up and what I believed. Tuscorara Academy in Pennsylvania taught me that. And it *was* the right thing. For both of us. And by dang, Chambers, if I'm called upon again, I'll go again."

"Not for Virginia, I 'spect."

"No, next time will be for the Union—for whatever she shall need—or for Idaho Territory."

"Such as?"

"I 'spect there will be a chance we'll need to round up some Indians in the future."

Charles raised his eyes. "Problems around here?"

Frederick Shearer interjected, "You still got settlers having a beef or two taken along with an occasional missing horse, but then I'm not too sure it's Indians all the time that's doin' all the taking."

"Maybe scum like the three we met on the trail today?"

Frederick nodded. "Another thing about the Indians. There's bands that didn't agree with the new treaty that shrank the Nez Perce reservation—Young Joseph's band in particular. Right now the government is leaving him alone in the Wallowas, but I can't 'spect that to remain so. This is traditionally some of their hunting grounds."

Charles told how he and Samuel met the Nez Perce and then asked in what campaigns George had fought. George began, and Mrs. Shearer interrupted.

"Samuel, would you like to join Mr. Shearer and me out here? Maybe have some cold buttermilk and let the men talk?"

Samuel glanced at his father. He wanted to stay and listen, but his father nodded. Despite the bad that had come from the uprising, the stories fascinated him, and his father rarely talked about the war.

Reluctantly, Samuel followed Mrs. Shearer into the living room. He found it also neatly decorated—a window with drapes, two rocking chairs, and a couple of other chairs with arms and cushions. A couple of rifles hung on pegs above a fireplace where a small fire crackled. A large rag rug covered the wood floor, spiraling outward in colorful patterns. Samuel felt strange. It had been months since he had been in a real home.

Mrs. Shearer handed him a glass of cold buttermilk and offered a plate that held oat cookies. Frederick Shearer helped himself to one as it went past.

"These are the best, Samuel. My missus makes a wonderful cookie."

"Thank you kindly." Samuel bit into one and took a swallow of the buttermilk. Its fresh, sweet taste surprised him. He tried to remember when he had last had some.

"Mrs. Shearer thought you might like a break," continued Mr. Shearer. "I don't mind, of course. My son doesn't usually run into a Yankee who is tolerable of the South, let alone one who actually fought in the war. Most of the folks out here avoided the war."

Samuel nodded. He found it awkward, knowing the man talking with his father was on the side responsible for his uncle Jake's missing leg; however, his father rarely spoke disparagingly of the South when he did talk of the war. He had explained before that they fought for what they believed.

"I came to this river the year the war broke out. I heard of the strike at Florence about twenty miles northeast of here. In '62, a party of men left there, crossed the river near here, and headed up into the country to the southeast. They made a good strike in some meadows. Called it Warren's camp after the party's leader, James Warren—unfortunately, a ne'er-do-well who spent most of his time showin' off his pearl-handled pistols than seriously mining.

"Anyway, as more men moved in, there were more Secessionists than Unionists, so they named the town Richmond after the Southern cause. The Unionists would have nothing to do with it and moved downstream a bit, naming their place Washington. Ain't no Richmond anymore, though."

Samuel set his empty glass down. "The Unionists run them out?"

"Nothing like that. Unfortunately for Richmond, or fortunately— depending on how you look at it—they found a heap load of gold under Richmond. It wasn't but two years before the town was completely dug up."

Samuel laughed.

"After the new strike, me and the missus realized the incoming miners would need a stopping place. More importantly, they would need a way to cross the river, especially during high water. So ... I built this ferry. The first couple years, I just rowed it back and forth or used a sweep."

"Weren't you afraid you'd get washed downstream?"

"That's why I like a sweep. It helps you keep the ferry at the right angle so the current just pushes you across." Mr. Shearer leaned back. "Didn't have much trouble except in high water like we got now. The wire we finally put up is just for safety in case I fall asleep at the rudder."

Samuel frowned and shook his head. "It seems the water should push something that big downstream."

Frederick Shearer smiled. "That's why I designed it with the two narrow boats underneath the decking. I figured out they don't catch the current as much. But the main thing is to angle the boat correctly." He held up his hands. "If the current is coming direct at you, the force hitting the boat will cause it to be pushed downstream, but if you turn it into the current at an angle, the current deflects off the side of the boat and pushes it in the opposite direction." He pushed his hands first one direction and then the other. "There, that's your engineering lesson for the day."

Samuel remembered how both George and Fischer had turned the bow to catch the current.

"Anyhow, I proved to be correct about this place. We've made a good living here operating a ferry, a boarding place, and now a post office. And my son just finished building a water-powered sawmill up Elk Creek. Used to be miners would come out of Florence down the trail across yonder. We'd go and ferry them over to this side, and they'd go up over Elk Creek behind us on up to Warren's camp. Now they just go up French Creek." Mr. Shearer leaned back.

"And the missus and I have planted a good garden, and now the fruit trees are producing. We have some produce we sell in the mining camps. Just a few years back, we got our first real good crop of apples. Boy, was that the best apple pie I ever had."

"I reckon it's about the best I ever had as well," Samuel replied and then hesitated, thinking. "Maybe excepting my ma's."

"Nothing beats a boy's own mother's apple pie." Mrs. Shearer, who was listening, winked at him.

Samuel settled back, feeling the warmth of the room, feeling comfortably tired, trying to remember the last time he'd had a piece of his mother's pie. He could not. Apples had been scarce.

"It was good when George showed up from the war in '65. Business was picking up strong. He was sure a sorry-looking sight, though. That Yankee prison didn't do him any good. His momma about had a fit. Took most of a year to get some meat back on his bones."

Samuel blinked, catching himself falling asleep, missing some of what Mr. Shearer had said.

"Mr. Shearer," Mrs. Shearer whispered. "I think Master Chambers should be turning in. They have a long trail ahead of them tomorrow. You might check on Mr. Chambers."

"Oh, heck, let them be, Susan. Let them talk." They had occasionally heard laughter and a few choice exclamations floating in from the other room.

"Then I suggest we let Samuel use the boarding room," Mrs. Shearer said. "I don't think he'll be able to make it out to their camp. What do you think, Samuel, about having a real bed to sleep in for a change?"

Samuel could not believe his ears. "But Pa, won't he—"

"Don't you worry about your pa," replied Mrs. Shearer. "I'm thinking Mr. Shearer just might join the men for a bit of a nightcap." She winked. "At any rate, he'll take care of things. Here, let me show you where to settle." Mrs. Shearer led Samuel to the back of their home into a small room.

Samuel soon found himself sinking into a wonderfully soft and warm bed. Hardly had he pulled the covers over than he slept.

WASHINGTON
AT WARREN'S CAMP

Chapter 9

Samuel felt a wave of joy as they turned down the main street into the town of Washington. A few people milled about. A couple of men were busily loading a pack train, lashing bundles tightly to the mules' aparejos. The sight refreshed Samuel's memory of the near disastrous encounter on the face of French Creek gorge, and he shivered.

Some structures were simple white canvas tents, tin pipes emitting white smoke columns, a single board sign slung above each tent's opening. Others were log buildings, and a few were saltbox structures built of rough-sawn wood. The first building, a substantial log structure, looked like a boarding house. Up a hill, there appeared to be the courthouse and jail. A US flag fluttered on a tall pole in front. Adjacent to the street below stood Ripson's Saloon, the Washington Hotel, and Hofen's Mercantile. The mules being loaded were partially clogging the street in front of Hofen's.

On the street's opposite side, a new-looking saltbox building with a sign announced, "*Raymond Hinley, Mine Assays.*" Adjacent to it stood another saloon, R. Sauxe Saloon, and a small log butcher shop, Jay Dubois, Butcher. Also near the butcher was Alexander's Mercantile and Mining Supplies, a tall saltbox structure.

Samuel could not make out the other buildings toward the southeast except the livery and blacksmith, where the large corral and horses identified it.

He was struck by the absence of wagons and carts, but then it occurred to him that there were no roads. It made no sense for a few hundred yards of town. This was the end of the trail. Nothing but wilderness lay beyond.

He gazed at the thick conifer-timbered hills rising what seemed only a short elevation above the town. A head frame with some buildings on the side of a hill and a pile of waste rock stood among the trees. He figured it was one of the quartz mines. He hoped it was not O'Riley's ledge already discovered by someone else.

A mother with her small daughter stepped out of one of the stores, a package in her arms, which surprised Samuel. He had not expected a mother and daughter.

He looked for the Chinese, half-expecting them to be swarming the street. Instead, they seemed to be at the far end along the side of a hill. Several moved about, dressed similarly in loose, blue cotton.

He suddenly felt odd. "What do we do now, Pa?" They had so long been on the trail, so long been heading to Warren's camp that it seemed strange they were actually here.

"Guess we need to get our stock taken care of. Find a place where we can picket them and pitch a tent. We aren't of a position for paying another night of lodging, no matter how great the bath is."

They pushed past Sauxe Saloon and the mules stamping impatiently and dismounted in front of Alexander's Mercantile. Samuel could now make out the next building down the street—C. A. Sears, Druggist. The two-story building next to it was another boarding house. A sign that said, "*Boarding, Baths, Hot Meals*," was tacked above the porch walkway. A smaller sign next to the door said, "*Meals, $1.00.*"

"Mind the stock, Samuel. I'll get us oriented." Charles headed into Alexander's Mercantile.

Samuel looped the reins around the rails. He noticed a few Chinese milling about a number of low-slung cabins. Built on partial stone foundations, the cabins were clustered around the hillside beyond the blacksmith and down along the creek. A larger, windowless, log building stood on the hill in a clearing among the lodgepole pines. He guessed the Chinese businesses and homes were largely located in that area, mostly separate from the white miners.

A couple of ladies approached, seemingly to Samuel to be trussed up more than they should be but at the same time not wearing what he would expect for going to church on Sunday. The youngest, a woman with reddish hair, was perhaps four or five years older than he was. The other, a dark-haired brunette, whispered to the younger lady as they came toward him, smiling. Samuel's heart caught at the sight of the younger lady. It had been a long time since he had seen such a beautiful woman.

The older lady, powder-blue dress and large feathery hat, weary face covered with heavy makeup, stepped up to him closely, broadly smiling. Samuel smelled her fragrant perfume, which was almost overpowering, and stepped back a little.

"You a newcomer to town?" she asked.

The younger lady, who was dressed in frilly pink and white and had a pleasant smile, laughed. She gazed intently at Samuel with bright hazel eyes.

"Yes, ma'am," he replied, touching his hat. "Me and my pa just got into town."

"Your pa as good a looker as you?" The brunette asked, winking.

Samuel blushed, embarrassed. "My ma says so."

The younger lady gushed, "Oh, you're so sweet."

"Well, welcome to Washington, traveler. I'm Hattie." The brunette held out her hand. The younger lady quickly added, "You can call me Lilly." She, too, held out her hand. Samuel took both in turn, feeling awkward but gave each a polite shake.

"Good to meet you, Miss Hattie ... Miss Lilly." Samuel nodded to each in turn, cracking a huge grin. Then, catching himself, thinking that was what a boy would do, he tempered his smile, stood taller, and said more strongly, "I'm Samuel Chambers." And as a quick afterthought, he added, "My pa's name is Charles."

The ladies laughed. Samuel could not help but notice that their bodices were low-cut, and they were remarkably full-chested. He flushed, hoping they had not noticed his glance.

"Well, I hope to meet your pa someday," Hattie said. "If he's at all as good lookin' as you."

"He's married, ma'am," Samuel said, catching her meaning.

"Well, if not your pa, maybe you?" She winked. "Maybe you're looking to meet a lady like me."

Samuel felt his ears burning. He found it difficult to believe what she had suggested, but he also found it slightly thrilling.

Lilly jabbed her, quickly interrupting, "Hush, Hattie." She addressed Samuel. "Don't you pay her no never mind, Samuel." She reached and touched his collar. "Samuel. I like the name Samuel. Like from the Bible. Sounds strong." Her hazel eyes twinkled, and her smile flashed. "If'n you like, you and I, we could get to know each other."

Samuel just stood, staring dumbly, burning with embarrassment but feeling a warm glow within.

Hattie nudged her. "Look who's talking now," she whispered quietly. She addressed Samuel. "You and your pa plannin' to do some placer mining or what?"

Samuel briefly thought a lady would not be asking questions about their business.

"I reckon." He was beginning to feel uneasy with the attention, but he liked Lilly. He wanted to hear her voice. "We're checking on some ground."

Hattie brightened. "I guessed. You're too young to be a hired hand. Maybe what? Thirteen?"

"I'm fourteen," protested Samuel, trying to stand taller.

"Hell ... I mean, heck, fourteen?" exclaimed Hattie.

"Fifteen in December."

A slight smile formed on her lips. "You come visit Hattie for sure."

Strangely, Samuel found himself wondering where Hattie lived, but he had no desire to go visit with an old lady unless she were serving apple pie and buttermilk.

Lilly gently interrupted, "*I* should be the one welcoming Samuel. Don't you think, Samuel?" She looked hopeful, beaming even more, if it was possible. Samuel thought she already sparkled from head to toe.

He nodded. He was unsure of what to say or do. Although he thought she was a bit odd, he *did* want to get to know Miss Lilly. He had not expected to come to a remote mining camp in the middle of Idaho Territory and find any civilization, let alone any women so beautiful.

Two sharply dressed men approached, one carrying a satchel. The ladies looked up. When they drew near, the men touched their hats, greeting them.

They returned the greeting with wide smiles and turned to leave.

"You are *so* welcome to Washington," Hattie called back over her shoulder. "It is *so* good to have someone new to brighten up the place."

Lilly blew Samuel a small kiss.

The men frowned but stepped back to let them pass.

"New in town?" The shorter man, who had black hair and a moustache, asked. His demeanor was businesslike. Dressed in a coat and vest with a bow necktie, he and his partner, who was similarly dressed, were the best-dressed men Samuel had seen since Fort Boise.

"Just got here."

"I see you're planning on staying awhile." He gestured at Molly.

Samuel anticipated the next question. "We hope to do some placer mining."

"Placer mining?" The man raised his eyes. "I'm surprised. Mostly Chinamen coming in now doing the placer mining. It's good to see someone who isn't Chinese." He set down the satchel and offered his hand. "I'm Matt Watkins. This is my partner, Ted Rankin."

"Pleased to meet you. I'm Samuel Chambers. My pa is Charles." Samuel shook Watkins's hand. When he shook Rankin's, he noticed the pistol at his waist and felt a bit uneasy. Rankin was younger than Watkins and had sandy-colored hair and light eyes. "My pa's inside checking on things." Samuel nodded toward the store.

"Just come from there. Saw a stranger talking with Mr. Alexander."

"That'd be him."

"You guys already got someone to work for, or are you planning on buying ground?" Watkins inquired. "Reason I'm asking is I know some folks who are willing to sell if you're buying."

"Why they sellin'?"

"Same as most around here, Sam," he replied. "Most of the ground is marginal and won't pay more than five or six dollars a day anymore. Owners are selling out, and the Chinamen are moving in. The whites are moving on or working for a few better-paying placers."

Rankin interjected, "Actually, most of the miners are workin' in the quartz mines now. That's the Little Giant up there you can see on the hillside." He pointed to the mine Samuel had noticed earlier. "You can try placerin', but if it don't work, don't forget the quartz mines. 'Spect you're a bit young for hirin' on for hardrock, though."

Samuel did not answer. He was tired of being too young.

"Leastwise, around here, some are leavin', and the Chinese are comin' in. But I know for a fact if you're willin' to work hard, most of the placers will pay well enough, and sometimes you can get lucky."

Watkins laughed. "Better listen to Ted Rankin, Sam. He knows what he's talking about. Found one of the richest placers ever at Florence, a thousand dollars in one day. Then he comes here and does the same thing. Now he has nothing better to do, so he gives me advice."

Samuel's head spun. He could not imagine one thousand dollars in gold. *Fifty ounces ... less, gold didn't run pure ... but in one day?* He felt disappointed. They had arrived too late. The gold was nearly gone. Now they talked of five or six dollars in a day as being good, maybe half an ounce. They had no choice but to find O'Riley's ledge.

"We plan to do some prospecting for a while," Samuel offered. "If we don't find any good ground, I reckon my pa will try to buy a placer."

"Be careful. I know a claim a fella bought and within a week of buying it, filled a pint jar full of nuggets. When he began flashing the jar around town, the former owner got mighty upset and insisted on buying the claim back. He did ... for double. Of course, after selling it back, the man promptly left town, considerably richer."

Rankin finished the story. "The owner's now packin' a good rope and out huntin' for the con man."

Samuel grinned.

"If you come to wanting to buy a claim, Sam, look me or Mr. Rankin up. We've been here a good amount of time and know most of what all these claims have produced. I know of at least two that should pay pretty well. I'm also the county recorder. If you do get one, see me about recording it. You can usually find me in the back of Hofen's." He gestured across the street. "Remember the name, Matt Watkins."

"Thanks kindly, Mr. Watkins. I'll let my pa know."

The men stepped away.

"Let me know what?" Charles had caught part of the conversation as he returned.

"That those two guys are selling claims." He watched them enter Hofen's. The mule train began pulling out. It looked like it was packed with mining gear. Probably for one of the new quartz mines, Samuel figured.

"Could be they know what they're talking about," Charles said. "One of them's the recorder, and I'm guessing he just carried about thirty pounds of gold dust or so past you in that bag. They just picked it up from Mr. Alexander." He nodded toward Alexander's Mercantile. "The outfit across the street owns that pack train. They have a store in Lewiston and supply some of the camps. And as you might figure, they take out some of the gold."

"That's what took you so long? Learning that?"

"Partly. Also trying to run down a place we can set up camp, at least temporary," Charles replied. "Anyone else say hi?"

Samuel was not sure he wanted to answer. "A couple of real nice ladies talked to me for a while."

Charles raised his eyebrows. "Family ladies or otherwise?"

"Otherwise?" Samuel was uncertain what his father meant.

"Later, son," he replied. "Been talking to Mr. Alexander. He's been here since the strike in '62. Knows what's going on. Says this season should be better than last. Last year, it was so dry the placers shut down early, and then the fires that got started chased everyone out of the woods, so not much work was done on the quartz ledges.

"He also told me about a place we can camp." Charles nodded to the north. "Down the meadows is a placer that belonged to a couple fellows he grubstaked, but they didn't do much with it. Says there's part of a cabin nearby with a spring, but it will need a lot of repair. Said there should still be some gold. We can stake it if we want. He said to remember him if we hit it big."

"But if there's still gold there, why doesn't he take it up?" Samuel could not imagine someone knowing where there was gold and not mining it.

"He said it didn't pay enough." Charles shrugged. "I'm quickly learning apparently there's gold all over this country, but most of it doesn't have water or isn't worth the time to dig it."

Samuel frowned.

"Mr. Alexander seems like a good man. He was glad to see us here instead of more Chinamen."

"Same thing the other men told me." Samuel shrugged. "Guess no one much likes the Chinese."

Charles swung up onto Buster and turned him from the post. "Didn't say he didn't like them. Just seems concerned they're flooding into the country and taking all the jobs.

"Got a letter from your ma." He showed it to Samuel. "It's been waiting for us for a couple weeks. Mr. Alexander almost sent it back."

Samuel's heart skipped as he reached to take it. *"Mister Charles Chambers and Son; General Delivery; Washington, Warren's Camp, Idaho Territory,"* it said. He clutched it, seeing his mother and sister, Elizabeth, back at the cabin in Iowa. He wanted to tear it open and read it, but he decided to wait until he had private time.

Muted thunder rumbled from the north. The sky had darkened.

"Guess we'd better find that cabin," Charles said, looking up.

Gray clouds flowed across the mountains to the northeast. The ridgeline, heavy with bright green conifers and broken occasionally by gray granite outcrops, was partially shrouded in rapidly moving clouds. Samuel guessed the mountains rose about fifteen hundred feet above them, similar to Steamboat Summit they had earlier crossed.

They followed Meadow Creek toward the north. Within several yards of either side of the channel, it was completely torn up and mined out. Barren piles of cobbles stood where meadow had once been. Not a tree or grass blade remained.

About half a mile up a finger meadow, they found the abandoned cabin, a small stream flowing nearby. Just beyond, a cut in the hillside showed where the men had placered. Undisturbed meadows extended beyond the cut to the edge of the timber.

"Plenty of grass for graze," Charles observed.

The cabin was little more than some rough walls. The roof had collapsed. No floor. Grass and brush grew up inside.

"Better pitch our tent till we can get this place looking more like a home," Charles muttered. "Might be better off building a new cabin."

They cleared and leveled a place for a floor, and then on the adjacent hillside, they cut some lodgepole pines for a frame for the canvas tent. Samuel decided the name for the trees was fitting. Rising perfectly straight, the narrow trees grew spindly, sporting sparse limbs near their crowns, yielding naked, twenty-foot poles.

It began raining while they pitched the tent, but recalling the tent at the freight-landing, they took time to dig a drainage ditch around its perimeter before hauling in their gear. The grassy floor was already becoming muddy, but for the first time since leaving Iowa, they were settled in one place.

"Feels strange to finally be here," Samuel said.

"That it does. Now we got to figure on how to go about things."

"Let's look for O'Riley's ledge."

"I agree, but we got to keep in mind taking care of ourselves as well."

Charles pulled out a piece of paper. "This is what I sketched."

Samuel had seen the map a hundred times, but he looked at it with renewed interest.

"This is where the creek comes into what used to be Richmond." His father pointed at the squiggly line. "Upstream—I don't know how far—should be a rock outcrop. Somewhere along a line between it and a bare knob should be the quartz ledge. The cairns O'Riley piled up should be somewhere downstream beside the creek and point to the outcrop." Charles pointed to a small triangle on the map. "Somewhere near here, I think."

"What if we can't find it right away?" Samuel gazed quietly at the thickly timbered hills shrouded in rain clouds. "What I mean is … we might have to hunt a long time, and we're going to need grub."

"That's what I meant about taking care of ourselves." Charles folded the paper and put it away. "I had hoped to have a bigger grubstake than what we got to live off while we looked for the ledge. That was the purpose of bringing Molly and buying supplies in Fort Boise. Might be I'll be looking for work sooner than expected, and you're going to have to do a lot more hunting."

*   *   *

After dinner, Samuel opened his mother's letter:

My Dear Charles and Son, Samuel

By now, you should have reached Washington. I hope you have found a nice place to stay.

Mother, Elizabeth, and I are as fine as can be expected.

Uncle Jake and Cousin Daniel have done a fine job tending the crops, and you will be pleased to know they are coming in fine. The corn is a couple of inches up, but I do not know if it will be knee-high by Independence Day. Nevertheless, I think we will have good crops this summer.

Daniel is growing to be a good young man. He packs the rifle with him wherever he goes and does some of the hunting. He shot a doe a week past, which was a welcome addition to the fare. Uncle Jake rode out to pack it in on his mule.

The weather has been mostly warm and pleasant. The other day, there was a fierce, twisting wind that went through over by the Wilson's place. They were all fine.

We are all praying for you to find Mr. O'Riley's gold mine and that there is still some gold remaining. I know you will use some gold to provide for yourselves; however, we will be thankful for any amount you can send home. Elizabeth asks every day if you have found the gold.

I know the country out there can be unforgiving. I pray God watches over you, but you must do your part and be careful.

Charles, I hope you and Samuel are eating good fare.

Elizabeth and I love you both very much and pray for your safe return soon.

Your loving wife and Samuel's mother,

Mary Chambers

A couple of spaces below she had written:

Samuel, remember to take a bath on the weekend and wash up your clothes. Remind your father as well. Your clothes will last longer.

He did not read that part to his father.

"I need to write a letter, Pa," Samuel said.

"I figured you would. When I saw we got a letter, I bought a few sheets of paper and some envelope makings." He handed the necessary items to Samuel. "Next time we're in town, you can post it with Mr. Alexander."

Samuel wrote a long letter back. He asked what his father wanted to say. His father was not much with writing letters, and Samuel had already figured he would be the one to do most of the writing. He was careful to avoid much about the Indians and the three men they met on the trail. It would do no good to get his mother riled up about such things. She was too far away even to appreciate things in the daylight where, naturally, they did not appear as bad. So he told her they had passed a pack train that was coming out and they had taken a bath at Burgdorf's. He was glad he could say that, figuring it would make his mother feel better.

CHAPTER 10

Saturday morning, they woke to a steady drizzle occasionally mixed with sleet. Water ran across the grassy floor of the tent, which was increasingly turning to mud. Their bedding was soaked.

"We aren't going to get much looking done during this kind of weather," Charles muttered, pushing up on the canvas to dump the water that had collected.

"Not much of anything we can do."

"We can put on our coats and start cutting logs for the cabin and get a better roof over our heads."

Samuel hoped his father would not say that, but he soon found himself in the timber on the hillside searching for suitable trees. Most were too skinny. As his father felled them, Samuel hitched them to Molly and dragged them to the cabin.

They cut and replaced most of the logs in the wall and then began work on the roof. Three evenings later, they had a new ridgepole up and finished covering it with a layer of small poles until it was relatively weatherproof. With other poles, they built two bed frames and wrapped ropes around each for springs. For mattresses, they filled gunnysacks with grass and laid them across the ropes. They dragged stumps inside for something to sit on and built a crude pole table. The floor was now mud. Water trickled under the walls and seeped up into their boot prints. Samuel guessed the previous owners had probably not spent a winter in the cabin but had given up after a single season. At one time, the cabin had probably contained a stove, but if so, someone had carried it off. For the time being, they continued their cooking on an open fire outside.

"Maybe we can take our tent in and trade for an old stove," Samuel suggested.

"Not yet. We might need it for a camp elsewhere. But I can ask around about a stove."

"We could cut some more poles for a floor. It would be better than this mud."

"Too slick when they get wet. We'd break our necks." Charles shook out his bedding and brushed off the mud spatters that had fallen from the roof. "For the time being, you can pull a couple boards from the remains of the sluice and use those."

Samuel had checked the sluice when they had first arrived, hoping to find some gold behind the remaining cleats, but nothing remained in the box. The wind and snow had decimated it.

Other than the mud floor, the cabin felt like home. Samuel gazed out across the meadow toward the grazing stock. "With all the grass and good water, this would make a good homestead, don't you think, Pa?"

"Only till the snow comes. Then this entire meadow will be buried under six feet."

*   *   *

In the morning, the clouds still hung heavily over the meadows. A soft drizzle fell. Nevertheless, Charles and Samuel rode out in search of the ledge.

"I've had enough rain already," Charles muttered, gazing toward the sky, "but I can't stand sitting around the cabin any longer."

"Neither can I." Samuel was giddy with excitement. Finally, they were heading out in search of the lost ledge.

By the time they reached and rode through Washington, the rain had ceased, and the clouds began to lift. Samuel's spirits lifted as well.

Often, he had dreamed of the gold. He imagined they would ride right up the creek, find the cairns, and walk right to the ledge. He imagined shining chunks of gold stuck everywhere in the rocks. He had tied a large canvas bag behind his cantle for such a thing.

He studied the Little Giant Mine, where steam and smoke rose. He now knew it could not have been O'Riley's ledge. It was too near town.

They headed upstream from Washington, passed the stone and log cabins where the Chinese lived, and continued on to where a tributary came in from the northeast. Dozens of Chinese were hard at work all up and along the stream. The trees had been stripped from the ground and piles of naked cobbles ran in rows up the creek. Pits were gouged into the hillsides. Several wooden flumes carried water through the gouges. Groups of Chinese slogged through the mud and water, working the sluice boxes. Silt and mud clogged the creek.

Charles muttered, "It's good O'Riley's ledge isn't in that direction."

The Chinese paused to watch them pass. Samuel felt uneasy.

"Your Celestial brethren hard at work." Charles nodded a greeting toward them.

Most were dressed like white miners—trousers and suspenders, gumboots, flannel shirts, wide-brimmed, western hats. A few still wore their traditional cone-shaped hats and loose-fitting tunics with baggy, short trousers that were now soaked wet and plastered to their bodies. Samuel guessed their traditional clothing did not last long in such conditions.

What struck Samuel the most was their industry. None rested. They were shoveling dirt, pitching rocks from the boxes with their sluice forks, or swinging picks to knock more rocks and dirt from the banks. Others hauled baskets of earth that were suspended from yokes balanced across their shoulders and emptied them into the heads of the sluices. Their constant chatter, a singsong, melodic talk, sounded pleasant.

When they passed, the Chinese cheerfully greeted them, smiling and waving.

"Hello," Samuel greeted and waved back. Curiously, when he did, they bowed politely.

"That must be the Rescue Mine." Charles pointed toward some buildings on a hillside above the creek to the south. "It's supposed to be one of the richest quartz mines in the district but seems to always be in litigation, according to Mr. Alexander. Right now, the owner, a Mr. Isenbeck, has a crew of about a dozen men running around the clock. Maybe things will look up for them." He nudged Buster past the upturned roots of a fallen tree.

"And I imagine that's the Pioneer Mill." Charles nodded toward another building with a tall frame and hoppers. It stood somewhat downhill closer to the creek.

"It looks dead," observed Samuel. "I don't hear a thing."

"Pert near *is* dead. As I understand, the Pioneer is down more than it operates."

They followed the trail about a mile and turned up a tributary that came in from the southeast.

"Hard to believe a town once stood here," observed Charles.

Samuel looked around. He remembered Frederick Shearer telling him how the early miners discovered gold under Richmond and dug it up. Low mounds and rows of rounded rocks spread in every direction across the narrow valley.

"Haven't seen any signs of buildings, have you? 'Spect the entire town was dug up?"

"Sure looks that way," Samuel replied quietly, his excitement had dimmed.

He realized that because of the amount of digging, there was little chance of finding any cairns.

They rode until the trail turned northwest up another tributary. The main creek continued toward the east. Charles paused and waved toward the heavily forested mountains that rose beyond. Several barren outcrops peeked through the trees. "So which outcrop is it?"

"I don't know, Pa. There must be dozens." Samuel felt dismayed. "Did O'Riley say which one?"

"He said it was a prominent outcrop on a hill above the creek. Said it couldn't be missed. The Charity is up this trail. Knowing our luck, that's where we'll find the outcrop. The good news is we must be in the right place. Most of the richest quartz leads have been found back up this direction."

"What do we do, Pa?"

"We start prospecting. Maybe we'll get lucky and no one has found it."

They turned their horses up through the timber and headed toward one of the outcrops. When they reached it, they paused to scan the country.

"Guess that must be the Charity." Charles pointed toward the tops of a few structures north of them in the trees. "They've got a stamp mill there as well. Good news—it's over that direction and not here where we're at. But I'm starting to think we could do this every day for a month and still be finding new outcrops," he said quietly. "And I don't see anything resembling a bare knob."

The rain picked up as they pushed through the brush and trees and searched the hillsides. From each outcrop they reached, they gazed west and northwest. They found a couple of rocky areas but no large knobs. *It couldn't be missed, O'Riley had said*, Samuel reminded himself.

Near evening, they reached an isolated outcrop far to the south. Charles dismounted and gazed back across the country, shaking his head. "It made sense to O'Riley because he saw the outcrop. He climbed it. He'd recognize it and could use it as a marker, but to us, it's just one outcrop among the many."

Samuel felt distressed. His hopes had vanished. He touched the canvas bag and hoped his father had not seen how naive he had been. "What do we do, Pa?"

"For today, we call it quits. I'm getting soaked. It's not good for the horses either. It's just one day. I'll rustle up some grub, and we can think about it. Maybe we should spend time looking for the cairns along the creek." He turned Buster back the direction they had come. "Maybe tomorrow the sun will make things seem brighter. The good thing is we've seen some of the country. The more we see of it, the more it will make sense."

By the time they reached the Chinese placers, the rain had increased in intensity, and it was near dark. Water ran freely from Samuel's hat brim, and when he leaned too far forward, it ran down his neck. Their horses' hooves sank in the mud as they slogged through Washington, streets now empty. The Chinese had also abandoned their work. Samuel felt chilled.

It was night by the time they reached the cabin. Wearily, Samuel fed and turned out the stock while his father started the fire and began some dinner. Samuel dragged wood to the camp on his way back. His father warmed some beans and corncakes and brought them inside the cabin to where it was somewhat dry.

Samuel felt numb. Now he knew he would not just walk to the ledge and begin picking up chunks of gold. He listened to the rain drumming on the roof and dripping through in places, thinking of his mother and sister back in his grandmother's warm cabin in Iowa.

CHAPTER 11

The next several days, they alternated between scouring the creek banks for the cairns and searching deeper into the hills for the lost outcrop. They found nothing but old placer tailings along the creek. In the hills, they found a few abandoned digs, which they carefully inspected. Samuel looked for traces of gold, but other than the bright yellow specks he had seen at Pete and Hallelujah's, he did not really know what it would look like, especially in a piece of rock.

From the ridgetops, they searched to the west for a bare knob or open meadows. The nearest bare knob appeared to the north beyond the Chinese placers in the opposite direction and along a different drainage. They frequently picketed the horses and searched the more inaccessible areas on foot. Nothing matched O'Riley's description.

Several miles to the southwest, they came upon the Knott and Hic Jacet mines. Several men were busy preparing a site for erecting a stamp mill. They paused a moment to talk. The men bragged that the ore they were finding would best the Rescue ore and were anxious for the mill to arrive. It was already en route and being packed in out of Lewiston by mule train.

"Not to worry, Samuel," Charles explained. "We're too far west for this to have been O'Riley's ledge. Besides, the gulch drains to the north and not into Meadow Creek."

"That's a relief."

"Keep it in mind, though. If we don't find O'Riley's ledge, this might be a good place to prospect."

Saturday morning, they woke to more drizzling rain.

"Nuts with searching in the rain, Samuel. Let's say we go into town. I've a mind to be asking a few questions."

Samuel was happy for the decision. He wanted to see more of Washington anyway.

The cold rain hammered a steady beat on them as they rode. They avoided

75

as best as possible the deepest mud holes in the trail and the creek of water that now ran down it. They stopped in front of the new assay building.

Inside, a couple of stools and a table stood near a counter. A work area with a furnace and shelves lined with glass containers, wooden boxes, and tins was separated behind the counter. A thick layer of light gray dust blanketed everything.

A man in his early thirties with short reddish brown hair came to the counter. "Good morning, gentlemen. How may I help you?" He peered expectantly through round glasses. His left eye twitched.

"I need a little advice." Charles got to the point. "Just got here a few days ago from Iowa with my son. We thought we'd do some prospecting. Frankly, I have no idea what I'm doing."

"Then may I welcome you to Washington," the shorter man said. "I'm Raymond Hinley." He dusted his hands on his work apron and reached out a hand. "Perhaps I can spare a moment."

Charles introduced himself and Samuel.

"I have come from Canada myself," Hinley said, adjusting his glasses. He had an easy smile.

"From Canada? Then what brings you to Idaho Territory?" Charles asked.

"I worked several mining camps. When I arrived here, I found the climate to my liking and relatively little competition. Overall, the work has been reasonably steady, and there seems a tolerable future with the quartz mines opening and coming into production." He paused. "May I ask what brings *you* here? If you're green to prospecting, Warren's camp is not the most likely destination."

Charles shrugged. "It's a long story. I can't really explain. Just know we're here and we're interested in hunting for gold."

Hinley grimaced. "I shall be direct. You are nigh on five years too late. The placers are on the downside, and not a few owners are selling out to the Celestials. I wager the best quartz ledges have also been discovered. The shining hope for Washington is bringing the quartz mines into full production, and I believe that shall happen. If not, then we have all arrived here a bit late."

"Doesn't sound optimistic," Charles said.

"If you are pursuing work, your best chance would be the quartz mines. I do not believe anyone would hire on your boy, however—too much a featherweight for hardrock mining. Someone might consider him at one of the placers if any of those are hiring." He glanced at Samuel. "I mean no offense, lad."

Samuel nodded. He understood.

"We're not looking for work just yet, and I don't think we're interested in a placer. We can see that everything's pretty dug up," Charles said. "How about any advice on hunting quartz ledges?"

Hinley shrugged. "You, sir, shall find it is a big country." He tossed some white rock fragments onto a metal plate.

"Look, I know you're a busy man. Any help would be obliged. I might have made one of the biggest mistakes of my life, but I'm here now. I owe it to folks back home to give it a go."

"Then I suggest prospecting south and east of here within four miles. There, you shall have your best chance for locating a quartz mine. All the producing mines are within that region."

Samuel felt relieved. That matched the information they had received from Kevin O'Riley. He also worried. One of the operational mines might well be O'Riley's ledge.

"You will discover most of this country has been hard prospected. True, there is always a chance another ledge remains to be brought to light. Indeed, this ore is from a recent discovery." He indicated the pieces of white quartz on the plate.

"Now if you decide to be looking for work, the Charity, Rescue, and Little Giant are all running crews around the clock. They may be to hiring, but those jobs are hard to come by unless someone gets injured or killed. When the Hic Jacet and Knott get their stamp mill put in, they may be hiring. Otherwise, you shall find coming by work around here quite slim."

Samuel poked at the quartz. "This got gold in it?"

Hinley adjusted his glasses and ran his hand through his red hair. "Aye, lad, and I shall be figuring out just how much. Like everyone, the owner believes he has struck it rich, and he wants to be learning the news yesterday." He picked up a metal mallet with a curved head and began rolling it back and forth, pulverizing the fragments.

"I thank you kindly, Mr. Hinley," Charles said, reaching to shake Hinley's hand. "I'll let you return to your work."

Samuel stared hard at the fragments on the plate. "What you doing that for?" He felt compelled to ask.

"Come on, son. Mr. Hinley has work."

"I shall oblige the lad." Hinley's eye twitched. "I am reducing these pieces of ore to a fine powder so that I may melt it down and determine the gold and silver values."

"Know where it's from?" Samuel asked. "Maybe you can tell me, and we'll go prospect there." He grinned.

"Now, lad, I would not be at liberty to divulge such, even if I could," Hinley said, winking. "However, after seeing samples from known locations and understanding the nature of ores, I generally have a good idea. I would wager this sample comes from near the Charity mine about a mile and a half south of here."

Hinley picked up a small fragment from the steel plate and handed it to Samuel. "Study on this. You should be able to see some gold."

Samuel held it close and spotted some tiny gold flecks as well as some black metallic specks. He realized this was what gold looked like in a rock and now wondered if he had missed it in the rocks he had been examining back in the hills.

"This is what you call free-milling gold. It is easy and cheap to process. All you do is crush it, float off the quartz, amalgamate the gold, then retort it down."

Hinley tossed the sample back onto the plate. He dusted his hands on his apron and picked up a tiny gold button. "Here's what you get when you fire it."

Samuel looked it over and handed the button to his father. "Is it pure?"

"Except for some traces of silver."

"I'm much obliged to you, Mr. Hinley." Charles handed back the button. "What do you say, Samuel? You ready to go look at more ledges?"

Samuel grinned. "I reckon I'm motivated."

Hinley laughed. "Well, Mr. Chambers, it appears the lad is beginning to catch the fever. Perhaps *he will* find you a quartz mine."

"That's why we're here," Charles replied. "And thanks. I'm obliged for your help, Mr. Hinley. What do we owe you?"

"It is appropriate to keep me in mind if you strike it rich." Hinley smiled.

Charles turned to leave.

"Look," Hinley said as they stepped toward the door. "I regret appearing less than optimistic. I see a young lad and you out here, Mr. Chambers, and I recognize the true nature of your likelihood of success. Most folks fail miserably. I believe if you have diligence and perseverance, you may succeed. I should like to see you both succeed. Visit again if I can be of further assistance."

"I appreciate your honesty. You've given us hope."

CHAPTER 12

Sunday, they resumed work on the cabin. They fashioned some peg-leg stools to replace the stumps they had been using, installed pegs to hang clothing, built a couple of shelves, and placed the bed frames up on short logs—all improvements to get up out of the mud and to help keep things dry. More importantly, they rescued an old stove from a man in town. They had to seal the stovepipe with clay, but by noon when they fired it up, it drew the smoke nicely.

Late that afternoon, Samuel returned to explore the cut on the hillside and to re-inspect the sluice. He dug down into the old dig where the miners before them had been working and carried some gravel back to the spring creek near the cabin for washing. Trying to remember how Pete had demonstrated, he submerged the pan, vigorously shook it, and then gently swirled the water around, washing out bits of gravel until a small amount of black sand remained. He was shocked to see a couple of tiny specks of gold. The second pan showed more. He figured it might be a penny's worth. Not much, but he began considering how he could repair the sluice and get water to it.

Most days, the mornings began fair, but by noon, the rain came, steadily increasing in intensity, often raining heavily late into the evening. Sometimes they tried to wait it out under the pines. Other times, they were forced to return to the cabin. The meadows had almost become lakes. The trails were small streams. Word was both the Salmon and the Columbia Rivers were flooding. Some of the ferryboats were shut down.

The cabin offered little protection. Water leaked in under the log walls. Their gear always seemed wet. They spent their evenings trying to dry it out. Keeping wood cut and the fire going were draining chores.

One evening, Samuel worked on building a checkerboard from a slab of wood. He had previously cut the round checker pieces by slicing up a limb. Drops of rain spattered through onto the board, smudging the charcoal he had used to make black squares.

"Might need to add more brush to the roof, Pa."

As if to make a point, rain rattled across it, sending down more spray.

"Yes, I'm catching drips in my cooking but not like if I was outdoors." He laughed.

Dinner was meager—corn mush and a few beans. Their supplies were dwindling.

The following day, they rode northeast of the cabin and hunted for game. They saw none until late afternoon when they caught sight of a yearling black bear. It entered a brushy draw where they lost it. Finally, they managed to jump a couple of cottontail rabbits near a rock outcrop. Charles killed them both.

"Won't last but a good meal, Samuel, but at least it's a bit of fresh meat."

Whenever the rain paused, they resumed prospecting to the south near the known quartz ledges. Systematically, they examined the rock outcrops. Samuel tried to remember what the ore Hinley had shown him looked like. Nothing he found matched the rocks. Sometimes he found white quartz, but none held specks of gold.

As they drifted even farther south, they reached two of the newer placer mines, the Martinace and the Keystone. Charles told Samuel the area was too distant to have been near O'Riley's ledge, but at least they were still in the drainage feeding into Meadow Creek.

South of the Keystone, they encountered a party of prospectors working along a gulch.

"Anything good?" inquired Charles.

"Got a bit of color panning in the stream below but no lode."

"Yet," added his partner. "We're just getting back at it. We had to shut down most of last summer due to the fires. They must have burned half of Idaho Territory."

"We've been hearing about them."

"Hey, I've seen you guys before," the taller man observed.

"Yep, I 'spect so. We've been out here a number of times prospecting."

"Well, the way I see it, I think you're lookin' for somethin'."

"Aren't we all?"

The man laughed. "You seem intent on this area, and I seen you studyin' the hills. Like you're looking for a marker. Ain't that so?"

"Can't say." Charles grinned. "Most of the time, I'm lookin' for a way back out of here."

"Well, it's okay if'n you are. More lost ledges in this country than wot's been found."

Samuel sat Spooky while the men talked. He studied the hills north of them—hills he had now memorized. He wondered how anyone could spot anything in this country. Timber and brush choked the hillsides, and thick meadow grass clogged the creeks and formed bogs. He turned and studied the burnt hills to the south, trying to imagine what it looked like when the woods were ablaze. The fire had revealed outcrops in that direction, but he knew they were too far south for any to have been O'Riley's. *Maybe one has gold anyhow. It doesn't have to be O'Riley's. These guys have found some gold. Why not us?* he reasoned.

Another day of fruitless searching and again being caught in an afternoon rain, they returned to the cabin. Samuel held his damp shirt before the fire, turning it as it dried, trying to enjoy the fire's warmth on his bare shoulders. Outside, the rain had become heavier, and drops spattered through the roof.

"Nuts." Charles shoved the serving spoon into the beans he was preparing and threw up his hands. "I'm beginning to believe O'Riley misled me," he said. "We've been at it how long? Almost three weeks ... and there's not a clue."

Samuel remained silent for a moment, feeling his father's distress. "Some things are like O'Riley described. The creek and the outcrops are right." He tried to dismiss the sinking feeling. "He had no reason to lie. It's just harder than we expected." Samuel put on his shirt, still damp but warm, and sat near his father.

"Unless I'm overlooking something pretty obvious, something's wrong."

"Could be O'Riley's ledge is now one of the quartz mines," Samuel said quietly. He knew the Charity especially matched the description, although they had failed to find any cairns in the creek bottom below it.

"I been thinking the same."

The sound of rain drumming on the roof increased. More drops sprayed through, causing them to shift around to avoid the drips.

"Damn rain," Charles muttered. "You'd think it would be summer by now." He brushed the drops from his forehead.

Charles spooned some beans onto a plate and offered them to Samuel. "I'm afraid we need to start thinking differently about things. We're out of grub. I'm going to see if anyone's hiring on hands. I'll get a bit of work to raise a little cash. Then we can—" He set down his plate. "Hell, maybe we should just call it quits and head home."

Samuel felt stunned. "Go home?" Rain spattered into his plate.

"I know it will mean we struck out. We'll go back empty-handed, tails between our legs."

Visions of finding gold evaporated. Samuel felt a terrible emptiness. "I don't want to go home, Pa. We still got a lot of places we can check. We spent near three months getting here. It's a long ways home empty-handed."

"It'll be harder to get our own place—that's all."

"I'm okay with trying longer, Pa. We hardly know what we're doing. We keep working hard, maybe we'll get lucky."

"I always thought it would be hard work that mattered. Now seeing how miserable it is around here—how miserable the weather is, always raining, always wet, always muddy—and seeing just what little gold there is, I just got to admit this was a wild-goose chase and concentrate on getting us home safely to your ma and your sister."

"What about finding our own placer?" Samuel pushed. "Maybe we should work this one. Fix up that old sluice. I found a little gold when I panned some gravel. You said we could try placering."

Charles brushed another drop from his forehead and looked up at the steady drip that had started above him. He moved again.

Samuel's mind raced. He needed to convince his father to stay. He could not bear the thought of the long trip back, and for what?

"We owe it to Uncle Jake. Part of it is his money."

His father remained silent.

"Ma would want us to keep trying," Samuel said quietly, almost choking. He knew of nothing else to say. Spray from the rain drumming on the roof showered him.

At length, Charles spoke. "You're right, son. Your ma would want us to keep on. I'm sorry. Maybe the sun will shine tomorrow, and things will look up. Maybe we can figure out something." He reached over and tapped Samuel's shoulder. "I know for a fact I need a job. At the very least, I need to have traveling money for when we do head out, and in the meantime, if you want to fix that sluice … that will take a few dollars for new lumber. You up to it?"

"You bet, Pa," Samuel said as he felt the rush of relief. They would hang on for a short while at least. "Maybe until then, I can keep checking some of the outcrops."

"You can, Samuel, but I'm not sure it will be worth your while. You've seen how everything good is staked—all the quartz mines—but go ahead. You can't sluice any gold till we fix the box, anyhow."

Charles took a mouthful of beans and then frowned. He picked a bean husk from his teeth. "Do some more hunting first. We could use something to eat besides beans and corncake."

CHAPTER 13

The grass was still soaking wet when Samuel rounded up the horses and brought them to the cabin the next morning. Steam lifted into the bright sunlight off the meadows. It was a good sign things would dry.

"I want to go with you while you look for work." Samuel threw his saddle onto Spooky. "I can go hunting later."

"Well, I don't mind the company, but I'm thinking it will be a lot of boring talk."

"Maybe the boring talk will pay off for us, Pa. Sometimes I learn things. When people are busy talking to you, they don't notice me."

Charles smiled and pulled his cinch tight. "Maybe, but I'm not sure what you could learn we don't already know."

They returned to Raymond Hinley's assay shop.

"Morning, Raymond."

"And to you, Charles and Samuel. What brings you to town so early?"

"I'm now looking for work."

Hinley frowned. "After my careful instruction, you have been examining ledges for nigh on two weeks, and it has not come to fruition?" His eye twitched.

Charles shook his head. "It was a chance we took. Now I need work so we can at least make grub. Samuel will keep up on the prospecting a bit and do some hunting."

"Then I will remind you of the quartz mines. The Hic Jacet should have its stamp mill running. They could be looking to put on a new hand."

"I'd prefer a placer. I'm figuring I'll be on the other side of the ground soon enough."

Samuel frowned.

"Aye, only two outfits I know of doing well enough they may hire— McLane and Osborn. Both have good paying claims in the Big Meadow." He took off his spectacles and polished them. "However, if you are interested in moving up into the hills, you have the Martinace and the Keystone. They each have crews, but I can't wager if they are putting on hands."

"I've been past them. Neither seemed to be much of an operation. What about any new strikes?" Charles asked. "Seems to me they would be the most likely to be hiring."

"I have heard nothing of new strikes. Except for an occasional short run by someone finding a rich gulch in the hills, the placers are dwindling. No one wants to hold anything that pays less than half an ounce a day, so they are selling out for a pittance to the Celestials. A few are filing on new claims, hoping they will come into pay when they reach bedrock, but most are just selling and leaving."

Samuel shot a glance at his father. "Maybe we could pick up an old claim, Pa. You and I could make it pay. We'd pay for it when we get enough gold."

Hinley glanced at Samuel and smiled. "Young Samuel appears to be a willing hand, Charles; however, I suspect he does not appreciate the amount of work a placer takes. For certain, I could not work twelve hours a day at his age." Hinley set a tin on the counter and pried off the lid.

Samuel recognized the rock as ore and leaned closer to get a look.

Charles shook his head. "I'm not interested in buying *or* a grubstake. Any ideas on who's doing the best placering?"

"That would be Mr. McLane. His crew is nearing bedrock, and they're sampling at fifteen cents a pan. However, you should know that once the word gets out, everyone else will attempt to hire on. Nor would I expect the work to last for any length of time. It takes a season to work down to bedrock. It takes a few days to mine it dry. Then it's back to work developing a new site." Hinley pulled a piece of paper from the tin and made some notes in his ledger.

Samuel tried to study the pieces of rock, wondering what made the owner decide to pick them up.

"If you do get hired, perchance you will receive your meals and a cot on top of your pay. I do not think they would have need for Samuel, however."

Charles nodded. "I thank you kindly. How do I find Mr. McLane?"

"Robert McLane. He is a few miles down the Big Meadow. His is the outfit you come to just past the Celestials." Hinley gestured north. "Now I would think twice about turning down work at the quartz mines. They pay about eight dollars a day. I think you shall be lucky to get five a day working for a placer outfit."

Charles tightened his jaw.

Hinley dumped the canister in front of Samuel. "Here, take a study. I can see in your eyes you have been wanting to."

Samuel flushed, embarrassed. "May I?"

Hinley spread the pieces in front of Samuel. "These are pieces coming in from a prospect the other side of the Secesh."

Samuel examined the rock. A swarm of black and silver specks ran in a band through white quartz.

"What you observe is mostly silver," Hinley said, adjusting his glasses. "Now should they bring in a mill that is able to reduce this quality ore, the prospector might have something. For the time being, he will need to wait."

"I thought you didn't know where the samples came from."

"Aye. However, once the claim is proved up, the mine owners frequently inform me. Each time they open a new vein, they have me run an assay to determine their production values related to costs. Milling and transportation frequently exceed the value of the ledge. In that likelihood, the owner may wait to join forces with other owners to bring in a mill. Such is the case with the Hic Jacet and the Knott. If this *is* Secesh silver ore, there may never be a way of getting it out or a way of milling it. It may just as well have been left undiscovered."

Samuel had never considered that finding a quartz ledge might not be what mattered most.

Charles tightened his mouth. "What about if we were to find something upstream of where Richmond was, southeast of here. How rich would ore have to be for bringing it out of the woods over there?"

"Richmond?" Hinley looked puzzled. "You're meaning northeast of here, up Slaughter Creek."

"No, southeast about two miles from here, up the tributary where Richmond was. What about another mile upstream of there or the country near there?"

Hinley shook his head. "I believe you are mixing information. Have you observed where most of the Celestials are working? Up that creek a short distance—perhaps a mile from here—is where Richmond once stood. And no, processing ore would not present a problem because the Pioneer Mill is directly across the valley—at least not a problem when it's operating."

Samuel felt a tingling rush up his neck. He glanced at his father. He could not believe his ears. The bare knob they had seen to the north jumped into mind.

"Right ... right," Charles said quietly. "Anything up in that country to the north?"

"Up above the Celestials' diggings ... I don't know of any lode gold being found per se. However, I would not doubt a quartz lode being up there somewhere. I did assays on placer gold that ran fifteen dollars an ounce from a couple of claims up in that direction. The gold had to have arisen in a ledge somewhere."

*   *   *

"We were looking up the wrong tributary, Pa!" Samuel hissed almost breathless as they stepped from the assay office.

"I reckon, Samuel, but now I know I'm looking for work. You saw how much of that mountainside the Chinamen have dug up. If O'Riley's ledge was there at one time, it ain't anymore."

Samuel felt like he had the wind knocked from him. That explained why his father had not seemed excited. Samuel clung to hope. "Pa, I doubt they've found the ledge. They aren't up that high! And maybe they missed the cairns."

"It appears to me they *are* up that high. And those cairns would have been the first things to go." Charles's frustration showed. "But you can look if you want. It's only right to make certain. I've still got to take on a job. We need to eat."

Samuel felt a rush of joy. "Good, because after I find the cairns, it'll be a different spot than where the Chinamen are. I'm sure of it. There are a lot of ravines. We learned that much already." Samuel was beginning to envision chunks of white quartz sparkling with lumps of gold. In his bones, he could feel the ledge was up there, still waiting to be found.

CHAPTER 14

Samuel could not get the vision of finding O'Riley's ledge out of his mind. He dreamed of it. It was so real he could almost put the pieces he was seeing into his pockets. Nevertheless, he held his excitement in check and rode with his father to Robert McLane's placer while his father sought work.

The placer was located on the shoulder of a hill above Meadow Creek a considerable distance northwest of their cabin. A giant gouge stretched dozens of yards out into the meadow to the creek. Much like the small prospects near their cabin, the placer cut into the gravelly hillside. Piles of waste rock snaked through the excavation, now about twenty feet below the original slope. A long, wooden sluice ran across the bottom. Tracks of wooden planks connected the excavation to the sluice. White canvas tents peeked from the nearby timber.

About ten men were at work. Some were swinging picks and breaking up the earth; others were shoveling it into wheelbarrows. Still, others wheeled them up the wooden tracks to the head of the sluice. There they dumped the gravel into a grizzly that separated out the large rocks before it allowed the gravel to feed into the head of the box and mix with the stream of water. The sluice worked much like Pete and Hallelujah's rocker, except that its length allowed the water to separate the gold from the gravel without rocking, and it washed it over a much greater distance. Samuel recalled watching the Chinese along Slaughter Creek. Two different cultures, but the process looked similar.

He stood back as his father shook hands with a tall man. They talked a moment before they turned to him.

"This is Mr. McLane."

"Howdy, son." McLane gripped his hand hard.

"Howdy, sir."

"You'd be welcome to work as well," he boomed. He was a big man who was better dressed than the other miners, with graying hair and deep creases about his eyes. "Always more fetching than a man can stand when you got this many parts working at once. I could use a runabout, but all I can pay is your room and board. If we get into some nuggets, I'd maybe spring four bits your way once in a while."

"Thank you, sir." Samuel glanced at his father.

"I explained you'd be tending our cabin—that we have stock to mind and work to get done."

"I understand that just fine," McLane boomed. "Also understand you might be starting up your own placer shortly."

"Yes, sir." Samuel felt his excitement surge. His father had purposely kept him freed up so he could still hunt for O'Riley's ledge and fix their own sluice at some point.

Charles shucked his shirt and picked up a pick.

"Expect me about dark, son. Mr. McLane wants us to work as long as possible, as long as we have water and light."

*   *   *

Deciding to take a roundabout way home and do some hunting as his father had been suggesting, Samuel turned Spooky and headed up the draw above McLane's. He followed the ditch that brought the water to the head of the sluice and shortly reached the main ditch from which McLane tapped his water. He followed it at length until he determined it brought water around the hill from a distant creek. This was similar to what the Chinese had done. By diverting water in a series of ditches stemming off Slaughter Creek and traversing the hillside, they had brought water to otherwise dry gravels. *For this amount of work, McLane had better be finding several ounces a day,* Samuel thought.

He pushed upward, now seeking game, until he broke out on top. He saw nothing but a few fool hens. He realized the entire time he and his father had been seeking O'Riley's ledge, they had only jumped a couple of deer and once the black bear. The country held little game.

In a clearing among the lodgepoles, he sat Spooky and pulled his leg over the pommel. He patted the horse. "Good boy." The animal twitched his ears. The two of them had nearly become one, it seemed.

It felt strange not being with his father. He was not nervous about being in the country alone; it just felt odd. They had been constant companions since the day they had left Iowa a terribly long time ago.

Puffy clouds drifted across the deep blue sky. He could make out a fire plume, hazy and orange brown, billowing up from behind the farthest ridges to the northeast. After all the rain, it should have been too wet to burn. Lightning ignited most of the fires, most of which were short-lived, except the one he now watched. It had smoldered all winter in one of the lower canyons of the Salmon and reignited when the woods began to dry.

Samuel turned Spooky downhill, wondering where he would find game. He was convinced the mining activity had scared it away.

He returned to the cabin and studied the placer and the hillside above, noting its similarity with McLane's. If he got the sluice repaired and water to it, he could operate it. He inspected the ditch that had at one time brought water from the spring. A couple of places needed repaired, but it would not take a great deal of work to redirect the water. The sluice was a different matter. They had used most of the boards for a floor to keep themselves out of the mud, and presently, there was no money to replace them.

He filled a couple of buckets with gravel and carried them back to the spring creek, where he panned them down. Again, there were only a few minute specks of gold in the black sand. *Unless the sluice works, there won't be enough gold here to get serious.*

He decided to build a spring box for keeping freshly killed game cool. He dug a large hole, lined it with rock, and fashioned it so a trickle of water came from the spring and flowed under the rocks lining the bottom. He used short logs for a cover.

Not knowing what else he could get done, he rode into town and dropped by Alexander's Mercantile.

"What can I do you for, young man?" A tall man with black hair and waxed moustache stepped toward him from behind a counter. He wore a dingy white apron over a blue-striped shirt.

For a moment, Samuel hesitated. He was not sure what he was thinking or why he was even there. "Just a couple of questions, if I may." Samuel judged the man to be in his late thirties, a bit older than his father. He had a few streaks of gray in his hair.

"I'm Scott Alexander, by the way." The clerk stuck out his hand. His eyes were blue gray and lively.

Samuel gripped it hard. "Samuel Chambers. Pleased to meet you, Mr. Alexander."

"Scott's fine by me, Sam. What's on your mind?"

"Been here with my Pa since end of May. Been stompin' around the woods, prospecting. Haven't had a lick of luck, so Pa went to work for Mr. McLane today."

"Yep, I've talked to your Pa a couple of times."

"I went hunting but didn't see any game. Is that on account of all the mining and the miners killing it off?"

"Not entirely," Alexander replied. He pointed at a stool. "Have a seat." He pulled up his own stool and pulled out a pipe. "Don't mind, do you?"

"No, sir. Thanks."

After a short puff, he continued, "There were some elk here when folks first arrived. They'd come down into the Big Meadow. A few moose as well. Now those animals got hunted out. The elk of course, they just took off. Sometimes you'll see one or two come through."

"What about deer? I almost never see any."

"This isn't the best deer country. Some does have their fawns along the edges of the meadows, and there is an occasional buck. But now that folks like Fred Burgdorf are bringing in plenty of cheap beef, the miners prefer it over venison." He blew out a puff of smoke and pointed with his pipe.

"As long as there's daylight and gold to be got, no one wants to stop and go hunting. Nor can they afford to." He studied Samuel. "So now your Pa's working the goldfields, he expects you to do the hunting, does he?"

Samuel nodded. "And mind the cabin and stock."

"Buy yourself some beef. You can pay me when the dust starts to come in. All the miners do." He pulled a ledger off the counter and showed it to him.

Samuel shook his head. He knew his father.

"Then my recommendation is to go over to the South Fork. That's deer country. A few folks are going down there to homestead but not enough to scare out the game."

"Reckon I will. Thank you." Samuel started to stand and then paused. "Uh, how do I get to the South Fork?"

Alexander chuckled. "There's a trail up Meadow Creek. Keep going until you reach the ridge. Then just follow the trail down. I'd plan on a couple days, though. It's a fair distance and mighty rugged. About like French Creek, if that's the way you came in."

"We did."

"How are you and your Pa gettin' along anyway, if you don't mind my askin'? We had a good talk the day you arrived."

Samuel felt a stab of regret. Suddenly, he wanted to confide in Alexander, tell him about O'Riley's lost ledge, see if he knew anything, and see if there was any hope.

"We're gettin' along okay, I 'spect. Not what we'd hoped for." He shifted on the stool.

"You expected to get rich?" Alexander grinned.

Samuel wanted to shout, *Yes, we were going to find a lost ledge and become crazy rich.*

"Only a little rich." He tried to smile. "We wanted to take something home to Iowa. Help get a new place of our own."

Alexander looked thoughtful and smoothed his moustache. "You came here with better reasons than most, I'd say."

Samuel stood, suddenly wishing he was not talking. "Well, mighty obliged for the advice, Mr. Alexander. I guess I should get going."

Alexander rose. "Don't be a stranger, Sam, and remember, it's Scott." He offered his hand again. "Check back with me. When the pack train comes in next week, I could use an extra hand unloading."

"Thanks, Scott." Samuel felt uncomfortable using Alexander's first name but warmed that the man treated him as an equal. "I reckon I can do that."

*   *   *

His father returned near dark. Samuel had some dinner waiting and reheated it while his father washed and pulled off his boots.

"How was it, Pa?" Samuel dished up a biscuit topped with gravy. He set a cup of steaming coffee next to the plate.

"'Bout like I expected. It's work."

Samuel lit the kerosene lamp. "Did you get paid? I want to see the gold."

Charles laughed. "Not till Saturday night, end of the week." He took a bite of biscuit. "So did you do any hunting?"

"Some. Didn't see anything. Went above McLane's. Saw how all the water was brought in by ditches. That's how we can bring water to our old sluice. There's a ditch pretty much already dug."

"Got to put these back on it first." Charles tapped the boards lying in the mud. "Or wait till we can buy more."

"I figured," Samuel said. "I also fixed us a spring box out of rock next to the spring and panned a couple more pans of dirt, but there wasn't much gold."

Charles nodded. "I'm thinking even if we do get the sluice going, we won't find much. Otherwise, others would have dug up that hillside before us. I think whoever put this cabin here did it for its location near the spring, not for the gold."

He scooped up the last of the biscuit. "Thanks for dinner."

CHAPTER 15

When his father rose, the stars had just begun to dim. Samuel built up the fire and put on the coffee, again thankful for the stove. It sure beat stepping outdoors and bending over a campfire, especially in the rain, although lately, there had been none.

His father pulled on his boots and peered to the east, where light began faintly streaking the sky. "Morning sure comes early. Maybe we should move into one of Mr. McLane's tents so I don't have to get up so blasted early."

Samuel stopped halfway to pouring the coffee. "And leave our cabin? All our hard work?"

"I'm kidding." His father ruffled his hair. "We'll keep the cabin, but I might stay out there once in a while if you don't mind. That way, I can put in a couple more hours mining ... *and* get another hour of sleep."

"If you need to, I can manage. Figure I might have to be gone overnight sometime hunting anyhow."

Charles took his coffee and sipped it. "How so?"

"I talked to Mr. Alexander. He says that the mule deer are more likely down along the South Fork. It's at least a day out and a day back."

"Mule deer? Not like Virginia deer? Virginia deer, why, they'd like the brush like in these meadows. Guess that's why we haven't seen any."

"Nope, Mr. Alexander says they like open hillsides and open brush. Don't spend as much time down along the creeks like Virginia deer."

Charles rose. "We'll do what we need to, but we need to plan so one of us is near the cabin if we can." He slipped on his coat. "The Shisslers, a family down the creek from McLane's, got some new aparejos stolen."

"Who would want those?"

"Someone who figures they can sell them for a couple dollars. People think it's Chinamen. Anyway, be cautious."

"I'm not planning on the South Fork yet. Might get a deer up here. Mr. Alexander says they come up to have fawns and travel through from time to time."

Charles stepped out the door. "See you tonight."

"Need help with Buster?" Samuel called after.

"Nope. You got your own horse to saddle."

Samuel watched as his father turned and rode downstream. He was alone, the cabin silent except for the crackle of the fire.

Abruptly, he stood and checked the rifle and then brought up Spooky. He told himself he was going hunting, but he knew where he was heading. Ever since he had talked to Hinley, visions of the ledge had pestered him.

Shortly, he was passing through the Chinese placer along Slaughter Creek. He could hear the *thump, thump, thump* from the stamps at the Pioneer mill, now finally running again. That was good for both the nearby Rescue and Little Giant mines that were bringing ore in to be processed. It would be good for him when he found the ledge.

As he followed the creek, Samuel watched for cairns. The entire area had been dug up. There would be none unless they were many yards from the creek in the trees. He frowned. O'Riley had said they were in the creek.

Samuel turned Spooky uphill and began a long traverse toward the summit. He soon cut across the ditch bringing water out of Slaughter Creek. Samuel followed it a distance, impressed with its rugged construction.

He turned back uphill and climbed until he topped out on the first summit. The lodgepoles and firs spread unbroken in all directions. No outcrops showed above timber, only the bare knob. He decided that would be a good place to begin and angled in its direction.

Immediately, he ran into trouble. Spooky was unable to work through the thick timber. Samuel made a few yards in the general direction of the knob and then had to backtrack. Downed timber blocked his way. He edged down into the draws to get around the densest areas but then became helplessly tangled in the thick brush. It was not long before Spooky began to tire, trying to climb back out.

Samuel scanned for rock outcrops. He saw none. He had expected some above the Chinese placers. He figured the gold had to be coming from a ledge somewhere above them and had worked its way down. But there were no ledges.

He pushed toward the west. The country was worse. He saw only a few boulders haphazardly scattered throughout the thick timber. He wondered if the ledges had deteriorated years ago and the gold had all washed downhill. Perhaps no quartz outcrops remained. He wondered where the placers Hinley had spoken of were located. Maybe some outcrops could be found above them. There were countless possibilities. He realized it would take weeks, if not months to explore this area.

Samuel did not have weeks. His father intended to earn enough money and head back home. An ache welled within his chest. He had hoped he would prove his father wrong. He would find the ledge. Instead, he stared at the hopelessly dense timber. If there were a quartz ledge up here somewhere, it would take a miracle to find it.

The following day was much the same. He reached the area he had last searched, picketed Spooky, and again examined the rocks. At last, he found a few shards of white quartz, the first he had seen. He dug at them for a long while, but failed to turn over any of interest.

By late afternoon Saturday, he discovered an area with several more outcrops. He again picketed Spooky and worked his way downward into the gulches below them, combing the hillsides. The heavy brush prevented him from seeing the earth underneath. Where the rocks were exposed, he again found only scattered pieces of quartz, and again the quartz was barren.

Maybe I should just forget it. Maybe Pa's right. In a week or two, he'll have enough money and we can head home.

Heart heavy, he turned to head back. No longer looking for outcrops, he headed east, angling across the ridges, trying to find easier traveling. When he reached a narrow, somewhat open ridge, he followed it downhill until he reached Slaughter Creek. He then headed toward Washington and the cabin.

*   *   *

Samuel fixed a dinner of corncakes and beans, their one staple meal. He longed for salt pork, for fresh greens, for fresh meat. He grew irritated with himself. Instead of looking for the ledge, he should have been hunting. He noted the coffee was nearly gone.

His father arrived after dark, exhausted. Samuel had begun to worry.

"No luck hunting?" Charles asked. He sopped up the last bit of sorghum with the last bit of corncake. "Maybe you need to head down to the South Fork. Take two days. I'll stay out at McLane's tomorrow night in that case."

"I didn't do much hunting," Samuel admitted. "Because of what Mr. Hinley told us, I spent the last couple of days looking for the ledge."

Charles raised his eyes.

"No luck, Pa. The country up north is worse than where we been looking. I didn't see a single good outcrop. Not one."

"That's about what I expected."

"I just don't know anymore, Pa. Maybe we *should* go home. I want to stay, but it doesn't seem like we got here at the right time." A crushing ache began overwhelming him. "I thought I could find O'Riley's ledge, but now

I don't think so. It's impossible country up there, and it's probably been dug up, anyhow." A sting had come to Samuel's eyes as he fought the realization that he had been beat.

"Whoa, now hold on. Weren't you just telling me a few days ago your ma would want us to keep trying and that we owe it to Uncle Jake?" Charles rested his hand on Samuel's shoulders. "I have a good job now. I can take back something. It won't be enough to buy what we wanted, but it will help us get going. We can keep most of what I get paid, assuming you start bringing in something other than rabbits to eat." He pulled Samuel close.

"Coming out here is like gambling, son. You gotta commit for a set amount, and if lady luck smiles on you, you gotta get out before she decides to frown again. You go on and do some hunting. Maybe look some more for that ledge. But let's agree we stick it out at least till the first snow. Deal?"

Samuel fought the burning in his eyes. An incredible relief flooded through him. They would make an honest go of it, no matter what came their way, at least until snow. "Sure, Pa. It's a deal."

"Here, Samuel." Charles rose and fished a tobacco tin from behind his bed and pulled out some coins. "Here's a dollar and four bits. I've been holding it in reserve. Buy us some cornmeal and sugar and something green if you can. We could use some fresh vegetables." He paused. "If there's something left, maybe buy a treat for us. We'll have it when I get home tomorrow."

Samuel raised his eyes.

"It's okay. We can spend it. I get paid Saturday."

CHAPTER 16

Samuel fixed breakfast while his father dressed. He threw the last handful of coffee grounds into the boiling pot and then shook out the bag into the water as well. "Maybe when I go to town, I should get some more coffee."

"Wait till payday. We can last till then. The money I gave you won't go far—not up here with prices as high as they are."

He saw his father off. Briefly, he thought about going back to sleep. None of the merchants would yet be open. But then he thought about it. His father counted on him to do his part, even if it was just being a runabout.

He grabbed the water pail, brought in fresh water, and put some on to heat. He split and stacked more wood. He washed out the breakfast dishes and put things back in their places. By then, the sun was peeking through the trees, casting long fingers of light across the meadow. Morning mist hung in the low areas. Samuel reflected on the beauty. *I wouldn't mind living here if, like Pa says, it didn't get six feet of snow.*

He took the rifle and some lead shot and walked along the meadow fringe scouting for small game. He figured a rabbit or two would make a fine stew with whatever new vegetables he found to buy.

Birds hopped and flitted among the trees, but none were of size. Squirrels scurried along the thin limbs, now lit by early light high in the crowns of the lodgepole pines, occasionally pausing to scold him as he passed below. A ruffed grouse exploded in front of him, wings hammering the still air. Startled, heart pounding, Samuel searched frantically about until he determined the source of noise and movement and spotted the bird. Flying awkwardly, the grouse swerved between trees until it settled into the brush a few yards away. Head jerking, it strutted toward a small rise.

Samuel quickly pulled the rifle to his shoulder, aimed toward its head, and squeezed off a shot. Feathers puffed into the air where the grouse had been. White smoke drifted into the forest. *Roast grouse is better than rabbit any day.* He picked up the dead grouse, head now missing. After he cleaned and plucked the grouse, he stored it in the spring box and headed for town.

*   *   *

Samuel found Scott Alexander just opening his store.

"Mornin', Mr. Alexander," Samuel called as he looped Spooky's reins about the post. He knocked his hat against his pants to dust it.

Alexander turned and greeted him. "Hello, Sam, but I'm fine with just Scott." He pushed the door open. "Didn't figure on you being back so soon. In town two times in one week."

"We're out a few things."

He followed Alexander into the store.

Alexander began setting items out for the day's customers. "What can I get you?"

"I'll start with about four pounds of cornmeal and a pound of sugar."

Alexander walked to a bin and started weighing out the cornmeal.

"I also need some fresh vegetables. What do you have? I got a grouse this morning and figured at least on green onions to go with it."

Alexander paused. "*Those* I don't have. I've got a few spuds and some dried onions, but if you're looking for something green, you'll have to visit the Chinamen."

"Uh, thanks." Samuel had not considered visiting any Chinese merchants and was uncomfortable with the thought of doing so.

"The Chinamen seem to be able to grow vegetables even in the snow. We have to pack ours in. I don't expect anything new until the week's end."

Samuel realized he had no choice. He wandered about the store and examined the mining gear. He thought about what he would buy when they had money. He needed a new pair of trousers, and both his and his father's shirts had holes in the sleeves. They also both badly needed underwear.

Alexander wrapped the sugar and began jotting in his ledger. "Four pounds of cornmeal at ten cents a pound … that's forty cents. One pound of sugar at thirty-two cents a pound." He smoothed his moustache and looked up. "Anything else? That comes to seventy-two cents."

"Better give me four bits worth of coffee." The thought of dinner without coffee was intolerable, and his father had said to get a treat.

Alexander gave him a curious look. "Four bits?"

"Pa gets paid at the end of the week. We'll get more then." He needed to save money for the green onions.

"I told you I could give you credit, especially since your pa is working. That's how business is done in a mining camp."

Samuel shook his head.

Alexander scooped out some coffee onto a square of paper, not even bothering to weigh it. He quickly wrapped it, tied it up, and handed it over. Samuel guessed it was more than four bits' worth. "Okay, Sam, that comes to a dollar and twenty-two cents."

Samuel handed Alexander a dollar and two bits in coin.

"I usually don't need to make change," he muttered. He reached into a box below the counter and handed back three Indian-head coppers. "You could trade these in for a few pieces of stick candy." He gestured at the jars full of colorful, striped candy sitting on the counter.

"Might. Want to check on the green onions first," replied Samuel, pocketing the coins. "Thanks, Scott. Next time we'll be paying with dust."

"If not, I'm putting you in the ledger, like it or not."

Samuel fit the parcel into a saddle pouch and turned Spooky down the main street. He turned off onto a side road lined by several low-slung Chinese cabins and a few larger, saltbox structures. These were the Chinese businesses. He noted a couple of saloons, a butcher, and a couple of mercantile stores.

Similar to Alexander, the Chinese appeared just to be opening their businesses. One Chinese who was leading a mule packed with mining tools hurried by and cast him a curious look. Two others moved quickly into one of the saloons.

Samuel avoided the largest mercantile and crossed the street to the smaller store. It had a saltbox front and a covered, rough-wood walk. A couple of chairs sat near the door under the overhang. In its window were crocks, brass pots, and glass canisters.

When he entered, a myriad of fragrant odors filled the air, more so than at Alexander's Mercantile. Instead of neatly stacked counters and shelves lined with boxes, colorful bottles and crockery were haphazardly crammed onto overflowing shelves.

An older Chinese gentleman bowed toward him slightly and smiled. He was dressed in a formal-looking red tunic with a high, stiff, white collar and cuffs and a row of gold buttons up its front. He wore a bowl-like cap, his braided queue hanging freely. His trousers were the same baggy, dark blue cotton that many of the Chinese wore.

He stood beside a counter, which was nothing but a couple of boards laid over a couple of barrels. It contained bolts of colorful silk cloth, reds, yellows, some deep blues; similarly colored handkerchiefs hung nearby amid spools of brightly colored ribbon. Samuel wondered who might buy such items in a mining camp. There were no Chinese women in the town—at least none he had seen.

"Howdy," replied Samuel. "Do you have any greens?"

"Hehwoh," the man greeted and then spoke rapidly in Cantonese, grinning and repeatedly bowing.

Samuel realized he did not understand English. Hesitantly, he chose to look around for himself.

Mining supplies—pans, picks, shovels, gumboots, and rope, similar to those items offered at Alexander's Mercantile—were piled high. Other shelves held stacks of trousers, shirts, and western-style hats. Quilted coats hung from pegs on a wall.

The food items differed. He recognized the fragrance of ginger and anise mixed with pungent incense wafting from the back. Bottles of oils and sauces lined some shelves. Open glazed crocks held unfamiliar bulbs and roots. Tight-lidded brownware pottery lined the shelves beneath. Samuel suspected they contained pickled vegetables and meats. Blue and white glazed bowls overflowed with rice, spices, and dry herbs.

He saw no fresh vegetables and began to wonder how he could communicate his wishes.

The man addressed someone, and Samuel looked up to see a Chinese boy about his age had entered the shop, a package under his arm.

"Hehwoh," the boy greeted. "How to help you?" He put the package down and bowed. He was slender, slightly built, and dressed in the dark blue, loose-fitting Chinese tunic and trousers.

"I am Sing Chen," he said, smiling, his dark eyes sparkling. "I help you."

Samuel instinctively began to offer his hand but stopped. The Chinese did not shake hands. "I'm Samuel Chambers," he said and impulsively bowed in return. It brought polite laughter. Samuel was slightly embarrassed but continued, "I'm looking for some green onions."

"Ah, we have some, Mistah Samyew," replied Chen. He said something in Cantonese, and the older man ducked away. "He is uncle, Sing Mann. He own store. I help in store." He pushed his tightly braided queue to his back.

"What else you like?" He waved around the store, his slender hands flashing.

"I think that's all. I needed some onion to spice up the grouse I shot."

Chen smiled but stepped to a shelf, his queue swinging. "Tea? We have many tea." He rummaged further. "Ah, wine, Mistah Samyew?" He pulled some dark olive green bottles from a shelf. "Beer? Chinese beer vehlie good." He lined some bottles up in front of Samuel.

"No, thanks." Samuel shook his head, but he could not help wonder how the liquid inside tasted.

Samuel was near laughter. The manner in which Sing Chen moved about, hands flying, uncovering items, showing him things, trying hard to make another sale, struck him as humorous.

Chen pointed at the mining gear. "Gold pan? Shuhvoh? We have alla things for you to mine."

Samuel shook his head and felt slightly relieved when Sing Mann returned with several bundles of onions. He handed them to Chen and then stood aside, his dark eyes following Samuel.

"How many you like?" Chen offered the bundles.

Samuel selected a large bunch. "This should do it."

Chen nimbly wrapped them in a type of rice paper and held out his hand. "Gold."

"I have some coins."

Chen shook his head. "Ohnee gold, Mistah Samyew." He pointed toward a balance.

Samuel felt dismayed. "I don't have any gold." He pulled the remaining coins from his trousers. "Two bits?"

Chen shook his head but gave Samuel the onions, pushing Samuel's fingers around them. His dark eyes flashed. "You keep. Bling gold in a few day. Buy more things, maybe." Both he and Sing Mann smiled politely.

"I can't—" But something felt wrong for him to refuse, and he nodded. "Okay, after my Pa gets paid, I'll be back."

Sing Mann reached into a jar, pulled out two pieces of red and white mint candy, and handed them to Samuel.

Samuel knew he could not refuse those as well. "Thank you. You are very kind." He nodded toward Chen. "Thank you, Sing. It was good to meet you."

Chen shook his head. "My name Sing Chen, Mistah Samyew. You call me Chen. Uncle is Sing Mann. You call him Mann."

Samuel nodded his understanding. "And you may call me, Sam." He recognized Chen had trouble pronouncing *Samuel*. He stepped toward the door. "Thank you. I'll be back soon."

"Bye, Sam." They bowed slightly. Samuel bowed in return and walked from the shop. Other Chinese had gathered nearby and had been watching from the street.

"Hello." He waved and bowed to them. They hurried away.

*   *   *

When he returned to the cabin, Samuel began cutting and dragging poles from the hill for building a corral. He lashed eight to ten poles onto Molly, allowing the butts to drag. Unlike dragging the logs, Molly did not like the arrangement and became rather contrary, braying and setting up a ruckus. When she realized she could not shake the poles, she decided to head to the cabin. Samuel more or less steered her in the right direction and then cut the poles loose after she arrived.

He cut several into six-foot lengths and began digging holes for the corral posts, intending to build a rail fence. He designed it so one corner would cross the spring creek, giving the stock access to water. While he dug the postholes, he took careful notice. More than one person had found gold in a similar manner.

He had a pair of posts set by the time his father came riding in from the north.

"Glad to see you're starting on that, Samuel." He dismounted.

Samuel helped his father remove Buster's saddle.

"How was today, Pa?"

"Glad the week has ended." He headed toward the cabin. Samuel could see he was tired.

Later, he dumped the gold dust into a pan. "Near an ounce. Some went to pay for tools."

Samuel's heart caught. He gently rocked the gold back and forth; he ran his fingers through it. The smooth, cold metal felt strange. He could not get over the sight of it. "It's not as shiny as you would expect."

"That's raw gold, Samuel. Not like the broken pieces you see in a rock like we saw at Mr. Hinley's."

"But it's real. This is real money." Samuel poured it from one hand to the other, feeling the weight. "I mean, you actually made money. Money that you can buy stuff with." He laughed.

"Don't get too carried away, Samuel. I spent over forty hours earning that."

"I know, Pa. But it's money. It's not a crop you have to grow and then sell. It's already money." No one could diminish the value the gold held.

"It *is* a good feeling." Charles nodded.

"So what are we going to buy first?"

"I'd say if we were the typical mining hands, we'd probably ride into town, buy a plate of grub, take a bath, and stomp to some music. Or if you're like Hallelujah, you'd go into town and spend it on wimin and whiskey." Charles winked. "I think we'll hold off on that, however, till you've growed some."

"For sure, Pa."

"Most of this will go for grub. After that, I don't know where to start. I'd like to get planks for a floor. I want you to fix the sluice, see if we can get a bit of a placer going here. With you and me going opposite directions, I'm thinking of another firearm. We both could use new long johns. My shirt is just about shot. Your trousers are falling apart. Is that enough?"

Samuel felt discouraged. The gold had seemed like a goodly amount. Now he recognized just how little it was. "But we got some money!"

"We do." His father began spooning the gold back into the pouch. "I saw you got a good start on the corral. What about hunting?"

"I got us a grouse. Also picked up some things in town—some onions to have with the grouse." He did not tell him about going to the Chinese store or about owing them some gold.

*　　*　　*

Sunday, they took Molly and rode out to Shisslers' mill for lumber. They put in a log sill around the base of the cabin and then ran several log braces across to lend support to the planks. They had the floor in by late afternoon.

Samuel was elated. It was solid. For the first time since they had left Iowa, they were up out of the mud.

"With the wood that's left, you should be able to fix up that old sluice," Charles said. "We don't have a riddle sheet, but if the box is long enough, the gold will separate out okay. Maybe you can work on that this coming week."

"I plan to, but I want to finish the corral. I'm tired of chasing the stock every morning."

They stashed the small amount of remaining gold in a tin and hid it behind a rock in the wall of the spring box. They reasoned that if someone broke into the cabin while they were away, they would not find the gold.

THE SWEET MARY

CHAPTER 17

The weather had warmed considerably. It finally felt as if summer had arrived. Except for thunderstorms that moved in during the afternoons, the days were hot and dry.

With the long light of summer and good water, Robert McLane wanted to work every possible minute. When the snowpack melted, the water drained quickly from the gravelly hills, and the small streams dried up, putting an end to many of the placer operations. Even with ditches diverting water for great distances, there was insufficient water seeping from the hills to supply placer operations much beyond mid-July. A few of the operations along the Secesh and other permanent streams could continue, but most of the workable gravel lay situated along the valley flanks where there was little water. As a result, Chambers had agreed to remain at the placer as many nights as possible.

Samuel worked in earnest on finishing the corral. He retrieved more poles from the hillside, taking Molly farther and farther, trying to first use the dead poles because they were easier to work with.

He set the posts in pairs about six inches apart and began stacking the rails, inserting one pole to run one direction and the other pole on top to run in the opposite direction. While he was working, images of a wide ledge of white quartz peppered with chunks of gold pestered him. As immense as the country was and as daunting the task, he knew he would renew his search. He worked feverishly until late evening he had finished the corral.

Samuel rose early the following morning, packed his gear, and rode directly to Raymond Hinley's assay shop.

"Good to see you again, Samuel," Hinley greeted him, squinting. "What can I do for you?"

"Heading out prospecting. Wanted to see that gold ore again and study on it some, if I could."

"Aye, you may." Hinley pulled out some of the specimens and then laid some additional rocks on the table. "These are pieces you should study as well.

You see their rusty appearance? That results from carrying sulphurets that break down and cause staining. On occasion, you can smell the sulfur."

Samuel held one to his nose and discerned the faint sulfur odor.

"These deposits are not as valuable because the ores are difficult to refine." Hinley adjusted his glasses.

"Then what's the use?"

"Should you find a large quantity, someone will build a mill. Besides, almost all sulphuret ore carries some free-milling gold. If the gold is sufficient, even with sulphurets, the deposit may pay."

Samuel examined the samples again. "Thanks, Mr. Hinley. When I strike it rich, I owe you."

"Aye, Samuel." He gave him a quick wave.

Samuel felt renewed confidence. He realized the best chance of noticing gold or silver in good ore was along a fresh break and not on a weathered surface. Not long ago, if he had been given a piece, he probably would have chunked it at a grouse, thinking it worthless.

He rode up Meadow Creek, south of Washington. The thumping of the stamps at the Pioneer grew louder as he approached. If he found ore to the northeast, the Pioneer would be the nearest mill.

When he reached the Chinese placer, he waved and several Chinese grinned and bowed in return. He marveled at their industry. Their pace never slackened. He turned uphill where he had descended the mountain from the time before.

From the first small summit, he could see the bare knob far to the north. He angled toward the peaks to the northeast. They seemed to have more rock than those to the west where he had previously searched.

The ridge he followed lay in a north-south orientation just above Slaughter Creek. He worked along both sides to the opposite end and then traversed lower until he ran into timber and brush, where he did not dare take Spooky. In those places, he scouted on foot.

He crossed to a second ridge where more rock was exposed and again began systematically searching its length. An unease and emptiness seeped in. This was immense country, heavily forested, and difficult to search—an area of about ten square miles. He had not even scratched the possibilities.

Late afternoon, a thunderstorm moved in, and the lightning forced his retreat to the cabin.

The following morning, he returned to the outcrops. He found quartz chunks, but when broken, they appeared sugary white. None appeared rusty. He finally collected a few pieces that held a few black specks, not knowing what else he could do.

Toward the upper end of the ridge, he found where someone had dug a small prospect. He closely studied it but failed to see what the prospector had found, if anything. The quartz was a thin stringer that ran through the hard, salt-and-pepper, textured granite.

Samuel paused for some dried meat. He had run out of water earlier. The ridgetops were barren and dry. He gazed north, noting a number of additional outcrops. Almost overwhelming, any of them could be O'Riley's.

He searched awhile longer, comforted by knowing at least one person had dug in the area. Reaching a knoll that overlooked the creek to the east, he wondered if the rich placers Hinley had mentioned were below. The creek actually separated the ridge he was on from the bare knob. It seemed a sizeable stream, and from the looks of the country, swung to the east and then south, entering Slaughter Creek to the east. It occurred to him if O'Riley had hunted along this creek, any markers would easily line up with the bare knob.

The country also seemed to be better game country, not as steep, more open. O'Riley would have favored this area for hunting. Moreover, it would have made sense for him to simply follow Slaughter Creek and turn up this tributary when he reached it. The gold could possibly lie along the creek, all the way to the Chinese placers. Samuel began feeling a tingling excitement. The cairns might still exist in the creek below.

Heart hammering, he dangerously pushed Spooky down the ridge until he intersected the creek. Madly, he looked along it for cairns. He found nothing. His excitement drained into frustration. If this were the right creek, every tiny gulch could be the correct gulch. Every ridge could be the right ridge. It would take forever to search the length of the creek and all its side gulches. An ache welled inside his chest as he turned for the cabin.

His father arrived near dark. Samuel was surprised at how anxiously he had awaited him.

"Mighty good looking corral, son," Charles said, stripping off and hauling the saddle toward the cabin. "Once you get some hay brought in, I can leave Buster for the evening and not have to chase him in the morning."

"Don't remind me about hay, Pa." Samuel grinned. "I'll be on it next." He intended to build a crib and stock shelter.

After dinner, his father sat quietly with his cup of coffee. Samuel figured the long hours of swinging a pick and shoveling gravel were wearing on him. He had hoped they would play a game of checkers.

"Thanks for dinner, Samuel. It's a comfort knowing I'll get something when I get home." He pulled off his boots and lay down.

*　　*　　*

Before daylight, with scarcely four hours of sleep, his father was up. Samuel fixed some breakfast and coffee and saw him off. At sunrise, he took the rifle and scouted for small game. A snowshoe hare was all he saw. He killed and cleaned it and stored it in the spring box. He moved the rock at the back of the box and checked to make sure their gold tin was still there. He figured it was safe. The few weeks they had been at the cabin, no one had ever dropped by. As far as he knew, no one had even been past the cabin. They were off the main trail over half a mile, although they could see where the main trail ran.

The remainder of the morning, he began repairing the sluice. He reused the boards they had used for the cabin floor and added some new pieces for those that had been ruined. Only a couple of the cleats were any good. He decided to try the sluice anyway.

He repositioned the box to near the ditch and dug a depression to catch and store water. Next, he traced the length of the ditch, shoveling out the debris and repairing the areas where the sides had broken down. He blocked most of the flow of the spring creek with large stones and diverted the water into the ditch. When the water reached the head of the sluice, he used a spare board to adjust the flow until he had a good stream similar to McLane's placer.

"Now we'll see." He threw in the first shovel of dirt. Carefully, he broke it up and allowed the water to carry the slurry of mud and gravel down into the box where it bumped over the few good cleats.

He shoveled for a few minutes, cut off the water, and anxiously gazed into the box. Similar to what he had seen in Hallelujah and Pete's rocker, a line of glistening black sand had gathered behind the first cleat. Three or four tiny specks of gold—so small he almost missed them—gleamed brightly. The pans of dirt he had washed earlier had held more.

But gold wouldn't come out of the ground by itself, he told himself. He enlarged his excavation, broke down the sides, and dug out some more gravel from around the cobbles.

He shoveled for a longer while, shut off the water, and checked again. The number of tiny specks of gold had increased. *Not even ten cents worth*, he figured, *but at least there's some gold.*

He resumed his work until late day when his arms ached and he could no longer swing his pick. His back was sore, and his hands cramped. He shut off the water and redirected it back into the spring creek. Scooping out as much of the black sand and gold as he could, he dumped it into his gold pan. Carefully, he panned the fines down until he had a string of bright gold. He spooned out what he could, trying to keep from getting too much black sand in it.

At the table with the kerosene lamp lit, he began separating out what gold he could from the remaining sand. He flicked the larger sand particles out by using a tiny wood sliver. The lighter material, he gently blew away. His first gold, he realized. Maybe six bits if he was lucky.

His father did not return that night. Samuel heated some beans. Stiff and aching, he could hardly move enough to undress and pull the blankets over himself.

He lay for a moment. It was clear why the previous owners had abandoned the placer. Maybe the recovery would be better after he made further repairs to the sluice. Maybe he needed to dig deeper.

*　　*　　*

Samuel woke early from nagging pain. He took his father's remaining gold and the gold he had recovered and headed to Alexander's Mercantile.

Scott greeted him.

"Hi, Scott." He remembered to call him Scott. "I need a few nails and some canvas to finish fixing up my sluice." He placed his father's gold on the counter. "Is this enough?"

"Let's see." Scott took the gold and poured it gently onto one of the pans of his balance. On the opposite pan, he placed tiny weights until the two pans balanced. "I take it your pa's down the Big Meadow, and you're taking care of the cabin."

"That's right. I did some repairs to the sluice and ran it a bit. It's no wonder the men you grubstaked abandoned the place."

Scott deftly whisked the gold he had weighed out into a small box that was stored beneath the balance. Samuel wondered how much dust the box contained but refrained from trying to get a peek.

"You didn't find much?"

Samuel shook his head. "Maybe six bits for all day."

"It's always the next shovelful, Sam." Scott laughed. "The men I grubstaked before you didn't seem to find much, either. At least not that I ever saw. At any rate, I only grubstaked them for twenty dollars."

"You grubstake many outfits?" Samuel was thinking.

"Not since the early days. There have not been any new strikes lately, so now my risk is greater."

"Anyone ever strike it rich?"

"I usually got my money back, but no one got rich that I know of." He eyed Samuel. "I'm counting on you."

"You haven't grubstaked me."

"I'm hoping you remember me for putting you and your pa onto that cabin."

Samuel remembered.

Scott pulled out a handful of nails. "This enough?"

"If I can still get a yard or two of canvas."

"You should. Your gold came to just over a dollar." He placed the nails on a large balance and jotted down the weight.

He measured and cut a strip of canvas that Samuel thought was adequate. "About two bits worth," Scott said, recording it.

"Anything else?"

"Could I get the remainder in coffee?"

"I think so." He weighed out some loose grind, watching the balance. "I can give you this much, if that will work."

Samuel nodded, surprised. It was more than he would have guessed. He wondered if Scott had added some extra like he figured he had done last time.

Scott wrapped the coffee, packaged up the nails and canvas, and handled the bundle over. "Let me know if you do any better with your sluice."

"Thanks, Scott. I will."

*   *   *

When he reached Sing Mann's store, Samuel paused. Several Chinese and Mann were gathered outside, inspecting some salmon. An animated discussion erupted with the men, all eventually following Mann into the store. Samuel followed and watched while Mann apparently negotiated a deal, first to buy the salmon and then to sell them. The Chinese all seemed pleased upon conclusion of the transaction, repeatedly bowing to each other. One slipped the salmon into a gunnysack, threw it over his back, and headed away, a smile on his face.

Mann recognized him. "Hehwoh, Mistah Samyew."

"Is Chen here?"

Mann smiled and shook his head. "No Chen."

Samuel was surprised with the English.

He pulled out a square of leather in which he had wrapped his gold dust. "For the onions," he said.

Mann's eyes lit with recognition. He smiled broadly but shook his head. "No, Mistah Samyew."

That was not acceptable to Samuel. "I'd like to pay." He pushed the dust toward Mann.

Mann again shook his head and gently pushed it back.

"Then I will find something else." Samuel began looking around, wishing Chen were present.

He examined the silks and thought of his mother. *Maybe when I'm heading home.* He examined the socks. *Too much for my gold.* At the dry tea canisters, he removed the lids and smelled each. He found one with a spicy, pungent aroma. "Is this a good one?" he questioned.

Mann smiled, vigorously nodding. "Good."

Samuel handed his gold to Mann. "I'll have this amount." He figured if Mann approved, he could always tell his father that was why he bought it.

Similar to Scott, Mann weighed out the gold and then poured it into a small box beneath the balance. On a larger balance, he placed a square of rice paper and on the opposite pan placed a weight for equivalent value. Mann sprinkled dry tea onto the paper until it balanced. It seemed a small amount, but Samuel figured the tea was probably more expensive than what he had guessed.

Mann wrapped and handed the tea to him and then picked out a couple pieces of candy.

"Thank you very much," Samuel said and bowed. He was not a little kid, but the candy was a treat.

He decided to visit Hinley. He wondered if anyone remembered O'Riley and if so, what they might be able to tell about him. As unlikely as it seemed, maybe someone had an idea where he had been hunting, or maybe someone had heard him say something about his ledge. He had nothing to lose.

He popped a piece of the mint candy into his mouth at the same time he turned the corner, nearly running into Miss Hattie.

"Hello, sweetheart," she cooed.

Samuel quickly stepped back, almost tripping, pulling the piece of candy from his mouth, whisking it behind himself, trying to be polite. "Sorry, Miss Hattie." She was dressed nearly the same as before. He could not help but again notice the strong perfume and her low-cut front.

"You must of got that from the Chinamen."

Samuel nodded. He flushed. He wanted to hide the candy in his pocket.

"Shouldn't be visiting the Chinamen," she said. "You in town with your pa?"

Samuel shook his head. "No, ma'am, he's working at McLane's. I just came in on business." Her perfume was almost overpowering.

"You're so sweet." She reached out and touched his cheek.

Embarrassed, Samuel turned away. "Uh, I got to go, Miss Hattie."

"Just Hattie. You call me Hattie." She smiled brightly. "Don't rush away, Samuel. We can talk. I like talking with you. It makes me feel nice." Deliberately, she looked him over. "So handsome."

Samuel blushed. He was afraid she was going to fall out of her dress. Then he found himself wishing she would and felt miserable about his thoughts. He glanced away.

Hattie leaned forward and whispered, "You're so good looking. I see you, and my heart flip-flops." She let her hand trace down his shirt. Samuel pulled back.

"Yes, ma'am. Mine too." He wished he had said anything but that. He was not thinking clearly. His mouth was dry.

"I got something that's much sweeter than candy." She winked, nodded toward the saloon, and reached for his hand.

Samuel was terrified. His ears burned. He could not help but think of what was possible, but he pulled back.

"Oh, there you are, Hattie." Samuel heard Miss Lilly's voice.

Hattie frowned. "Hi, Lilly. Remember Samuel?"

"I certainly do. How are you, Samuel?" She held out her hand.

Samuel felt his heart melt. Miss Lilly was the most beautiful woman in the world. He touched his hat. "Hi, Miss Lilly."

Hattie scowled more strongly. "Samuel and I were just leaving," she said quite loudly.

"*Oh really?*" Lilly hissed.

"Oh no, Miss Lilly. I was just saying hello," Samuel quickly said. "Anyhow, I have business to attend."

"Yes … we were just talking," Hattie said. "You can visit anytime, Samuel." She stepped toward the saloon, where Samuel knew she sang. He also guessed what else might take place upstairs.

"Don't you pay no never mind to Miss Hattie."

"No, ma'am. I reckon not." Samuel much preferred Miss Lilly's company. Miss Hattie was really quite an old lady despite the makeup hiding her wrinkles.

"Sometimes I seen you ridin' through town."

"Yes, ma'am. I've been hunting and such up the creek."

They stood for an awkward moment.

"I reckon you know where to find me as well, Samuel." She looked at him. Her eyes showed a hint of hope but also pain.

Samuel wanted to reach out and touch her. He stopped himself, a cold feeling filling him. "I'm sorry, Miss Lilly. I got to go."

"Maybe visit someday, Samuel." She looked hopeful.

"Maybe." Samuel could not believe he said it. He wanted to say it. Why was it this way, he wondered.

She smiled. "Thank you." She walked away, glanced back over her shoulder, and blew him a kiss.

Samuel found himself staring. All sorts of confused feelings stormed through him. Thoughts of visiting Hinley vanished. He wanted only to get back to the cabin but could not shake the thoughts he was now having about Miss Hattie and especially about Miss Lilly.

*   *   *

Saturday afternoon, his father returned from McLane's placer and dumped his week's pay into the pan. It was about two and a half ounces, maybe thirty dollars. Samuel felt rich.

"Hey, Pa, I got the sluice repaired and got a little gold myself."

Charles's eyes went up. "How much?"

"Maybe six bits." Samuel tried to laugh. "Went to town and got nails to work on the sluice and some more coffee. I also bought some tea at the Chinese store with my dust. If you want, I'll fix you some."

"What you doing at the Chinaman store?"

Samuel gulped. He had not intended to tell his father. His father did not think warmly of the Chinese. Meekly, he told him about not having dust to pay for the onions from before.

"It's good you went back and did what was right, but I don't know if we need to be doing business with the Chinamen, Samuel."

"Meaning?" A cold feeling went through Samuel. He added the tea to the water to steep.

"They're heathens. It's best not to get mixed up with them."

"Yes, but they *are* bringing in good vegetables, and they *are* willing to do the laundry. We don't exactly have many white women around here doing that."

"True." He slid the two coffee cups to where Samuel could reach them. "Keep your head about you. Half the time they're opium-crazed. They'd just soon as chop you up as look at you. I heard one poor Chinese fellow over by Florence was blamed for taking somebody's grub. The others went after him with hatchets and made short work of him."

Samuel cringed. "Just for taking food?"

"Well, you see, Samuel, they needed more stew meat and that gave them an excuse."

Samuel looked up, not believing his ears. "Not funny, Pa."

"Well, it is true they get opium-crazed, and it is true that the fellow got hacked to pieces."

"You know the British forced them to open their ports to the opium trade, don't you?" Samuel poured the tea. "The British fought two wars with China over it. They wanted a market for their growers in India."

Charles sipped the tea. "Not bad." He eyed Samuel. "I mean, not bad for *tea*."

Samuel poured himself a cup.

"Well, son, they've brought their opium with them. A number of whites are coming into town on Saturday night for more than wimin and whiskey." He shook his head. "I can't figure. Just remember, just because it's around, doesn't mean you have to participate. Like whiskey, you can choose to drink or not, and choosing to get drunk is a man's fault, no one else's."

"I reckon, Pa." Samuel shrugged. He had not seen any Chinese yet who were not working hard or who appeared drugged, but he had seen some wandering the street outside the saloon, obviously drunk.

"Best not to associate with them, if you can help it. Bad stuff going on, and you don't want to get pulled into it."

*　　　*　　　*

Sunday, they rode into town. His father visited Alexander's Mercantile and bought an old Colt pistol. With their remaining money, they purchased a few beans, salt pork, and wheat flour.

Two men stomped in, loudly talking.

"Well, if you think it's still your placer, Ben, take it up with Attorney Poe. Otherwise, I consider the Chinese are there legally."

Samuel caught sight of a pistol under the man's short frock coat and the glint of a badge.

"You know where I stand, sheriff," the other man spoke. "They're all thieving yellow heathens." He looked up and paused as if noticing Alexander and the Chambers for the first time. He nodded weakly and left the store.

The sheriff tried to explain, "You know how it is with Ben Morton. Everything bad is the fault of the Chinamen. He just won't own up to losing his claim through his own blasted fault." His eyes flicked to Charles and then settled on Samuel.

"Howdy, Charles. This is your son, I take it." He extended his hand. "I'm Harold Sinclair, sheriff of Idaho County. I met your pa out at Mr. McLane's."

Samuel shook hands. "Pleased to meet you, sir." The sheriff was younger than his father was.

"Heard you been out all over these hills, prospectin'."

Samuel nodded.

"I've told your pa this. Keep your eyes open when you're out and about. Not all the neighbors are friendly."

"I'm okay." He had not felt threatened.

Sinclair flicked his eyes to the Colt that Charles had laid on the counter. "Expecting trouble?"

"Not if I see it first." Charles explained, "I'm usually going one way, and Samuel's going the other. I just need a bit of reassurance."

"Not a bad idea." Sinclair nodded. "Hey, you two are coming into town for the big celebration, aren't you?"

"Independence Day?"

"The ladies are fixin' a meal won't be the likes of ever seen again. There'll even be some horse racing. Now that ought to be something you should be doing." He winked at Samuel.

It was the first anyone had said anything about an Independence Day celebration. In Iowa, they had a dinner but little else. Samuel felt a rush as he tried to imagine an entire town celebrating. He glanced at his father.

His father seemed not to hear what the sheriff had said. "Guess this ought to do it, Scott." He threw a rope onto the pile of items they were buying.

Sinclair studied the stack of supplies. "How's the mining going otherwise?"

"'Bout like you see, sheriff. This equals what I dug last week."

Chapter 18

Monday, with his father back at McLane's, Samuel finished repairing the cleats on the sluice, nailing on an additional two. He laid the canvas along the bottom of the last three feet of the box and folded it up each side about an inch. Using the last cleat, he anchored it into place. The canvas should help trap the finer particles of gold before they washed back out.

He returned to his pit, dug more gravel, and began carefully washing it through the box. After a couple of hours when he did a quick check, he found the same steady run of colors as before. *Not much, probably two bits,* he figured.

He was surprised when his father returned late afternoon, short of a full day.

"We shut down early for Independence Day celebration."

Samuel leaned on his shovel, staring. Yesterday, everyone in town had been buzzing about it, but his father had said nothing.

"What? You thought we weren't going to celebrate?" Charles grinned.

"You kept it a pretty good secret." Samuel whooped and ran to his father, helped with Buster, thrilled his father was home, thrilled they were going to attend the doings.

That evening after a dinner of cottontail rabbit with a bit of salt pork, they took baths—more or less. Samuel dumped the black sand he had been collecting from the sluice out of the tub onto a pile on the ground. The gold would not wander very far, he reasoned. He heated water and poured it into the tub, a tub large enough for two feet up to the ankles. They each soaped up, and using a cloth, they washed up the best they could.

"Not quite like Burgdorf's, is it, son?"

Samuel shook his head.

"We start getting ahead in this game, we might take a trip or two up there for another swim."

*   *   *

Except for Christmas, Independence Day was the only day when the mines shut down. Father and son slept an extra hour before they rose to make up breakfast.

The meadows warmed quickly, and the sky shimmered blue, hinting of a hot day. Smoke from the ongoing fires tainted the otherwise clean air.

"If they let me, you gonna let me race Buster, Pa?"

"Nope, he's too long in the tooth. We need him to get back to Iowa. If you want to run a horse, run Spooky. He's full of spit and vinegar. You been riding him all over this country anyway."

"He isn't as smooth as Buster. If he doesn't run straight, he'll lose."

"He might surprise you when he's running alongside another horse."

Samuel tingled with the excitement. Since they had arrived Washington, his father and he had taken no time off. This day, the entire town was celebrating.

As his father shaved, Samuel slicked down his hair. He wondered if anyone would come to town from elsewhere, like that girl from Slate Creek. He wore his blue shirt and dark brown vest, which was what he wore for going to town. Although frayed at the edges, his blue shirt was in better shape than his work shirt. His trousers were not as good. Another hole had opened in a knee and needed patched.

"Instead of that pistol, maybe we should have bought you some new trousers," Charles said, eying him. "I swear those are growing shorter by the day. You were tripping on them when we left Iowa."

Samuel washed some of the dirt from his hat. At least it still looked intact.

When they reached town, they staked their horses in the meadow with other people's stock and then joined a number of people who milled about a recently built platform that was draped with red, white, and blue bunting. A couple of men shouted directions. Costumed men and women and horses began gathering. Shouting and prodding, a couple of men quickly formed them into similar groups and herded them into a line heading south toward the opposite end of town.

Half a dozen men, some blaring away on brass instruments, a few playing violins and banjos, led the parade with a recognizable march—to Samuel's surprise. Important people, Samuel guessed, including Sheriff Sinclair, Attorney Poe, and Mr. Watkins, but others he did not know, followed after. Then came several brightly costumed dancehall ladies, bustling and bouncing along. Several horses that were brightly decorated followed, prancing and tossing their heads.

Bringing up the rear amid cheers were several Chinese in white costumes fringed with gold and red tassels. They waved poles trailing bright red and yellow silk streamers and weaved them into flowing patterns of color. Samuel now realized who purchased the bright silks from Sing Mann. One Chinese beat incessantly on a couple of gongs while another vigorously shook some tambourines. Two more tossed out pieces of candy and firecrackers that hissed and popped into showers of sparks to the glee of a couple of small children who raced alongside. It struck Samuel as strange that people foreign to America would participate in its celebration of independence.

The parade looped back at the end of the street and returned to the place it had begun near the podium, where the townspeople gathered for patriotic speeches and songs. A small girl sang "My Country, 'Tis of Thee." A group of four men followed, singing "Hail, Columbia." Mr. Riebold, the owner of the Little Giant Mine, spoke about the great opportunities America had to offer.

A man whom Samuel did not recognize followed and reminded people of the recent war, commenting on the people on both sides who had fought or died. He asked for a show of hands for each side. About three to one had been Southern sympathizers. Samuel watched his father's face as the hands rose, but his father did not turn to look. He noticed more than one stony stare and wondered if it had been a good idea for people to identify sides from a bitter war that had ended scarcely six years earlier.

Mr. Timberlake, a store clerk at Hofen's, took the podium, and in a strong voice, read the Declaration of Independence. Samuel noticed he mostly recited it from memory. He found himself remembering many of the words from his own school studies.

At noon, people moved to the meadow, where some pines offered some shade and the ladies had set out dozens of dishes of food on plank tables that they had covered with fancy linens. Samuel had not seen such food in his life. Plates were stacked to overflowing with beef, ham, and chicken. Others held potatoes, brown beans, breads, and steamed vegetables. Best of all were the dozens of pies.

An elderly woman shoved a plate into his hands. "It's clear on your face you been waitin' for this. Dig in, young man."

Samuel stacked a plate as high as he dared and looked for some shade.

"Better not overdo it, Samuel, if you don't want to weight down Spooky." Charles had caught up to him.

Samuel followed his father to where he sat with some of the men from the McLane placer. Samuel sat outside the circle. He recognized the men but did not know them.

He hesitated about eating the last piece of chicken. His father was half right about not overdoing it for when he raced Spooky.

After dinner, men and women sat among the trees, many taking an afternoon nap in the heat. White, billowing clouds rose on the horizon.

The horse races would begin in about an hour. Samuel rose and dusted his trousers. "I want to look around a bit," he told his father.

"To where?" Charles raised his eyes.

"Don't know. Just looking to visit with folks." He wondered if he could find Miss Lilly.

Samuel had never seen this number of people all gathered together at one time. He estimated there were about two hundred men and an untold number of Chinese. There were half a dozen women and about six or seven little children, the number surprising him because he never saw any about. Several small children were running, playing tag. The others were infants in their mothers' arms—the "newly hatched ones" to which Jenkins had referred. He figured none of the families lived in town, except for the Manuels, who owned the Washington Hotel, and another family who owned one of the saloons. He learned two of the families had come up from their homesteads on the South Fork.

The Chinese had retired to their own side of the field, where they also had a spread of food. Samuel looked around for Chen but did not see him. He saw no Chinese women—he never had—and he had never seen any Chinese children, except Chen, whom he figured was about his age and did not count.

He did not fit with the families or with the working men. Strangely, among all the people, he felt alone.

Finally, he spotted Miss Lily with a group of similarly dressed women and a few men. Because of the men standing nearby, he declined to go over and bring attention to himself.

A pistol shot signaled the time for the races. His heart caught. He now wondered why he had agreed to race. He caught up Spooky, saddled him, and checked the cinch twice. He wanted to at least be mounted when they crossed the finish line.

"Hey, kid, you really expect to race that cayuse?" The man calling to him led a sleek black that pranced and shook its head.

"I do."

The man just laughed, shaking his head.

He led Spooky to the starting area, where several men and their mounts were gathered. The winners would race the winners and the losers, the losers, until one remained, undefeated. They drew pairings from a hat. Samuel and

Spooky were matched against a white mare ridden by a man unknown to Samuel. They drew the second heat.

The first heat ran two gelding bays, which were similar to Buster. It was a dead heat until the corner when one animal went wide, nearly spilling his rider. The winning horse walked across the finish. Samuel worried about Spooky making the corner. He was a good running horse and cornered quickly, occasionally too quickly. Samuel had been unseated before.

He mounted up and brought Spooky up to the line beside the mare. Spooky shied a bit, and Samuel nudged him back. He nodded to his father standing down the line.

"I got two bits on you, son," he hollered. "Better win this one."

"Listen up." The man with the starting flag waved at them. "The moment you see the flag drop, you run. You get one miss-start, and then you're out." Samuel wet his lips and gripped the reins more tightly. He nudged Spooky up closer, feeling the animal's tension.

"Easy, boy. Easy." The horse quivered.

Samuel knew he could do this. The race was a straight run to the other end of town and then a large loop out and around some barrels. It was then a mad dash back to the start.

The flag dropped. "Go, boy!" He dug his boots into Spooky's flanks. "Get up, Spooky. Get up." He dug again as the animal jumped, exploding down the line. Samuel buried his head low and held on. Spooky hammered down the track, pounding hard, the mare crowding his left flank. Samuel did not look up. He held tight until near the corner and then pulled firmly on the reins. Spooky cut sharply left, cutting in front of the mare. He held the corner tight, his heels digging into Spooky, and then gathering speed, he thundered out. *Wide.* He quickly nudged Spooky back into line, aiming for the far end of town.

He heard cheering. "Come on, kid. You got him! Come on." He dug his heels into Spooky. The horse surged on.

Head low, glued to Spooky's powerful frame, Samuel thrilled at the feel of the horse's muscles exploding, recoiling, exploding as they raced, thundering down the track.

He won the first heat by several lengths. Spooky heaved and shook as he came to a halt. People clapped and cheered. "Way to go, kid."

"Bah," the beaten rider complained. "If I was a light banty weight of sixty pounds, he'd have had no chance."

Samuel started to take exception but saw that the man grinned. "Well done," he said.

"Good horse you got, son," another man said. "He from good blood?"

"Don't know," replied Samuel. "He's an Iowa farm horse."

People laughed and turned back to the start of the next heat. Samuel felt good, warmed by his success. His father came by. "You earned us two bits. Do it again, and I'll buy us dinner."

Samuel grinned. He realized the worst he could now place was fourth. That might be good for a couple of dollars prize money.

When the winners of the first heat had lined up to run again, Samuel was matched against the black. Spooky ran well but was edged out at the last. The black moved on to win the day.

Samuel won the final heat, which was good enough for four dollars in dust and enough in bets to cover those that his father had lost on the second heat.

"Maybe we ought to take up horse racing," Charles told him. "I have to work near all day for that kind of money."

Samuel shrugged. "Lucky." He patted Spooky, who still heaved from exertion. "Kinda like mining. Never know what will turn up."

"Maybe you ought to start carrying the mail around here." A man approached him and offered his hand. "I'm Warren Hunt. I'm the expressman."

"Pleased to meet you, sir," Samuel replied, shaking his hand. He remembered the story of Mr. Hunt at Shearer's ferry.

"If I had more horses like yours, I'd be less likely stopped by road agents."

"A youngster like him on a good horse like his just might be what we need," the man with the black agreed. He angled away with Hunt. Samuel could tell he was trying to discuss something.

The celebration moved back to the platform for an evening dance. Charlie Bemis and Rube Besse took up violins. Nate Jenkins played his banjo. Charles Brown played an old accordion. And Peter Beamer, who had written up some of the music, played a flute. Samuel thought it was great music.

He felt a bit strange being at a dance, however; he hardly ever danced. His grandma had tried to teach him a few times back in Iowa after Sunday doings, but he had not taken to it.

He noted the men outnumbered the ladies about ten to one, but none of the men hesitated to swing each other around, loud and raucous. Samuel joined in. They danced arm in arm, meeting one partner after another, stomping away to link arms with a new partner—rarely a woman—dancing, clapping, and stomping away in a large, noisy circle, kicking up dust from the street.

The line dancing paused, and a few men took to the platform to dance in singles or pairs, hopping and bobbing about to great cheers from their fellow men. Mr. Hofen, the Prussian, took the platform, dancing, jutting his legs out one at a time, dropping lower and lower each time to the accompaniment of Charlie Bemis's violin. Slowly, he began and then more rapidly as the music increased in tempo. Arms folded, he bounced on one foot, knee bent, his other leg flung outward. Then he switched legs. Moving faster and faster until he was a blur of flying legs and flapping arms, he ended in a thunderous applause. After that, no one else tried to match his effort.

The music slowed. The few remaining women looked exhausted. Somehow, Samuel found himself dancing with a pleasant-looking woman named Marjorie Reynolds. "Ma Reynolds," she told him to call her. She reminded him of his own mother, and he felt a knot in his throat. After his dance with Ma Reynolds, the other ladies sought him out. One by one, they introduced themselves and said how good it was to see a decent young man in Warren's camp. He thanked each, and each told him how handsome he was. His ears burned, but he felt comfort in their warm presence.

Evening fell. Lanterns were lit. People paused for pie and coffee. When the orchestra began again, only a few dancers returned. The families had drifted home. The bachelor miners remained.

"These men will go all night, Samuel. I have work tomorrow."

Samuel reluctantly agreed. "Got to get Spooky and Buster back. Reckon we can buy Spooky an extra helping of grain?"

"And then some," Charles agreed. "Work around the cabin tomorrow and give him the day off to rest."

CHAPTER 19

S amuel had been thinking of O'Riley's ledge again, but he had decided to work the cabin placer and see if the changes to the sluice would help any. To him, the gravel looked good, much like McLane's. There should be more gold than what he had been finding. He decided to try two or three spots, sampling each by digging as deep as possible and then running gravel from each spot for at least a couple of hours.

He swung his pick into the earth, gouging out clumps of grass and roots. These he threw to the side, knowing there would be little gold in them. Below the thin soil, the ground became rocky. Every swing he took, the pick bounced off buried rocks, jarring his hands.

All too soon, his sore muscles returned, and new blisters cropped up on his callused hands. All too soon, the ache returned to his shoulders and lower back.

He pulled the cobbles from the hole and stacked them to the side. The larger boulders, he pried loose and rolled out. Those he could not move, he dug around, scraping out the small quantities of gravel from between them. When he had enough loose material to load his bucket, he carried it to the sluice and stockpiled it.

He paused frequently and stretched, trying to ease the strain on his shoulders and back, trying to pace himself for a full day's work.

Although he knew he was in the company of dozens of men doing the same, he felt strangely alone. The country around was silent except for the birds and the wind. It was a big country, which swallowed up men. Many were scattered throughout a dozen gulches several miles from Warren's camp to the southeast. Thus far, these strikes were short-lived, providing a few men with a living for a season or two at most. Other than the quartz mines, it was only the big placers, like McLane's and Osborn's, where men were doing well.

He gazed at the unbroken, grassy meadows to the north. Everyone suspected that large quantities of gold had settled to the bottom of the gravels deep beneath the meadows, but it was not possible to work them without the benefit of a grade. The best some had done was as he was doing only on a larger scale—dig the gravel and carry it up to the sluice boxes where water and gravity could do the work.

The spring creek from which Samuel diverted water seemed to be steady, but it was not large. Its flow hardly moved the gravel through the box, and by the time the water reached around the hill to where Samuel was working, most had seeped into the rocky ground beneath the ditch.

He spent a couple of hours enlarging the small pond where he trapped the water. As before, he kept the water from entering the sluice with a section of board while the pond filled. In the meantime, he continued to dig and stockpile gravel near the sluice.

Satisfied he had enough, he pulled the board and allowed water to flood the box until he had a strong flow. Carefully, he shoveled in the gravel, sprinkling it into the water, watching as it moved it through the box, watching for any small nugget to be trapped behind the cleats. He saw only the same tiny specks as before, pieces about the size of thin cornmeal grains.

Disappointed, he began a second hole to the side of a boulder located lower on the hill in a small gulch. Again, he lugged buckets to the sluice until he had enough to run. This time, more black sand showed, sprinkled with more tiny bits of gold, a couple of them the size of flattened grass seeds. Samuel felt encouraged. He scooped out the black sand and added it to the pile he had already saved.

The day warmed until uncomfortable. Samuel removed his shirt, welcoming the breeze that occasionally interrupted the dead heat. White billowing thunderheads gathered to the northwest, but they failed to bring any relief.

He began a third hole. This one proved to be nearly barren. Nevertheless, he stayed at it until late day, not giving up despite his sore muscles and blisters.

Satisfying himself he had done what he could to check the three new prospects, he turned the water back into the spring creek and returned to the cabin with his bucket of fines. He would pan them down later and pick out what gold he could. Based on what he found the previous times, he did not figure he had much more than a dollar. He had worked an entire day for a dollar.

He glanced to where Spooky and Molly grazed across the meadow, lazily switching their tails at the flies, thinking momentarily of the easy lives they led—well, at least for now.

In the stillness of the evening, he started a fire and put on a kettle of water to heat. He stretched, trying to ease the pain from his muscles. He remembered the swim at Burgdorf's, how the hot water would help ease the pain. He thought of looking for the ledge in the morning but instead vowed to give the placer one more day.

*   *   *

After he finally fell asleep in the early morning, trying all night to get relief from his sore shoulders and back, Samuel slept past sunup. He took his time preparing some breakfast and tending to the cabin before he returned to the sluice.

He turned the water back into the ditch but was dismayed to find his pond nearly dry. The rocky ground held little water.

As he had done previously, he began digging some new holes, looking for better gravel. He no longer bothered washing the first several feet. The amount of gold found in the grass clumps and topsoil was insignificant. When he was down about three feet, he began collecting and running the gravel.

By late day, he was again so sore he could hardly move. His back and legs ached. He could no longer open his cramped fingers.

There was no longer any excitement when he shoveled the dirt into the box and watched the water wash it through. Only tiny specks of gold lined up along the upper cleat—the same meager amount and size he had been finding in all the holes. Dutifully, he collected the black sand and separated out what gold he could.

Late afternoon, he returned to the second hole from the previous day. He enlarged it, exposing a number of boulders. He wrestled the smaller ones out of the hole, but the largest, he could not budge. He dug in front of them. If he ever did get behind them, they would slide down into the hole out of his way.

He stockpiled a few buckets of gravel next to the sluice and then released the water. Carefully, he shoveled in the dirt. He was encouraged. The bits of gold showing in the black sand were better. One the size of a cucumber seed gleamed at him. His heart raced as he picked it out. *This was good gold!*

Dusk had gathered. Samuel was grateful. He was too sore to keep mining. At the cabin, he ate some cold corncake before he stretched out on his cot. In two days, he figured he had mined about two and a half dollars, not counting the tiny specks yet trapped in the black sand. It was not much, but it was real money. He opened and closed his hands, trying to work out the stiffness and get some feeling back into them. He felt a great sense of accomplishment.

The excavations had answered his question. With both his father and him working, they might get five dollars in gold a day, but the diminishing water concerned him.

His father did not return that night. Samuel knew they were working as long as possible while they had light and the water held. It had not rained for several days, and now the creeks were simply draining dry.

Samuel decided he had done as much as possible with the placer and would return to look for the ledge.

CHAPTER 20

Morning, he was on the trail early, heading up through the Chinese placers, up along Slaughter Creek. The Chinese smiled and bowed and waved as usual as he passed. They then immediately returned to their work.

He turned up the tributary—Bare Knob Creek, he was calling it. Over three feet in width, it had a good, strong flow and contributed much of the water in Slaughter Creek. As usual, he watched for cairns and swept his eyes along the ravines for any outcrops.

He followed the creek a couple of miles and climbed upward until the timber and brush began to thin and more loose rock appeared. He turned Spooky east and worked his way upward toward the ridgetop far north of where he had last been.

On top, he thought he smelled a faint trace of wood smoke. He glanced to the northeast to where he could see the fire cloud. The main fire had crossed the Salmon River and burned toward Montana Territory. Some said it would burn until winter.

Samuel noted several promising outcrops and noted that the bare knob was clearly visible to the west. Perhaps he had discovered the correct ridge. He spent most of the day searching. In the few rocky places he discovered, he searched on foot, painstakingly checking for quartz. The quartz was isolated and consisted of a few pieces of snow-white chunks, showing no indication of mineralization.

Late afternoon, he had reached where the ridge intersected another. It descended toward the southeast. More rock showed as he began following it downward. The wood smoke came to him again. He guessed prospectors were below him in the creek—maybe one of the placers Hinley had described. He pushed Spooky down through the timber toward the camp, eager to say hello.

He broke out into a clearing. A tent had been pitched against a rocky hillside where a seep emerged from under the talus. He spotted three shabbily dressed men, their horses nearby, but dismissed studying them. His attention was caught by the nearby outcrop. *They had found O'Riley's ledge!* But they were not mining. Loud arguing had erupted.

One man brandished a pistol. Another man in a black frock coat watched. A younger man staggered backward, eyes bulging white and frantic; his hands clawed the air. He turned and ran, stumbling toward the horses. Two quick explosions from the pistol shattered the silence. The man went spinning, stumbling into the dirt, clutching his side. The camp filled with white smoke. The downed man began crawling back toward the gunman, pleading, one arm raised over his face.

Like a mallet slamming into him, stunned, disbelieving seeing the man shot, now remembering the three men, Samuel pulled back on Spooky.

Quentin Dudgin deliberately walked up to Clay Bender, raised his pistol, and fired. Particles sprayed from the back of Bender's head. Face gone, he crumpled into the dirt. The explosion echoed through the basin.

Samuel could not breathe. "God, God, God," he heard himself saying. He tried to turn away, not look. He could not move. He shook. "God, no." He was vaguely aware that Ramey Smith had turned toward him, coming his way, hollering words he could not hear. He felt like stone. From somewhere else, he was looking at himself sitting on Spooky, looking at Smith reaching up to him, seeing him pull him from the saddle, watching Spooky sidle away.

Only when he hit the ground did he come to his senses.

"It's that damn wet-nosed kid," Smith said, glaring down at him, black, matted beard, stinking breath. "So scared he wet himself." He laughed.

A cold, icy shock washed over Samuel. These were the scum his father and he had met on the trail.

"Grab his horse." Dudgin stumbled past and lunged wildly for Spooky. The horse bolted, heading up through the timber, branches snapping.

"Damn it, Ramey. Why didn't you grab his horse?" Dudgin brandished the pistol.

"What the hell—" Smith snapped. "You rather I let the kid get away? His horse'll be back."

"If it gets to Washington without a rider, it won't be alone in coming back." Dudgin cursed again and kicked at the dirt.

"The wet-nose saw it all, Quentin." Smith pushed Samuel into the dirt.

Dudgin came over. He smelled as bad as Smith. His clothes were even rattier than before. Samuel shook, his heart hammering in his ears. He felt he was choking. He tried to calm himself.

"What you doin' up here, kid?" Dudgin demanded. His yellowed eyes flashed.

Samuel remained silent.

"Damn it—talk." He threatened with the pistol.

"I-I was prospectin', same as you." Samuel tried to think of something. He had already seen the aparejos. These were the scum preying on the miners around Warren's camp. This was their camp, and they were not Chinese.

"We ain't—" Dudgin said and then paused. "Anyone with you?"

"M-my pa. He's behind me. We were supposed to meet up top of this ridge—" Samuel did not see the cuff coming until after he was spitting dirt from his mouth, tasting blood, trying to sit back up.

"Damn liar, you are, kid."

"No, he's prospecting the other ridge over." Samuel stuck to his lie. He could think of nothing else.

"If that's so," Smith interrupted, "put a bullet in him, and let's get out of here."

Dudgin hesitated. "Bender double-crossed us. No one's gonna miss his hide, not even his own mama, and this kid's pa *ain't* here." He waved the pistol at Samuel. "Ain't that so?" He cocked the hammer.

"Y-yes, I'm alone." Samuel braced for the bullet, wondering if he would feel anything.

"What'd I tell you? Damn kid's a liar. Your pa ever tell you what happens to liars?" He waved the pistol again.

Samuel nodded.

Dudgin burst out laughing. "You end up like us two, don't you?"

Samuel refused to acknowledge. "People will be looking for me."

"We're done here," Smith snapped, making a move toward the tent. "We can hightail it."

"Shut up," screamed Dudgin, jumping up and pushing his partner away. "Gotta think."

The men moved off, arguing loudly. Samuel fought to slow his breathing. If Dudgin had meant to kill him, he would have already done so. He glanced at Bender's body and shuddered. It lay still, unmoving, his skull a bloody mess, blood seeping into the dirt. Samuel felt sick. His heart hammered until he thought it would burst. *Please, dear God,* he prayed.

Smith came up to him, a length of rope in his hands. He leaned into his face, black eyes gleaming. "One wrong move, wet-nose, one word ... it will be your cussing last." He pulled his skinning knife and laid it against Samuel's throat. "'Twas my choice, you'd already be dead meat."

Smith's breath stank so bad Samuel tried to turn away.

Smith turned him back, the stubs of his missing fingers poking into his neck. "Give me another excuse, pretty boy, and you will be." He pushed the point in. Samuel winced and squeezed his eyes shut. "Is that what all the ladies say to you ... pretty boy?"

Samuel shook his head.

"Pretty boy … pretty boy." He pushed the blade around. "You know what happens to pretty boys?" He breathed heavily into Samuel's face.

Samuel tried to pull away.

"So pretty boy doesn't like me, does he? What? Think I'm ugly, do you?"

Samuel felt panic. He choked out, "N-no."

"You're lyin' again, boy. I can see it in your eyes." He laughed and hollered at Dudgin. "This wet-nose thinks I'm ugly, Quentin. Now what do you think about that?"

Dudgin did not reply.

"Think I'll just have some fun with him. What you think, Quentin? Use him up like that squaw woman up in Montana Territory?"

"They'll hang you for it." Dudgin stood above Samuel, looking down.

"After what this wet-nose just seen, we're both gonna hang." Smith laughed, pulling his hand with the stubs through his beard. "The hell of it is, we can only hang once. I say we enjoy it while we can." He grabbed Samuel's face and turned it toward him. "Whatcha think about that?"

Samuel could not talk. Smith's eyes frightened him. They danced, revealing his pleasure in cruelty. Samuel could not think. "I-I won't say anything."

Smith laughed loudly. "Look at that, Quentin. He's beggin'." He turned Samuel's face again. "No, you won't say a thing," he spat, "or you'll end up like that double-crossin' cuss." He tossed his head in Bender's direction.

"That's enough, Ramey. We got work to get done."

A cruel grin, Smith hissed, "Soon enough." He jerked Samuel's hands up and bound them until the rope cut in, making them go numb. Samuel winced.

The men struck camp, packing some of the items onto the horses.

"Could sure use that kid's horse," Dudgin muttered. "Going to have to leave some of this." He threw the aparejos into the brush.

"We were ready to go anyways," Smith reminded him.

Dudgin exploded and went for Smith. "You want to join Bender? *I* decide when I'm ready." He moved about recklessly, angrily throwing items, shoving others into packs.

Samuel tried not to watch as they dragged Bender's body into the rocks. He heard a few clatter and guessed they were hiding it. Evening approached. He studied the basin, trying desperately to figure a way to make a break for it.

Smith approached him, leading Bender's horse. "Get up, wet-nose. You're comin' with us." He grinned and tapped his skinning knife.

Samuel felt himself go numb. He scrambled to his feet. He was able to reach the pommel, get a foot into the stirrup, and hoist himself up. He had enough give in the bonds to hold the saddle horn. He tried to flex his hands. They were turning purple.

"You've cut off the blood in my hands," Samuel managed.

"Won't be the only thing we cut off, if you don't shut up." Smith laughed.

They rode out—not downstream but uphill toward the northeast, toward the South Fork divide. Samuel rode between Dudgin and Smith. He kept working his hands, trying to loosen the rope, trying to increase the circulation. He prayed Bender's bay was sure-footed. The country, he knew, was similar to French Creek. He realized they were trying to put miles between themselves and their old camp. If Spooky did wander back to Washington and people came searching, he and the outlaws would be long gone.

It was near dark when they reached the ridge overlooking the South Fork. The first stars had emerged. They angled downward across the tops of several ridges until they reached a basin. Samuel smelled elk and guessed they were near water.

"You can get down, kid. We're staying here tonight," Dudgin muttered and spat. "Try running, and I'll put a bullet in you." He brandished his pistol.

Samuel studied the canyon of jagged gray shapes below, thankful they would not try going down in the dark.

The two men threw out their blankets, seemingly oblivious to Samuel.

He approached them. "I got to pee." He held up his hands.

"Go ahead." Smith laughed. "You already done it once."

Samuel turned and walked toward the trees, burning with shame.

"Go with him," Dudgin snarled.

"Come here, pretty boy," Smith muttered. He undid Samuel's ropes.

Samuel flexed his hands and tried to get some feeling back into them.

"Get your business done, wet-nose."

"My hands ... I can't feel anything," Samuel replied. He kept rubbing, finally feeling some tingling, reaching for his suspenders.

"You got one minute." He shouldered up beside Samuel and began undoing his own trousers.

A jolt ran through Samuel. He stared ahead, an icy chill coursing through his body. He studied the rocks; a rib descended from above. He broke for it, sprinting. Springing from one rock to the next, he hurled himself up and over the rib.

"He's running." Smith cursed, fumbling with his trousers, scrambling for Samuel, tripping.

Cursing and yelling erupted below Samuel. He veered to his left toward the canyon, snapping branches, flying downhill. He knew one slip would send him tumbling—probably kill him. His breath came hard, lungs aching. The cursing behind grew more distant.

He reached the ravine and flew down it. Gray shapes of rocks raced past him, and black tree trunks came at him. He hit one branch that almost took his wind. He slowed. If they could not hear him, they could not follow. They could not see him or catch him now. He gasped for breath, trying to slow his breathing to hear where the men were.

A few shots sounded, and he flinched as the rounds buzzed above him. *Not aimed.* He was satisfied. He hoped they would think he continued downward. He listened and then began a wide circle back up and around the men. When he could hear them arguing, he paused in the cover of the trees and darkness.

"He has to go back through Washington," Dudgin muttered. "Otherwise, he'll end up on the South Fork with nowhere to go. We can catch him in Washington."

Smith cursed unintelligibly. "I got unfinished business with him."

"You let him get away."

They both exploded into loud arguing again. Samuel slipped past but was unsure how to proceed. If they returned to Washington, they could easily intercept him. He scrambled upward. As long as he could hear them, he was safe.

He climbed, not knowing exactly his direction, but knowing he would come out on the ridge. If he were far enough to the south, he would immediately drop into Slaughter Creek drainage. If not, he would cut the ridges he had been prospecting. The ravines and creeks would eventually come out at Washington. He located the North Star and headed west toward Washington.

Exhausted, he stopped and listened for the men. Eventually, he heard them below, coming upward, riding. As long as he knew where they were, he was safe. But they moved more quickly and soon passed him. Now out of hearing, he could no longer be certain where they were. They could hole up anywhere along the trails or in Washington. He would never see them until it was too late.

He decided to swing wide to the north, to circle around Washington and return to his cabin. At least on foot, he could travel where their horses could not. More importantly, he could hear the horses coming.

Samuel could not get a good grasp of time. He knew total darkness lasted only a few hours. It had been so for some time.

He angled downward, believing he was in the Slaughter Creek drainage.

When he reached a trickle of water, he paused to drink. His stomach turned. He wished for food. He wondered if a hungry animal might be hunting *him* for food, and a chill washed over him. Without a rifle, without a knife, he felt naked and alone.

The stars in the sky hung like brilliant, glittering crystals. He sought out the North Star again and angled southwest.

Exhausted, unable to continue, he paused, shoving himself back up against an overhanging rock. The creek had now grown to a good flow. It had to be Meadow Creek. Washington had to be a short distance downstream. He listened for the men who were now beyond him, probably somewhere along the trail into Washington. He strained to hear horses coming, any noise. He needed rest and sat down. His energy was gone. He could move no farther, and he closed his eyes.

*   *   *

Thuds in the night woke him. He strained to see from where the sounds originated. They drew nearer and paused. A horse snuffed and rattled its bridle. *They've found me!* Samuel tried to push himself back out of sight, shaking uncontrollably, an icy chill enveloping him. The shape loomed up above him and nickered.

"Spooky!" Samuel reached up to take the animal's head. "Thank, God, Spooky." He stroked the animal. He checked to see that his saddle was still there, as was his rifle. An immense relief flooded him.

He dragged himself up onto Spooky, pulled his rifle, checked it, and rested it across the pommel. Softly, he urged the animal down the creek. Flickering kerosene lamps from the Rescue mine appeared. Not daring to continue closer, he turned uphill until he was above the Chinese placer. Something told him the men were below, just below the spot where he had turned uphill. He tried to calm the overwhelming feeling urging him to bolt and instead pushed ahead quietly through the timber. A trace of light had come to the sky. Soon, the hunters would be able to see their prey.

He cut through the timber above Washington, crossed the numerous ravines that came off the hills, and feeling he was finally safe, returned to the trail. He made it to his cabin in the gray light of the new day, unsaddled Spooky, and dropped exhausted into bed. He kept his rifle near.

He slept a couple of hours before he woke, terrified, dreaming that the men had found him. Catching up Spooky, he made his way back to Washington, where he found Sheriff Sinclair and told him what had happened, concentrating carefully on describing the men.

"Description fits what Shissler said," Harold Sinclair muttered, putting down his pencil. "Sounds like the same three snakes all right ... now two."

"What are you going to do, sheriff?"

"I'll get a few men and go after them. Based on what you say, though, I'm betting they're past Burgdorf's and heading down into the canyon. Doubtful we can catch them before they get out of the country."

"You think they'll come looking for me?"

"Not unless they've seen you around and know where your cabin is."

"Me and my pa saw them last spring. They know us," Samuel explained.

"Better chance then that they'll keep going."

"Should I take you to their camp?"

"What you need to do is get down to Mr. McLane's and see your pa. I know the country where you been. If it's the basin I think it is, I've been through there."

*   *   *

Fuzzy from exhaustion, Samuel reached McLane's placer and told his father the story.

"You think they'll come after me?" The more Samuel had thought about the possibility, the more uneasy he had become. He was beginning to believe they knew where he lived, especially since they had been hanging around Warren's camp.

"They might come after both of us, but if they don't want their necks stretched, they'll be smart to keep on going."

"I hope so. I haven't slept much."

"Use my cot, I'll wake you when it's time to head in. Come on. I'll show you which one. Maybe we can knock off a little early."

Samuel felt washed with relief. "I don't understand, Pa. How can men do such evil?"

"Some men give their souls to the devil. They no longer care what happens to them here on earth."

Samuel remembered Smith had said something like that.

He felt somewhat better knowing others would be watching for Dudgin and Smith. He doubted they would come for him, but he knew if they did, he would never see them before they put a bullet in his back.

*   *   *

When they reached their cabin that evening, Charles and Samuel scouted the perimeter for any sign of unwelcome visitors before they headed in. Nothing appeared disturbed. They had a simple dinner and turned in.

Samuel was exhausted. He tried not to think of Dudgin and Smith, but visions of Bender's bleeding body plagued him. He was clawing, gasping for air, struggling. He remembered his father telling him to go back to sleep, that he was dreaming.

*   *   *

Samuel was surprised to see the sun full up and his father not around when he woke. His father had let him sleep. Later that afternoon, they rode into town for weekly supplies—some apples, potatoes, and cheese. They bought new long johns. For the first time, they had a small amount of gold remaining. Not being prone to spend their money on "wimin and whiskey," as he remembered Hallelujah had put it, they were able to resupply. Come Monday morning many of the other miners would again be broke or further in debt. Still, Samuel knew his father and he were scarcely making grub since coming to Warren's camp.

"Next week, maybe we can buy you some quicksilver for you to start panning down those fines you're getting off the placer."

"I hope there's more gold in it than what I can see, because it sure won't do as is," Samuel admitted.

CHAPTER 21

Samuel packed some of their gear onto Molly and accompanied his father back to McLane's the following week. Both wanted to make sure Dudgin and Smith had left the country and showed no indications of returning.

Robert McLane quickly agreed to give Samuel room and board for helping as a runabout. Samuel did the small things that helped free the men up to work more efficiently. If ever any of them needed something, he delivered it or carried it away.

For most of one day, he gathered firewood. He took Molly and rode Spooky up into the timber away from the placer until he located a substantial deadfall. After he got a rope around a tree at a time, he dragged them to the camp. He found an ax and began splitting the wood, watching in satisfaction as the pieces flew apart.

"That's more wood than I've had around here since filing the claim," McLane boomed.

"I've had a lot of practice hauling poles to our cabin." Samuel patted Molly. "Old mule is getting pretty good at it by now."

One of his main tasks was helping the cook, Gabe Whitman. He was a short, stocky man with balding hair. Samuel figured he was better fit as a saloonkeeper than a cook. There were no frills about him. He cooked up whatever grub was handy, simple and quick.

"Now maybe I can get more than ten minutes of sleep a night," he barked when he shook Samuel's hand.

Soon, Samuel was tending the fire, hauling water, peeling spuds, and helping serve the men. Only after they had eaten did he and Gabe have a chance to eat. Sometimes little remained. Even so, it was considerably more than what he and his father usually ate, and for the first time in a long while, he felt he was being filled up.

"I'd feed them more if'n Mr. McLane allowed me more on the spendin'," Gabe once apologized.

"I think this is great, Mr. Whitman."

They had large slices of fried beef with potatoes and gravy and on occasion, baked salmon. The fish were running strong, and plenty were available. He helped Gabe split the fish and tie them to wooden stakes, which they leaned over a bed of coals to bake. The only frill Samuel could discern with Gabe's cooking were the apples he served with the salmon—nothing like Mrs. Shearer or Mr. Burgdorf.

The men, including his father, did not seem to mind. They came in exhausted and ate whatever Gabe set before them.

Gabe worked him hard and barked a lot, but Samuel saw through it. The man was happy to have help. But to Samuel, Gabe seemed to be out of place. He wondered how he ended up a cook in a placer camp, but he never had the heart to ask. Like many, Samuel figured he was thankful to have some work.

Samuel appreciated being able to eat and he knew the men welcomed his help, but he soon tired of doing camp chores. He had hauled more water, tended more fire, and washed more dishes than he cared to think about.

Although the mornings began cool, they quickly heated until they were almost unbearable, especially in the pit where the air sat unmoving and the sun reflected hot from the white cobbles. Every hour, Samuel ran water to the men and kept buckets filled and nearby. During those times, the men paused and kidded with him, and during those times, he took time to check the cleats of the sluice boxes for gold. There was far more than what he found at the cabin, but more than ever, it made him impatient to be running his own sluice and finding his own gold.

Late one afternoon, Sheriff Sinclair and another man rode up. "There's somebody I'm glad to see," Sinclair said, nodding toward Samuel and dismounting. "I rode by your cabin and couldn't find hide nor hair of you and got a bit nervous. Those were some bad snakes you ran into. How you doing?"

"I'm good. Just being a runabout for a bit," Samuel replied. "You catch them?"

Sinclair shook his head. "We found their camp where you said it was. Looks like they were using up most of what they stole to keep alive. Maybe if they had worked as hard at mining, they could have made a decent living. Being out in the woods like you've been, you're lucky you didn't run into them earlier."

"Maybe if I had, it would have saved Bender's life."

"Probably not. You'd likely be the one dead. They would have killed you and just gone on robbing folks. No telling where they would have dumped your body."

Samuel cringed, seeing images of his own bleeding body in place of Bender's.

"I'd like to think Washington is civilized—certainly more so than Florence or Elk City—but we got our bad element. And there's always lowlife hanging around the gold camps, looking for easy pickings." Sinclair studied Samuel. "You might consider sticking closer to civilization."

"Thanks for the advice, sheriff," Charles answered for Samuel.

"What were you doing way up in that country, anyway, Samuel? No gold strikes been found up there."

Samuel hesitated. "Some hunting. I figured if I could get over onto the breaks, I might get a deer closer than going all the way to the South Fork."

"I did see good elk sign up there," Sinclair affirmed. "Anyway, I think we got them on the run. Some miners reported seeing them on the trail to Florence. If they're smart, they won't stop until they reach Canada. I don't think you need worry about them anymore."

"Thanks, sheriff," Charles said. "I appreciate you coming out here to tell us."

"Just wanted to make sure everything was okay." He turned away. "I'll let you get back to work." He paused a moment and visited with McLane.

*   *   *

That evening when they shut down, Charles rode with Samuel back to their cabin. They decided Samuel would be more useful watching their own gear and minding the stock. Samuel was immediately thankful. He had not come to Idaho Territory simply to be a runabout; he wanted to find gold.

The following morning, after his father returned to McLane's, Samuel resumed work around the cabin. He worked some on a hay crib and a stock shelter before he grew impatient and returned to the placer.

He studied the hillside above it, convinced more than ever that the placer was much like McLane's. It only lacked water. On the west side of the Big Meadow, men had tapped into a substantial creek, ditching it around the hills in order to draw water for running the sluices. Here, he had no creek to tap into other than the meager spring creek. Samuel reckoned had there been water, men would have mined these gravels years ago.

He studied on how to improve his water supply. He began by enlarging the catch basin, working for most of the day on it. He avoided digging too deeply. The soil, when turned to mud, acted to seal the bottom, but he found that if he dug too deeply, the water seeped into the gravelly soil below. When he realized the problem, he re-dug a portion of the ditch as well, leaving more soil in its bottom to help seal it. He partially filled some of the gravelly places. It was more important for the water to reach the catch basin than to have a large flow.

Late afternoon, he released the water back into the ditch, watching anxiously as it flowed along and began collecting in the catch basin. When it had covered the bottom, he felt satisfied and returned to the cabin to prepare some dinner.

He was surprised but happy to see his father riding up.

"Guess I don't like the idea of you being here alone." He dismounted and turned the reins over to Samuel. "Got any supper?"

"I can fry up some squirrels I got in the spring box right quick."

When he returned with the squirrels, he found his father just sitting. He built up the fire and put on water to boil.

"You okay, Pa?"

"Just fine, Samuel. Just worn out. And to be honest, a bit worried about you. Not sure I trust this country much anymore. Maybe you should come back to the placer with me. It was good to have you as a runabout."

"I'm fine, Pa. If Dudgin and Smith show up, they can dry-gulch me at McLane's just as easily as here."

"Now that's a nice thought."

"Maybe you should work here, pa. I think this placer could be as good as McLane's."

His father raised his eyes. Samuel began frying the squirrels. He explained how he had enlarged the catch basin and how he intended to work around the boulders where he expected to find more gold.

"If anyone's going to find it, you are." Charles spread his hands. "Thanks for the squirrel." He began picking the meat from the tiny bones. "Maybe you can rustle up something a bit more growed up someday."

*   *   *

After his father again left for McLane's, Samuel eagerly returned to the placer. He was elated. The catch basin held water.

He returned to the lower pit, dug more around the boulders, pried out the smaller rocks, knocked off the dirt, and tossed them onto a growing pile of cobbles. When he had a good amount of gravel, he released the water and began shoveling it into the box, carefully washing it through. When finished, he replaced the head gate to shut off the water and anxiously examined the box. A fair amount of gold showed. He felt giddy. The gold was not nearly as much as at McLane's, but it was the most he had yet found. A thin line of bright yellow had accumulated behind the first cleat.

Eagerly, he returned to the excavation and began expanding it, pulling out the rocks, carrying more gravel to the sluice, washing it through. He completed two more runs before the water level dropped too low. He spooned out the gold he could from the sluice and saved the fines.

Overnight, the catch basin again filled but not as completely. Samuel continued prying out the cobbles and working down beside the boulders, trying to get beneath them. The quantity of gold was improving the deeper he dug. If he could get under the boulders or hit bedrock there should be a good accumulation of gold, hopefully larger pieces. He envisioned rolling out a boulder and seeing a dozen nuggets.

It did not happen. He made two runs, and the water was gone. He cleaned out what gold he could and shoveled the black sand into a tub to save for later processing.

A lone rider turned up the trail. Samuel felt a cold panic. The rifle was inside the cabin. He set down the tub and began to run but then relaxed when he recognized the sheriff's broadband hat and his bay. The bay reminded him of Buster.

"Howdy, sheriff," he greeted as the man drew near.

"I hoped someone would be here," he replied and swung down. "Your father still at Mr. McLane's?" He flicked his eyes past Samuel and around.

"Yes, sir."

"No unwelcome visitors?"

"None I know of." Samuel felt his chest tighten, expecting the sheriff to tell him Dudgin and Smith were back.

"Good. I'm pretty sure those snakes have skedaddled, but you can't be certain." They shook hands. "You got a few minutes?"

"Certainly." Samuel felt a wash of relief, but he wondered what was up. "Do you want to come in? I can heat some coffee."

"Not today. Everyone I meet's been giving me coffee." He shook his head and gazed around. "Quite a place you and your pa have fixed up. Last I saw it, it was just a shell of a cabin."

He took out a pencil and notebook. "Just a couple of questions, and then I'll be off. You authorized to speak for your pa?"

"I don't know."

"We'll pretend that was a *yes*." Sinclair flipped a couple of pages. "What do you call your place? The Chambers' placer?"

Samuel began to agree but then hesitated and replied, "We're calling it the Sweet Mary ... for my ma."

"Sounds fair." He marked in his book. "And you'd say you're a producing placer?"

"Not hardly. Most of my time is spent hunting or working on the place, but I've dug a little. Did halfway good today."

"I'll put you down for intermittent production." He scribbled something. "Then it's safe to say you don't employ any Chinamen?"

Samuel laughed. "Unless I qualify."

"Don't think you'd want to. I'd have to collect a tax on you. I wager from the looks of you, you're already eating your pa out of house and home."

"He says I eat my fair share," Samuel agreed. "What tax?"

"Foreign miner's tax—five dollars a month. That is, if I can catch them." Sinclair flipped his book shut. "Used to be I could get about half a dozen Chinamen a day, but now they see me coming and skedaddle for the woods. Gettin' tired of chasing them. When I do catch them, they give me all sorts of excuses about paying up. Most of the time, they tell me they already paid, that I got the wrong Sing or Sang, or whatever. Then they show me the receipt, but I know dang well they're just passing it around." His jaw tightened. "Maybe I can hire you and that fast horse of yours and get a jump on them."

Samuel grinned. "Maybe so."

"About all I do anymore is worry about Chinamen. Although I will say you caused a bit of excitement jumping those snakes. And we did have the De Rocher homicide a year past on the South Fork. That kept me busy a bit."

"De Rocher homicide?"

"Last year. Abe Harpster killed him."

Samuel raised his eyes.

"It was quite the event. Harpster and another Frenchman got to fighting over a card game. The Frenchman's friend, De Rocher, intervened, got the better of Harpster, and knocked him down. That should have ended it, but Harpster came back at De Rocher with a knife, so De Rocher brained him with a chunk of wood. Somehow, Harpster recovered, and he went back after De Rocher. Knifed him in the heart, he did. I had to go down there and investigate."

Samuel felt a hollow chill.

Sinclair remounted. "Oh, nothing happened. Harpster turned himself in, and the justice acquitted him. Said it was self-defense. Everyone knew Harpster was a pretty honest, hardworking man. De Rocher was a hothead, ne'er-do-well. About like those three snakes you had the run-in with."

Samuel nodded, but he was bothered. Either man could have chosen to walk away alive.

"Anyway, since they voted to allow the Chinamen in, all I do anymore is chase them down. At month's end, I start all over. We must have dang near four hundred in Warren's camp alone, twice as many as whites, and this is a big county."

Samuel whistled. "That many?"

"That was this morning." He turned his horse back toward the trail. "By now, it's probably five hundred."

Samuel had no idea about the numbers of Chinese flooding into Warren's camp. He thought of the placers he had seen. It was astonishing to believe the Chinese had dug up as much as they had in such a short time, but with the numbers Sinclair mentioned, it now seemed more possible.

He thought about De Rocher and Bender and an uneasiness overcame him. Death with little reason was no stranger in this country.

*   *   *

His father returned late evening.

"You're still here," he said half-seriously. "I guess you can take care of yourself if need be."

Samuel could not help but grin. "I got a bit of dinner, Pa, and something else to show you." He set the pan containing the gold he had collected down in front of his father.

Charles shook his head. "I'll be— You must have dang near an ounce."

"I figured so, and most of it's from just two days."

"Two days and an ounce—that's almost worth it."

"It's going to get better, Pa," Samuel claimed. "Tomorrow, I'll show you."

*   *   *

In the morning, Samuel showed his father the boulders he was trying to move.

"I know if we can get under them, there will be a lot more gold."

"Sometimes that's the way it's been at McLane's," Charles replied. "We've had to use powder on boulders this size, though."

Samuel frowned. "We should do it then."

"I don't know if we've got the money or the time. I'd need to buy some drill steel and hammers, and powder ain't cheap."

"But if nuggets are under them, we'd be rich."

Charles laughed. "Don't mean to disappoint you. Just as often as there are … there ain't. It mostly depends on how much deeper the bedrock is." He glanced at the catch basin. "Besides, I don't see a lot of water. What are you planning to wash with?"

"That's been the problem, Pa," Samuel replied weakly. "I can only run a few buckets before I have to wait for more water to collect."

"Maybe we just wait till spring when there's more."

Samuel looked up.

"I'm kidding," Charles said. "But if we were really making a go of it here, we'd stockpile the gravel and wait till spring. Some of the placers do that."

Charles jumped down into the pit. "Let's see if I can help you get some of these rocks out of here."

They worked for a couple of hours, trying to excavate some of the boulders. The two largest continued to grow in size as they dug around them. A flash of lightning and reverberating thunder interrupted them. Threatening thunderclouds had filled the valley.

Charles straightened and looked up. "If you get some rain out of this, maybe you can run a bit longer."

"Hope so."

"Come on. That was the good Lord talkin' to us. We're supposed to take it easy on His day. I got a few supplies to pick up."

Samuel was disappointed to leave the placer but thankful for the help his father had given. He was happier to be heading to town.

Chapter 22

The next day after his father left for McLane's placer, Samuel debated about running the Sweet Mary. Not much water had collected. He decided to take Spooky instead and head toward the South Fork. As his father had hinted, it was time to get something *more growed up.*

He stayed along Meadow Creek beyond the Chinese placers and then cut uphill until he reached the summit above Warren's camp and the South Fork, south of where he had walked out when he had been hunted by Dudgin and Smith.

He sat Spooky and studied the surrounding country. Meadow Creek—some folks now called it Warren's Creek—flowed almost due north and emptied into the Salmon River. The canyon it cut en route to the Salmon was too treacherous and steep even for a foot trail. Instead, an old route came up from the Marshall House and up over Marshall Mountain into the Secesh drainage and then over the mountains and down into the Big Meadow. From the west, the trail came up over French Creek, crossed into the Secesh drainage, and then went up and across Steamboat Summit, where it dropped back into the Warren's camp basin—the trail they had used when they had come into the country. Other trails existed. An old one came up from Shearer's ferry over Elk Creek, and now a newer one followed the Secesh south of Miller's camp and went over the summit into the Payette drainage and down through Long Valley to Fort Boise.

He gazed east across the South Fork canyon. Nothing came from that direction. The country was so incredibly cut into rivers and canyons that Samuel thought it was impossible for the good Lord to have crammed any more into the area. It was 150 miles across of unexplored land. What it held was anyone's guess.

He picked up the trail and headed down toward the South Fork. The country quickly steepened into precipitous slopes. The north and west faces were heavily timbered and covered with thick ceonothus shrubs that allowed easy passage downhill, but like a gate fixed in a single direction, they prevented travel back uphill. In contrast, the south and east faces were open, covered with scanty grasses.

Samuel hesitated to push Spooky. Instead, he cautiously angled across slope, carefully avoiding the draws. Frequently, he paused to check the ridgelines below. It was midday. Deer would more likely be bedded under the pines along a spur ridge. Patiently, he worked his way downward toward the river, wondering if he would even be able to spot the game in the heavy underbrush.

A tawny coat and white rump flashed just as he caught the sound of thudding hooves and cracking brush below him. "Easy, Spooky." He jumped down and stepped quickly toward a clearing where he could spot the running animals. He pulled his rifle to his shoulder. The deer, four does, moved into thick brush before he could settle a shot. "Nuts. Not ready for that, Spooky, were we?"

He remounted, balanced his rifle across the pommel, and nudged Spooky across the top of the ridge, following where the deer had crossed. He turned Spooky downward, hoping he could catch them bottled up below. The timber thinned to towering yellow pines and sparse grasses, but the terrain turned to rocky outcrops and shattered talus. Bitterbrush and sagebrush grew in the draws amid the rock.

Samuel had dropped a great distance. He figured he should soon spot the river. If he killed one of these deer, it would be a long climb back.

He came out onto a narrow ridge, the sides steeply falling away, a rocky precipice at its end. He eased Spooky out along the edge of the rocks, trying to get a better view. He figured the deer must be below in the draw.

Spooky's ears flicked, and he shied just as Samuel heard the rattlesnake's angry buzz. A massive snake was on the other side of a rock near Spooky's hooves and instantly struck. Spooky reared, unbalancing Samuel. The rifle flew, clattering into rock. Frantically, Samuel clawed to stay in the saddle but fell. He slammed into the rocks. His left arm buckled underneath him, erupting in blinding pain. He felt himself jerked up, his foot caught in the stirrup. He was slammed across rocks, through the brush, into trees. Broken limbs on a snag punctured his stomach and leg. Searing pain flashed through his body, and he felt himself go numb as his breath rushed out.

Spooky plunged ahead, dragging him through the timber. Samuel grabbed about and caught a branch with his good hand. It ripped through, tearing his flesh. Wildly, he grabbed again and again at the snapping limbs, his body screaming in agony.

Spooky stumbled, staggered, wheezing, eyes rolling; he was pinned against downed timber.

Samuel grabbed the pommel and hoisted himself, trying to release the strain on his foot. Spooky began moving. Panic flooded Samuel. He was keenly aware more people died from being dragged by their horse than by anything else. Frantically, he again pulled himself up. This time, his foot slid free. He slid to the ground and tried to sit up, but the world spun about him. He slumped back.

Blood seeped from seemingly everywhere, soaking his clothing. Gingerly, he tested the holes where he was punctured. The one inside his left thigh bled freely. His finger slipped inside the one that opened near his stomach. A wave of nausea swept him. His leg bled worse. Samuel ripped a piece of his shirt and pushed it against the wound, desperately straining to slow the flow. His trousers had become soaked with blood. He looked for Spooky. Somehow, he had to get to help. The horse had moved off.

"Spooky," he called, his voice broken. He called again. The blue sky dimmed and slowly spun about. Pain flooded his body and drew him into a black cloud.

*   *   *

Strange voices and smells filled Samuel's senses. Dim light filtered through his eyelids. He tried to open them but could not. He rocked his head to the side, trying to see. Pain washed over him. Slowly, he realized he was in a bed in a dim-lit room, a rock hut of sorts. A Chinese leaned over and spoke unknown but comforting words.

He tried to sit up, forgetting his injuries, and immediately fell back, racked with pain and nausea.

The man, speaking gently, patted his chest and then rose and departed. A new voice came to him. A familiar voice, Samuel struggled to place.

"Hehwoh, Sam. You hurt bad." Chen came into his view.

Samuel tried to speak but could only cough. He reached out, tapping Chen's hand and nodding.

"You at Sang Yune home." Chen pulled up a stool and sat near Samuel. His dark eyes sparkled, etched in concern.

Samuel studied him, wondering how long he had been unconscious, where he was exactly.

"Sang Yune fix you up. He is good doctor."

Samuel carefully moved his head to examine himself. He felt nauseous. It was as if he were looking at someone else's body. He lay on top of blankets on a bed of fir boughs, naked except where some bloodstained cloths covered him. His left side was skinned and raw with blood. The puncture wounds were covered. His left arm had an awkward-looking splint; his right hand was bandaged.

Yune returned, carrying a pan of water. He set it on the table near the doorway.

"I catch your horse," Chen continued. "He by the spring." He pointed a thin hand out the door uphill. "Hard to catch."

Samuel tried to talk again. "T-thank you." His throat was dry. He pointed at the water pan and mimicked drinking.

Chen filled a porcelain bowl and handed it to him. Samuel sipped it, sitting up enough to keep from spilling it all over. He drank more, feeling its coolness, realizing how thirsty he was.

Yune watched. Nodding, seemingly with understanding.

Samuel handed back the bowl. Chen refilled it, and he drank more. Chen was dressed as before, except he now wore a western-style hat with a flat brim. His black queue hung over his shoulder.

Yune reached over and carefully pulled back some of the cloth, examining Samuel's wounds. Eyes bright, he spoke rapidly to Chen.

"Yune say now you awake, he fix again," Chen explained. "It hurt like dickens, but is good stuff." He grinned.

Samuel nodded weakly. He did not know if he was ready for more pain.

He wondered how long he had been here, if his father was out looking for him.

Yune mixed what looked like a moldy soup and began sponging it onto one of his skinned areas.

It stung. "H-hurts like a bastard," Samuel gasped, grimacing, "and stinks."

Chen laughed. "Yes, stinks. But is good stuff. Yune is good doctor."

Samuel tried not to watch as Yune continued his work. But with each application, there was a new sting, and the cumulative effect was becoming intolerable. His entire body felt like a burning coal.

"H-how long have I been here?" Samuel wheezed.

"Two day," Chen explained. "I come here and see horse come up hill. I first think you just fall off, but you don't come, so I go to find you. You behind a log, so hard to see. I think you are dead. Blood everywhere. I can't carry you, so come back for Yune. I catch horse and come and get you. At first, we think you will die, but Yune patch you up."

"Thank you, Chen," Samuel said, his head pounding. "Thank you and Yune very much. Please tell Yune.

"Where is this place?"

"Sang Yune making gardens here. I come for vegebows to take to uncle's store."

Samuel bit his lip, trying to block the pain.

"How come *you* here, Sam?"

"I was hunting. Snake spooked the horse, and I got thrown." He rolled his head. "C-can you get my pa for me?"

Chen nodded. "Now you awake, I will go. Yune will take care of you. I will be back tomorrow."

"Take my horse. You will be back this evening."

"I walk. Not good for horse. Already almost night."

Samuel wondered if he could bear to wait. He had no choice.

"You know my cabin? No, wait. My pa will probably be at McLane's placer."

"I know both. I will find him." Chen turned to leave. "You get better." He bowed briefly and, stepping through the door, broke into a jog, heading uphill.

All Samuel could do was wait. The throbbing in his head was nearly unbearable. Yune finished with the last of his wounds and began replacing the bandages.

"What is it you put on me?"

Sang Yune smiled, shaking his head.

Already, Samuel missed Chen. He laid his head back, thankful for Chen and for Yune. He thanked God they had been nearby. He prayed for the pain to subside. He closed his eyes, thinking of the cabin, thinking of his mother and sister ... the others back in Iowa. He wondered how they would have taken the news had he been killed.

*   *   *

Samuel woke to darkness except a small flame sputtering from an oil lamp on the table. Fragrant incense filled the hut. Again, he was thirsty. His head pounded. His arm throbbed, and his side burned. "Sang Yune," he called. "I need water."

A shadowy form near the lamp stood up. Yune's face became visible in the lamp's glow. Samuel felt humbled, realizing the man had remained at his side.

He mimicked drinking. Yune promptly brought him the porcelain bowl and held it for him. The coolness to Samuel's lips was comforting, and he drank deeply.

Yune touched Samuel's head. Murmuring quietly, he unfolded wet cloths over him.

*   *   *

Samuel woke to daylight. Again, he asked for water. The throbbing was incessant. He wondered how much more pain he could take.

Men's voices and the sound of horses filtered in.

His father as well as Raymond Barnes, a man Samuel recognized from McLane's, stumbled in.

"How are you, son?"

Samuel tried to sit up, tried to smile. The joy he felt in seeing his father flooded through him. "I hurt, Pa," he managed. "All over ... I hurt."

"I'll get you back. Dr. Sears will know what to do."

"Yune and Chen have done a good job, Pa. They saved my life."

Charles turned to them. "I am very grateful. I will not forget this." He turned back. "This is the Chinaman boy you told me about?"

Samuel nodded.

"I thought he worked at the store."

"He comes here to get vegetables."

His father nodded and studied Samuel a moment. "Can you sit a horse, if I hang onto you?"

"I can try. I might spring a leak, though. I got a couple good holes in me," Samuel tried to joke.

"That's what I understand." Charles's mouth tightened.

His father helped him sit up and managed to pull his shredded clothing back on him.

"Maybe we can borrow a blanket," he muttered.

Chen handed him one. "I pick up when in town."

"Much obliged." He took the blanket. "Where's the rifle?"

Samuel shook his head. "Probably down the cliff where the rattler struck at us."

"I'll look later."

Chen interrupted, "I will find. I know where Sam fall." He nodded vigorously, smiling.

"Thank you, Chen." Charles offered his hand; Chen bowed.

The men bundled up Samuel and hoisted him onto Buster. Charles swung up behind. "I think I can hold onto you. Let me know if you're about to fall."

Leading Spooky, they headed uphill back toward Washington.

"Too bad Chen is a Chinaman, Samuel. Being your age, he'd make a good friend for you."

Samuel could not reply.

CHAPTER 23

Samuel remembered little of the trip out of the canyon back to Washington. The first thing he clearly remembered was being carried into Marjorie Reynolds's boarding house and being laid on a bed. The Reynolds had one of the placers at the upper end of the meadow, and several miners boarded with them. He thought they had a young son but was uncertain. His head throbbed.

Dr. Sears, properly dressed in coat, high-collar shirt, and string tie, had arrived and greeted him. "How's your pain?" He removed his coat and laid out his medical kit.

"I hurt bad," Samuel managed.

"Here, then." Sears held a glass. "It's laudanum. Comes from opium. It will help you sleep, if nothing else."

"Why aren't we at the cabin?" Samuel implored, taking the laudanum and turning toward his father.

"People here can take better care of you. Mrs. Reynolds has agreed."

She smiled at him. "I'll be tickled to have you, Samuel," she said, patting his hand.

"Thanks, Mrs. Reynolds," Samuel managed, turning to look at her, graying hair, lines across her face, appearing older than her years, yet she had a pleasant face. He remembered the dance with her.

"Ma Reynolds is good by me, remember?"

"Yes, 'um." Samuel nodded.

"And from the looks of you, young'un, you'll not be a-goin' home all that soon. You got lots of healin' to do."

Samuel was already thinking about the doctor's fees and now Ma Reynolds's care. He squeezed his eyes. He had been good for next to nothing on this trip. Now he had become a burden.

Dr. Sears began examining him, asking questions, cutting away his clothing, probing, looking. Samuel was vaguely aware Ma Reynolds stood by. He began to feel woozy.

"You're damn lucky to be alive, son. Lucky you didn't get your skull cracked open when you hit those rocks," Sears muttered.

"I reckon." Samuel winced, feeling stabs of pain as the doctor dug around inside his wounds.

"Can't really sew these up. Probably won't help anyway." He looked at Samuel. "You say that Chinaman put something on them ... said it would stop the blood poisoning?"

"Sang Yune. It burned like crazy ... and stank," Samuel offered. He fought to stay awake. "Looked like moldy soup—"

"Probably put more poison in you than took out." Sears muttered, shaking his head. "Pray to God you survive."

Samuel came momentarily awake, frightened—more frightened than he had ever been in his life—hearing the doctor suggest he might die. A panicky feeling flooded him. He shook his head, trying to clear the clouds. He feared falling asleep—that he would never again wake.

"Better let me look at that arm." Carefully, Sears removed Samuel's splint and gently probed from his wrist to his elbow.

"I'll be," Sears muttered, "I think that Chinaman must of got it set okay."

Carefully, Sears put on a new split, wrapping bandages around it, firmly immobilizing Samuel's wrist and lower arm.

"You are a lucky, lucky lad."

"I reckon I am," Samuel managed. "If Chen hadn't found me ... I'd be coyote bait."

"More likely cougar bait," Charles corrected. "Now you just look like bait."

Samuel smiled weakly.

Sears pulled the covers up and addressed him, "If you don't get blood poisoning, you're going to heal up just fine. Biggest problem is those holes you got. Luckily, I don't think anything inside of you was punctured—just cut up your insides a bit. If you don't move around much, they might close up okay."

Sears stood. "That means you aren't going to be doing much hunting for a while, and you aren't going to be getting far from this bed for a while." He glanced at Charles and Mrs. Reynolds.

Samuel slept.

*   *   *

The fever hit hard shortly after Samuel reached Ma Reynolds's place. He faded in and out of consciousness. Some of what he remembered, he thought had been a dream. He remembered Dr. Sears cursing the Chinese for doctoring him. He overheard him cautioning his father to prepare for the worst.

The light filtered in and out. He missed Chen and Yune. He felt Ma Reynolds's presence rather than saw her, poking at his bandages, caring for him. Strange voices drifted to him frequently. He slept.

Once he remembered Miss Lilly visiting. She sat next to his bed, touching his shoulder, talking to him. He remembered nothing she told him, and he did not remember anything he might have said to her. He just remembered her warmth and that she appeared to him beautiful—like a regular woman, not a dancehall lady. He remembered a deep ache in his chest as if he were crying. He wondered about the reason.

Then it passed. He woke and felt focused. He sat up and looked around. He was alone. From the light seeping under the curtain, he knew it was day. "Hello?" he called.

"You're awake." Ma Reynolds came through the door and immediately kissed his forehead. "No fever. Thank the Lord, Samuel. Thank the Lord. I'll run and get Doc Sears."

Samuel lay alone for some time. He realized that the pain and throbbing had subsided. His arm even felt better. He looked around the room as if he were seeing it clearly for the first time.

Dr. Sears came in and also touched Samuel's forehead. "Good. First time you've been cool in a couple days."

His father arrived. "I'm glad to see you've returned to the land of the living." He smiled.

But Samuel could see the exhaustion and strain under his smile.

"You had us worried, son." He sat.

"How long have I been out of it?" It seemed like ages. Maybe he dreamed most of it. Maybe he dreamed about Miss Lilly.

"The better part of three days."

Samuel wondered if any of what he remembered was real. It seemed ages ago when he got hurt.

"How's McLane's going, Pa?"

His father shook his head.

"I'm sorry, Pa." Samuel realized his father had not been at work.

"You just put your mind on mending. We'll be okay."

"We won't. How do we pay—"

His father tightened his jaw.

"I shouldn't have come, Pa." Samuel felt the knot in his throat as his eyes misted. "I've done us no good." He felt a tear he could not stop.

"No, Samuel," Charles said. "You've done all I've asked—taken care of the stock ... taken care of the cabin. Just sometimes, we're dealt a bad hand. Nothing you can do about it. Just thank the Lord you're alive."

Samuel nodded, but he could not shake his thoughts. He pushed his bandaged hand across his eyes.

"Now you're through the worst of it, I can leave and go back to work. Mrs. Reynolds can take care of you until you're fit."

"I'm fit now. I'm going with you." Samuel swung his feet off the bed and tried to sit up. "I—" A stabbing pain racked him, and he doubled over, gasping.

"Not so fast, lad," Sears caught him. "You're over the worst of it, but you aren't going anywhere until I say ... and not until those holes are completely healed. You also still only got one wing, if you haven't forgot."

Samuel slumped back.

Charles added, "It's okay, son. Your job now is to heal up. We still have plenty of time before the snow hits. Remember our deal?"

Samuel nodded.

*   *   *

A couple of mornings later, Samuel woke to Ma Reynolds emptying water into a big tub she had positioned beside his bed. With a start, he realized what was intended.

"Doc Sears says for me to get you a real bath instead of those rags I been moppin' you with. Maybe help you heal up some better." Ma Reynolds set the bucket aside.

Nervous, Samuel sat up.

"Come on. We're gonna scrub you up good. Then I'll redo those bandages." She stepped to the bed. "Here, let me help you up."

Samuel pulled away, embarrassed, realizing he was about to be seen by Ma Reynolds in all his glory. "I can take a bath by myself," he protested.

She shook her head. "A little bashful, are we?"

"No ... I mean yes. I can do this. You're not my mother."

Ma Reynolds shrank back. "No, son, I'm not, and I won't pretend to be. But Doc doesn't want you to slip and hurt yourself. You only got one hand at best to scrub you and half a leg to boot. He's off helpin' other folks, or he'd be puttin' you into this tub himself."

Samuel cringed.

"Besides, whether I'm your mother or not, yours ain't here. And no matter how old you are, we all need our mothers at some time or another. Right now, I'm just going to have to do."

Samuel felt a wash of sorrow for what he had said. "I mean, Ma Reynolds, I'm not a little boy."

"I know you ain't, but you ain't a man neither. I know. You're at that age where you're embarrassed by what you got one minute and then proud as a peacock the next. Kinda like them gals you see about your age. Scared as the dickens at what they're sproutin' and proud as heck of them the next. Young'un, there ain't nothing you can do about it—you're in the best of years and the worst of years."

Samuel started to laugh but stopped short from the pain it caused in his side. She had about summed it up. "I'm sorry," he murmured.

"Now I know about things like that, and there's nothin' you can do about it, so let's get outta that bed and into this tub. I'll pretend I don't see nothin'." She shook out a large towel and held it up. "Besides it ain't somethin' I ain't already seen."

"What?" Samuel pulled the blanket more firmly about his middle.

"Who else do you think it was that put all those patches on you, if it weren't me?"

She took Samuel by his good arm and let him lean across her as she helped him stand and step out of the bed.

"Now you get in nice and easy." She steadied him on his good leg while he dragged his other over the side.

"How's that feel?"

"It's hot." Samuel leaned on her, and in a shower of pain, he quickly slipped into the water. His legs bent up, but the water covered him.

"Hot is good."

Samuel had been nauseated when he first saw his body raw, scraped, and bloody. Now it was black and purple and badly bruised. He propped his splint out of the water the best he could.

He did not mind Ma Reynolds's hands, which were remarkably soft, sponging his back and shoulders. Suddenly mortified, he realized Ma Reynolds intended to wash the all of him. He recognized what could happen if his middle got undue attention. That sort of thing happened these days. Desperately, he tried to get his thoughts elsewhere. He pushed farther down into the water.

"Uh, Ma Reynolds, how's your baby?"

Ma Reynolds did not seem to notice the question. She was intent on scrubbing him.

"Huh? Oh, George. He's almost two. Getting into everything."

"Is the placer going well? The one Pa's working is drying up."

"We're doin' just fine. We're in the main creek, so water hasn't been a problem."

He squirmed and pulled away when she began soaping lower.

"Oh, I see." She paused and handed him the soap. "Here. Think you can do the rest of you?"

Samuel was immensely relieved. He fumbled with the soap in his mangled hand but managed to somewhat finish washing.

"Your head." She poured a bucket of water over him.

Samuel lost his breath a moment. The heat was luxuriant.

She lathered his hair. "When was the last time you had a bath anyhows?"

Samuel felt embarrassed. "We scrub up on Saturday nights when we can," he replied. "I smell that bad, huh?"

"Nope, you're a darn sight cleaner than some of the men who've ended up on my front porch. For them, you'd be stretching it nice to say it were a couple months. And even after a good cleanin', most often their clothes just get burned." She poured on more water. "Lean forward so it don't get it in your eyes. Now let's get you out and redo those patches."

Gently, Ma Reynolds replaced the dressings, first putting a salve back on the skinned areas. Each application burned, making Samuel wince and grit his teeth. Getting in and out of the bath had also aggravated his injuries. His entire body throbbed.

"Ma Reynolds," he managed, "I-I'm hurting pretty bad."

"Okay." She handed him the glass with the laudanum solution. "I wanted to wait a bit, but I guess you'll be okay."

Samuel took it. "Thanks."

"Lord, I hope you don't get hooked on that stuff."

Finally done, Samuel lay in bed, the burning beginning to ebb. Never had he felt so helpless. Never had he owed so much to others ... and to his father. He thought of Chen and Yune. He owed them his life.

He turned to where he could see a sliver of sky through the curtained window, dark pines etched against the blue sky. Somewhere out there was a lost quartz ledge. Maybe God had preserved him for a reason.

CHAPTER 24

Samuel spent another day in bed, withstanding the pain until late afternoon when the throbbing became unbearable, causing him to ask for more laudanum. Ma Reynolds had a fit when he did, so much so he did not ask for any the next day, even though his injuries throbbed again. Instead, he forced himself out of bed and walked about the room. His leg did not bother him as much as the hole near his stomach. He avoided any sudden moves or bending that might tear it open.

It seemed everyone in town had heard about his accident. Some came by to visit, including Harold Sinclair and Raymond Hinley. The sheriff reassured him that no one had seen the two at-large desperados. Hinley encouraged him to keep prospecting. He told him a new arrival brought in some good-looking ore of a nature he had not seen before in the region.

"I say poppycock." Hinley adjusted his glasses. "He may have brought it in from California and is planning on salting an area and selling a salted claim to some unsuspecting greenhorn. I informed him I would like to examine some additional pieces."

One morning, Samuel overheard voices fussing outside his door. He recognized Miss Lilly's voice, and his stomach flip-flopped. Quickly, he checked the bedcovers.

Lilly came bustling in. "Hello, Samuel," she cooed. "I've been meaning to visit you. Mrs. Reynolds don't think it proper and all, but I'm asking *you*."

Ma Reynolds stood in the doorway. "It's not that ... it's—"

"It's okay, Ma Reynolds." Samuel did not want to disappoint Miss Lilly. Despite she was a dancehall girl—despite what he now knew—she was still the most beautiful woman in Washington and the one nearest his age.

She wore her pink frilly dress, her reddish hair seeming more red than usual, her hazel eyes sparkling even more brightly, and her perfume stronger than he remembered.

"I'm so sorry you nearly got yourself killed." She leaned over and kissed him. Samuel felt a new surge of excitement and butterflies in his middle. "I couldn't stand it if the most handsome man in camp was killed."

"Thank you, ma'am," Samuel said and blushed.

"I came by to visit you once, but I don't think you remember."

"Sort of." So she had been by. It was not all a dream.

"Now I just wanted to visit you and see you are going to be okay." She patted his shoulder. "You running into those murderers and now this, you just seem to be getting into more than your fair share of trouble." She pulled the chair over to where she could sit close.

Samuel could not help but notice her low-cut bodice. He looked away. *Why does this happen to me?* he wondered, but he felt warmed with her presence.

They visited for a while, and before he knew it, Samuel found himself telling Miss Lilly things he had not shared with others—how he wished he was not hurt, how he was letting his father down, how sometimes he missed his family. He did not know why he told her these things. It just came easy. And Lilly listened. She did not make him feel foolish. She gently patted his splinted hand and softly traced along his fingers.

Presently, Ma Reynolds came to the door with an expression Samuel could not quite read.

"She's telling me it's time to go, Samuel." Lilly laughed quietly. She brushed his hair from his eyes and stood. "Well, I just had to come see you, Samuel. You're just about the nicest man here. I sure want to see you get well soon."

"Thank you, ma'am." Samuel blushed. He wished she were a different person, not a dancehall lady, not what she did. He wondered if she could change. He wanted to talk to her about it, but the thought paralyzed him. "I like you too, Miss Lilly. A lot," he whispered and touched her hand.

A sadness appeared in her eyes, and she pulled away. "You come visit me sometime, Samuel?"

Samuel did not know how to respond. A confusion of feelings washed through him. "Yes, ma'am." He wrestled with what he had blurted out.

Later, Scott Alexander dropped by. Samuel was sitting up, flexing his fingers on his broken arm, studying the splint. He kept accidentally banging it into things and jarring his arm.

"You look like hell warmed over," Scott said. "Heard you had a run-in with some rocks. Didn't think you'd be looking this bad, though." He sat down.

"I don't feel so bad except I gotta watch the hole in my stomach and keep it from opening up. I'd get out of here except Doc Sears doesn't trust me about that."

"I expect he's right."

"Besides me just about getting myself killed, anything else going on?"

"Fred Burgdorf was in from his hot springs. He's let everyone know he brought some cows into his meadows and has beef and milk available." Scott stretched his hands. "We got plenty of beef but milk cows—cream, cheese—that's going to be good. I got my order in."

"How about anyone striking it rich?" Samuel could care less about the cows.

"You know how that is. Every time someone finds a tiny little nugget, it's a major strike." Scott laughed. "I *am* hearing more is opening up around Miller's camp at Ruby Meadows. There's starting to be a real settlement up there. In places, there's some good, deep gravel."

Samuel felt a rush and then frustration. He was lying here. He wished he were at Ruby, finding his own placer before they were all staked.

"Also a few more folks settling down on the South Fork. I'm guessing about five homesteads down there now between the Secesh and the wire bridge on the main Salmon. Did hear they're doing some serious placer mining at James Raines's place. George Dyer, Amasa Smead, and George Woodward are all down there helping him."

Samuel recognized Dyer's name. He had been helping at McLane's placer. Like his father, he suspected these men were taking advantage of work wherever they could get it. "I guess that's a few miles downstream from where I got hurt. Makes me realize how big this country is. Also makes me realize I'm not doing any good lying here. I could be down there looking for gold myself."

"Heard a hell of a thing about Smead," Scott continued. "A few days ago, Raines sees a party of Indians riding their way. Everyone scrambled for their rifles, thinking their scalps were about to be sacrificed, but the Indians were just out hunting. Must not have been doing any good. They offered to trade Smead one of their young girls."

Samuel felt his stomach turn.

"Smead traded a horse and a bag of flour for her. Maybe all of twelve years old, she is."

No different than buying a slave, Samuel thought, but he realized the Indians might give up a girl child if they thought they could not feed her. *Maybe they simply thought she would have a better life with the whites.*

"Now Smead claims they needed help at the place, cooking and washing and such—and I really don't know him—but some folks are insisting his intentions are no good. He's not married, you see." Scott raised his eyes. "Pony Smead—some folks are now calling him."

"I can think improper thoughts as well," Samuel said quietly. "I suppose any man can, but I'm of a mind to think Mr. Smead's honorable. What would say he isn't? Maybe when the girl's of age, he'll marry her. Maybe he's keeping her from starving to death."

Scott laughed. "I can't fathom you sometimes, Samuel. You always think the best of people."

"I guess I'd like them to think the best of me." He was wondering if anyone knew Miss Lilly had visited him.

Scott quietly replied, "I believe I can say they do, Samuel." He rose to leave. "Thank you."

Samuel wondered what the *thank you* was all about.

*   *   *

Dr. Sears frequently dropped in to inspect his injuries. He continued to express amazement that the puncture wounds, especially the ones in his leg and near his stomach, had not given him blood poisoning.

"That's where the Chinaman put on that poultice?"

Each time, Samuel confirmed it. "All over me. All my cuts."

Each time before Sears left, Samuel insisted he was ready to go home, but Sears would not listen. Samuel took solace that his father was working at the placer. They would be able to pay for his care; however, he reminded himself he was contributing nothing, and it pestered him.

He moved about Ma Reynolds's boarding house, refusing to stay in bed. He tried to assist in the kitchen, but she would have nothing to do with it. He did manage to persuade her to let him watch George for a bit from time to time. Mostly, George followed Samuel around as he moved about the house. Often when he walked out into the yard, George and he stood and watched the people in the street, the pack trains moving about, the Chinese carrying their bundles. Samuel listened to the thumping of the stamp mill up the creek.

"See, George," Samuel said, pointing to the north. "A long ways that way is the Salmon River in a deep gorge."

"Me?"

"No, a hole in the earth. A deep canyon."

George giggled.

"And up there is where the bad men were." Samuel pointed and stared northeast. *That's where I need to be—looking for that ledge, not here.*

CHAPTER 25

On the day Dr. Sears released him, the doctor's instructions burned into Samuel's memory: "Watch the holes, that you don't try heavy lifting and somehow open them again. And watch your arm. It probably feels fine to you now, but you put any strain on it—*any*," he emphasized, "you'll break it again. You do that, and I'll confine you here the rest of the summer."

Samuel had taken careful note. He was not about to spend a single day longer cooped up.

"And you come by my place next week so I can check you over."

His father had helped him swing up into his saddle. It felt good being on Spooky, heading home at last. He patted the horse. Spooky pricked his ears forward as if to welcome him. Samuel felt so fine that he thought of running Spooky; however, as they moved down the trail, he felt mounting discomfort from the jostling and declined.

It seemed like he had been at Ma Reynolds's for months, not a couple of weeks. He wondered why Chen or Yune had not visited but learned later it was understood they were not encouraged. The white community tolerated them. The Chinese were to mingle only through limited commerce or service.

At the cabin, Samuel eased himself out of the saddle; the discomfort had grown to a throbbing, dull pain.

Charles eyed him. "You doing okay?"

"Better than being in bed."

"We don't have to push it. Stay here today, but I've arranged for you to join me back at McLane's." He helped Samuel down. "You can be a runabout, and I can give you a hand if you need one while you're still on the mend."

Samuel did not argue.

When they entered the cabin, it was much like when Samuel had left it over two weeks ago, except some of their gear was gone. *At McLane's placer*, he figured.

In the morning, they packed their necessary belongings, leaving the cabin mostly empty. Samuel gave it a quiet look before he mounted Spooky and turned north.

"I know you'd rather be out prospecting, Samuel, and I know you're probably feeling as worthless as teats on a boar hog, but in a couple weeks, you'll be back at it."

"For sure, Pa."

When they reached McLane's, Samuel reacquainted himself with the men. From the dozen before, six remained, including his father. Samuel was not surprised to learn Gabe Whitman had left—to where, no one knew. Others like George Dyer and Hanscomb had left for other placers. As Hinley had said, it took a season of digging to get to bedrock and then a short while to clean up. When the cleanup was good, the placer operations were long on volunteers. When the digging began again to clear off more gravel, those weakest of heart were often off to richer diggings. Some left with good reason. Every placer operation had its compliment of high-graders. Some made it a practice to hire on at the well-producing placers when the gold was flowing—just long enough to pilfer the boxes and move on before they were caught. His father suspected Hanscomb had done so.

Samuel helped get their gear settled as best as possible. He felt better, but the ride down the meadow from their cabin had again aggravated his stomach. A dull, deep pain had set in, bothering him.

"Here, you might want this in a couple weeks." His father brought out his rifle—good as ever, except for a few scuffmarks. "Chen found it." Samuel vowed to pay Chen a visit as soon as he was able.

*   *   *

Samuel soon found his main chore was not to reinjure himself. The worst part was getting up into his saddle. He could throw it over Spooky and get it cinched down well enough with one arm, but it was his stomach he worried about. He forced himself to take it easy whenever mounting or dismounting. He found he could get a good grip with his right hand and get his left foot into the stirrup and then swing up. He had to baby his stomach was all and keep from snagging his splint.

He resumed his duties as a runabout—gathering firewood, tending the fire, carrying water, and doing dishes. He was pleasantly proud to notice a good portion of firewood remained from his previous efforts. With Gabe gone, the men relied on him more for cooking. Except for cutting meat, Samuel found he could manage most of the meal preparations and took over much of it by himself.

"We should have thought of this earlier," McLane said one evening. "Not bad salmon you've baked for us, Samuel."

Samuel grinned. He had served it as he remembered from Burgdorf's, with a berry sauce and Dutch-oven wheat bread.

McLane turned to Charles. "I think the sprout has been hiding his real talent, Pa, making us think he was no good so he could sneak off and go hunting."

During the day, Samuel made it a point to carry drinking water to the men or to fetch tools as he had done before. It gave him an excuse to examine the findings in the sluice box. A steady line of fine gold built up over the day, but there was seldom a particle larger than a cucumber seed. When so, the men cheered, and McLane picked it out.

Samuel recognized that the flow of water had lessened, and it continued to diminish. Water from the snowpack had drained from the surrounding valley walls and seeped into the gravels under the meadow. The meadow itself was most likely at one time a lake about a mile wide and extending to the north for several miles. Over the millennia, it had filled with rock and sediments and, most importantly, gold.

McLane collected the fines from the week and panned them down. He never showed the men the results, but Samuel knew it had to be more than three ounces a day; otherwise, he would be going into debt. He paid his men from the coarse gold, the gold he could scoop out without getting much black sand in it. The remaining fines he ran through another sluice lined with mercury and amalgamated it for later refining.

It was usually midafternoon Saturday by the time McLane finished panning the week's fines. He then promptly paid the men. That gave those men who wanted to head to town sufficient time to get there. At least one man remained behind with McLane to guard the placer. Chambers had done so when Samuel was laid up.

After receiving his pay, Charles handed the pouch to Samuel.

He hefted it. "This is great, Pa."

"Unfortunately, I'll spend it tomorrow."

Samuel frowned. Without his father saying, he knew it was for his injuries and care.

"It's okay, son. Another few weeks, we'll be getting ahead."

By then McLane's would be dry. *His father must know,* Samuel reasoned. There would be at least another week, maybe more, but after that—then what? They did not have gold enough to return to Iowa.

SOJOURNER

CHAPTER 26

It was late summer. The days turned hot, and the woods continued to dry. The pungent odor of pinesap and the earthy fragrance of late-summer flowers hung in the still air. Afternoons clouded over, and thunderstorms moved through the meadows, sometimes dumping heavy rain, refreshing the air with the smell of wet grass and sweet, evening blossoms. Other times, no rain came, only flashing lightning and reverberating thunder. The resulting fires burned for a few days, most going out within a short time. Others continued. The renewed fire from the previous summer continued to gain in intensity, throwing a dense cloud of billowing white smoke towering to the northeast, causing red morning skies. Smoke drifted over Warren's camp. Last season had seen the worst fires since the camps had opened. Men mused that the continuing fires would burn what remained, leaving nothing but a devil's playground.

Sunday was a day most miners could rest. Mine owners conducted business and resupplied. Miners came to town for a bath and a meal and then the stag dance, where they stomped away to the music of Charlie Bemis's and Rube Besse's violins and Nate Jenkens's banjo.

Usually on Saturday night, Samuel and Charles did their best to clean off the week's grime, using a tub of hot water and sponging themselves down. Sunday, they washed their work clothes, and in the meanwhile, they wore their Sunday best while they bought supplies, worked on upkeep of the cabin, and cared for the stock—the necessary things that could not be addressed during the long workday.

When he and his father rode into Washington on Sunday, Samuel explained he wanted to see Chen. "I have to thank him."

"You do, and thank him for me as well," Charles replied. "I'll probably be at Alexander's Mercantile when you get back. Otherwise, I'll see you back at the cabin. Need anything?"

"A new arm."

"Doubt he has one of those."

Samuel headed toward the Chinese cabins. They were constructed along the south end of Washington, upstream of the town along the creek, up and around the hillside. Most were ramshackle affairs sunk partway into the earth, partially built from rock and partially built from logs. Almost none had windows.

He found Chen's cabin. Except for a sputtering oil lamp, it was dark inside. Samuel called from outside the door. He noticed a couple of Chinese nearby, watching.

Immediately, Chen came to the door. "Sam," he smiled broadly and then quickly bowed, dark eyes curious. He pushed his queue to his back.

"Hello, Chen." Samuel returned the customary greeting. "May I visit?"

"Here? This is Chinese place. We go to store." Chen gestured nervously toward the town.

"Here is fine."

"I was getting ready to go to store." Chen motioned him in.

"Only a moment." Samuel entered.

The cabin was tiny, perhaps six by eight feet, scarcely room for the two beds, simple straw-filled mats on the floor covered with bedding. A washbasin rested on a rough table next to the oil lamp. There was no stove or source of heat that Samuel could discern other than the lamp.

"You are well, Sam?" Chen inquired. He motioned to Samuel to sit on one of the peg-leg stools.

"I'm still stove up a bit, but I'm good." Samuel gestured with his splinted arm. "That's why I came."

The oil lamp's flickering caused shadows to jump about the tiny room. Clothes were hung on pegs adjacent to the door. A pair of gumboots stood beneath them.

"I have something for you." He handed Chen his skinning knife. "Thank you for what you did for me, Chen. I owe you my life."

Chen looked down, appearing uneasy. "Thank you, Sam. I cannot take knife." He pushed Samuel's hands away.

"I want you to have it," Samuel insisted.

"You say *thank you*. Is enough for Chen."

"I owe you."

Chen shook his head. "Maybe you teach me about Ahmelicah." He smiled.

"I would like that, Chen." Samuel felt humbled. Here Chen was, a stranger from a foreign land, asking for nothing more than to learn about America.

Samuel began to feel uneasy. The hut did not seem a home. It was where one slept, nothing else.

"Uh, Chen ... how do you fix dinner in such a small room?"

Chen laughed. "Not here, Sam. Come, I show you."

On his way out, Chen scattered some red papers laced with tiny holes into the opening of a small cairn that stood near the door.

Samuel paused, confused.

Chen smiled. "If devil find us, he take us to hell. We leave paper with holes. He have to crawl through alla holes before he can go in. Too many holes. He get lost."

They crossed the street, followed a path up the hill, and entered a much larger stone and log building. Smoke poured from the chimney and with it, a mixture of spicy, almost overpowering odors. Apparently, this was where many of the Chinese ate their meals—a communal kitchen of sorts.

The room was dark, except for one small window set high in the wall and a few burning Chinese tapers that cast flickering light. Two men squatted on the floor, talking, eating from porcelain bowls. They paused and looked up when Samuel entered. Another man who had been dishing rice from a large metal pot resting on the coals dropped his bowl into the pot and stood up in a submissive gesture.

"This my friend, Sam," Chen introduced him first in English and then spoke in Cantonese. The men exchanged rapid comments and then went silent, eyes on Samuel.

"They say okay."

Nervously, Samuel gave a quick bow.

"Ah." The men nodded and smiled. Immediately, they returned to eating and talking but with occasional glances toward Samuel.

"You want to eat?" Chen picked up a bowl off a table cluttered with cooking utensils.

"No thanks, I already ate." Samuel wondered if the concoction tasted like it smelled, almost overpowering. Not to be impolite, he quickly offered, "I'll have some tea, if that's okay." Another pot on the coals held what he presumed was tea.

Chen handed Samuel a bowl-like cup and poured him some.

Samuel sipped it. "It's good. Thank you." It was not as overpowering as its spicy fragrance, he decided.

Samuel watched while Chen nimbly scooped his bowl full of rice and patted it down. The kitchen walls were dark and smoke-covered. Utensils hung from hooks or were stacked high on a few board shelves along with baskets, rice cake molds, wine flasks, glass bottles, and kettles.

Chen lifted the lid from a crock, scraped out what appeared to be a vegetable relish, and spread it onto his rice. From another, he scraped out what looked to be some dried fish. He sat down next to the other men and began rapidly eating, scooping the mixture to his mouth with his chopsticks. Patting the ground next to him, Chen eyed Samuel. "Sit."

Samuel tried to squat but then stood. "Sorry to be impolite, Chen, but I still have a hole that's mending. Makes it hard to squat."

Chen nodded.

Samuel watched, amazed at Chen's dexterity with the chopsticks and suddenly happy he had turned down the meal. He would have looked the bumbling fool. He studied how Chen used them and decided it would be wise to cut a pair and practice.

Samuel poured himself more tea, studying the crockery and baskets, all presumably full. "Where do you get all this food?" he whispered, bending down.

"Some China. Some we grow."

"From China?"

"We get fish, vegebows pickoed in soy sauce, sometime honey," Chen explained. "Pack train bling from Lewiston."

Samuel looked around at the crocks lining one wall. *Must have had a recent pack train come in,* he reasoned. "What's in all those?"

Chen rose and lifted some lids. "Pickoed cucumber, pickoed turnip, pickoed bean. You try." He handed Samuel a green bean.

It was surprisingly tangy and crunched. "It's good." *About six weeks from China, not counting the time from Lewiston, and it still tastes good.* Samuel was impressed.

Chen finished eating, wiped his bowl, and placed it back on the table with the others along with Samuel's cup. Samuel cringed.

As he left, Samuel politely bowed toward the men, now joined by several others. He noted two with a newspaper, reading, conversing, smoking their long-stemmed pipes. The paper looked wrinkled and well used like all newspapers in Washington that the men read and reread. He surmised that the Chinese were no different. They wanted to keep up on events back in their homeland.

*   *   *

On Monday, his father and he returned to McLane's placer. Samuel tired of cooking meals and hauling water and firewood. One evening, with his father's help, he figured out how to load the rifle and hold it with his good hand. He could rest it over his broken arm.

He resumed hunting for a short time each day. The first few times shooting at something, he missed. Finally, he hit a rabbit.

Each day afterwards, he hunted, usually getting a rabbit or grouse. Then he struck out searching for quartz ledges. He reasoned there could be one near the McLane placer as easily as elsewhere. He found where other men had worked and dug several pits, but he never found any rocks resembling ore. Although tempted, he avoided being gone overly long. He did not want to shirk his job as runabout.

As he was returning one time, he heard excited shouting from the excavation. His father and Raymond Barnes were peering into the head of the sluice. Other men dropped their tools and scrambled toward it. Samuel hurried to join them and immediately saw the glitter of gold. Several nuggets had caught behind the uppermost cleat.

"A beautiful sight, eh, Samuel?" McLane boomed. "Go ahead and pick those out of there."

The men watched as Samuel scooped out the small nuggets. In turn, McLane passed them around for the men to examine.

"Now it begins, fellows. We're on bedrock. We're into rich diggings," McLane fairly shouted.

In a fevered pitch, the remainder of the afternoon, men worked to bring up more gravel from around the boulders they had unearthed. Each run brought new cheers as more small nuggets caught behind the cleat. By evening, McLane had cleaned the cleats three times.

"A bonus for you all." He passed around a few small nuggets to each man, even giving Samuel a share. "Now if we had days like this every day, we would all be rich men."

Alone in the tent later with his father, Samuel fingered the nuggets. "Sure was nice for Mr. McLane to give us these."

"I'm grateful. He didn't have to. I'm sure some days he hardly covers expenses, and I know when we're digging off overburden, he's borrowing from what he's previously mined to pay us."

"Just the same, he has to be getting rich—all that gold."

"Perhaps *he* is. Remember, all I get is a wage. At the rate we're spending it, even if this placer keeps going, we might break even."

Samuel was shaken. "What are you saying?"

"I'm sorry, son," Charles said quietly. "I misspoke. I can still get a few dollars before first snow flies. Who knows, maybe we'll really hit it rich here and get a few more nuggets to spread around."

Samuel was silent for a moment and then whispered, "That's why we need to dig up those boulders at the Sweet Mary."

Charles glanced down at Samuel's arm, started to speak, but then was silent.

CHAPTER 27

Monday morning, Samuel did not return to McLane's. He had tired of being a runabout. It was useful work, but it did not find gold. Seeing the men finding the gold had only frustrated him.

He tried running the sluice, but with his arm in a splint, he could hardly dig, and he was unable to pull rocks from the excavation other than the smaller ones. Patiently, he stockpiled gravel and then released the water. With one arm, he shoveled dirt into the sluice. The process was slow and wasted water. He kept catching things with his splint, and in doing so, he remembered Sears's warning. He had no intention of being confined the remainder of the summer.

In frustration, he gave up, stowed his gear, and took Spooky into Washington. Raymond Hinley always seemed to have some mining news, and he could always stand a little motivation by studying the pieces of ore lying about. He was getting good at recognizing quartz that carried values. Unfortunately, the only pieces he had seen were at Hinley's.

"I'm pleased to see you up and around, Samuel," Hinley greeted. "What may I do for you?"

"I got tired of being a runabout at Mr. McLane's. Just wanted to see what was happening."

"I certainly don't mind your company. Perhaps when you have mended, I could put you to work here a mite." He adjusted his glasses.

"I'd like that." However, Samuel felt frustrated. He turned on the stool where he sat and waved toward the hills. "But I want to be up there. It's gotta be there."

"I will say you're getting a little competition. I cannot say when I have seen as many new faces."

Samuel looked up, puzzled. He had not noticed, but then he had not been around.

"I have had at least six parties of prospectors drop by and ask about likely areas."

"What you telling them? I hope you're not telling them where I'm going."

Hinley smiled. "You have not exactly informed me of where you've been searching."

Samuel realized he had misspoken. As far as Hinley or anyone knew, he was prospecting toward the south, near the quartz mines. "I figured you knew." Suddenly, it no longer seemed to matter if Hinley knew or not. "It's where I ran into those scum, north of here."

"I suspected as much." Hinley pulled out some crucibles. "You need not worry. I have not encouraged anyone to head north. I do not believe there is much gold in that country. Most of the prospectors are heading down the Secesh or over toward Miller's camp."

"But you said yourself the gold in the Chinese placer had to come from somewhere."

"Aye, but the source may be long gone." Hinley began scratching numbers on the crucibles and setting them in a rack. "I strongly believe you would have a better opportunity southeast of here. Frankly, I wish to see you find a paying ledge."

"I appreciate that, Mr. Hinley. I still plan to. Please don't tell anyone I'm looking up north."

"Aye. However, if you do find ore up there, you will have more difficulty getting it to a mill. The Pioneer just sold at sheriff's auction. I have no idea what the new owners plan, but I do know they will relocate it. I also don't know if the former operators were ever paid. I strongly expect it will see more litigation." Hinley began measuring out flux for the crucibles.

Samuel shrugged. "Doesn't seem to make much difference. It hasn't run much since me and my pa have been here, anyway."

Hinley laughed. "Aye, it was always a spotty affair, not even producing half the values from the ore it processed. Mr. Isenbeck was running it last year when he was reprocessing ore from the Rescue and claimed he was still getting fifty to eighty dollars a ton. Certainly makes you wonder what remains in those tailings."

Samuel briefly entertained the thought of reprocessing ore.

"The district still has two good mills—the Charity and the new one at the Hic Jacet. And I do hear William Bradshaw hit good on his Summit vein near the Keystone. He's now bringing in a mill that will be able to reduce silver ores."

"So I now have permission to find silver ore?"

"Aye, you do."

*　　　*　　　*

The next day, Samuel packed his pick and rifle and headed east toward the South Fork. He would shoot a deer if he saw one; otherwise, he intended to visit Sang Yune.

He came out above the garden and was surprised to see both Chen and Yune working at the end of a good-sized terrace. The terrace extended around the knoll of the ridge directly below the stone hut. Tall willows spaced about six inches apart formed a fence of varied height around one end. Water ditched from the creek ran across its length, dropped down, and ran back across the hill below. Vegetables grew luxuriantly. Samuel could not fathom how one man could have done so much work in such short time.

He hollered to get their attention before he picketed Spooky.

Yune jabbered excitedly when Samuel reached them.

"What does he say, Chen?"

"He say you look like devil when you go. He worry alla time that you will be okay. He is vehlie happy to see you." Chen's dark eyes flashed.

"Thank you, Yune," Samuel said and bowed. "Tell him what I told you, Chen. I owe him my life. I will always be indebted. If I can ever do anything for him, just ask."

Chen hesitated, spoke, and then interpreted Yune's response. "He says you already do much for him. You are friend for Chen and tell him about Ahmelicah."

Yune smiled, nodding.

Samuel felt regret. He had told Chen very little about America. He had been unable since he had been hurt and at McLane's placer. "Tell him I will do more."

Samuel waved his good hand at the terrace. "This is incredible."

Chen nodded. "We work hard."

"What are you growing?"

"Alla things grow this year." Chen pointed out the different vegetables. "Onions, radish, beans, peas, cabbage, beets." He gestured uphill above the stone hut. "Also have fruit trees. Cherry, apple, plum, pear. We plant them when you get hurt." He pointed beyond the stone hut. "And we plant grapes."

Samuel could see the new vines climbing wooden frames built against a rock wall. "So in a few years, you will have fruit." It struck him to realize the Chinese intended to stay. Maybe they knew the placers were not as exhausted as everyone thought.

"You Chinese eat all this?" He wondered at all the strange vegetables.

"Yes, in China where not much food, we must eat everything … rats … glasshoppah even."

"But we have plenty of food in America—beef, pork, chicken."

"That is good thing about Ahmelicah, but we still eat everything."

Samuel shrugged, marveling as they pulled large, white, Chinese radishes from the rich soil. One broke, revealing its striking red center.

"Need a hand?"

"You ohnee have one hand." Chen laughed.

Samuel frowned. "I'm getting pretty good with just it, and the other is close to healed." He pulled a radish, enjoying how it popped out of the ground, long, white, and miraculous.

They cut some pea vine tips, pulled garlic, and gathered leaf cabbage. These, they packed in cloth soaked in water. Sang Yune took other bundles of vegetables, wrapped them carefully in layers of canvas, and tied them onto a pack on the mule.

"I take these to store and then go to sell," Chen explained. "Go now before it gets dark."

"You should ride. It's much faster."

"Have to sit on vegebows. No good."

"I'll walk with you a ways." Samuel retrieved Spooky.

The two turned up a faint trail that descended from the ridge. After they made their way along the winding path for a couple of hours, they topped out on the summit above Washington. Samuel found it strange to walk when he had a perfectly good horse, but he was also surprised at how little time it took by following the trail.

Near the Chinese kitchen, Chen said farewell. "I take vegebows tomorrow and sell. Be gone two days."

It was past dark when Samuel reached his own cabin. His father was not home. It did not surprise him. After they hit the rich pay streak at McLane's, he expected the men would be working as late as possible, even lighting bonfires to work during the night, attempting to uncover more gravel while they still had water.

*   *   *

At first light, Samuel rode back toward Washington. He wondered if he could accompany Chen, maybe to be of some help and, if nothing else, to see new country. He caught Chen leaving his uncle's store, leading the mule, now fully loaded with vegetables as well as other items.

"Howdy, Chen. Mind if I come along?" Samuel had packed his bedroll and provisions.

Chen hesitated. "Maybe tell me more about Ahmelicah?"

"Maybe you tell me why you came here?"

They headed south toward the Secesh.

"So why *do* the Chinese come to America, Chen?"

"This is the land of golden mountain. In China, there is war, no food, no land. Chinese come to Ahmelicah for gold and land."

"Chinese cannot own land in America."

"Chinese come here and send money back to family. Family buy land in China. Then Chinese go home. Pay boss big dollah to come here. Owe boss money. When we pay boss, we earn more money. Then we go home to China." Chen nodded adamantly.

"So how much did it cost for a kid like you to come here?"

Chen shook his head. "Born here. Born in San Francisco, but it cost fifty dollah, sometime more to come to Ahmelicah."

Samuel stopped short. "You weren't born in China? Then you're an American."

"No, not allowed. Even born here, not Ahmelican." Chen shrugged.

Samuel tried to understand. "Why go back to China, if it's not where you were born?"

"My father Chinese. My mother Chinese lady in saloon in San Francisco. Go back to China, or saloon boss take me."

Samuel felt a cold chill and struggled to understand. Chen's mother was a Chinese prostitute—a slave girl, they called them. Chen actually belonged to the saloon owner. "That's why you're here with your uncle. You're hiding."

"Yes, hide. My father killed by Chinese boss."

Samuel felt his skin crawl. Chen's tone made it sound like an everyday event. "I'm sorry." He was thinking.

"Then is Sing Mann your real uncle?"

Chen shot a quick look at Samuel and then returned his gaze down the trail. He shrugged. "I am Sing, so I call him uncle. People think he is my uncle so I can stay with him."

They walked in silence.

"Please don't tell." Chen looked at Samuel, eyes pleading. Samuel realized that for some reason Chen trusted him—trusted him to know things he had probably told no one.

"I won't, Chen. I give you my word." Then Samuel wondered, "Do you understand what it means to give your word?"

"Same as for Chinese. Blake word means you go to devil."

Samuel laughed. That summed it up. "Thanks for trusting me."

"I help Sing Mann at store. He send money to China to his family and to buy land. He also send money for my family. Someday, we pay boss man and go home to China. We sojourners. We don't stay. Ohnee a few are lucky to go back to China."

It struck Samuel that he and his father were no different. They intended to send home money and eventually return home and buy land. He felt a stab of regret. Thus far, they had scarcely made grub.

"I hope you succeed, Chen." Samuel could say nothing else.

"Don't tell. If you tell, I have to be with other Chinese men." Chen's eyes were frantic. "If they know Sing Mann not real uncle, they treat me like slave girl."

Samuel felt his stomach turn, and a coldness enveloped him.

They walked in silence until they came to a small placer to the side of the trail, one Samuel remembered from their trip in.

Chen cried out, "Vegebows. Vegebows."

The men put aside their tools and quickly gathered around while Chen spread out the vegetables for them to see.

"When was the cabbage picked?"

"One day," Chen answered.

The man asking took a bundle of leaf cabbage and a bundle of green onions.

For each sale, Chen used a small handheld balance and weighed out the gold for payment. As Mann had done for Samuel, Chen put a weight equivalent to the price of the vegetables on one side of the balance and sprinkled dust on the opposite pan until it balanced.

"Good?" Chen always asked, making sure the men agreed before taking the gold and adding it to his pouch.

One addressed Samuel, "What you selling, Sam?"

Samuel recognized the man from the Independence Day celebration and remembered his name was Ripley. "Nothing." Samuel shrugged. "Just tagging along."

Ripley frowned.

"What do you need?" Samuel was beginning to get an idea.

"Chawin' tobacco and fresh bread."

"Maybe next trip then."

"If that's so," someone hailed, "how 'bout bringin' some wimin and whiskey?"

"He's too wet behind the ears to know 'bout them things," someone chided, and the others laughed.

Samuel blushed, feeling uncomfortable. He knew about Miss Lilly.

"How about fresh buttermilk or cheese?" Samuel remembered Fred Burgdorf would be bringing some in for Scott Alexander.

"Say, that wouldn't be bad, if'n you could swing that and the buttermilk don't turn on ya." They laughed.

"I do need a shovel. If'n you're serious. Want me to pay you now or when you get it to me?"

Samuel was not prepared to take gold. "When I bring it."

Shortly, they continued on, Chen happy with his sales, Samuel thinking. On horseback, he could travel farther and more quickly than Chen, and he could use Molly for packing the goods. But then he realized he would not feel right competing against Chen.

"At this rate, Chen, you won't even make it to Mr. Burgdorf's." Burgdorf's and the freight landing were the last two places Samuel knew of before the trail descended French Creek to the Salmon River.

"I go to Miller camp. Next time, I don't stop here. I go to Burgdorf."

Samuel realized Chen had a pattern. While vegetables were in season, he roamed the district, visiting each camp every few days.

They camped past the Secesh River on a small stream off the trail that headed into Miller's camp. Samuel felt somewhat uncomfortable camping with Chen. He did not know his customs. If it were he and his father, they would make dinner, usually some cold corncake and some hot beans with salt pork. They would talk for a while and then roll out their bedding under the trees.

He helped Chen unpack the mule. They hobbled the animals, not wanting them to wander too distant during the evening. Samuel built a fire and began preparing his meal. Chen joined him, producing a crock from one of the packs. It held rice with a topping of dried fish. Another held bamboo shoots in a thick relish. The spicy fragrance quickly filled the air.

"I can boil water if you want tea," Samuel offered, "or we can share my coffee."

"You have tea with me." Chen produced a small kettle, filled it with water, and set it on the fire. "You tell me about Ahmelicah?"

Samuel wondered what to say, where to start. At last, he began talking about the War of Independence.

Chen listened, nodding, but after a length of time, he said, "That is good, but I want to know about Ahmelicah now. I want to know about big city. About rayroad. About steamship."

Samuel stopped. He tried to explain, but then he quickly found the more he talked, the more he did not know about America himself.

Even so, Chen listened, occasionally asking questions. "You tell funny stories," he once commented.

Samuel remembered the paper with holes and what Chen had said about the devil. He kept his thoughts to himself.

After the questions died, Chen took a flute from his pack. "I play, okay?"

Samuel was surprised. He would have never suspected that Chen would play a musical instrument. "Of course."

"White people complain sometimes when Chinese play music."

Samuel understood why. Often it was brassy and loud, but then he reasoned that it was no louder than the violins and banjos he often heard coming from the saloons.

Chen began playing. Samuel marveled at his nimble fingers. The tone was high-pitched and the melody hollow, echoing, almost lonesome-sounding. Samuel found himself picturing what China must be like—a strange land, an ancient land over eight thousand miles away. He had a strange yearning to see China.

"You play well, Chen."

"You play?" He offered the flute.

Samuel shook his head. "Someday, I'd like to play a fiddle like Charlie Bemis, but I don't think that will ever happen."

"Why not?"

"I need a fiddle." Samuel laughed and then was silent. "Chen, you said your father was killed. What about your mother?"

"I never hear from her after saloon boss take her away."

Samuel wanted to ask how he knew the man he called his father really fathered him. He could not bring himself to ask.

"My father love my mother. They go away so no one know where they are. My father work at gold mine. My mother cook and help the miners. When I am small boy, the saloon boss discover where we are and send men to kill my father. My mother hides me, but men take her to be saloon lady again. Sing Mann find me and bling me here, far away. We are safe here."

"You said you have family in China."

"I do. Uncle and grandparents. I hear from Sing Mann. I send letter to them. That is why someday I go back to China."

"I understand, Chen," Samuel said. "I am sorry for what happened to you."

"No, I am happy. I live free in Ahmelicah. I learn many things. Now you teach me more."

"I will try."

They rolled out their bedding. Samuel no longer felt uncomfortable. He knew he would learn far more from Chen than Chen would ever learn from him.

*   *   *

Early morning, they reached Miller's camp. It was located on Ruby Creek, a small stream that meandered through a meadow high above the Secesh. Samuel noted several small placer operations scattered across the small meadows. Miller's camp was smaller than Warren's, but he had heard several of the placers were deep and rich.

Ruby Creek received its name from the plentiful garnets found in the sluice boxes during cleanup. Hinley had informed him they were a good sign. Garnets were heavy, somewhat like black sand, and often found associated with gold. They were also sometimes problematic. The sluices quickly clogged with the bright red grains, forcing more frequent cleanups.

They came to a placer situated along a tiny stream tumbling down a lodgepole-lined gulch that appeared newly opened. A couple of white canvas tents were pitched among the lodgepoles. Several men were busy constructing a sluice from fresh, rip-sawed lumber.

"Vegebows. Vegebows," Chen called out.

The men paused in their work and made their way down. In short order, they purchased the remaining vegetables.

Samuel pinched himself to keep his mouth from gawking when the men brought out their gold—small nuggets with little dust. Chen did not comment but calmly weighed it. He had trouble achieving an exact balance because of the gold's coarse nature. Samuel also noted he charged them less than he did the men back at Ripley's placer.

They inquired about Samuel's presence. Samuel again asked what they needed.

"Could use another pick," one replied. "Don't want to trek all the way to Washington to get one."

"I could use another wash pan," another said.

Chen turned to him. "I know what think, Sam. Remember, it lot easier to bling vegebows than know what tool to bling." He headed back down the trail, still walking. "Vegebows are not heavy."

"How come you're not riding the mule?" Samuel wondered. He figured that now the vegetables were sold, Chen would ride.

"Mule don't like me to ride," Chen said and then grinned. "Besides, I not look like you when you fall off horse."

Samuel shook his head. "All the more reason to ride." He stopped and brought the mule around. "Here, I'll hold her steady. You get mounted. She should follow Spooky, same as our mule does."

Reluctantly, Chen climbed onto the mule. The mule balked for a moment, but when Samuel led off, it promptly began to follow. Chen held on tightly, eyes glued to the trail.

"By the way, I noticed you gave them more for their gold here. How come?"

"Better gold. Gold here ... fifteen dollah. Gold at other place ... twelve dollah." Chen did not look up.

Samuel pondered what he had heard. "How do you know?"

"Color. Learn color of rich gold is yellow. Color of cheap gold is not so yellow."

"But how do the men know you're correct?"

"*They* know how much their gold worth. And they trust me."

The mule began scampering and bounded into the lead.

"Whoa, mule. Whoa," Chen called, eyes wide, frantically holding on, bouncing along, long queue flying.

"Doesn't look like that mule much trusts you." Samuel laughed and chased after.

CHAPTER 28

When Samuel reached his cabin, he saw Buster in the meadow. Elated, he raced Spooky the remaining distance.

"Where you been, son?" Charles's voice was flat.

Samuel explained.

"I worried you had found more trouble," he admitted. "You should be cautious about being with the Chinamen, even Chen. Trouble's brewin'."

Samuel sat, uneasy.

"There's a lot of folks cussin' the Chinamen, Samuel. Sayin' they're jumpin' peoples' claims and stealin' anything not tied down, thinking it's theirs for the taking. A fellow left his outfit near where he was prospecting, and it disappeared. Only people around were Chinamen."

"I owe them my life," Samuel said quietly.

"I know," Charles replied. "Just keep your head." He rose and got a plate. "Here's some beans. Didn't know if you'd be back, but I can split this plate."

Samuel took it. "Thanks, Pa." He was surprised at how hungry he had become.

"Most folks don't look on the Chinamen as human but as something less," he continued. "Don't know how I look on them, myself. They're mighty peculiar, praying to their gods and to the devil and such."

Samuel was stone silent. Chen had become a good friend, and Samuel had promised to help him learn about America. Although he did not know about their beliefs, he was pretty sure they were as much human as he was.

"Got some other news, Samuel." Charles put his plate down and leaned forward. "Today was my last day."

Samuel knew it. He had sensed something wrong. "I figured it was close, Pa. I could see the water drying up."

"At least Mr. McLane kept me on to the last. I owe him for that."

"Any plans?"

"Nope. Not at present."

Samuel studied his father's face. It was drawn, strained. He felt even more miserable for having been injured—for the weeks that he had been worthless, the cost of doctoring, even the cost of new clothes.

"I got an idea today, Pa."

"I'm listening."

Samuel explained his thinking.

"Might work a bit. Where would you get the money for merchandise?"

"I think I can get it on loan and bring back what doesn't sell. When I get a chance, I'm going to talk to Mr. Alexander." He did not call him Scott in front of his father. Adults were still *Mr.* and *Mrs.* until he became one, and Samuel was not sure when that would be.

"Worth a try." Charles rose. "Coffee? I didn't fix any of that Chinaman tea you got. Guess I'm particular for coffee."

"Sure." Samuel got his cup. "Either is good with me."

"Guess I'll go upstream where there's still water. Maybe one of the outfits will hire me on until winter. Some of the men have already left for the Salmon River. If they survive until spring and can still stomach it, they'll be back up here next season."

Samuel jumped in. "I saw a new placer today, Pa." He could hardly contain himself. "Over in Miller's camp on Ruby Creek. You wouldn't believe the nuggets they were getting."

Charles swirled his coffee. "Always one day late and another behind," he said. "Maybe they're hiring, but we'd need to move. That's near a full day's ride."

"I reckon we been doing okay as we have most of the summer. I can get along. I'd maybe pay a visit and try selling stuff. You can come back out on Saturday like you been doing."

Charles put his cup down and ran his hands through his hair. "I'm sorry, son. I didn't want it to be this way. Maybe they'd hire you on as well. Your arm's nearly healed. You can do a man's work. If not, they might could use a runabout."

"For sure, I don't want to be a runabout anymore. And I don't think they'd reckon I was man enough yet." He remembered the comments about women and whiskey from the one camp. "Though, I reckon I could do the work."

Samuel was quiet for a moment. He was thinking about his accident. "That's kinda a funny notion. Only people care if I'm growed up or not. This country really doesn't care what people think. I still just about get killed by it no matter how old I am."

"Well, I'm guessing you're right about that." Charles laughed. "But I 'spect you're pretty much growed by now anyway." He thumped Samuel on his shoulder. "By me, you carry your weight, arm or no arm, and that's pretty much what it takes in my book."

Samuel felt a knot in his throat. He knew he was not carrying his own weight, and he certainly was not bringing home any pay.

"Got a letter from your ma." Charles handed it to Samuel. "I already read it."

"Are things okay?" Excitedly, Samuel took the letter, feeling a little trepidation.

"Everyone seems fine. You can read it."

Samuel took the letter to where the light was better.

The crops were looking good. Daniel was a big help. Everyone was fine. They all missed him and Pa.

Samuel could not help but notice how much his mother wrote about Daniel. He felt he should be there. Maybe Daniel was becoming something like him in his mother's eyes. He felt strange over the thought, but he was better than sixteen hundred miles away.

He could tell from the tone that she worried. He could also tell she missed his father.

"When we write, we'd better tell her we're fine," Samuel said. "How much should I tell her about my accident?"

"Since you survived, I'll let you write about that," Charles responded. "I'll also see if I can get some money for some of our gold and slip it into a package with our letters. Wrap it good so no one suspects."

Samuel wrote a long letter to enclose with his father's. At first, he wondered how much he should say. He avoided mentioning the run-in with Dudgin and Smith. That was better shared when he returned home. He mentioned the accident, mostly stressing he was well and now looking for the ledge again, that he had a pretty good idea how to find it. He told her how he went on a selling trip with Chen. He did not mention Miss Lilly. His mother's tone told him they were concerned over food. The farm was not doing well enough to feed eight people, even though some were little children. That was why his father talked about sending a few dollars home, even though they had only a few.

*   *   *

On Sunday, his father helped him run gravel through the sluice until the water was gone. Very little now trickled into the catch basin, and it did not completely fill. The string of gold they washed from the gravel looked good.

Some was about the size of flattened grass seeds, but without being able to keep washing, it did not add up to more than a dollar.

"If we had more lumber, we could have built a flume," Charles observed. "We wouldn't lose the water soaking into the ground before it got to your sluice."

"Now it's too late."

"You keep watching it. When the basin fills again, wash what gravel you can."

They headed back to the cabin, Samuel carrying a pan of black sand with gold. "Do you want me to buy some quicksilver and amalgamate the fines I've been saving?"

"Yes, or we could just try to sell the fines outright." Charles glanced around then threw up his hands. "Hell, maybe we ought to just sell the Sweet Mary. We ought to be able to get a hundred dollars for it and the cabin. We could head home, if you'd like."

Samuel shook his head. "It's a long time till first snow, Pa. We agreed to stay in the game till then."

"That was when you still had two arms."

Samuel raised his splinted arm. "And I got some proving to do."

"I reckon you're right."

*   *   *

Early morning, they headed west to inquire about possible work at other placers. They packed some of their gear and took Molly, not knowing how soon they would return to their cabin.

A few of the placers along Steamboat Creek had already shut down. Only those nearest the creek were still operating. A couple of parties of Chinese were working rockers down near the water, carrying gravel to them from excavations many yards away.

One party of whites still mined up in the timber where Samuel remembered from before—Ripley's placer. They recognized him and greeted him. A man asked if he had brought his shovel.

"Not yet," Samuel replied. "We're looking for work now."

Ripley quickly told Charles they did not expect to be operating much longer. He was letting men go as the water dwindled.

That evening, they camped near the base of Long Gulch near the Secesh River. Samuel looked for salmon. There were none. Apparently, the run was over.

"When Chen and I came through here, there were still a couple salmon. I thought maybe you and I could get one. We never did fish for any."

"I'm not too disappointed. We had plenty while at McLane's. Even when you weren't there, it seemed someone was always bringing one into camp."

The next morning, they turned down the Secesh, looking for placers. Being adjacent to the river, these could operate until winter. Most were small, operated by a couple of men at most, all wary at their approach. Without exception, someone cradled a rifle while they talked.

"Guess being way out here does that to a man," Charles said.

"It wouldn't take much for some scum like Dudgin and Smith to rob someone and skedaddle before anyone could catch them."

"Nope." Charles nudged Buster back up the bank onto a small bench. "I had heard there were a number of strikes down here, but it looks like they're just getting underway. It doesn't look like any have amounted to enough for anyone to be doing any hiring."

"I can't think of a harder place to run a placer," Samuel observed. "It's all rock. All you'd be doing is moving boulders and then scooping out a cup or two of gravel from under each. The Sweet Mary is better than any of these."

"Except these have water." Charles led the way out of the river bottom. "Tomorrow, we'll head over to Miller's camp. If we don't have luck there, we're going to need to talk."

Samuel did not reply.

They traveled until they found an area with good grass and water for the stock. Samuel built the cook fire and began preparing dinner.

The following morning, Samuel led the way into Miller's camp. A number of the men he recognized greeted him, glad to see him back, asking how his arm was doing. Some wondered where Chen was and asked if he was coming back with more vegetables.

Charles explained the reason for his visit. The answer was the same. The crews had trimmed down to match the amount of work.

"We can try the new placer I told you about," Samuel suggested. "Maybe they're into something rich and need a spare hand."

The men greeted Samuel, remembering him from the day he and Chen had brought items to sell. Samuel introduced his father and stood aside while they talked. From the shaking heads, Samuel figured it was like the other placers—too little work, too late. He noticed there appeared to be only four or five men working. Before, there seemed to have been about a dozen. He did not consider that a good sign.

When his father came back and said he got the job, Samuel did not believe him. "You sure?"

"I asked about you, Samuel, even though I know you don't think much about being a runabout. Mr. Thomas wanted to hire you but figured you'd not be able to do enough with your bum arm. I said your arm was just about good to go. He said maybe later."

"That's all right, Pa." Samuel was secretly pleased with the news. Now that the Sweet Mary was dwindling, he was aiming to return to hunting for O'Riley's lost ledge.

"Stick it out for the rest of today and head back in the morning," Charles said. "I can still use you taking care of things at the cabin. Start bringing in some hay. Maybe you can start prospecting again."

"I intend to."

The next morning, Samuel took his time before heading back. He helped Thomas fix the chow. The morning had been cold so he decided to take some coffee to the men as they worked. No one had ever brought coffee out to them before, and they asked if he did not want to stick around.

Alone, Samuel rode back to the cabin deep in thought. Although Dudgin and Smith had left the country, he flinched at any movement—even at the sparrows flitting through the willows. He could imagine the two scum materializing from the brush. Nervous, he pulled the rifle and carried it across his pommel.

He reached their cabin after dark, took care of Molly and Spooky, and sat on his bed without moving, too exhausted to make up some dinner, but he had been glad to accompany his father and give some help, and he was thankful his father again had work.

CHAPTER 29

amuel woke before sunup, hunted until he killed a couple of rabbits, and clumsily cleaned them. He then ran what gravel he could through the sluice and began panning down the fines he had been saving. As the gold accumulated, he took a twig and scraped it out onto a piece of leather. He picked out the largest pieces, slowly accumulating some dust. He dumped the remaining black sand back into a tub.

He rode directly to Alexander's Mercantile.

"I need to buy some quicksilver, Scott."

Scott nodded and lugged out a canister, heaving it onto the wood counter. "How much?"

Samuel shrugged. "Don't know. I've been saving the fines from our sluice, and I need to amalgamate them. I figured I could swirl a pan with some quicksilver and the fines."

"Most people line the riffles of their sluice and run the fines back through with a good stream of water."

Samuel shook his head. "Don't have enough water anymore to do any good."

"Panning can work. It'll be harder and take longer, especially with one arm." He grinned. "Two pounds ought to get you started."

"What's a pound cost?" Samuel dragged out the folded leather and began to open it.

"Three bucks."

Samuel just stood. He had no idea mercury was so expensive. "I-I'm sorry, Scott. I can't do it." He had collected less than two dollars in dust from the fines. He began refolding the leather.

"Not so fast." Scott took out his pipe and lit it. "How much do you figure you have in fines?"

"I don't know. I've got a good tubful of black sand and some more I've been piling up on a piece of canvas."

"Would you say an ounce?"

"For sure an ounce. I'm hoping at least three."

"Okay." He tapped his pipe. "I know you haven't figured out how things work around here, but here's what we do. You take the quicksilver. I know you have the gold in your sand. You pay me when you've refined the gold. It's simple as that."

Samuel hesitated.

"I'm not going to argue, Sam. This is between me and you." He smoothed his moustache, carefully poured some mercury into a smaller canister, plugged the top, and handed it to Samuel. "And when you're done amalgamating, you know Raymond Hinley can retort it for you, don't you?"

Samuel nodded and thanked Scott. Two pounds of mercury was such a small amount that he wondered if it would do the job.

When he reached the cabin, Samuel filled a tub with water and poured some of the fines into the pan along with a few ounces of mercury. He swirled the pan and watched the mercury quickly sink. He tilted the lip into the water to keep the black sand submerged as he shook. In this manner, the gold would settle to the lowest point of the pan where the mercury now rested and be drawn into it.

It was not easy work. He vigorously shook the pan and then rested a moment. Without another hand to share the burden, his good arm quickly grew weary and numb. He propped the pan at an angle using his injured arm, but he knew not to do more than that. His arm now felt fine, but he knew the mending bone could easily pull apart.

After he ran several pans, the lump of mercury began to appear frothy, almost spongelike, bright and sparkling. Samuel was not certain how much more gold it could absorb, so he scooped out the lump and replaced it with clean mercury.

He quit working on the fines late afternoon, his shoulders and back aching. Most of the mercury had been used. He stored the amalgam in a separate canister, deciding he would say nothing about it to his father until he had paid for the mercury.

Long after dark, his father arrived home.

"Before you ask, I won't get paid till end of next week," he said, smiling, hanging his hat on a peg. "It's really good-looking gold, though."

Samuel laughed. He was looking forward to seeing the coarse gold.

"I got a rabbit for dinner. You can have it with vinegar and potatoes or with beans."

"Potatoes and coffee."

Samuel soon had the rabbit sizzling and the potatoes heating.

"You know the real reason I got the job, don't you?"

"Because we're both so sorry-looking?"

"Could be, now that you mention it." Charles smiled. "No, a couple of the hands quit. There's a new strike at Houston Creek."

"Houston Creek?"

"Downstream of McLane's placer about a mile west up a draw."

Samuel turned the rabbit. The odor filled the cabin.

"John Keep hit an incredibly rich pay streak. He pulled out several one-ounce nuggets ... and two that topped five ounces."

"Five ounces!" The rabbit spattered as he dropped it. Samuel was incredulous. At the same time, he felt as if he had just been punched in the stomach. He felt a terrible disappointment and emptiness.

"Wish it had been you that found it, Samuel."

"So do I," he whispered. He could not help thinking that his father and he had chased one rainbow after another since they had arrived. Strikes had been made all around them, even the new ones being worked along the Secesh that were liable to prove up; yet, they had found nothing. Maybe the Sweet Mary would prove up, but now they had no water. He ached to be prospecting or even shoveling dirt through a sluice. He was tired of just one arm.

*   *   *

After his father headed back to the Ruby placer on Monday, Samuel caught up Spooky and headed toward Washington. It was time to resume his search for O'Riley's ledge. The Sweet Mary was done. He dropped off the amalgam with Hinley.

"Can't get to it for a few days, Samuel. Drop by later in the week. Maybe you can watch."

Samuel was disappointed. He wanted to pay back Scott right away. He turned Spooky toward the south end of town toward the hills.

Lilly stepped from the saloon porch. Apparently, she had been watching for him. He pulled up and touched his hat, feeling his heart trip up. "Howdy, Miss Lilly."

She smiled broadly. "I was hoping to see you. I heard you been down at the McLane placer, but they shut down for the season."

"We're out at Miller's camp now. At least my pa is."

She stroked Spooky's muzzle, looking up at Samuel. "How ya been?"

"I'm fine, ma'am."

"You ain't mad at me, are you?"

"Uh, no, ma'am." He remembered her invitation, and his stomach knotted. "I just been mighty busy."

She touched Samuel's leg. "You healed up good now? I see you still got your arm in a splint. When you gettin' that off?"

"Soon. When I next see Doc Sears." Samuel sat Spooky, thinking the polite thing would be to dismount but knowing he had better not.

"Soon's you get that splint off, maybe you come visit me." She winked.

Samuel gulped. "Yes, ma'am."

She laughed. "Don't call me ma'am, Samuel. You call me Lilly."

Samuel felt burning in his face. "Thank you, ma'am ... I mean, Lilly."

"And you promise to come see me?"

Samuel did not know what to answer. A promise was mighty sacred. He felt caught. "Okay," he whispered. He felt himself go weak. How could he have possibly promised? He turned Spooky. "Got to be going, Lilly."

"Bye." She blew him a kiss and waved.

Samuel waved back and noticed at least a couple of people in the street watching. *God*, he prayed, *I hope I'm not as red-faced as I feel.*

*   *   *

Samuel rode up Slaughter Creek and turned up Bare Knob Creek toward the north. He felt as if he had been absent for ages and wondered how he could have been gone for so long.

By midday, he had reached the ridgeline where he had last searched, but he found he was having difficulty concentrating. All day, his thoughts had been plagued with Miss Lilly. Sometimes his mind wandered about the possibilities, and then he felt miserable thinking about it. How could he have said what he had said—that he would visit her?

He searched along both sides of an ascending ridgeline, concentrating on areas from which Bare Knob Creek was visible. If O'Riley had built cairns below, they would be on line with the barren knob.

The country he searched became familiar, and he recognized the area where he had witnessed Bender's murder. An uneasiness washed over him. He felt as if the men were still there—that they would emerge at any moment. He watched about himself, looking, searching, and feeling an unaccountable chill. He knew he should check the rocks to where Dudgin and Smith had dragged Bender's body and partially buried it, but he could not bring himself to do so. He argued with himself. That was probably where he would find the outcrop. A wide gold-laced quartz vein probably streaked the rocks, he told himself. Still, he could not force himself to look.

The chill followed him, sending shivers up his neck as he turned west— more to get out of the area than to look at something new. The bare knob was to the north. Before, he had found almost no outcrops to the west—just thick timber and downed trees. This day was no exception. By late afternoon, frustrated, he turned back toward the cabin. He did not desire staying out overnight, but he realized he would soon be too far to make a trip in a single day.

He returned the next day and resumed his search this time to the north until he found a quartz seam. He dug down alongside it for several hours before he gave up, having seen nothing that appeared mineralized. Walking its length, he noticed a rusty spot he had missed earlier. He decided it was common granite that had been stained and prepared to turn back.

What's the difference? Samuel thought and kicked at the rubble. A couple of chunks of rusty quartz turned over. Disbelieving, he broke several pieces and closely examined them. There was no distinct sulfur odor, but he discerned a few black, metallic specks.

When he reached Washington, he dropped the pieces off with Raymond Hinley.

"These are looking better, Samuel. They may even carry some values." Hinley took out a small glass and studied the specimens. "The iron staining is largely from sulphurets." He pointed to a small brass-colored cube. "That's pyrite. It may carry some gold, but as I informed you before, unless you discover a thick seam, it is unlikely to be of value."

"Guess I keep looking." Samuel smiled, pleased at last he had found some mineralized quartz. Maybe his luck was changing.

"Want some coffee?" Hinley set out the coffee cups and brought the pot over to pour.

Samuel nodded and sat. It was Hinley's way of talking on the mining doings.

"I'm hearing that more companies are selling out to the Celestials. Biggs and Company sold theirs on the Big Meadow just down from McLane's placer, and Mr. Ripley says he is selling his over on Steamboat Creek at the end of the season. At least Mr. Biggs is filing on more ground farther downstream. I don't know what Mr. Ripley is doing."

Samuel remembered Ripley. He was surprised. It looked like they had good ground. All he had to do was wait out the winter for more water.

"Several of the placers actually did well this year despite the low water. Church and Company hit some good pay on their claims right before they ran out of water."

"That's what happened at McLane's. I was out there with my pa when they hit a good pay streak. Gold was everywhere."

"Aye. Quite a thing to see, isn't it?" Hinley smiled. "Even so, the quartz mines are doing the best. The Hic Jacet is now crushing ore night and day.

I assayed some of their rock, and it is running remarkably good values. But yesterday beat all. Someone from the Rescue brought in some samples that were almost solid gold. They have hit their best quartz vein ever. It is running a thousand dollars a ton."

Samuel almost dropped his cup. "You're funnin' me." Mentally, he calculated about six pounds of gold per ton. A pile of rock approximately three feet tall weighed a ton.

Hinley laughed at his reaction. "I surmised you would appreciate that information."

"And I can't even find ore that runs ten cents." Samuel pushed at his cup.

"Do not forsake hope, lad. You may very well be the person who finds the next Rescue ledge. I keep assuring you hardrock is where the future of this camp is. Oh, there will be more placers found, and they will shine like the first glint of gold in your pan, but that glint will quickly fade. And it remains that a road by which we can bring in machinery is yet a long distance in the future—Warren's camp still resides at the end of the world—but the day will come, and this camp will be booming. Mark my words, Samuel, the real hope for our future is the quartz mines. Keep faith."

CHAPTER 30

Samuel was surprised when Chen came to his cabin in the morning. He had the mule loaded with vegetables.

"I go to Houston Cleek. You come?"

Samuel could not believe the opportunity. Since he had heard of the strike, he had wanted to visit the camp. Quickly, he packed his gear.

Again, they walked, leading the animals. They talked about America, but Samuel wanted to know more about China.

"We soon have big doings," Chen said. "This is celebration of Guanyin Pusa, Buddhist goddess birthday. That is why I go today."

"What sort of celebration?"

"We eat and dlink alla day. Play music. I play flute. Sing. Eat and dlink more and pray."

They turned up the creek from which McLane's placer drew its water, now only a shallow trickle. By midday, they had crossed over a low summit and reached John Keep's placer on Houston Creek. This creek flowed northeast and dropped through a treacherous gorge into Meadow Creek. Samuel could see why it was a late discovery. It was near impossible to come up through its lower gorge.

A huge yellow and red excavation opened into the hill, a strongly flowing creek running through its bottom. High ridges of tailings bordered on each side of the creek, extending upward along several small gulches into the timber. A dozen men worked, swinging picks and shoveling gravel and earth into a long tom that connected to a sluice toward the bottom of the excavation. Smaller excavations were visible through the trees scattered along other gulches.

The men paused to greet them. Samuel recognized a couple of them from the Ruby placer and a couple of others from the McLane placer. They asked how his father was doing.

John Keep was a friendly man but wore a pistol and acted guarded. He and some of the miners purchased most of what Chen had brought and paid well in heavy, coarse gold. Samuel hoped the men did not notice how he stared. Miller's camp gold was coarse. This was coarser.

He studied the gulch; it looked no different from others he had seen. Why was gold here? From what ledge did it come? He remembered Hinley saying there might no longer be a ledge. It could have completely worn away, leaving the gold deposited in the low places along the gulches. But mostly, he wondered if there was another rich gulch still undiscovered. It had taken nine years to find this one. There was no reason for him not to find the next one.

That evening when they returned to Samuel's cabin, Samuel asked Chen to come inside. "I can make some tea."

Chen politely shook his head. "Not Chinese cabin."

Samuel was too surprised to insist.

*　　*　　*

The following morning, as early as he dared, Samuel rode into Washington to see Dr. Sears. He was quite nervous, fearing the doctor would insist he keep the splint on longer. Samuel had not exactly favored his broken arm.

Sears examined his arm, probing and twisting. "No pain?"

"None." Samuel had expected to feel some and, out of habit, favored his arm.

"We'll leave off the splint but keep the sling handy. If your arm starts aching, put it back in the sling."

"You bet." Samuel was exhilarated. He was finally free. He flexed his arm.

"You won't have full strength for a week or so. I recommend you exercise it a bit."

Sears had Samuel remove his shirt and pull back his trousers so he could get one last look at his scars. Again, he shook his head. "Wish I knew what those Chinamen used on you. Still can't believe you didn't get blood poisoning."

"Why not ask them?"

Sears looked disgusted. "Doubt they know. You were just plumb lucky. They put so much stuff in their concoctions, I doubt anyone will ever figure out what does the good and what kills you, and I'm not in the mood to experiment on folks, unless you want me to start with you."

"No, thanks."

Sears eyed him. "Well, I guess you're fit to go."

Samuel pulled on his shirt and rebuttoned it, slipping his suspenders back into place. It felt strange having full use of both arms.

"How's your pa doing? Did he get another job?"

"He's out at Ruby Creek. They got a good strike going there."

"That's good." Sears wrote a few notes in his journal.

Samuel guessed that his father had not completely settled with the doctor. He offered no further comment.

"I suggest you and your pa add some buttermilk and cheese to your meals. It will help your bones as well as your strength. You're growing up tall as a weed, Samuel, but you don't have any *out* to you. At your age, you should be starting to fill out some, if you reckon what I mean."

Samuel flushed. He need not be reminded that he was skinny.

"Now I don't want to be seeing you again, unless you're just dropping in to say hi." He shook Samuel's hand. "Hope you and your pa have some better luck."

"Thank you, sir."

Samuel had to tell himself it was okay to use both hands to swing himself up onto Spooky. He was giddy with joy and wanted to shout.

Samuel reached the assay shop.

"Well, glory be, the lad has his splint off. How does it feel, Samuel?"

"Great. Now I can get back to mining."

"I apologize for not having your amalgam run," Hinley said. "I have had a run of folks needing work completed yesterday. This is a good time to do so, if you like."

Samuel nodded. Hinley was already in the process of dividing the amalgam sponge into several crucibles.

"The science behind this process is almost evident. Mercury has a low boiling point, which means it volatizes rapidly. Therefore, you simply heat the amalgam in an oven until the mercury boils away."

Samuel frowned. "It's three dollars a pound."

"Aye." Hinley smiled. "You condense the vapor and collect the mercury in another flask. The gold and silver are left behind."

"Silver?"

"It stays combined with the gold. The amount is generally not substantial. We are able to part it with nitric acid, leaving essentially pure gold. If you desire to recover the silver, there exists another process, but it is usually not worth the cost."

Hinley stepped outside behind the shop with Samuel following.

"Kindly fetch a bucket of charcoal." He nodded toward a pile.

While Samuel filled a nearby bucket, Hinley began setting the crucibles into a rack in a small compartment in the upper part of a furnace. A metal tube emerged from its top and sloped down through a tub of water and out into a separate container.

"The principle is like a whiskey still," Hinley explained. "As the mercury vapor settles down along this tube, the water cools it, condensing it back into a liquid. The gold-silver buttons remain behind in each crucible." He packed some charcoal into the burn box, lit it, and closed the door.

"Now let's get out of here."

Samuel hesitated.

"Mercury vapors are deadly poisonous. I have taken extra precautions to seal this system; however, we shall return indoors and allow it to cook itself out. If you breathe mercury fumes, they eat your brain."

Samuel got the message and quickly led the way back.

"How long's it take?"

"You shall have your mercury back in three hours."

Samuel looked at Hinley.

"Of course, I can also just give you some fresh mercury." Hinley brought a flask from the back room. "Your mercury weighed out at about a pound and a half, including the gold. I will give you that much new. You may have an ounce of gold is all."

"Okay." Samuel was silent.

"Is that not acceptable?" Hinley pried.

"I was hoping to get the gold now to pay Mr. Alexander. He loaned me the mercury."

Hinley laughed. "Do not inform your father."

Samuel looked at him. "Actually, I'd appreciate it if you didn't."

"Aye, Samuel. Your business is with me." He brought out some small gold bars. "For the moment, will a half ounce be enough?"

Samuel took the bar. "Sure, but what's it worth?"

Hinley laughed. "The lad asks *what's it worth*."

"Ten dollars." Samuel felt silly. He had momentarily forgotten there was such a thing as pure gold.

"Aye." Hinley laughed. "We shall settle up my fees and the difference later, if this meets with your approval."

Samuel nodded. He was beginning to figure out how commerce in a gold camp really worked.

He took the gold Hinley loaned him and paid Scott. He talked to Scott about his idea of doing a selling trip.

"Be here tomorrow morning, Samuel. Might be you paid me a little too quick."

*   *   *

In the morning, Samuel took Molly and dropped by Alexander's Mercantile. Together, they loaded the merchandise consigned to him. Samuel felt good about having two arms; still, he avoided pulling too hard or lifting too much. Samuel thought it was a mighty fine deal when Scott offered to give him 10 percent of anything he sold. He was a bit nervous about weighing out the gold. He had to borrow a pocket balance from Scott for that as well.

"What if it's fourteen-dollar gold?" he asked. "How do I know for sure so I don't short anyone?"

Scott laughed. "Tell them you'll weigh it at twelve. They'll be quick to tell you if it's fourteen or more. Trust them. Then if you do this trip a couple times, you'll know which placer is paying what. 'Course you already know the placer your pa is working is fifteen-dollar gold. That's good gold. Wish I had that placer."

Samuel headed out in the direction of Miller's camp, leading Molly. When he reached the remaining placers along Steamboat Creek, he thought he had made a terrible mistake. He hardly sold a thing, including the shovel for the man at Ripley's placer. The man had been let go since the placer was closing down. The shovel was just over twenty dollars, the most expensive item Samuel carried. He also figured out later, being it was Friday, most of the men would head to Washington come morning for a hot meal and bath and to do their own resupplying.

He had some buttermilk in a canister that he and Scott had wrapped with wet cloths, thinking the evaporating water would keep it cool. He resoaked the cloths whenever he crossed a creek; however, the day was warm, and he worried the buttermilk would go bad.

At the bottom of Long Gulch, Samuel turned downstream along the Secesh. It seemed a few more tents had sprung up, although a couple of earlier diggings now looked abandoned. Samuel worked his way among the small camps but again sold very little, mostly buttermilk. A few men asked him to return in a week and gave him some specific wants. The most common request remained "wimin and whiskey."

Late afternoon, he turned toward Miller's camp with the shovel and most of the fresh goods still intact. When he camped for the night, he shoved the canister down into the nearby creek, hoping to keep the buttermilk fresh.

Midmorning, he found better luck when he reached Miller's camp. He had sold most of the items by the time he reached the Ruby placer, where his father worked. Samuel spotted him, his back toward him, shirtless, swinging a pick seemingly effortlessly. He felt proud. His father was a strong man and a hard worker.

Another man filled buckets, took them to the head of a sluice, and dumped them in. Still another raked the gravel with a sluice fork and sorted out the larger rocks.

It struck Samuel that all the men were indebted to the owner for their wages. As long as there was gold, they were paid.

He thought about the Sweet Mary and the weeks he had invested there. What he had recovered had paid for a few onions and some mercury, certainly not enough for grub. That was the difference, Samuel realized. If you worked for someone, you got paid but generally not much. You worked for yourself, you got nothing, or you got lucky rich. His father had given up on becoming lucky rich. Instead, he worked for grub and perhaps a little to take home.

"Here comes the Warren kid now," he heard someone say.

Charles turned and broke into a broad smile when he spotted Samuel. When he noticed the splint was off, he patted his arm, and raised his thumb.

Samuel dismounted. "Anybody be needing a shovel? I got a spare to sell." They shook their heads. "How about some fresh buttermilk and bread? Although it might be butter by now."

The men set aside their tools and crowded around. "Give me a drink of that buttermilk. Warm day like this, I'll pay you double."

Samuel was stunned. Quickly, he spread out his remaining wares and bartered with the interested men. He was careful not to take advantage. The Ruby placer was too far to quickly trek to Washington. The fresh goods were most welcome.

His father watched as he weighed out the gold. Samuel guessed it appeared that he almost knew what he was doing, and he felt a stab of pride.

He quickly sold the remaining goods, including the shovel after all, making the new owner a good deal, so he did not have to carry it back. The other sales more than covered the small loss.

Samuel liked the feel of the weight of gold now in his pouch. He pinched the bag approximately one tenth the amount, trying to figure what 10 percent would be. It was not a great deal, but the feeling was exhilarating.

Samuel took up a shovel and helped alongside his father for a while. He was so relieved to be unburdened by the splint that he wanted to test his arm some.

"Looks like you're doing all right with that arm. How's it feel?"

"Great. I keep thinking I need to go easy on it though."

"Probably your muscles will tell you the same tonight."

Early afternoon, Thomas came up to where they worked and handed Chambers his pay, allowing him to leave early, knowing he would not reach Washington until near dark. A couple of other men also shut down about the same time. Others who camped on site would work through, maybe taking a few hours rest on Sunday, if any.

Samuel rode with his father, leading Molly.

"Looks like you done good trading, son," Charles said. "Looks like it was a good idea you had."

"I think so."

"It was a good week all around, Samuel. This is a rich placer. I got paid well, about five dollars a day after grub, including today. For last week and up through today, should be better than three ounces."

Samuel grinned. He wanted to see the gold. He remembered the small nuggets from before.

"We got good water here, so I figure we can work up to snowfall." He clucked at Buster. "Then we'll see about heading home."

They rode in silence for a short distance. His father was happy. Samuel decided it was a good time to tell him what was on his mind.

"Pa, I met a woman I like mighty powerful."

Charles pulled up and sat Buster. "I presume you speak of Miss Lilly."

"I reckon." Samuel also halted.

"She visited you when you were laid up." Charles sat quietly, his face expressionless. "You know what kind of woman she is?"

"Yes, sir," Samuel said miserably. He adjusted himself in his saddle. "I think I do, but she can change, can't she?"

Samuel saw a flash of disappointment cross his father's face.

"It's happened before, but I don't think it's that easy." He turned and looked at Samuel. "You know I want the best for you, son, but I don't think this is the woman for you or the time. You still got some growing to do."

Samuel immediately felt defensive but bit his lip. His father had always shared his thoughts and respected Samuel's.

"I reckon I should tell you some things—some I probably should of said before." Charles looked toward a distant peak. Samuel looked as well but could not see anything other than a small white cloud drifting against the blue.

"Being together—a man and a woman—it's a pretty powerful feeling. Heck, I know an insect, down south they had them, called a prayin' mantis. The male starts to mate, and the female starts eating on his head. But the drive is so strong he goes on mating even after he's dead."

Samuel's stomach turned.

"But you ain't a prayin' mantis." He eyed Samuel. "The good Lord gave you a head. You just got to remember to use it." He set his jaw. "Just don't go letting the wagon lead the horse around—if you know my meaning."

Samuel tried to laugh, but his thoughts were flooded with Miss Lilly. Thankfully, the wagon was still where it belonged.

"You become a man physically, but that doesn't make you one. Believe me, the world is full of losers that can father a young'un. A real man is one who's going to love his wife and provide for her. And he's going to love her even more when that young'un comes along. And then he's going to love the both of them even more, more than anything in the world, more than anything he can imagine."

His father went quiet. Samuel knew his father realized what he had just said.

"A real man is going put that wife and family of his first and make sure he can take care of them properly. That's when he's ready to marry."

Charles turned to Samuel. "I know what you're thinking, son, and you're right. It's been real hard to be away. And I know your ma misses you too. But we're out here because of them. And we're out here for your uncle Jake. He did the right thing by fighting for the Union and paid for it—coming home without a leg. Now that I'm into some gold, maybe we can do right for him as well."

"You done the right thing too, Pa," Samuel replied. "You paid the price too. We lost everything."

"Hell, Samuel," said Charles. "I was young then. I figured we'd lick ol' Johnnie Reb and be home by Christmas. We all did. Losing our place never crossed my mind." He was quiet a moment, remembering. "None of us figured we'd be gone for four bloody years. We're luckier than blazes that *any* of us came back."

"But you still did the right thing, Pa."

"I hope so, son," He clucked to Buster and turned back down the trail. They rode in silence for a short distance, the trail wide enough for them to ride alongside each other.

"Just remember, son, knowing and doing the right thing is what counts. Lots of men know what's the right thing to do. Only a few got the strength to do it."

Miserably, Samuel thought about Miss Lilly. He also remembered his promise. How had life become so complicated?

*　　　*　　　*

At the cabin, Samuel eagerly examined the Ruby placer gold. The size of flakes and small nuggets sent his heart racing.

"Any dust?"

"Mr. Thomas amalgamates it and pays us the coarse gold."

"This is better. I like seeing this."

"So do I. I only wish it was from our own claim."

They rode to town to get supplies. Scott informed Samuel he had a choice of a credit from the sales if he wanted to apply it to the day's purchases, or he would pay him his share of the dust.

Although Samuel wanted to see and hold his pay, he realized it did not matter. "I'll take the credit."

His father decided Samuel needed boots. They both did; however, his father would get his boots next.

The supplies and boots took nearly all their gold, including Samuel's credit.

Later at dinner, Samuel offered his thoughts. He knew what his father had to be thinking. "We aren't getting ahead, are we, Pa?"

He shook his head and speared a potato. "Not yours to worry, son."

"I've been around long enough, Pa. I got a part in all this as well."

Charles paused, giving him time to speak.

"I could join you at the Ruby. We could make more."

"You'd be paid your grub, and that's about it, son."

"We'd get a bit farther ahead than we are now."

Charles shook his head. "And it still wouldn't be enough."

Samuel shrugged. "Then I don't know what to do. The Sweet Mary is dry. I can't find the ledge." He looked up. "Remember how Hallelujah talked about not wanting to work for someone, how he wanted the chance to get lucky rich? We wanted it as well. I guess we aren't going to get it."

Charles smiled. "You must have forgot why I brought you. Unless I'm missing some news, O'Riley's ledge is still out there."

Samuel looked up, disbelieving what his father was saying. He was throwing the chips on the table.

"Either you make it happen, son, or we go back the way we came," he said. "And if that's the case, then that's not so bad either. But you seem to have forgot, it hasn't snowed yet, and it's still a ways off."

CHAPTER 31

The meadow grasses had turned amber and russet. Birds feasted on the ripening seeds. Chokecherries hung in clusters of bright red purple and clumps of elderberries had turned from green to red to almost black. The September heat pulled the sap from the pines and firs, making the woods rich with their tangy fragrance. The pungent odor of smoke from the fires lingered. On some days, the sky was hazy, shrouding the country in an eerie orange cast. Evenings sometimes had a nip.

Charles returned to the Ruby placer. Although the water was holding, the deposit was proving to be shallow. Already, they had stripped the gravel down to the bedrock along the main channel. They now worked upslope along the small draws until they found no more gold or the concentration dropped below an ounce average per man per day. The placer upstream of them was already finished. Charles doubted that work would last until winter, but he had not shared this with Samuel.

Samuel had prepared for an extended search for O'Riley's ledge and took Molly to pack the additional gear. His father's words were fresh. Only if *he* got lucky rich would they get ahead. Without water, the Sweet Mary was now no help. Only if he found the ledge did they still have hope.

He did not miss the two trail-worn horses outside Ripson's Saloon, a dun with a white blaze and leg bars and a black with a white sock. Two men came spilling out, appearing ragged and unkempt. A chill washed over Samuel. At first, he thought he was seeing Dudgin and Smith, especially the man with the black coat, but he calmed himself. The horses were not right.

The men talked loudly, something about one of the girls. Samuel thought about Miss Lilly and felt his hackles rise.

"I've a mind to leave you here to face the music," spat the shorter, red-haired man. He was properly dressed in a dark gray vest and high-collared shirt, although his clothes were dirty and ragged.

"I was doin' fine, Reuben, honest to hell, till that other gal got her nose bent out of joint." The man spoke loudly, his speech slurred, jerking the sleeves of his coat back into place, adjusting his hat. "It warn't her business."

205

Samuel had a feeling the man was referring to Miss Hattie.

"Damn it, Orwin. I was remindin' you we been in enough trouble. Don't need to be gettin' run out of here either."

They began to mount up.

"There warn't no harm," Orwin whined. "That's the kind of thing those kind of wimin like."

Samuel tried to ignore their comments but could not. Something told him Reuben had been bothering Miss Lilly.

"What the hell you starin' at, pup?" Orwin glared at Samuel. He appeared lanky, almost goonlike, but Samuel sensed a wicked mean streak in him similar to Smith. A white scar crossed the bridge of his nose.

"You're new in town," Samuel replied. Quickly, he approached them. "Welcome to Washington." He reached his hand up toward Reuben. Something told him he needed to pay attention to these two. "You must be comin' in to do some mining. I'm Samuel Chambers. Need a hand with anything?" Samuel moved to where they would have to pay attention to him or ride through him.

Reuben fidgeted a moment but held back his hand. "Well, now that you mention it, kid, would you know any mines that're hiring?"

"No, sir, I don't, but Mr. Rankin and Mr. Watkins might know some. They'd be at Hofen's store if they're around." He purposely avoided mentioning Hinley.

"You know how any of the mines are doin'? I hear the Rescue is the best one around. They hiring?"

"Well, I'm not sure the Rescue *is* the best." He got a funny feeling about Reuben's questions. "One day it is ... the next, it's another mine. The Rescue has litigation troubles."

"How about now?"

"Guess it's doing about as well as any of the others." Samuel knew they were fishing. Hinley had told him they had found the richest ore yet. "I'm sorry. I didn't catch your names." He reached his hand out again.

"I'm Reuben Finney, and this here's my partner, Orwin Culler." Both of them ignored his offer. "We come lookin' for work."

"Good to meet you gentlemen." Samuel offered nothing useful. Trusting a man who did not shake hands was like trusting a rattlesnake not to strike. "The Rescue is doing good, but so's the Knott, the Hic Jacet, and a couple others south of here. The quartz mines are doing well, but most of the placers are done." He avoided mentioning Houston Creek. "I think you'd do best to hire on at a quartz mine."

"Thanks, kid," muttered Reuben Finney without enthusiasm. He clucked to the black and headed down the street. Orwin Culler followed, his dun sidestepping a bit, protesting.

Samuel continued to study the two. Finney had light, watery eyes, and he carried a pistol as if he knew how to handle it. Culler carried a rifle. His dark, cold eyes matched his hair. He guessed he would see them again. Maybe he was wrong. Maybe they *were* looking for work.

He entered the assay office.

"I don't think those two are up to any good," Samuel told Raymond Hinley.

"Aye." Hinley watched down the street. "I've had the unpleasant experience of meeting them, and your assessment is accurate. They are scoundrels of the lowest sort." He adjusted his glasses. "They inferred as to be looking for work, but each time I shared a possibility, they sought to know the mine's performance. They ventured it was important they hire on with someone prosperous. Poppycock. They're looking for some easy pickings."

"You mean you think they'll dry-gulch someone?"

"They will not take a fellow's life, but they will take whatever else they can get their hands on. I shall give Sheriff Sinclair my assessment."

He turned to Samuel. "So what is my pleasure of your visit today?"

"I'm pondering a man named Kevin O'Riley. Is there anything in your records about him?"

Hinley looked puzzled. "I have no claim records. You would need to see Matt Watkins for those."

"Yes, I was hoping you might have some old assays."

Hinley raised his eyes. "I do, but perhaps not all. I acquired this business from another fellow."

"How about anything when the camp was struck?"

"Would that be when this man, Mr. O'Riley, submitted ore for sampling? Mr. Eames was doing assays out of a tent in those days." He turned toward the back. "I shall see what records survived."

Samuel heard him clumping around in the back room. He looked over the samples lying around out front, tempted to look at them more closely. He decided against it.

Hinley returned with a sheaf of yellowed papers. "How is it you are looking for something on Mr. O'Riley?"

Samuel declined an answer.

"What year?"

"Had to be fall of '62."

Hinley began shuffling through the papers, turning them around, his eye twitching as he squinted. Samuel waited patiently, glancing outside to see if Finney and Culler were still around.

"Nothing in '62. At least not among these records."

Disappointment flooded Samuel, but if an assay had been run, what would it tell him, anyway?

Hinley began going through the next stack and did not get more than a few sheets down before he paused.

"O'Riley? Kevin O'Riley?" He adjusted his glasses, pulled a piece of paper, and spread it out.

Samuel saw O'Riley's name on the paper. A strange feeling came over him. The piece of paper was the first proof that the man they had chased all the way from Iowa had actually been here at one time. *O'Riley had really existed.*

"Kevin O'Riley submitted samples for assay on April 12, 1863." Hinley looked up. "I'm in a fix as to how he did so, beings it had to be under a dozen feet of snow."

"He found it in the fall but must not have brought it in right away."

"Perhaps." Hinley traced his fingers across the faded paper. "*Copper, trace. Lead, one ounce. Silver, 10.1 ounces.* Silver is certainly respectful. *Gold, 6.4 ounces.* Blazes, Samuel, that's rich! And you checked with Mr. Watkins? Mr. O'Riley did not file on this? That would be a mystery."

Samuel felt a rush of excitement. "Any clues on where it's from?"

"Based on the assay, I have an idea," Hinley replied. "The high content of silver and trace of copper. It could be south across the Secesh, or it could be north of the basin, perhaps up Slaughter Creek coming from a ledge up in that country." He glanced at Samuel. "That's where you've been looking, have you not?"

"It's not from across the Secesh. O'Riley wasn't there." Samuel's heart raced. He now wondered if it were farther north of the bare knob. For some reason, he had always envisioned it being west.

"You and your father came here to search for this fellow's strike, did you not?"

"I shouldn't say," Samuel began, "but it doesn't matter anymore, and you've been a kind help, Mr. Hinley."

Patiently, Samuel related the story. "My pa learned of the strike direct from Mr. O'Riley. He probably left here in April of '63 after he got the results."

"Aye," Hinley mused. "I always speculated why a strapping lad like yourself did not just work at a placer with his father—before you got hurt that is—and why you were always asking to study samples. You had a ledge you were searching for."

"Yes, sir." Samuel grinned. "And you just confirmed I'm not chasing ghosts. So I think I still do."

"Perhaps this may help. You recall the samples you brought me a couple of weeks back? I informed you that I did not think they held any values? Well, I proceeded to run a partial assay. It came back with some decent silver and some minor gold."

"What?" Samuel could hardly contain himself.

"Aye, it was just a trace of gold, but you might collect some more samples in that area."

"I knew it! That's where O'Riley had to be." Samuel was fairly dancing with excitement. "I'm going to find it!"

Hinley returned to studying the O'Riley assay, muttering quietly. "To blazes. Of all the assays I've run that I knew were from that country, they all ran high in silver but not much in gold. It appears Mr. O'Riley discovered the area with the gold." He shuffled the assay back into the stack.

A thought suddenly silenced Samuel. "Do you know of any claims up there? Even old ones that have been abandoned?" He remembered a couple of pits but had never found any blazed trees.

"None," Hinley replied, "but confirm that with Mr. Watkins. He has records from what were recorded."

"Thank you kindly, Mr. Hinley." Samuel raced from the building, his heart hammering.

*   *   *

At Hofen's Mercantile, he was pleased to find Matt Watkins in his office, a room at the back. He sat at his desk, papers stacked high, a pipe in its stand.

"What can I do for you, Sam?" Watkins reached out to shake. "Haven't seen much of you. Not since we recorded your placer." He offered a chair for Samuel to sit. "It doing any good?"

"A little. Fact is I haven't worked the placer on account of my arm. But now it's good as new." He raised his arm, gesturing. "'Course, now we're out of water. Besides, I spend a lot of time hunting and taking care of the stock."

"Yes, I heard about your hunting accident. You're back at it okay, I see."

"Finally." Watkins was one of the few people who had not been by to see him. "I've also been doing some prospecting."

"I figured that's what you were up to when you ran into those desperados. But I couldn't figure why you were up in that country. No gold there."

So two people had guessed. Samuel nodded. "Are there any claims up there?"

"None," Watkins quickly replied. "I can tell you that without looking. At least not any within a couple miles."

"How about abandoned ones?"

"Unless I know the name of the claim or who filed it, it's difficult to look up, unless you just want to go through the records."

The only name Samuel knew was O'Riley. "How about Kevin O'Riley?" He blurted it out, not quite knowing why. His father said he had never filed on it, but what if he had?

"It looks like you're looking for a lost claim."

Samuel told himself it no longer mattered. His father had turned finding the ledge over to him, and he was getting close. "Actually, I am. Did you ever hear of a man named Kevin O'Riley ... ever hear of him finding a quartz ledge?"

Watkins studied on the question a moment but shook his head.

"Back when Warren's camp was discovered," Samuel continued and briefly told the story. Afterward, Watkins rummaged through the early records.

"Sorry, Sam. Nothing." He paused. "You say it was up above the Chinese on Slaughter Creek? Well, I imagine that gold had to have come from somewhere. But no one's ever located a ledge. Could it be where they're mining now?"

"It's possible, but I don't think so. Mr. O'Riley was working a placer and accidentally found the ledge while he was out hunting."

"Ain't that the way it always is?" Watkins grinned and pushed back in his chair. "Do you know the name of the placer he worked?"

"Only that it was on Slaughter Creek near Richmond."

"Then the reason you two showed up was to find a claim Mr. O'Riley told you about?"

"In short, yes."

Watkins stood up. "I need to tell you something, Samuel. That's the Chinese placer that's operating on Slaughter Creek that you're talking about. It's the only one it could be. And based on what you just told me, you could probably challenge the Chinese claim. It's clear to me O'Riley had an agreement with your father, and beings he and his brother are both dead, your father probably has a prior claim to that placer—more so than the current owner."

"The Chinese?" Samuel asked.

"No, Lance Baroon. The Chinese don't own the placer." Watkins began pacing. "They can lease claims or buy the mining rights, or they can work for someone, but they can't own the ground. The truth is the claims on Slaughter Gulch went inactive a while back, presumably exhausted. A couple years ago, the Chinese convinced Lance Baroon to file on that one for them." He glanced at Samuel. "You haven't met Baroon. He's a drunk. He could care less about mining. He just cares about the next dollar for the next shot of whiskey." He frowned. "Your father and you probably have more legal right to that placer than he does."

Samuel was surprised.

"You should consider filing for ownership and remove the Chinese."

Samuel hesitated. "I don't think I could do that."

Watkins shook his head. "I don't understand your thinking, Samuel. It was clear Mr. O'Riley and your pa had an agreement. In a sense, your pa is his heir."

Samuel grew frustrated. Watkins had not been listening. "It wasn't the placer he found. It was a ledge—somewhere else on a mountain where he was hunting."

"Forget the ledge a moment. You have a right to that placer." He shook his head. "I can't figure you. Forgive me for saying this, but everyone knows you and your pa are making grub by a whisker. Your accident had to eat up any gold you've earned. Now you have some chance of getting a break, and you don't go for it?"

"I understand what you're saying, Mr. Watkins, but I don't see that by Mr. O'Riley telling us about a placer he once owned, it gives us any right, particularly since he was talking to my pa about a different spot."

Matt Watkins sat back down and eyed Samuel. "Maybe it's because you're getting a mite friendly with the Chinese. I'll talk to your pa."

Now aggravated, Samuel spoke sharply, "You mean well, Mr. Watkins, and I sincerely appreciate your help. *I* will talk to my pa and consider what you told me."

"I'm sorry, Sam. Perhaps I'm a bit out of line. However, you should worry someone else might try it. I'm seein' more and more of the type of thing Mr. Baroon is doing. Can't be but trouble a brewin'. Other whites have had their claims jumped by the Chinese, and they aren't doing a thing about it. Figured they were played out so they don't care. Trouble is the Chinese are going to run us over. The gold they're mining is ours. It's American soil and American gold, not Chinese."

Samuel considered his last comment. "Okay, Mr. Watkins. Suppose someone was thinking about filing on the Chinese. Is there any way I could get some kind of warning?"

Watkins shook his head. "I'm bound by the law. I have to take what comes first." He smiled slightly. "Of course, my partner, Mr. Rankin, isn't similarly bound. I know he sometimes has trouble keeping his mouth shut ... and it does take me a couple days to draw up the paperwork."

Samuel smiled, relieved. "Mighty obliged, Mr. Watkins."

"Oh, no, don't thank me. Thank Mr. Rankin."

CHAPTER 32

again taking Molly to pack his extra gear, Samuel headed up Slaughter Creek, eager to get back to the last place where he had found the rusty rock and had taken the samples. He felt renewed determination, now knowing Kevin O'Riley had not made up a story. He had actually found and taken in specimens to be assayed, and they had been rich.

He became aware that the Pioneer was again silent and briefly wondered what was going on. Apparently, there were unpaid bills, and though recently sold, it was again in litigation.

As he passed through the Chinese placer, some men paused, greeting him as usual. Many now knew him. He had come to know them as hard workers. Most would never realize their dream of going home to China. Many would never fulfill their debts to the persons who had paid their passage to America, but none would quit trying or quit dreaming of again seeing their families or their homeland. Maybe the gold *was* going to China. *They* were still being left behind.

He felt strange now he knew the only reason they had the claim was because of some drunk named Baroon—a drunk who could care less about actually developing the claim but only about getting a few dollars a year to lease it. That was good for the Chinese, but he knew it caused anger among a number of whites.

He sat Spooky and watched the Chinese, marveling at their industry, marveling at how they seemed happy despite their slim odds for success. Men swung picks into the dirt, wrenched out the alluvial cobbles, and shoveled the dirt into baskets. Others carried the baskets suspended on the ends of yokes across their shoulders to the heads of the sluices, where they washed the dirt and gravel through, releasing the tiny bits of gold, trapping it behind the riffles. The water carried the mud and gravel out the other end, slowly building up a fan of debris along which the sluice would eventually be extended.

For the first time, he noticed that the Chinese collected the cobbles, carried them to the sluice head, washed each rock in the sluice, and then stacked them in neat, long piles. *That's how they're making these worn out placers pay. They're washing the rocks, collecting the tiny specks of gold that cling to them.* The Chinese were taking the gold the whites had already thrown away.

Samuel clucked to Spooky, moved up Slaughter Creek, and then turned up Bare Knob Creek. He returned to the area he had searched a few days ago, to where he resumed his search for outcrops and quartz veins.

Just beyond his last spot, he found several new outcrops, but none held quartz stringers. It was the most barren granite he had yet encountered. Despite his new hopes, nothing had changed, and he quickly became discouraged. *Where is it, God? O'Riley was here. He found gold. Where is it?*

He surveyed the country. A few aspens had turned yellow, their leaves trembling in the wind, their shadows tracing intricate patterns across the rock. Their beauty struck him. Inexplicably, a calm enveloped him, and he remembered his father's words: *It hasn't snowed yet.*

For the next several days, with a stubborn determination, Samuel began retracing his route back almost to within the shadow of the bare knob. He studied the country east and west. More rock appeared toward the east, but he had found nothing in that direction. That day, afternoon clouds began to build, creating intermittent shadows, and with them, there came cooler breezes. Samuel watched the clouds, figuring rain was likely. He turned his face to the wind.

The *skr-e-e-e* of a red-tailed hawk caught his attention. He glanced toward the call. A couple of hawks circled high above a rock outcrop, catching the updraft and riding it. One sideslipped the wind, dropping, and then, with outstretched wings, caught the draft and rode upward, rocking itself, feeling for the draft. He rode toward the hawks, watching, jealous of their flight. *Sure would make looking at this country easier,* he thought.

The hawks peeled away, soaring farther along the ridge where the air currents lifted them upward.

A twisted tree grew from the base of the outcrop. Several of the lowest branches were missing, as if they had been broken away, as if someone had disturbed the tree. Scattered pieces of quartz rested against the rock. Samuel dismounted and carefully examined them. To him, it appeared as if they had been disturbed before. He began digging, following the bits of quartz.

A gust of wind hit him, spraying him with droplets of cold rain. Gray tendrils had reached downward from a heavy-bottomed cloud and a cold, spattering squall marched across the ridge. He moved away out of the wind into a draw where there was good grass for the animals and sat under some heavy timber until the clouds raced past and the sky cleared. The hawks returned to hunting along the ridge, calling to one another. Evening approached.

He prepared a meal of dried meat and cold corncake. While he ate, Samuel could not help but recall Watkins's words about just hanging on, implying they were practically starving. He was not starving. True, he always felt hungry, but he figured that was normal. He flexed his arm, the one he had broken, and examined himself. He *was* pretty skinny, he decided. His legs poked out from his trousers, showing his bony ankles.

He hobbled both Molly and Spooky and watched the sky fade from orange to inky blue as darkness gathered. Finally, he rolled out his bedding. It was then that the disturbing thoughts of Dudgin and Smith and Bender's broken body began to haunt him. He shivered and built up the fire against the evening chill. Early autumn had arrived. Samuel swallowed. He might have a month remaining. The first snow was not too far distant.

He curled up in his bedding and tried to sleep, bothered by the ghosts and bothered by his failures. He felt warmed by thoughts of Miss Lilly, the friendship he felt when she visited him, but these thoughts, too, became bothersome as he remembered his promise and his father's words.

*   *   *

Morning broke. A squirrel busily scolded him. Apparently, he was lying beneath the squirrel's favorite tree, or so it seemed.

After a meager breakfast of corncake and coffee, Samuel headed back to the hawk outcrop where he had found the scattered quartz. If he had not thought about being hungry, maybe he would not be, but now his stomach protested.

Clouds had drifted in, and the sun remained hidden. A cold chill penetrated his clothing, and his hands and fingers were clumsy numb from the wet cold.

He discovered a large area strewn with broken pieces of quartz and traced them to an area of snow-white quartz about ten feet in diameter. Samuel had heard of quartz blowouts. Unlike veins, they rarely carried any values. Nevertheless, swinging his pick, he diligently broke apart some pieces, examined them one at a time, and seeing nothing, tossed them down. He broke another, picked it up, and automatically tossed it down before the shiny black spots he had seen registered. Prickles washed over him. Shaking, he picked the rock up and slowly turned it, expecting the specks to be gone. They remained. He broke another piece and revealed a swarm of black and gray specks running across the broken face. Silver flashed from the fresh break. His heart began to race. Samuel remembered the pieces of ore Hinley had showed him from across the Secesh. Maybe this was silver. If so, it likely carried some gold.

Most of the mineralized quartz seemed imbedded in the center of the blowout where it emerged from the ground. Samuel tried to dislodge more pieces. His pick bounced crazily, ringing his hands, barely chipping the rock. Stubbornly, he continued swinging. Eventually, he managed to pry loose a couple of large slabs. He loaded what he could into Molly's saddlebags and packed his tools, preparing to head back.

He built a small cairn near the outcrop and tried to memorize the new area. He knew country looked different from each direction it was viewed. The area was almost due north of the bare knob, a lot farther distant than where he always envisioned O'Riley's ledge to be.

It started raining before he made it back to Washington, gentle at first and then a steady drizzle. He stopped by Hinley's to drop off the new samples.

"Got these today, Mr. Hinley. Some of the outcrops where these came from looked more promising. I'll be headed back to check some more." He handed the largest chunk to Hinley. "I think this one contains something, but I couldn't get it to break much."

"So you brought back the mountain." Hinley laughed and then examined the piece under his glass. "It certainly carries some metals. It appears primarily to be galena, a sulfide of lead. When broken, it appears silver; however, you can observe the cubic shape under the glass." He scanned the rock slowly, flipping it, turning it. "Also, possibly, tetrahedrite, a silver mineral. There presents greenish discoloration, so there could be a hint of copper. I do not see any gold."

Samuel's hopes sank. "Is it worth doing an assay?"

Hinley studied him. "Aye, lad, it is certainly worth an assay. I believe it to be largely lead ore. However, you may have some silver and possibly gold which is not observable."

"How long will it take?"

"For you, I shall accomplish it by next week."

"Monday would be fine. I might take another sales trip with Chen." Samuel no longer felt optimistic. The rain matched his spirits. Maybe he would never find O'Riley's ledge.

Hinley wrote him a receipt for the samples and put them aside.

"Now, some good news." Hinley handed him a small bar of gold. "Here's what I refined from your amalgam."

Samuel hefted the small bar, disbelieving.

"I recovered more than two ounces. What I have given you is adjusted for my refining fee and the ten-dollar loan." He pushed a piece of paper over to Samuel. "Here, you may review my figures."

Samuel studied them, not because he did not trust Hinley but because he wanted to see how he did the work. "Looks good."

"You can understand these numbers? Most folks cannot," Hinley said, smiling. "Perhaps I *could* use you some around here."

"So you got 2.3 ounces out of my amalgam?"

"Aye, you did a fine job washing the gold into your mercury, Samuel." Without asking, he brought out Samuel's cup and poured him some coffee. "I presume you have saved your fines. You may have oversaturated your mercury and missed some gold."

"Yes, I've saved them. I figured if we got a good flow of water before freeze-up, I'd run it all at least another time." He rubbed the gold, enjoying the feel and weight of the metal, feeling immensely proud. The hours and hours of work and one-handed panning suddenly no longer seemed as bad. He put the small bar into his pocket.

Later, when he left the assay shop, it was nearly dark. He glanced in both directions for Miss Lilly, although he did not expect to see her. She would be working. He glanced at the saloon—noise, flickering lights, loud music. His stomach tightened. She could be a good person, if she had met someone to marry. Someday, he might ask why she did what she did, but he was afraid of the answer. He knew she liked him. He liked her and felt drawn to her. He turned Spooky toward the cabin. "Come on, boy. Let's get you and Molly out of the rain."

SHEEPEATER
THE GHOST PEOPLE

Chapter 33

Samuel was too discouraged to return to the ledge. He had spent two weeks prospecting and taking back anything that remotely resembled ore and had found nothing but galena. He decided to head for the South Fork to go hunting.

The crew Charles worked with at the Ruby placer opened another small gulch. It did not have as much water, but the gold remained rich. Charles was finally bringing home more gold than they were spending. He had also been pleased with the gold Samuel had recovered from the Sweet Mary amalgam. He told Samuel, "We know it can be done. If we get enough rain, we might be able to run a bit more."

Samuel packed extra gear, fearing the weather could change, but as he looked at the bright blue sky and felt the warmth of the day, he found it difficult to believe. A hint of smoke still clung in the air, but the recent rains had nearly quenched the fires that had burned all summer.

Up Meadow Creek toward the summit, the aspen leaves were a solid blaze of yellow; the shrubs underneath were turning orange and scarlet. The days had become noticeably shorter. Summer had slipped away.

He crossed the summit and dropped into the canyon, taking the trail that wound to the bottom just out of sight of Yune's gardens. When he had nearly reached the bottom, he began keeping a sharp eye out for rattlesnakes, avoiding places they might be. Over four thousand feet lower in elevation, it was much warmer in the canyon.

The river stretched wide, sparkling in the sun. Its gravelly bottom showed out to the center, giving a sandy appearance to the stream. He thought of Amasa Smead and the Indian girl and James Raines's ranch downstream toward the main Salmon. He could see why people were coming here to homestead. The canyon was protected, and grass-covered benches that were ideal for grazing and gardening bordered the river. Yellow pines that were perfect for lumber towered along the banks in open stands.

He had seen no game, but now that he had reached the South Fork, he began thinking other thoughts. Beyond was largely unexplored country. He had never heard of a strike in the country to the east. Impulsively, he decided to cross and at least examine the ridge beyond. The huge nuggets that John Keep found at Houston Creek and the rich ore at the Rescue spurred him onward. Maybe it was his turn to get lucky rich.

He waded Spooky out into the moving stream. The current was surprisingly strong, and Samuel became nervous. He scanned carefully to avoid any deep holes. Spooky pushed ahead without trouble and splashed out onto the far bank. Much earlier in the season, the ford would have been impossible.

He headed up one of the tributaries that emptied from the east into the South Fork. It was a good-sized stream, and trout scattered as he rode past. A trail wound its way along the north edge. Ahead, the pine- and grass-covered gorge rose toward a thick blanket of dark timber and a number of scattered outcrops. The trail looked used, but he saw no horse prints. *Probably a game trail,* he reasoned.

The canyon shoulder pitched upward, and he entered a broad, protected basin at its base. He paused. Shelters of some sort appeared out of the shadows, much in disrepair, scattered throughout the basin. *An abandoned Indian camp.* A shiver raced over him. He inspected one of the shelters. It resembled a large brush pile covered with pieces of tattered hides. Beneath the skeleton of poles was a hollowed-out pit, its lip surrounded by stacked rocks. A few stone bowls were stored neatly inside along with what he took to be a type of fishing spear.

He wondered what people had used these shelters. He had heard mention of the Sheepeaters. Supposedly, they inhabited this region, but few whites ever encountered them. The shelters appeared primitive, and clearly, they had not been used for some time; however, the manner in which items were neatly stored indicated whoever had built them intended to return.

An eerie feeling washed over Samuel. Unlike the Nez Perce, here were a shadowy and hermitlike people. He wondered if any still lived. Maybe they had all died from a disease. It seemed that way. The feeling became stronger. He could not remember the last time someone in Warren's camp had reported actually seeing a Sheepeater Indian, and what stories he had heard were from the earliest days.

He continued past the camp, following the trail, clearly one used by these people. It traversed upward along the gorge above the stream, and he followed it a distance, surprising himself at how quickly it climbed. He now felt driven to continue onward and became more intent on following the trail than in looking for gold.

Evening overtook Samuel by the time he reached the head of the stream near the summit, where it bubbled out from beneath boulders into a small, grassy basin. He figured it might be the last good water, so he picketed Spooky and unrolled his blankets.

He wondered about being here. He could not explain the feelings he had. When he left Warren's camp, he intended to get a deer and return home. Then he had decided to do some prospecting. Now he felt compelled to move eastward, to cross this mountain, to follow the trail of these ghostly people.

He glanced west but could not see the summit above Warren's camp. He was too far east and now in country he had never seen, perhaps in country no white man had ever seen. His gaze traced several descending ridges downward, now sprinkled with golden aspens and black spruce, spilling downward into the purple shadows of the South Fork canyon.

The last rays of the September sun slid from the rocks above him, turning from rosy orange to dull copper until they became broken patches of gray etched against the steel blue sky. With the fading sun came the mountain chill, and he started a small fire for company and a bit of heat. He felt strangely comfortable in this country, unlike a few days earlier when he camped near the outlaws' camp. He glanced to where Spooky quietly cropped the thick grass along the tiny stream.

Slowly, the stars spilled across the canopy above. When he finally rolled into his blankets, Samuel lay a moment and listened to the coyotes yapping before he slept.

*   *   *

Shielded by the mountain flanks, the sun lit the peaks across the river, their brilliance waking him. Samuel wondered at first where he was and then remembered his strange journey. *Maybe not smart,* he told himself. He should be back at Warren's camp, maybe taking more goods out to trade with Chen. But his father would understand if he told him he was prospecting. At least that was what he told himself as he resumed his journey.

The trail soon crossed a grassy summit and disappeared. He paused, spellbound. The sky stretched endlessly. Every direction he looked, there were mountain peaks. Some were of barren rock with snowfields; some were covered with heavy timber; all were brilliantly lit and etched in gold by the morning sun. Patches of yellow aspens and deep green conifers carpeted them. Shadows marked the ragged ridges where they plunged off into the emptiness of the canyons below.

What incredible land, Samuel mused. *Nothing but river canyons and mountains as far as I can see. And no people. Land that is untouched, that is undiscovered.* But he thought of the trail he followed, the one that had seemingly disappeared. It had been made over the years, not only by game but also by people.

He let Spooky wander along the divide until he caught sight of a lake in a small basin below. Granite walls surrounded one end of the lake, and broken talus filled an avalanche chute that descended to the lake from a ragged peak that rose above it. He turned Spooky downward to investigate.

The lake was too shallow to hold fish. The rock-covered bottom showed sharply through the crystal water. Elk prints pocked the muddy shore. He headed for the far end to where the cliffs emerged along the far hillside.

Partway, he surprised a covey of ptarmigan. He pulled his rifle, loaded a round of shot, and quickly killed one for his dinner. The sound of the shot echoing throughout the basin surprised him. Almost irreverent, he felt.

When Samuel reached the outcrop, it took only moments before he located a quartz vein. His heart quickened. It looked identical to those he had found near Warren's camp. He scoured the rock face and examined the fragments strewn about the grassy hillside. With this much quartz, chances were good some might be mineralized.

He located a second vein that held a few rusty chunks. Trembling, he rolled out a piece from the moss at the foot of the outcrop and noted some metallic gray specks similar to the rock he had recently taken to Hinley. Bits of pyrite protruded from red and yellow stains. He swallowed in disbelief. Hinley had explained that sulphurets might indicate gold.

Samuel looked about and noticed that the veins appeared to extend around the hillside toward the next basin. He began to envision a ledge peppered with masses of gold. *Why not? Others had found them.* He shook with excitement and urged Spooky across the shoulder, following the general direction of the veins.

A narrow ridge ended abruptly at a massive outcrop. White quartz, some stained red and yellow, lay scattered about. A tingling sensation began to envelope Samuel; his throat was dry. Recklessly, he pushed Spooky forward. He knew what he was seeing.

He reached the spot, dismounted, and fairly ran to the face. He grew uneasy. Something about the rocks—some seemed disturbed. *This doesn't make sense. Somebody's been here, but that's not possible.*

Frantically, Samuel scanned the rock face, wondering if the rocks had been knocked loose by others falling. He decided they had not. Too much had been removed from the face. Too many pieces were chipped. A band of gray cut across the wall, obviously worked. He pried a chunk loose and immediately caught the unmistakable glint of tiny gold specks. It was rusty ore, but it had free gold. *Gold!* His heart raced, pounding in his ears. Somebody had been here but had long ago abandoned the spot.

He studied the nearby bench. It could have been a campsite—good grass and water from the creek near the outcrop. He strode toward it. Unmistakably, there had been a camp. He found the remains of a fire pit and a rusted coffeepot, some stacked decaying wood, a rusty pick and shovel, the handles gnawed by animals. He glanced around for other tools and then froze, a chill racing through him. The pile of rocks and its meaning were unmistakable. *A grave.* A weathered piece of wood and what could have been the crossbar to a cross marked the grave. A man was buried here. He began to feel uneasy.

Something had compelled him to come here. He was meant to discover the old camp, the gold, ... the grave. Inexplicably, an eerie feeling washed over him, and a shiver prickled his neck. He glanced around, half-expecting to see something, but not knowing what.

He returned his gaze to the rock face. It looked rich. Why had no one come back? Perhaps getting ore out would have been impossible.

A nearby stack of rock caught his attention. Grass and shrubs had grown up around the pile. Whoever had been mining had stockpiled some of the ore. He picked up a couple of pieces. Tiny specks of gold sparkled back.

Disbelieving, he studied the rocks in his hand, staring at the gold, closing his eyes and opening them, checking to see that the gold did not vanish, and telling himself that he was not dreaming. So many times he had dreamed of finding a ledge only to wake and find it had vanished, he had to check. He found himself shaking. This was real.

An incredible tingling wash of joy spread through him. He wanted to yell. His father and he had dreamed of this strike. He danced a silent jig, found himself crying and laughing, found himself kneeling in the grass. He was lucky rich.

Calming himself, Samuel realized that he needed to take his time and carefully collect samples. Hinley had taught him the importance of careful sampling to determine the true value of a strike. He also wanted to take enough of the stockpiled ore to mill out a couple of ounces if he could.

He unsaddled Spooky and set out his gear. Maybe he would stay another night, but he felt odd doing so with the grave nearby.

He started a small fire and began roasting the ptarmigan. Its odor made his mouth water.

The eerie feeling came back. Cautiously, Samuel raised his eyes and again scanned the surrounding basin. He spotted a man squatting under a small fir. Cold prickles rushed through Samuel. *An Indian.* Instantly, he scrambled up and glanced around for his rifle. It leaned out of reach against an aspen.

The man slowly rose, raising his hand as he did so. A young boy stood with him.

Samuel choked back his fear. The man seemed friendly. He could have already killed him had he wanted. He was not Nez Perce. Samuel knew he must be a Sheepeater. More ghost than real, some of the miners claimed, but this man and boy were real.

Heart hammering, throat dry, Samuel edged back toward his rifle. The man approached, the young boy with him, eyes wide but unafraid.

Samuel reached his rifle and closed his hand around the muzzle. The man shook his head. Samuel could see he carried a fine bow but had not notched an arrow. He also wore a knife strapped to his waist—a white man's skinning knife.

A feeling told Samuel he was not in danger. "Hello," he called. Shakily, he raised his hand.

The man replied, "*Hej.*" He stood a dozen paces from Samuel, eyes keen and sparkling black. His charcoal hair with a blue stone ornament braided into it above his right ear gently moved on the breeze.

At first glance, the Sheepeater had appeared ragged, but Samuel could now see the breechcloth he wore and his leggings were of fine leather. His moccasins were bootlike and furry. He wore no shirt but carried a bundle about his waist, probably a robe. The boy, seemingly six or seven, was similarly dressed.

The man spoke, but Samuel understood nothing. He peered intently at Samuel, studying his eyes until Samuel became uneasy.

"I'm Samuel," Samuel said, patting himself on the chest.

The man replied, "*Dosa-kwinaa.*" He tapped his chest as well. He pushed the boy forward. "*Yahnai Natuipittsi.*" He pointed to himself.

The man's son, Samuel guessed.

The man's face was smooth except for heavily etched lines at the edges of his eyes and mouth. His body was lean, strongly muscled, bronzed by the sun. Samuel figured he might be approaching thirty, judging by his son's age. The boy's eyes flashed brightly as they darted between his father and Samuel. He wore a yellow and red ornament.

Samuel's unease faded. He held no fear of the Sheepeaters, nor did they appear fearful of him.

Impulsively, Samuel made signs for eating and pointed to the ptarmigan. He pulled it from the fire, pulled off some pieces of flesh, and offered it to them. The man stripped apart the meat, giving some to the boy. "*Aishenda`qa,*" he replied. The three of them quickly devoured the bird. Samuel wished he could offer more.

The man squatted, studying Samuel. He pointed to Samuel's eyes.

"*Dugumbaa`naa Buih-nee`*," he spoke slowly. He pointed to the sky, to his own eyes, and then back to Samuel's eyes and repeated the words. "*Dugumbaa`naa Buih-nee`*." Samuel felt strange hearing the words. The man stood the boy and brought him closer. The boy stood unafraid. "*Dua` Dugumbaa`naa Buih-nee`*."

It struck Samuel that the boy's features were slightly different. His face seemed less rounded, and his cheekbones were not as pronounced. His eyes appeared slightly washed, and his skin tone was lighter. *The boy was part white.*

A thousand thoughts stormed through Samuel. *The son of the man who is buried here. Or maybe it was his mother.*

Samuel pointed to the grave, then back to the boy, and questioned, "His mother?" He made a rocking motion as if he held a baby.

The man shook his head. He pointed toward the grave and back to the rock outcrop, made a digging motion, and said words that Samuel figured were the man's name.

More questions spilled into Samuel's head. This Indian had known the man now buried here, but some other white man must have buried the man. Indians did not bury their dead. They certainly did not mark them with a cross. Perhaps it had been two white prospectors, and one of them had had a Sheepeater wife. He knew that trappers or prospectors sometimes had Indian wives. Amasa Smead might have an Indian wife in a few years if he liked the girl for whom he traded. It would explain the age of the dig. Maybe the Sheepeaters killed one of the prospectors. Samuel shivered. He would never know.

Presently, the man stood. He pointed to the sun on the horizon, beckoned to Samuel, and pointed east toward the canyon. Samuel believed the man invited him to his camp. He had a strange yearning to go, considered it for a moment, but could not make himself do so. He could not be this long gone.

"Someday," he replied. He pointed back toward Warren's camp. "I must go back as well."

The man seemed to understand and nodded. He took one of his arrows. "*Dugumbaa`naa Buih-nee`*," he repeated and gave the arrow to Samuel.

A gift, Samuel realized. "Thank you," he replied. He fumbled for a cartridge to his rifle and handed it to the man.

The man fingered it before he handed it to the boy, explaining something to him. The boy studied it, smiled, eyes bright. "*Aishenda`qa*," the boy replied.

The man and boy turned and faded quietly into the dense timber. Samuel stared after them, questioning if they ever existed; yet, in his hand, he held the arrow.

Samuel found himself shaking, found himself confused. Somehow, the man as well was the boy were tied to this place. He pondered what it meant as he finished gathering samples and packed Spooky. Then he found himself thinking, *Maybe I shouldn't take this rock. Maybe I should just leave. Leave this grave and leave these people. Maybe that's what the man wanted.* But if that was so, what had led him to this place?

CHAPTER 34

ater, when he recrossed the South Fork, Samuel jumped a couple of
does. He killed one, dressed it, and packed it onto Spooky. He climbed
out of the canyon, topping the summit late in the afternoon. A cool
front had moved in, and he rode the final hour toward the cabin in a frigid
rain. He arrived late evening and was pleased to find his father home.

"Good timing, son." Charles offered him a cup of coffee. Then he saw
the doe. "Good hunting. Glad you're not coming home empty-handed. I was
getting a bit worried."

"Lot more to it than the doe. I'll tell you." But he struggled with what he
would say. On the return trip, he could not shake the thoughts of the grave
or the Indians he had met or especially the gold.

He took the coffee, thankful for its warmth. His father also shared the
remainder of his corncake and beans. They fried up some venison and ate
again, hardly pausing for words.

"Had a good finish to the week mining," Charles said. "We were paid an
extra half ounce."

"That's great news, Pa. Does it look like it'll last?"

"It just might. The gulch just keeps going. You wouldn't think it by
looking at it. It's skinny and winding, but we just keep finding good gold."
He took a bite of the venison. "I'm glad you were able to bring this home.
Anything else?"

Samuel produced the arrow. "I got this."

Charles quit chewing, took the arrow, and studied it. "Hope it wasn't
shot at you."

"No," Samuel said and grinned. "I went to the South Fork, planning on
hunting, and saw nothing. Got to wondering if there were outcrops similar
to here on the other side of the river, so I went prospecting. I found an old
Indian camp and eventually a couple of them found me, actually a man and
a boy. They were friendly."

"I 'spect so, or you wouldn't be sitting here talking."

Samuel caught an edge of concern. "Not sure what got me going. I just ended up going and going. The country up high is incredibly rugged and beautiful."

"Find any good prospects?"

Samuel was not sure how to answer. He was not sure it was right to go and dig the gold. In some ways, it was sacred ground. A man was buried there. In practical aspects, no large amount of ore could be hauled out, which would make it too costly unless it proved very rich. But more important were the Indians. These were the ghost Indians—the Sheepeaters. Maybe only a few remained. He wanted to meet them and to know them, partly to solve the mystery of the grave but also to solve the mystery of the boy.

"I found an outcrop that I'm pretty sure has gold, but I won't know how much until I get an assay done."

"You don't seem excited."

"Unless it's very rich, it isn't going to pay to get ore out of there. The river is hard to cross. It's low now, but other times, you'd need a ferry or bridge. I might go back and do some more prospecting, though."

"Probably, you're right, and probably, we don't have the time. Isn't that the way?" Charles studied him. "I'm not sure I like the idea of you being gone that far, Samuel. I know you're capable, but I almost lost you once. I couldn't stand to go home without you."

"I reckon you're right." Samuel felt relieved. "Someday, maybe we'll both go."

"In the meantime, I still have a good job, and you still got a ledge to find."

"I did find some more rocks that I took to Mr. Hinley before I went to the South Fork. I thought they had silver in them, but he thinks it's mostly lead ore."

"Keep at it. One of these times, you'll find something worthwhile. You've worked hard enough at it." Charles shifted himself. "You're still doing good as a merchant, aren't you?"

Samuel grinned. "I'm figuring on another trip this week."

"Since I earned a bit more this week, how about you and I go to Mrs. Reynolds's tomorrow? Have us a real bath and a home-cooked meal. Make a day of it?"

Samuel could not hide his grin. "Sure we should spend the money? I can heat water for us here tomorrow."

"The good Lord tells us to take a day off, Samuel. Neither you nor I have in some time. I say we do it."

*   *   *

Morning, they headed in as early as they thought prudent. The rain had quit. The trail was still muddy, but the sky was a brilliant blue, the day, cool. Samuel checked the mountain ridges, half-expecting to see snow.

"It's coming, Pa."

"I know." He clucked to Buster to pick it up. "I'd like to get a few more ounces. It's not near as much as we need but good enough to get some things going when we get back."

"Sure you want to do this then?"

Charles sniffed his arm. "I think we're both in need."

Several miners were already at Ma Reynolds's. They waited their turn. Mr.Reynolds and another man brought in buckets of water as soon as they had been heated and put them inside the room, taking the empties back to fill and heat anew.

Samuel took his bath first. He was a bit embarrassed when Ma Reynolds stuck her head in, wanting to check to see how he had healed up.

"Good as new." He showed her the scars but nothing personal.

She seemed satisfied. "Lord Almighty, Samuel. We thought we lost you for sure. But you lookin' pretty good now."

"Thank you, ma'am."

"You and your pa ought to get by more often, though. You both as skinny as spring chickens." She gave Charles a hard look. "You two might be takin' somethin' out of the ground, but I'm fearful you're puttin' some of you in it with every shovelful you takin' out."

"Thanks, Mrs. Reynolds. Samuel and I feel we are about to turn the corner. That's one reason we came in today."

"Well, I'll make sure to load you two up with a little bit more grub. You *are* having some fixin's, aren't you?"

Samuel paused as he soaped himself and glanced at his father to make certain he had not changed his mind.

Charles nodded. "Been meaning to for some time. We'll be out soon as we can."

Charles poured a bucket of water over Samuel's head and shoulders. Samuel let out a yowl. "Hot, hot."

"Sorry."

"Feels good, though." He lathered his hair, which was longer now. They needed to give each other another haircut.

"Ma Reynolds is sure a nice lady, Pa."

"Yes, it's good she's brought a bit of a woman's touch to a camp like this."

He dumped the rinse water over Samuel's shoulders. Samuel stood to step out of the tub and exchange places.

"It'll be nice having your own ma help with this when we get home, don't you think, son?"

"Yes, but I usually have to heat and haul all the water."

*   *   *

Shortly, they sat down to a breakfast meal. It was more a dinner aimed at filling up anyone who needed filling. There was cornbread, sourdough wheat biscuits with various jams, slabs of ham, fried eggs, some beefsteaks, and cold buttermilk.

Samuel ate until he was stuffed.

"Now you did have some huckleberry jam, didn't you, Samuel?" Ma Reynolds pushed the crock toward him.

"Yes, ma'am, but there might be room for more." Huckleberries were a bit like whortleberries, only larger and tastier. He lathered some onto another biscuit and washed it down with more buttermilk.

Following breakfast, they left Ma Reynolds's and crowded into the Sauxe saloon for church service. Reverend Weatherspoon had come to town. Samuel noticed someone had turned the pictures to the wall and covered the bar, turning the place into a rather respectable church for the attending families. He noticed the Manuels had their baby daughter and the Osborns had their three small children. It made him feel as if he were back in civilization.

They tried a couple of hymns to which everyone knew the words, as there were no hymnals. Neither was there a piano. No one had figured a way to get one in over a hundred miles of mountain trail.

Reverend Weatherspoon read a couple of passages. Samuel would have liked to follow on, but the serious absence of Bibles prevented it. Afterward, he preached on being a good neighbor. Samuel thought it was to discourage some of the thievery still going on—mostly missing tools and such. All in all, Samuel thought it was a fine service. It had been a long while since he had been to a service, and he felt he needed a bit of preaching.

The remainder of the day, they cut and stacked wood. Sunday or not, when the ox was in the ditch, you had to get him out, and Sunday was the only good day for working around the cabin. Come tomorrow, they would both return to work.

PROVING UP

CHAPTER 35

Monday morning, Samuel rode with his father toward Washington. Where the trail forked outside of town, they said farewell to each other. Samuel guessed that his father would be home Saturday night if the water held. He headed toward Raymond Hinley's assay office.

"Good morning, Mr. Hinley." Samuel swung the canvas bag holding the Sheepeater samples onto the counter. "Got some more for you."

Hinley raised his eyes. "Aye, lad, and I have something for you."

Samuel felt a surge. *The assay must be finished*, he thought. "Is it good news?"

Hinley smiled. He placed two cups on the counter and filled them with coffee. He pulled out a piece of paper and slid it across the counter.

"Remember I believed the sample you brought in might have some silver? It does."

Samuel picked up the paper and turned it so he could read the numbers:

Sample C-023, submitted by Master Samuel Chambers, September 13, 1871
Silver: 5.4 oz.
Gold: 2.7 oz.
Lead: moderate
Copper: trace (by observation)
No other remarkable metals. Sulphurets are present in moderate quantities.

Samuel felt his hand shaking. He read it again.

"As you can see, Samuel, it also has gold."

The report was signed: *Raymond Hinley; Washington, Warren's Camp, Idaho Territory.* Slowly, he lowered the paper.

"Gold, 2.7 ounces. You mean ... the sample I brought in last time. You mean this is the assay. There's really gold in that rock?"

"Aye, Samuel. If you did not rediscover Mr. O'Riley's ledge, you have discovered one which is quite respectful—that is, if it holds up. You shall need to prospect it quite thoroughly and submit at least half a dozen samples from spots along the ledge for me to develop an accurate assessment."

Samuel thought about it. He remembered no length to the outcrop, only the blowout where he had found quartz protruding from the earth. "It'll take a bit of work, but I'll get them."

"And you have other work as well. It will take some doing to get it recorded. Actually, your father needs to record it, but I shall walk through things with you so you are able to post it. Perchance, does your strike have a name?"

"What do you mean?"

"Every mine has to have a name. You put papers on it. It has to have a name."

"Guess it should be called the O'Riley. He's the one who got us out here."

"Fair enough." Hinley adjusted his glasses and lifted his coffee cup. "Here's a salute to the O'Riley."

Samuel raised his cup in return, smiling. "To the O'Riley." Coffee had never tasted better.

"What now have you lugged in?" Hinley gestured at the canvas bag.

Samuel had almost forgotten. He undid the tie and dumped the contents across the counter.

"Are these from the same area?"

"No, a new spot." Samuel figured Hinley would know when he saw them that they were from a different ledge.

Hinley laughed. "You keep bringing them in."

"I try." He had refrained from bringing all of the ore. He was thinking of crushing and washing some of it himself. Hinley would have been suspicious had he brought in very much.

Hinley examined a piece, and his eyebrows shot up. "To blazes! This is plenty rich. If you cannot see gold in this, you're plumb blind."

Samuel laughed. "What do you think?"

Hinley retrieved his glass and studied the piece more closely. His eye twitched. "This is damn good."

He handed Samuel the glass. Samuel could see a swarm of tiny yellow specks scattered through the white matrix. "Jumpin' Jehoshaphat!"

"It always looks better through the glass, but it is still damn good." Hinley scribbled on some papers. "You're starting to set me behind, lad." He put the samples into a new bag and slid it behind the counter. "Just as soon get these out of sight. You do not want to chance someone coming in and seeing what you have—not this."

He handed Samuel the receipt. "So how did you discover this one?"

"Like Mr. O'Riley found his, I was out hunting."

"You stumbled onto it," Hinley exclaimed. "A little luck is never bad. By the way, that offer to grubstake you is still good."

Samuel laughed. "Maybe."

"This presents a problem. Your father can have but one quartz claim. I have little doubt this one shall come in stronger. I surmise you will post this one instead?"

Samuel shook his head. "I'm still planning on proving up the O'Riley and then selling it. I doubt anyone's going to find my new spot." Samuel knew no one would, and he was not certain he would file it, even if it did prove richer.

"Spoken like a true prospector. Sell one, find another, sell it."

"Could I ask when you get this new assay, can we keep it quiet from my pa? I told him I found some new rock, but I didn't tell him how rich it looked."

Hinley tightened his jaw. "Aye, it is your assay. When you pay for it, it is between you and me."

"There will be a later time."

"Aye." Hinley took out a piece of paper and began writing. "I can help you with the paperwork for the O'Riley if you get me this information. I need length of claim, angle of vein off north, location of corners, and location of discovery pit. Most people do not obtain all of the information, and it can lead to trouble later."

"How do I get all this?"

"You can estimate the angle off north by using the North Star, assuming you know the number of degrees in a right angle."

"Ninety."

"Therefore, the angle will be between zero and ninety degrees west or east of north."

Hinley sketched a couple of wandering lines and drew a rectangle around them. "Your claim will run lengthwise along the vein. The vein should emerge from each end. Give yourself at least sixty feet from the center of the vein to each side. Expose the vein for as long a distance as you can but not more than two hundred feet."

"That's a big area."

"Aye. The main mistake folks make is they do not thoroughly investigate the vein. They miss the main pay streak, and someone else files a claim either above or below them and strikes it rich." He drew some circles at each end of the vein. "You can mark each end with a pile of rocks. Find a tree at each corner and put a blaze on it. Put a sign on the vein at its center. That shall be your discovery point."

"What if I can't track the vein for two hundred feet?"

"You likely cannot. Estimate the direction the vein runs and pace it off." Hinley sketched while he talked. "Are there any prominent landmarks nearby? You locate the claim by describing the heading and distance from a known landmark. Can you do that?"

Samuel nodded. He had the bare knob in mind.

"Good." Hinley handed him the piece of paper. "Now if you should go bust as a miner, you can take up staking and selling mining claims for a living."

Samuel figured staking and selling the O'Riley would suffice for now.

*   *   *

Back at the cabin, Samuel prepared to head back to the O'Riley. Chen came by with his mule loaded with vegetables.

"Go to sell, Sam?"

"I'm sorry, Chen," Samuel said. "I have a claim to mark. I finally found a quartz ledge."

"You did?" Chen replied, surprised. "Alla time you go up in the hills, you find something?"

"Yes, I got to take more samples, but one sample Mr. Hinley ran says it's good."

"I understand." Chen nodded. "You go to hills, Sam. Then file claim. I would file claim but not allowed."

"You know a place?" Samuel was interested. "I could file it."

"Maybe someday." He turned down the road. "Go to sell. Bye, Sam."

"Hey, Chen." Samuel stopped him. "Are you going by the Ruby?"

"I can if you want."

"Can you give a note to my father?" Samuel found a scrap of paper, scribbled on it, and handed it to Chen.

Chen studied it.

"Don't let anyone see it, please."

"What does it say?"

"It says I found a good spot and I need his help."

"I don't need note. I could say that for you."

"I also wrote down some assay numbers," Samuel continued. "I don't want the others to know."

"Sure, Sam." He carefully folded the note and put it in his shoe.

"My pa has to file the papers, but I can do the sampling and lay it out."

Samuel watched as Chen headed back down the trail, his long queue swinging. He returned to packing. He figured on being gone several days. He took the pot of beans intended for the week, some corncakes, and salt pork. He packed his tools, including the gold pan for sampling soil near the ledge for any colors. If it was a good ledge, placer gold could be downslope of it.

*   *   *

Late afternoon, Samuel reached the area where he remembered the outcrop but could not find it. He retraced his steps but still failed to see it. He began to wonder if he was on the wrong ridge. He crossed to the next ridge, and after a while of fruitless searching, he continued on to the next and again finding nothing, returned. It had to be where he came up the ridge.

He searched for another hour, widening his circles around the last point he remembered, becoming more and more frustrated. He began to panic. *Lord, it has to be here. It can't just vanish.*

Desperation and anger seeped in. Despite his effort to memorize the new spot, he had searched so much, so often in this country, it had all begun to look familiar. Angrily, he rode higher up the ridgeline, frantically looking for outcrops. He rode directly into the cairn. He shook his head, choking with relief. He did not remember it being this high.

He cussed himself. It was not where he remembered it or how he remembered it. How it could change in his memory so quickly mystified him, but it caused him to pause. Having this much trouble on a spot he had just marked, it seemed reasonable O'Riley's cairns might still be intact.

Samuel studied the massive quartz, trying to determine which direction, if any, the vein ran. The swarms of gray seemed to form a band. He walked about fifteen feet in the direction they were oriented and began digging down, trenching across what he hoped would be the vein. He found nothing. He went to the opposite side and repeated his efforts. Again, he found nothing.

Then it doesn't matter which direction I lay out the claim, he told himself.

He began pacing off the distance across the ridge, figuring on marking the sides first. A couple pieces of milky quartz rested in the soil. He immediately began digging around them and then deeper until he hit a thick ribbon of quartz. The pieces he broke showed some gray and black specks. By luck, he had found the vein.

He walked in the opposite direction near one of his first digs and began another trench. He extended the ends of the trench and dug more deeply.

Nearing four feet, he finally hit quartz. He looked back along the three small pits. They were roughly in line, indicating a promising vein, not just a simple blowout.

Working steadily, Samuel enlarged the hole until he had exposed a good section of granite with quartz. He chipped free some of the pieces and washed them to see if he could see any mineralization. Only black specks appeared. For now, the northwest end seemed to have heavier mineralization.

He walked another fifteen feet on line to the south and began another trench. He continued digging until dusk but failed to hit quartz. Satisfied the vein did not extend farther to the south, he put his tools up.

He felt sore and exhausted, but he felt good. This was honest work. He looked back along the strike of the vein, envisioning how it ran. If it held up, it had the potential of extending a good distance and holding a lot of gold.

*   *   *

Samuel took Spooky and Molly down the hill about a quarter mile until he found good grass and a trickle of water. A few aspens, their leaves golden and beginning to fall, and chokecherry shrubs, flame orange, lined the forest edge.

He fixed a fire to heat some water for coffee and to heat a small bit of corncake with beans. *Not much of a meal.* His stomach rumbled.

Feathery clouds moved beyond the farthest ridge, still catching the fading light, etched pink and orange. The air had turned frosty cold, and he could see his breath. He breathed deeply the muted fragrances of damp autumn leaves and grass.

Samuel rolled out his bedding next to some rocks, keeping them to his back for protection. His muscles ached from swinging the pick, and he examined his hands, turning them. Despite his old calluses, they were red and raw.

*   *   *

For the next couple of days, he continued tracing and sampling the vein and laying out the claim. He estimated it to be about thirty degrees off north, bearing west. Most of the vein appeared northwest of the discovery point, although the original dig showed the most quartz. He marked an area about forty feet northwest of his initial dig, deciding to mark it as his discovery point, centering the better quartz along a two-hundred-foot line.

There was no creek below the ledge for sampling to see if gold had worked loose and settled in a placer. Nevertheless, he dug a couple of pits downhill of the vein and took pans of gravelly earth back to his camp for washing. The pans showed a few minor specks. Either the ledge was newly exposed, or it held very little gold. Samuel hoped it was newly exposed, meaning more gold would be found deeper in the vein.

He marked the claim boundaries—first the end points with rock cairns, each a hundred feet out from the discovery point, and then the corners, sixty feet perpendicular to the end cairns. For three of the corners, he blazed trees. For the southwest corner, he built another cairn holding a post. Lastly, he built a cairn above the discovery point and erected a post in its center on which he had carved "*O'Riley Lode.*"

He stood back, examined his work, and felt a great sense of accomplishment. This was his claim. The gold that was here was his. All he had to do was dig it out of the ground.

*   *   *

Later, Hinley studied Samuel's notes. "These appear adequate. I think I have what I need to write up the O'Riley."

"Here are more samples." Samuel swung the bundled pieces onto the counter. "I got seven places where I exposed quartz on the vein, about eighty feet before I lost it."

Hinley whistled. "That is well done, Samuel. I thought maybe you'd bring in one or two samples like most people."

"I need to know if the O'Riley's any good."

"Aye. If these assays do not hold up, you shall still have time to file on the other strike before it is buried under snow. I shall do my best, but I have several assays at the moment. Perhaps you could assist."

"I gotta take the stock to the cabin and check up on things. My pa could be finishing at the Ruby anytime now that things are freezing up. I had frost on me last night."

"Get here when you can." Hinley began writing up the new samples.

"By the way, Mr. Finney and Mr. Culler were back. They produced some placer gold, requesting that I promptly refine it. They professed to have been working a placer down on the South Fork. However, they could not give a claim name. Therefore, I just as promptly told them it would not be possible to refine their gold."

Samuel laughed. He knew Hinley would never reduce ore that he suspected was high-grade.

"Mr. Culler did not take kindly to my decision." Hinley put a slip of paper with one of Samuel's samples. "As I understand, they proceeded to head over to Ripson's saloon and imbibe until they were thrown out. At least that is what I understand. I had retired for the evening by then."

Samuel wondered if they had bothered Miss Lilly again.

"I later informed Sheriff Sinclair, and he acknowledged a miner on the Secesh reported his sluice pilfered." Hinley peered at him intently. "Just keep an eye out for those two, will you, lad?"

"Sure, Mr. Hinley." Samuel was struck by the man's concern. "After Dudgin and Smith, I've grown another set of eyes."

Hinley laughed. "Well, no man can be too careful in this country."

Samuel reached the cabin, turned the stock out, and cut some wood. He began to heat up some water. There was no food at the cabin except some cornmeal and dry beans. The beans would take until midday the next to prepare. He mixed some cornmeal into the hot water and began cooking it.

He added some wood to the stove.

"Hehwoh camp."

It was Chen. Samuel jumped up and opened the door. "What you doing out here? Come on in." He motioned to him.

Chen hesitated. "I am Chinese."

"Chen, you're my friend. You come in and sit."

Chen did so, but Samuel sensed his unease.

"Please feel welcome. Can I get you some coffee? I'll have some corn mush soon, if you'd like to join me."

"Thank you. Ohnee tea."

"I have tea," Samuel said, somewhat pleased. "I still have some I bought from Mann." He poured hot water into a cup, sprinkled in some tea leaves, and handed it to Chen.

"Did you see my father?"

"He give you this." Chen handed over the paper.

Samuel quickly scanned it.

"What it say? Read it to me."

"Sure," Samuel replied. "It says, 'This is great news, Samuel. Go ahead and start staking the quartz claim. I will file it when I get back. I do not know how much longer we will be working this gulch. The water is frozen in the morning; however, the pay has been good.'"

Chen studied the paper. "Which word say *Samyew*?"

Samuel pointed to his name.

"Sure look funny."

"Well, to me, Chinese looks funny."

Chen sat back, his dark eyes studying Samuel. "I live all my life in land of the golden mountain. I want to learn Englees to read."

"You want to learn how to read?"

Chen nodded. "And to write."

Samuel raised his eyes. "You're a sojourner. You'll go back to China as soon as you can."

Chen shook his head. "Not for long time. Goon Lui at saloon knows how to read and write Englees. But he no good for my people."

"Your people?"

Chen explained. There were two major Chinese factions in Warren's camp. Additionally, the merchants composed a third, smaller faction, including Sang Yune, Sing Mann, and Chen.

"We help our own tong," Chen explained. "But we are small tong."

"What's a tong?"

"Like a family. We help each other."

"But not the other tongs?"

"No, they fight each other. Too much gambling ... too much opium ... slave girls."

Samuel had heard about white gangs trying to control whiskey and such. It sounded similar.

"When I can read and write Englees, I can help my people. We do business with white people and Chinese and do not need Goon Lui. We do not trust him." Chen smiled. "Do much business. Make much money. Send home to China for family."

"I will do my best, Chen. I'll see about getting a book we can read, but you teach me about China."

"No, you tell me about Ahmelicah, then I tell you about China."

Samuel laughed. "Okay," he said and stuck out his hand. "Deal?"

Chen hesitated and then shook. "Deal."

Samuel was pleased. If Chen was going to learn about America, the handshake was an *Ahmelican* custom he should practice.

CHAPTER 36

Samuel woke to a gray sky. The morning air was damp and cold. Clouds sifted in, their bellies low, catching in the dark pines. Frost had carpeted the meadow grasses and edged the pines. Steam rose from the creek, its edges frozen in ice. Spooky billowed steam as he rode into town. Samuel picketed the horse in the meadow and walked to the assay shop, intending to help Hinley for however long he could.

"You going to run my assay from the new spot?" He joked.

"Are you going to file that new spot instead of the O'Riley?"

"No."

"Then I shall do the O'Riley assays first; however, I am quite behind with all these others."

"That's why I'm here."

"Good." Hinley brought out one of the canvas bags with one of Samuel's samples from the O'Riley. "First step is easy. You turn these rocks to powder." He pointed at the metal plate with the rounded hammer. "That instrument is known as a muller. You shall use it to powder your samples."

Samuel examined the hammer.

"I shall walk you through the process." Hinley dumped some fragments of ore onto the plate. Deftly, he hammered them into small pieces and then ran the muller back and forth over them, quickly reducing them to a coarse powder. "The crux to a fire assay is obtaining a representative sample. Most miners inadequately sample the vein. They frequently sample the richest area, and as a result, the assays are misleading. Second, you need to work cleanly and precisely. I cleaned the plate before you got here. If there were any gold particles on it, I would get erroneous results."

"Even a speck?"

"Aye. You shall see why in a moment." He mixed the crushed fragments, scooped them into a pile, and then patted it down into a pie-like shape. "I obtain this splitter and do what we call quartering. I shall continue doing so until I arrive at between two and four ounces of powdered sample." He took a

246

straight edge and cut the pie in half and then into quarters. Deftly, he removed the opposite quarters and dumped them into a bucket.

"You just threw that away."

"I shall process it later, but generally, the gold is insufficient to pay my effort." He adjusted his glasses. "As you can observe, our sample is much more than a few ounces, and it is still quite coarse, so I quarter it again." Hinley spread the remaining sample on the plate and ran the muller over it for a few more minutes, further powdering it. "The additional mulling improves the mixing. Now, lad, it's your turn."

Samuel scooped the sample into a conical pile and carefully flattened it into another pie. He took the splitter, and following what he had observed Hinley do, he split it in half and then measuring ninety degrees, quartered it. Carefully, he discarded the opposite quarters.

"Good," Hinley replied. "Do it again. We still have more than what's needed for a couple of assay-ton samples."

"Assay-ton samples?"

"Aye. It's a sample that is proportional to the number of ounces in a ton. I shall explain." Hinley took ten pieces of ore and lined them up on the table. "Presume these are identical in size and content. Now presume I have determined a single piece contains precisely half a gram of gold. How many total grams of gold would be in the entire lot?"

"Five."

"Aye, but I only measured the actual content of one piece. I use the same principle when using an assay-ton sample."

Samuel nodded. He was beginning to understand the basis for an assay.

"There are exactly 29,166 troy ounces in a ton. An assay-ton is exactly 29.166 grams. Therefore, if you determine you have half a gram of gold in your assay-ton sample, you multiply by one thousand and come up with five hundred ounces per ton." Hinley smiled. "I doubt the O'Riley runs five hundred ounces per ton or even five. That's why you need to have precise measurements and no contamination."

Samuel smiled, but he could see a number of factors which could affect an assay. If the sample contained a large piece of gold, the results would be high. Similarly, if gold concentrations were widely scattered, it would be possible to have a low assay from a rich mine. He had wondered why Hinley insisted on him chipping pieces to sample from across the entire vein. Now he knew. "That's why it's important to powder and mix it well."

"Aye," Hinley confirmed.

Samuel worked the last sample longer before he quartered it.

Hinley scooped up about four ounces and took it to one of the balances where he sat down.

"This is the pulp balance for somewhat coarse measurements. It gives hundredths of grams. I'm actually going to measure out a half an assay-ton or 14.58 grams." After he checked to see that the balance was level and zeroed, he placed a weight on the left pan. "This weight weighs exactly 14.58 grams, so now all I have to do is balance it with an equivalent amount of the powdered sample."

Hinley gently spooned some of the sample onto the pan on the right side. When the balance came close to the zero mark, he used pincers and added minute quantities until it balanced.

"We shall use the button balance for our final results." Hinley nodded toward another balance. "It weighs to an accuracy of a milligram—one thousandth of a gram—which means if we make an error, it will be multiplied by a thousand."

"That's why the glass cabinet?" Samuel noted the balance was enclosed behind glass.

"Aye. Dust and a breeze will affect your results. However, for this part of the process, we can use hundredths."

Hinley seemed satisfied with his measurements and poured the sample into a clean crucible. "Often, with the small amounts of gold we find in the quartz around here, I shall do two assays on the sample. That is why I saved a couple of extra ounces. It gives us better numbers." He placed the crucible in a stand.

"We shall melt the sample and bind most of the material with a chemical flux to form a glass. Any metals in the sample will melt down with the lead from the litharge that we add. When the mixture cools, I break off the glass, leaving a lead button that also contains any silver and gold. Now an interesting thing—" He turned to Samuel. "Do you know much about how glass is made?"

Samuel shrugged. "I know it's made from heating sand with some chemicals."

"Aye, but if you just took sand and heated it, how much heat do you think you would need to melt it?"

Samuel shook his head. "I've never seen sand melt near a campfire."

"Precisely. I could heat this sample all day in this furnace and never melt it. The secret to making glass was the discovery of a flux. I add three: soda, borax, and litharge. They enable everything in the sample to melt at a much lower temperature. The soda combines with the silica to form a glass. The borax combines with the metal oxides and also becomes a glass. The litharge partly combines with the borax and partly becomes molten lead. The lead is what traps the gold and silver."

Samuel wondered how Hinley knew such stuff. His head was spinning, trying to keep up.

A couple of men came in. Hinley promptly went to the counter and greeted them, talking a bit. He pulled out some papers and gave them to the men along with a small canvas bag with what Samuel presumed to be the remains of a sample.

They inspected the papers and nodded. Neither showed much emotion. *Like poker players*, Samuel thought, but he noticed they kept keen eyes on him until they had left.

Afterward, Hinley turned to Samuel. "This shall be a good time to tell you some things. You work for me, lad. Everything around here is tight-lip secret."

In a rare moment, Samuel recognized a threat in Hinley's voice.

"Not with your father, not with Mr. Alexander, no one—just me."

"Yes, sir."

Hinley began measuring powdered flux into small tin cups. "We do not need to weigh the amount of flux because the required weight fits exactly in these cups—twenty-five grams of soda, fifteen grams of borax, and so on. The most significant variable is the litharge. My experience for ores from around here is to use about eighty grams." He dumped all but the borax into the crucible and mixed it with a spatula. "I shall add the borax last. By being on top, it helps prevent the metals from volatizing." He brushed his hands on his apron.

"Now we shall fire this along with some other samples that I have waiting."

Similar to the mercury retort, Hinley packed charcoal into the furnace and lit it.

"I shall add the crucibles in a few minutes after the charcoal settles. In the meantime, you may proceed with your mulling."

Samuel began working down some more ore. Following Hinley's example, he hammered it into small fragments and then mulled them into a coarse powder.

Hinley watched until the furnace reached proper temperature and the charcoal settled. Opening the top, he took a poker and packed the charcoal down. With a pair of tongs, he then carefully inserted each of the six crucibles, packed more charcoal around them, and closed the lid. "We now wait until the material melts."

Hinley positioned a set of molds near the furnace. "After each crucible comes out of the furnace, I shall pour it into one of these molds where it will freeze up. Then I'll show you how to separate the glass from the button. Remember what the button is?"

"It's mostly lead with any gold and silver from the sample."

"Precisely."

Later, Samuel helped Hinley remove the crucibles from the oven. He watched in amazement as Hinley poured the smoky, fiery orange liquid from each into the molds. After each cooled sufficiently, he turned the mold over and tapped it with a hammer. Six cones of slag with metal broke free. Hinley showed one to Samuel. "See the separation of glass and metal?"

Samuel nodded. A cone of bright silvery lead was capped with dull green glass.

Hinley set it on an anvil and cracked it with a small hammer, breaking off the glass. He kept tapping until all the tiny pieces of glass had separated from the button.

"The next step is cupellation. We put the button in a hot cupel and put it back in the furnace until the lead is volatized or absorbed into the bone ash of the cupel." Hinley placed a button in each of several small bone-ash cups about an inch in diameter and placed them into a small chamber in the furnace. "So after all this, what should remain?"

"The gold with silver."

"Aye," Hinley confirmed. "And what would we do next?"

"You could weigh it. That would give the combined amount of gold and silver per ton."

"Keep going."

"I remember you said you could part the silver with nitric acid. That would leave just the gold."

"You remember that, lad?" Hinley beamed. "Aye, we part the silver with nitric acid. Now what?"

"You take the combined gold and silver weight and subtract the weight of the gold. That gives you the amount of silver. Am I right?"

"Precisely." Hinley laughed. "You sure you don't want to do assays?"

Samuel shook his head. "I'd rather be finding the gold, if I can."

"Why do I ask?" Hinley laughed again.

Later, for the completed sample, they determined 7.3 ounces of silver and 1.2 ounces of gold.

"That is just about break even," Hinley explained. "If you get ore with an ounce of gold per ton, it might cover the cost of mining and milling."

CHAPTER 37

Hinley handed him a broom when Samuel arrived the next morning. "If you're going to assist me, one of your chores will be to sweep and tidy up. The only things you won't tidy up are the balances. You probably appreciate how delicate they are by now. Those are off limits. When you have your own assays, I'll help you weigh them."

Samuel spent the next hour cleaning, tidying, and dusting. He figured Hinley had put off such a chore more often than he had done it.

Hinley called him to the bench and spent some time talking about fluxes and what minerals were pulled out of a sample by what. The main idea was to oxidize or reduce all the minerals except the ones being measured—generally the gold and silver. Other assays for copper, zinc, and lead were possible.

"The primary sulphurets in this district are galena and pyrite. The pyrite breaks down under heat, sometimes popping and spraying the molten sample, so you need to watch it, but generally, it is burned off. You can smell the sulfur. The lead will combine with oxygen, forming litharge. Because of that, you occasionally need to adjust the amount of litharge you add. That is the reason I use eighty grams. The litharge combines with the siliceous gangue and the other metals, releasing them from the sulphurets. Someday, I can show you with a pencil and paper if the chemistry interests you."

Samuel was surprised at how much it did interest him.

A man Samuel had not seen before entered and set some sample bags on the counter. Samuel picked up the broom and returned to sweeping, being respectful of the business Hinley needed to conduct.

"Good morning, Carl," Hinley greeted.

"Howdy, Ray. I see you finally got some decent help around here." The man, who was tall, dark haired, and rugged, spoke loudly.

"Aye, the lad is turning out okay."

The man surveyed the floor. "First time it's been swept out for what? A year?" He offered his hand to Samuel. "Howdy, young man, I'm Carl Isenbeck."

251

Samuel knew the name. He owned the Rescue mine. "Hello, sir. I'm Samuel Chambers."

"Figured so. Only youngster your age hereabouts. I've heard about your run-in with those outlaws up north. You're lucky as hell to be alive. Heard their partner wasn't the only man they've put a bullet in. How'd you manage to get away from them anyhow?"

Samuel had spared sharing the details. "It was near dark. I made a run for it and got into some rocks where they weren't able to follow."

"You're lucky they didn't put a bullet in your back." He turned to Hinley. "Well, Ray, this man know how to keep secrets?"

Hinley nodded. "Aye, he's been instructed."

"Not that we have any secrets at the Rescue." He laughed.

Hinley opened his ledger.

"We have a vein over two feet thick we're on now. I'm up to a crew of twenty men working round the clock. Best lookin' ore I've ever seen, as far as consistency."

"And how are you milling it now the Pioneer has been sold?"

Isenbeck laughed. "Just as well. I lost more gold out the tailings from that mill than I ever recovered. You know how I did last winter reprocessing some of it."

Hinley nodded. "You did well." He examined the bags of samples Isenbeck had brought in, checking the papers that were inside. He began writing up receipts and making notations in his ledger.

"No, I got a contract with the Hic Jacet a while back when the Pioneer went under. We've already packed out two hundred tons of ore—most of our summer's work. Trouble is it's six miles back in the woods and mule strings don't come cheap. Good news, though, they should be starting on Rescue ore this week. We should finally have some money coming in instead of just going out."

He turned to Samuel. "Don't get into mining, son. You just throw all your money down a hole."

Samuel was careful not to reply.

The two men talked for a short while. Samuel caught bits and pieces about consistent assays, wages, plans for working all winter. When Isenbeck turned to go, he addressed Samuel. "Now if you want to swing a single jack all day, you can come work underground. I pay eight dollars a ten-hour day."

"You just said don't get into mining," Samuel managed.

"Hell, the men working are the ones who get paid," he boomed. "We mine owners, we just hang on hoping to hit the really good stuff and finally make a buck. Everyone out there thinks we got it made. In fact, it's the working stiffs that got it made."

Samuel knew there was some truth to his words, at least while there was work to be had. "My pa worked for Mr. McLane until the water quit."

"Oh, don't mind my grousing, Samuel. Mining is a fickle thing for all of us. Everyone in this town knows it. I thought we hit it big earlier when that high-grade came to light, but then things settled down. Maybe the next foot—" He turned to Hinley. "And now maybe with some decent help, Ray can get more of my assays done, and I can convince investors the Rescue has a future. Then I can get the capital I need."

There was silence for a moment after Isenbeck left. Hinley began setting out crucibles. "Something to keep in mind, lad. If you and your father do hit good on the O'Riley, you shall need to line up a mill. I do not believe it too early to consider contracting with Mr. Bradshaw for when he gets his mill operating. He's an old Grass Valley, California miner whom I respect. I mentioned before that his mill will be able to reduce silver, and from that first assay I ran, it seems you might have a considerable amount."

"I'll talk to my pa about it."

"Keep this under your hat, Samuel, but Mr. Isenbeck has his hands full. As he said, he's been running a crew around the clock; however, I know for a fact none of them have seen a red cent in pay since the Pioneer was sold back in July."

"How they living then?"

"Mr. Isenbeck has stretched his credit. For now, he's managing to provide his men a meal and a cot, but unless he gets capital coming in soon, I expect he will have miners quitting on him. I am sharing this just in case you're considering that eight dollars a day." Hinley brought out the tin cups for flux. "His men are essentially running on faith and my assays. About every week, Mr. Isenbeck brings in new samples to keep checking the vein they're working, always hoping for better news. I am the one telling them they're still finding good ore. So far, the ore is running well, and as he said, it's consistent."

Samuel raised his eyes. "How good is it?"

"Good enough. You do enough assays around here, you shall catch on."

"I'd like to stick around and find out," Samuel said.

Hinley looked at him. "Perhaps this shall work out, Samuel. You're a good hand."

"But just till I get my assays done."

"Damn."

*   *   *

When Samuel reached the cabin, his father had just arrived. They both unsaddled their horses and turned them out.

"How was the week, Pa?"

"We're still mining. What about your quartz ledge?"

"I spent a couple of days on it, getting the samples and putting up the markers. Mr. Hinley is working on the paperwork. I'll bring it to you to sign when it's done."

They walked to the cabin, and Samuel lit the cooking fire.

"I also helped out Mr. Hinley at the assay office. Learned how to run some assays."

"That's good. What about the first assay? That the only one you got?"

"That's why I'm helping Mr. Hinley. We'll finish some others this week." Samuel handed him the report. "I'll save us some money if I help."

Charles glanced at the paper and clenched his jaw. "This is a good assay. You didn't say anything about silver. That's at least another six or eight dollars a ton."

"Right now it doesn't matter. None of the mills can process for silver. The one Mr. Bradshaw is putting in won't be running until next spring."

He handed the paper back to Samuel. "It seems we were too late for some things and too early for others." He lay back on his bed while Samuel began some dinner.

*   *   *

Sunday, they caught up on chores around the cabin. Samuel heated water, and they washed clothes. Afterward, they spent time cooking for the coming week, mostly for Samuel because his father was at the Ruby. They fried up some corncakes and boiled some beans and potatoes. Those two vegetables could be reheated at any time.

Dinner was a little better since they had spent the day cooking. They had rabbit with salt pork flavoring, potatoes, and some green onions.

"I thought it was going to snow the other day," Samuel admitted. "I thought it was the first snow."

"It did snow for a bit out at the Ruby."

"Are we still going to go back?"

"I'll work till they let me go or they shut down. The pay is dependable, and you and I are now getting ahead a bit. I think you should keep on doing what you've been doing. Keep us in meat. Take care of things. Go sell with that Chinaman boy."

"What about the O'Riley?"

"The way I figure it, son, we have to prove it up before it's any good. I don't know if we have time."

"That's what Mr. Hinley says," Samuel said. "A mine isn't a mine till it's been proven up."

"And no one's going to be interested in buying it if it hasn't been." Charles pushed his hands across his knees and studied Samuel. "I know there's not much chance between now and winter, but you've been chasing the dream since before we got here, and I'm proud of what you've managed, bum arm and all. I'm not going to tell you to give it up, but we'll be lucky if the O'Riley pans out. Do what you can to get some assays. If they show strong, someone might buy it as is."

Samuel nodded. Deep down, he did not want anyone to buy it. He knew with time, it would prove up. He wanted to see the gold coming out of the rock. It did not make sense for him to have found it otherwise.

"You going to come out and see it?"

"I would have today if we hadn't had so much to catch up on around here," Charles said.

CHAPTER 38

Charles returned to the Ruby placer. The gulch continued to produce. Samuel returned to the assay shop, anxious to finish the other assays on the O'Riley. They finally finished three. The one closest to the discovery point showed just over three ounces of gold and six ounces of silver, similar to the first assay. The other two from the south end proved to have less than an ounce.

"That's not good, is it?"

"Actually, it may not be all that bad," Hinley replied. "How much of the vein does this represent?"

"About forty feet."

"If the discovery point is strong, there's a fine chance the values will average out over the length of the vein. Just taking half an ounce and three ounces gives an average well over an ounce. Possibly, that would interest an investor." Hinley adjusted his glasses. "When we finish those additional samples, they may prove better."

"What if it's good only on the discovery point?"

"Often enough, that shall be the case. You informed me you didn't placer out any significant colors. That is evidence the lode may strengthen in depth. My advice is to go as deep as possible and submit more samples."

Samuel paused in his work. "That mean I'm done here?"

"Aye." Hinley laughed. "I would prefer not, Samuel. I have welcomed your help, but I recognize you have much work to accomplish in order to prove up the O'Riley before winter."

"Thank you, Mr. Hinley. I've learned a lot." Samuel would miss doing assays. He found them challenging and fascinating.

Hinley took out some papers. "Review these. They should be correct. Have your father sign them and submit them to Matt Watkins for recording."

Samuel took pride in seeing *O'Riley Lode* written at the top. Before it had only been a dream. Now they had a gold claim. "Much obliged, Mr. Hinley."

*   *   *

The moment Samuel stepped into the street, Lilly stepped from the saloon and headed his direction. Samuel's heart skidded. He remembered her invitation. He remembered his father's words. He knew the feelings at night when he thought of her.

She immediately came up to him. Samuel touched his hat, nodding.

"Hello, Samuel," she cooed. "I've seen you a couple days now but haven't had a chance to say hi."

"I've mostly been mining, but now I'm helping Mr. Hinley run some assays. How are you, Lilly?"

"Mostly fine. Some days better than others." She walked with him.

Samuel wondered what she meant. He felt awkward. He wanted to talk, but he did not want folks seeing him on the street with her. "I hope things are well."

"As much as possible." She smiled. "We should visit."

Samuel felt weak.

"Are you busy now?"

"I'm sorry, ma'am. I can't just now."

Almost imperceptibly, she stuck out her lower lip and fluttered her eyes. "I visited you."

"Yes, and I am grateful," Samuel replied. "You were a real pleasure to talk with."

"You were a real pleasure to be with," she spoke softly. She let her hand caress his shirt. "Well?" She raised her eyes, smiled, and nodded toward the saloon.

Samuel felt a strange flutter in his stomach. He stood, wavering. She was beautiful despite all the makeup and heavy perfume. He wanted to be with her. He felt his heart hammering. He glanced at the saloon doors. "Okay," he croaked. He stepped toward the saloon, and thoughts of what might happen flooded his senses. Maybe no one would notice.

He heard his name called and turned to see Scott on the boardwalk in front of the mercantile. Scott waved.

"I'm sorry, real sorry, Miss Lilly. I like you a lot. I truly do. I appreciate all you did for me, but I got to go. Mr. Alexander and I have some business to attend."

Her face fell. "I-I'll be waiting Samuel Chambers," Lilly said. "Just don't forget me."

"I won't." He turned and almost ran to Alexander's Mercantile.

Scott followed him into the shop. He had his pipe and drew a puff. "I thought you could use a hand, Sam, or did I just make things worse?" He gestured toward the stools and sat.

"Yes. I mean, no. It's okay, Scott. Thank you." Samuel sat down, not knowing what to say or think.

"You know, it's pretty obvious she likes you."

"Yes, but I can't ... you know what I mean," Samuel blurted out, shifting himself.

Scott raised his eyes. "I 'spect that's your business." He grinned.

"Why can't she be a real lady?" Samuel asked. "She's not that much older than me."

Scott was quiet for a moment, tapped his pipe. "Don't get me wrong, Sam. She *is* a real lady. Under all that ... despite who she seems to be now ... she's a real lady. Believe me, she doesn't want to be where she's at." He drew on his pipe. "I don't think any of them do."

Samuel felt troubled. "When I was hurt, she came and talked with me. Ma Reynolds didn't approve, but she was real nice to me. She had a lot of good things to say. It was easy to talk. I like her a lot."

Scott did not reply. He packed his pipe and drew another puff.

"When I first realized what kind of woman she was, I thought maybe if I struck it rich, I could take her away from here, and she'd be okay. We'd be okay."

"It's happened before."

"I don't know, Scott. I don't know what to think. I just know how I feel," Samuel said and pushed his hands apart. "Hell, I think I need to go back to mining."

"That's happened before too," Scott replied and laughed. "Now what can I do for you?"

"Chen and I are going to head out again tomorrow."

"Good. I got a couple deliveries for you to make." Scott smoothed his moustache, stood, and began gathering up items and bringing them to the counter. "How *is* the 'getting rich' part going by the way?"

"Pa's still out at the Ruby placer. I'm waiting for more water to run the Sweet Mary. We haven't struck it rich yet. Don't worry. I'm keeping you in mind for when we do."

Scott laughed. "Way it's going, you'll be the only white placer miners in these parts. Another long-timer, John Mathison, just sold eight hundred feet of his claims to a Chinese company. As far as I know, he's not refiling. I swear, there won't be any Americans left here by end of next season."

"I disagree, Scott. The quartz mines are going stronger than ever, and the Chinese won't touch them."

"That's because they have cave-ins whenever they try." Scott laughed again. "But even that's only a matter of time before they figure it out. They have their own laundries, butchers, blacksmiths, livery, merchants, pack trains, saloons—you name it."

"You forgot their gardens."

"Especially those," he agreed. "You wait. Soon, they'll be flying the Chinese flag over the town just like they did up at Elk City."

Samuel shrugged. "I doubt it. Most of them just want to go back to China."

"You believe that?" Scott looked at him.

"Yes."

Samuel began loading up the items Scott had pulled—cheese, coffee, some tobacco. They loaded the parcels for which the men had requested. The miners knew Samuel would deliver items if they could get word to Alexander.

*   *   *

Early morning, while Samuel finished packing Molly with the remaining stock—fresh buttermilk, bread, and some beef—Chen arrived, leading his heavily packed mule. The morning was cold.

They headed northwest toward the trail junction at Steamboat Creek.

"You still want to learn about America?"

Chen nodded vigorously. "Many freedoms in Ahmelicah. Men do what they want. Say what they want. Live where they want. How can that be and men not fight each other alla time?"

The question caught Samuel by surprise. He would have never guessed Chen thought about such things. "In America, you can do what you want as long as it's not hurtful to someone else. If you treat people how you want to be treated, it works. Men don't want other men to steal from them. They don't want to be treated with disrespect. They don't want to be hurt."

"But if men ohnee do what they want, they selfish. Other men not have as much."

"I think that is one of the best things about America. You can do as much or as little as you want. And no matter how much we have … or don't have, we help our neighbors. We respect others."

"Chinese respect elder. We must do what elder wants, no matter what he wants. Sometime elder is bad. Then it is not good. But I must do what elder want. I do that until elder die or I go away."

"We respect our parents as well, but when we grow up, we're on our own. It's not so much our parents tell us what to do anymore. They let us do what we want, but because we respect them, we listen to them and do for them what they want and need." Samuel heard his father's words in what he said.

"There are many good things about Ahmelicah. I like that you can work hard and keep your money."

Samuel wondered about keeping money. He and his father scarcely made grub.

They walked for most of the day, resting infrequently. Only one of the placers along Steamboat Creek was operating. A few one- and two-man operations were still working along the Secesh. The men wanted fresh goods, and both Samuel and Chen sold well.

They again camped in a small meadow outside Miller's camp. Chen was not comfortable with camping near the white miners, but he accepted camping with Samuel. Samuel knew this and did not insist they continue on to Miller's camp.

The aspens had passed their peak, and their lingering leaves fluttered to the forest floor. Huckleberry bushes and the smaller whortleberry shrubs yet blazed red orange on the open hillsides. The willows along the streams had turned a somber yellow and brown on reddening twigs. Cattails were beginning to turn deep brown, their slender, spearlike leaves turning golden.

The sun slipped quickly behind the timbered hills, and any lingering warmth went with it. The evening chilled quickly until their breaths hung in the air. Samuel built a fire against the chill.

"Soon, it will snow, Chen," Samuel explained. "I can feel it." He was thinking of telling Chen he would be leaving when it snowed.

"Yes, but the snow not stay long," Chen said. "Last year, it snow before this time and leave deep snow. But then it melt, and we have many warm days before it snow again."

"We call that Indian summer in Iowa." Samuel was quiet a moment. He declined to tell Chen what he had been thinking.

They sat, talking, keeping company until the moon's glow began lighting the trees to the east.

"Soon, we have festival of moon," Chen said, nodding toward the rising, near-full moon. "You come to town in two day. We have festival of moon."

"Tell me about it."

"Vehlie good Chinese festival, you will like. It is when Houyi visits moon goddess Chang'e, when moon is round and bright. Brighter than all other moons."

The hunter's moon or harvest moon, Samuel reflected. The light being so bright, farmers sometimes worked by its light to continue the harvest. He realized the corn in Iowa should be ripe.

The moon, now breaking into full view, cast a surreal light, sending shadows cascading through the darkened pines about them.

"Houyi, he immortal. He love Chang'e, a beautiful girl who work in palace of Jade Emperor in heaven. Evil immortal tell lies about Houyi and Chang'e, and Jade Emperor send them to earth. The rabbit help them. Houyi build a palace on the sun and visits Chang'e one time a year at her palace on moon. That is why moon is most beautiful. That is why we have festival. You come. Bling father. It will be a happy time."

"I'd like that, but I think my father will still be working the placer."

*   *   *

In the morning when they reached Miller's camp and later, the Ruby placer, they sold their remaining goods. Samuel delivered the packages he had brought, some on credit. The men would pay Alexander later.

Samuel found his father digging farther up the gulch than the other men. He watched as he lugged buckets of gravel down to the sluice and dumped them into the head box. Samuel could not help but think he was working harder than the others. He joined him and helped carry a few buckets. At least his father was getting good pay. They were beginning to stay ahead of their expenses and even stash some of the gold, figuring on taking it with them in a few weeks.

When they broke for lunch, Samuel handed his father the claim papers. "These are from Mr. Hinley. You need to sign them."

Charles looked them over. "Looks kind of nice seeing this come true."

"I felt the same."

Charles borrowed a pen and ink from Thomas and scribbled his signature. "Now we just need to prove it up enough that we can sell it."

"I finished three more assays with Mr. Hinley. Two came out poor, but the third came out about the same," Samuel explained. "Mr. Hinley says that's not all that bad because we need an average over an ounce."

"Then it's good news."

"When I get back, I'll take more samples. He thinks I should dig down as far as I can on the discovery point. But it's solid rock. I need your help."

"We can discuss it this weekend. I'm not sure it's a good idea to give up this job as long as the gold is holding up and I'm getting paid."

"I guess I can work around the cabin. I'll cut some hay in case we're here much longer."

"Maybe you can get another deer."

Samuel said farewell to his father, and he and Chen rode back to

Washington, reaching it by midafternoon. Samuel dropped off the remaining merchandise and gold with Alexander and then said farewell to Chen.

"Remember, tomorrow is festival. Good time. You come see."

"I'm planning on it."

Samuel entered Hofen's Mercantile, hoping to find Watkins. He was in the back, talking with Hofen, but he paused when Samuel came in.

Samuel handed him the signed papers, and the one dollar fifty in gold dust for the recording fee.

Matt Watkins glanced at Samuel. "The O'Riley, huh? You sure?"

"Close enough."

Samuel briefly told them the story of the discovery.

CHAPTER 39

As he headed home, Samuel turned Spooky down along Meadow Creek just below Ripson's Saloon. He recognized the two riders who emerged from between some buildings and turned downstream ahead of him—Reuben Finney and Orwin Culler. Kan Dick, an older Chinese, squatted beside the creek. Samuel remembered Kan Dick from Mann's store, where the man frequently purchased herbs. The Chinese considered him to be a doctor of sorts.

A queasy feeling overcame Samuel. He did not really think Finney or Culler would do Kan Dick any harm, but they were heading directly toward him, and Culler had begun shaking out a loop in his rope.

Culler threw the loop, lassoing the man. Kan Dick struggled up, thrashing around. Culler whooped, "Wal lookie what I catched. I done catched me a Chinaman."

Finney rode up, laughing. "Looks like you got a big 'un."

Culler's dun backed up, taking up the slack, throwing Kan Dick to the ground, and dragging him.

Samuel felt a crawling, burning feeling rise in his chest. He trotted Spooky toward the men. "Let him go," he shouted. "You're hurting him."

Kan Dick struggled, choking, his face bleeding from the rocks. Samuel knew what it was like to be dragged.

"Well, if it ain't a Chinaman lover." Finney blocked Samuel. "If I was you, sonny, I'd mind my own business."

Culler continued to back his horse, further dragging Kan Dick. "Lookie thar. Just like roppin' a steer. Hey, Reuben, you ever seen a better snubbin' horse?"

The color had drained from Kan Dick's face. Gurgling came from his throat as he clawed at the rope.

"Let him go, you bastards!" Samuel yelled. "He can't breathe." He spurred Spooky toward Kan Dick.

Finney drew his pistol. "Better git, sonny, if you don't want to get hurt."

Samuel came up short, staring in disbelief at the pistol, anger flooding him. Samuel knew the pressure from the rope squeezing the older man's chest could kill him. The man was not built like a steer. He turned Spooky and galloped for help.

Finny laughed. "Yellow, just like his friend here." He holstered his pistol.

Culler dragged Kan Dick farther up the bank. "Reckon I ought to brand him?"

"Naw," Finney remarked. "I think the rocks have done him just fine."

Kan Dick bled from several gashes.

Samuel found Sheriff Sinclair coming toward him.

"They roped Kan Dick," he blurted. "Down by the creek. Ya gotta stop them."

"Scott Alexander already told me, Samuel."

He turned and raced back toward Kan Dick. Culler had removed his rope and stood to the side recoiling it. Samuel jumped off Spooky and ran to the downed man. Kan Dick rolled his head, his eyes nearly closed.

"He's hurt," he called. He spotted Scott Alexander and a couple of Chinese making their way down toward them.

Both Finney and Culler stood by with amused looks. "He ain't *that* hurt," Finney insisted.

"Why'd you do it?" Samuel yelled at them. "He wasn't bothering you."

"I needed some ropin' practice, pup." Culler shrugged and spat, laughing. "He's a Chinaman."

"You two can leave now." Sinclair stepped down toward Kan Dick.

Samuel looked up. "You gotta arrest them, sheriff."

"For what?" taunted Finney, adjusting his derby. "For ropin' a Chinaman? Ain't no law I know that disallows it."

Samuel jumped up and headed toward Finney. Scott grabbed him. "Sam, it's okay. He's right."

Finney began laughing. "The sprout wants to tangle. Let him try."

Samuel looked at Scott and tried to pull away. "They pert near killed him, Scott," he whispered, his eyes burning. "There's no reason for what they did."

"It will be okay, Sam," Scott said, trying to calm him.

Sinclair stepped between them. "Might not be a law against it specific-like, Mr. Finney, but there is a law of human decency."

"Since when's a Chinaman human?" asked Culler. Finney and Culler again laughed.

The sheriff glowered at them. "Look, you two haven't exactly graced this town with your presence. You pull one more stunt, Chinaman or not, and I'm running you out."

Culler backed off. "Sure, sheriff. We was just a funnin'. Got to have some fun somehow in this hellhole of a town."

"Why don't you two try getting jobs and work for a living?" Sinclair asked, irritated.

The bemused look drained from Culler's face. "Them yellow heathens you're so bent on protectin' have them all, or haven't you noticed?"

Samuel could not help himself. "You could do just fine if you were willing to work as hard as they do."

Culler turned on Samuel. "Seems to me the sprout don't know his place, do he, Reuben? Where I was brought up, a young'un didn't speak unless spoke to. Makes me wonder about his daddy."

The burning, crawling feeling overwhelmed Samuel. He lunged toward Culler. Again, Scott grabbed him. "Easy now, Sam."

"Now the pup wants to tangle with me," Culler spat. "Let him. See if he's big enough to match his mouth."

"Take it easy, Mr. Culler, or you'll be tangling with me," Sinclair interjected.

"Oh, you're all Chinamen lovers now, ain't ya?"

"I'm here to keep the peace. Now your welcome's run out. Get out of my sight, or I'm running you in. If not for this, for a couple more questions on that Secesh gold, if you haven't forgot." Sinclair pulled his pistol.

Culler's face blanched, and he turned toward Samuel. "Pup, you just made the biggest damn mistake of your life. You and I got some settling."

"Come on, Orwin. He ain't worth it." Finney turned and trotted downstream, laughing and shaking his head. "Upstaged by a sprout."

Culler followed, stone silent.

Two Chinese attended Kan Dick. One turned to Samuel and said quietly so others watching could not hear, "You good boy, Sam." They helped Kan Dick to his feet and helped him limp toward the Chinese cabins.

"Samuel, I appreciate you coming to get me," Sinclair said. "But you got to be careful about the Chinamen. Some folks around here take getting involved with them real personal. You might get yourself caught in a crossfire, if you know what I mean."

Scott stood aside, arms folded. Samuel knew his feelings were not all that strong in favor of the Chinese. The Chinese cut into his business.

Samuel bit his lip and nodded. He did not agree, but he knew many in Washington felt threatened by the Chinese. There was reason enough. Of those who had come to the land of the golden mountain, some were hardened criminals and would prey on others given an opportunity. Chen said he could name a few Chinese who were waiting for the chance to slit a person's throat, white or Chinese, if they thought they could get some gain. A couple of Chinese had been hacked to pieces by their countrymen for gambling debts.

Samuel knew some men did terrible things. It did not matter what color their skin was.

*   *   *

The following day, Samuel remained near the cabin. The late September sky was deep vivid blue, and the day had warmed. He cut hay, cut some wood, and brought in water. He could not get the bitter thoughts of Finney and Culler out of his mind. Only thoughts of the festival of the moon consoled him. He headed into town to see about the assays and help Hinley if possible.

When he reached the assay shop, he mentioned the festival.

"Festival of the moon," Hinley exclaimed, adjusting his glasses. "I do say our Celestial brethren have brought some interesting customs to town. It takes little for them to find an excuse to celebrate—feast for the dead, Chinese New Year, other celebrations I do not fathom, even our own Independence Day." He began setting out crucibles. "I can see why they seek festivities. I would not wish to be living like them in misery and squalor."

"I don't think they're that unhappy," Samuel replied. "Things in China aren't so grand. I know a good number would be beheaded if they returned. That's the reason most of them are here."

Hinley studied Samuel. "That Chinese boy tell you that?"

"That's Sing Chen. He knows a lot, even though—" Samuel almost said he was born in America but instead continued, "—he hasn't gone to school."

"I will concede that. He seems a smart lad." He started measuring out flux. "Shall we proceed with these assays, Samuel? Perhaps we shall finish a couple of yours from the O'Riley as well."

Samuel spent the remaining time until evening assisting with assays.

*   *   *

When he stepped from the shop, the sun had set, and the dark evening shadows were fast approaching. The pungent and spicy fragrances of food cooking, more than the usual, mingling with burning joss sticks drifted from the area of the Chinese cabins and communal kitchen.

The Chinese were moving about, lighting candles in the dozens of colorful paper lanterns that now hung everywhere—several on each of the Chinese cabins, many on their businesses, some on tall poles lining the street. Other lanterns had been suspended from tree limbs and swayed, flickering in the breeze.

The townspeople gathered to watch, Samuel among them. Chinese singing and music filled the air with singsong voices and hollow flute and guitar. Samuel guessed Chen played his flute.

The lanterns now lit, the sky now dark, the faint light of the moon could be seen to the east above the timbered ridge—the point where it would rise. The gathered Chinese began lighting their individual lanterns and began a twisting parade through the streets of town, led by the lanterns' luminescent glow.

Some lanterns weaved among the others, forming the illusion of moving water. Samuel watched, spellbound. The living lights bobbed and glowed, wandering down through the town and then up through the Chinese cemetery, accompanied by singing and music. Ascending the hill, the lights floated eerily above the ground, flowing, bouncing. Slowly, the lights gathered into a dancing swarm and then began a bobbing, weaving journey back down the hill.

The moon slid into view, orange and then pale luminescent yellow, slowly rising through the black, spidery tree branches, at last free of the earth, hanging suspended, a brilliant, pale globe glowing brilliantly, slowly ascending.

The Chinese broke out food and passed it out among themselves. Samuel was surprised when Chen found him.

"You take this." Chen handed him a small, round pastry. "It is moon cake."

"What's it for?"

"You share it with family and friends."

"Thank you," Samuel said respectfully. He did not ask what was in it; he had learned the Chinese were apt to put dog meat or some strange mushroom in it.

"Duck eggs," explained Chen. "I know you not ask."

Samuel laughed. It was not an unpleasant taste.

"Look, see the moon?" Chen waved toward the luminescent globe. "Rabbit is on the moon, Sam. See his ears near top of moon and round body and belly below."

Samuel decided the shadows on the moon did somewhat resemble a rabbit.

"Rabbit still help Chang'e so someday she come back to earth. Houyi will come too. Happy time for alla earth when they do."

"Thank you for the story, Chen," Samuel replied. "I fear I am learning more about China than I think I am teaching you about America."

"Not true, Sam. Every day when I see you, you teach me about Ahmelicah." Chen nodded.

"The lanterns are beautiful, Chen. The breeze makes them bounce around like they are alive. I wish Pa could have seen."

"Next year," Chen replied.

Samuel wondered how he would explain there would not be a *next year*.

*   *   *

Friday morning, high, thin clouds blocked the sun. By noon, heavy gray clouds had flooded in beneath them. The temperature dropped. Samuel watched from the cabin. He had originally planned to return to the O'Riley and work on obtaining new samples. When the weather began closing in, he thought better of it. It was a cold, penetrating chill. The first snow flurries began early afternoon. By evening, three inches stood on the meadow.

Samuel watched as the snow continued to pile up the next morning. About the time he figured he might be of help at the assay shop, he saw his father coming up the trail, a gray blur in the thickening snow.

Samuel went out to help him unsaddle Buster and stow the gear. He pulled down some hay he had been gathering, glad now he had done so. Both Spooky and Molly had made their way to the stock shed. Samuel pulled the poles across the corral.

"I'm glad I got some hay put up and finally finished that roof."

"So am I, son." Charles put his arm around Samuel, and they walked to the cabin.

Inside, it was good to have a good warm fire against the snow. Samuel began heating some water.

"I don't know if we're done or not," Charles explained. "The snow hit us early, and I didn't think I wanted to stay the entire weekend camped out. Got worse than I thought it would. It's a lot deeper on Steamboat Summit. Buster had trouble pushing through it."

"It's the first snow, Pa." He handed his father some coffee.

"I know. I thought about it the whole way here, and I'm not sure it changes anything." He threw his pouch on the table. "We've been able to stash a bit for a couple weeks, but I'm not sure it's what I hoped for. We might have a week left. What do you want to do?"

"I haven't been back to the O'Riley. Mostly, I helped Mr. Hinley. The assays are okay but not great. He doesn't think they would interest anyone enough to buy the O'Riley."

"I was afraid of that."

"I'm going to hit it hard this coming week, Pa."

"That's a good idea. I expect the weather will warm, and we'll have a couple more weeks of Indian summer. Is it good by you if we last through it?"

"For sure." Samuel felt a rush of joy. Maybe he still had time to prove up the O'Riley.

Chapter 40

I t was early October. Charles had returned to the Ruby placer, and Samuel had set up camp at the O'Riley. He had worked in the main pit, digging it out and expanding it until he reached unaltered granite. The quartz vein was now sandwiched within the hard rock.

He slammed his pick against the vein, chipping small fragments free but not much else. *No way I can dig a pit into this rock without drilling and blasting.*

He began digging beside the rock. Hinley had told him they needed a discovery pit to help prove up the mine. It did not necessarily need to expose ore. He worked alongside the vein downhill slightly and discovered he was soon following the bulge of the rock and no longer getting any quartz. The vein was above him. It was impossible to break through the hard granite and into it. If he had drill steel and a hammer, he might be able to break more pieces free and get a better sample. He wondered about blasting the rock.

He gave up on the pit and spent the remainder of the day breaking out samples from other prospects along the vein. Although he carefully examined the pieces, he could not discern any gold. The pieces still held swarms of gray and black specks so he reassured himself the gold must be there.

Back at his camp that evening, Samuel found himself thinking about Bender's murder and seeing his bleeding body. An uneasiness enveloped him. He hoped O'Riley's spirit was present. He had come to believe O'Riley's spirit would watch over him.

The cold that night kept him from sleeping well. He woke frequently and rebuilt the fire a couple of times. Before light came to the eastern sky, he rose and knocked the frost from his blankets. He pulled on his boots, but his hands stung with cold afterward. He warmed them over the fire. Its heat was welcome against the autumn chill, and he was reluctant to leave its warmth to resume work.

He collected the chips from his prospects and labeled the samples. He then walked off the distance from the main discovery to each spot and recorded the distances. He figured he could extrapolate values based on the distance. At last, he decided he could do no more and headed back toward the cabin.

When he reached it, he wondered about continuing on to the Ruby to talk to his father about buying drill steel and hammers. But he also remembered his father's concern that they could not afford to sink more into the mine than what they might be able to sell it for.

He checked the sluice, hoping to see water. Unlike quartz ore, placer mining was easy. The gold needed little processing. What was found was already gold.

Scarcely a trickle ran in the ditch, and only a couple of inches of water stood in the catch basin, far less than what he needed. He studied the boulders where he had previously dug, remembering the gold he had been finding. If he could only go deeper, there had to be better gold. Maybe another storm would move through and the catch basin would fill.

Later, he visited Scott. He checked the prices on drill steel and hammers.

"Thinking of some real mining?" Scott asked.

Samuel explained their dilemma.

"I think your pa is right. You'll probably spend all the gold you've mined and still not be able to sell the O'Riley. Now's not the time to be trying to sell anyway."

"What if I was able to go down two feet and hit ore worth eighty dollars a ton like some of the other mines around here—it's possible."

"What if you don't?"

"What if I wanted to just do a little drilling and blasting? Maybe enough to get a couple tons of ore out of there?"

"Unfortunately, you can't just go about doing a little mining. You start hardrock mining, you have a big upfront investment." Scott grabbed some items. "You need powder, fuse, and fuse caps. You need a healthy supply of steel and a couple hammers—unless you want to come in every other day to the blacksmith and get the steel sharpened or to replace a handle." Scott began piling the items on the counter. "And this is just a start." He heaved a hammer and pick onto the stack. Samuel felt nervous when he tossed the dynamite and fuse onto the counter as well. "There. That might take you down a couple feet into solid rock, an eight-by-eight hole."

Samuel was dismayed. He already knew the cost of many of the items from carrying them out to the mines.

"This will run you about a hundred and fifty dollars," Scott said. "I know I offered to grubstake you before, but this late in the season ... not a good idea."

Samuel stared at the floor. If his father and he had half that amount, he would be surprised. He wondered if there were some other way.

"I'm sorry, Sam," Scott said. "You have spirit and perseverance—always did have—this is not the time to start mining. You might get enough assays with busting out some rock and be able to sell it as is."

"Thanks, Scott." Samuel quietly left the shop. He did not even have the heart to visit Hinley.

He had a promise to keep, however, and went to visit Ma Reynolds. Soon, he was headed to Sing Mann's store, looking for Chen. He greeted the two Chinese who often gathered in front of the store, where they sat and smoked their long-stemmed pipes. They politely bowed and left. He entered and found Chen.

"If I'm going to help you learn to read and write, I need a place we can work."

Chen spoke rapidly with Mann, explaining. Mann smiled and bowed and gestured toward the back of the store where there was a small table and a couple of chairs.

Samuel opened the book he had picked up from Ma Reynolds. He was not sure where to begin, so he began with the alphabet, writing the letters and having Chen copy them. Afterward, he began teaching him the sounds each letter made.

Chen looked puzzled. He drew some scratchy marks on the paper. "Chinese don't have letters. We have picture marks that say what something is."

"Does that mean the picture marks stand for something, but don't represent sounds of what it is?"

Chen nodded and drew some more. "There, this is bird."

"What kind of bird? Eagle, duck, pigeon?" To Samuel, the ink scratches did not even remotely look like a bird.

"Just bird." Chen added some more marks in front of the symbol. "Now it is duck."

Samuel wrote *b-i-r-d*. "These letters say *bird*. Each letter has its own sound. Some have different sounds for the same letter, but I'll teach you that later. You put the sounds together represented by each letter and get *ba-ih-er-da*. Say it faster, you have *bird*."

He wrote another word *b-a-d*. "This says *ba-a-da. Bad*."

"Bad," Chen said and smiled. "I like Englees. Vehlie easy."

Samuel did not think so, remembering his struggles in school. He wondered if Chen would think it as easy when he learned that the letters could be written cursive or block and that there were capital letters and small letters for each letter and two or three different sounds for each as well.

*   *   *

Samuel spent the next day working at the assay shop. Hinley had still not done any further assays from the O'Riley or the Sheepeater sample. Samuel did not want to seem impatient, but he knew without them, they could not sell the mine. And though he knew the Sheepeater ore had to be good, he could make no decisions regarding it either.

Similar to before, he swept the floor, arranged and stored tools, and brought in charcoal and water.

Late afternoon, they finally ran a couple more assays on samples from the O'Riley.

"These weren't much deeper or from much different locations, were they?" Hinley asked.

Samuel shook his head. "I wasn't able to break much rock, but I took better notes of where they came from. I might be able to get better numbers."

"They run about the same as before. I would guess this one is from near your discovery point. It is running about three ounces."

Samuel was relieved. At least the samples were consistent. None had decreased.

"What about the rich-looking ore I brought in?"

Hinley shrugged. "We know *that's* good. You wished to prove up the O'Riley; therefore, those samples have been my focus. I shall get the others done for you by Monday afternoon."

"I'd be much obliged. I might change my mind." Samuel had been thinking hard.

*   *   *

His father reached the cabin about an hour after he did. Samuel began heating some dinner.

"I only got a couple new assays done, Pa," Samuel explained. "The one from the discovery point is about the same—three ounces—and the other farther along the vein was about one and a half, so the vein is holding up. I tried working the pit but couldn't budge the rock."

"Probably going to need powder."

Samuel shook his head. "I don't know about that, Pa. I talked to Mr. Alexander already. He says we'd need about a hundred-and-fifty-dollar investment to do any drilling and blasting."

Charles did not reply.

"Maybe we can bust out enough rock with just some drill steel and a hammer. When you're done at the Ruby, you can help me."

"I *am* done," Charles said. "We called it today. The gulch is still going, but the ground's pretty much froze, and the water's gone." He was quiet a moment.

"I don't know, son. I don't want to invest all our money back into mining—even just for some steel and hammers," he continued. "Maybe we should just put it up for sale and hope we can get a few dollars to go home with."

Samuel felt his heart sink. After he had discovered the O'Riley, he wanted to mine it. He wanted to see the gold coming out of the ground. If they sold it, sure, they might get a hundred dollars or so, but what if the mine held thousands of dollars in gold? He shook his head, glancing out the window.

"Don't like that idea?"

Samuel tried to explain. "I guess when you get assays saying you found gold, good gold, you want to see it coming out of the ground. You want to hold it. Then you want to see what the next pick will turn up. Like the Sweet Mary—you want to see what the next shovel of dirt will hold."

His father studied him. "Remember when I said mining was like gambling? Each card you turn over might be a winner. It also might be a loser. You have to know when to leave the game."

Samuel felt miserable. He did not want to abandon the game.

Charles laughed. "You certainly did catch that disease old Hallelujah was warning me about." He pushed his hands apart. "Tell you what. We'll go real easy in making this decision. We got time. The weather should warm for a while, but it won't hurt to put out some feelers to see if there's some interest. We can do some checking tomorrow."

Charles reached into his pocket, pulled out his pouch, and handed it to Samuel. "Here, you can add this to our stash."

Samuel hefted the leather pouch with the gold dust. "It's more than two ounces."

Charles smiled. "Pretty soon you aren't going to need a balance to sell things by. We got about a half-ounce bonus."

Samuel opened it and looked in. "It's the best-looking gold yet."

*　　　*　　　*

Sunday, they went ahead and purchased a few pieces of steel and a hammer for single jacking, reducing their money again to a few dollars.

"We can get our investment back when we sell the O'Riley," Charles explained.

Charles went to talk to several people about possibly selling the mine. Samuel left to find Chen.

Sing Mann waved across the street toward another shop. "Chen there."

Samuel had not been in the other shop. Blankets strung across the midsection separated it into two rooms. It carried more tools and gear. Glass lanterns with silk tassels lined one shelf. An urn held a spray of peacock feathers. Samuel studied the iridescent colors. He liked the ornamented vases and urns covered with dragon and fish designs in fiery red, edged in gold.

Chen stood at a counter, waiting, watching a man whom Samuel presumed was the storekeeper manipulating an abacus. Another man stood by.

The storekeeper acknowledged his presence, bowing slightly, and then returned to the abacus. Samuel watched as the man rapidly moved the rows of beads and arrived at a total. The customer laid out some Chinese coins as well as some dust. They were the first Chinese coins Samuel had seen—brass-colored, round with square holes in the center.

An unfamiliar sweet odor wafted from the back room and mixed with the customary incense and oils. Loud, excited voices erupted.

Chen picked up a package wrapped in rice paper. He waved to Samuel and then politely turned and bowed to the storekeeper.

"We go now," he addressed Samuel.

"What's up?"

"They play fan tan and pak kop piu. Lose alla their money."

"What do I smell?"

"Also smoke opium. Lots of opium here. They send it in mail, also pack train, so plenty opium."

"Doesn't the expressman know?"

"Put in tobacco can."

Samuel shook his head. "What's it like?" Samuel wondered.

"Never have any," Chen replied. "Men do not offer it to me. Say it is bad for me. Some Chinese have too much and are no good. Chon Hai is always sleeping. Too much opium. He is no good mining. Opium make you no good."

Samuel nodded. "Then why do they use it?"

Chen laughed. "No Chinese women."

"So?"

Chen shot a puzzled look at Samuel and then shrugged. "Make men feel sleepy. Don't care about problem. Opium make you think there are no problem." He laughed. "But uncle tell me when you wake up, problem still there."

Samuel agreed.

*   *   *

A letter had arrived from his mother. His father and he sat at the table, eager for the news from home:

> *My beloved husband, Charles, and son, Samuel,*
>
> *I am glad to get the news you are well, although I fretted when I heard about Samuel's accident. I would feel more at ease if you both hunted and worked the mining together, but I trust your decisions when you allow Samuel to be off on his own.*
>
> *I do worry about Uncle Jake's and Cousin Daniel's health. Uncle Jake is simply unable to keep up with the work. Cousin Daniel is as thin as a wisp. The boy works from before daylight to after dark and falls asleep in his dinner. He is completely exhausted. He helps Uncle Jake in the fields, hoeing the crops and irrigating. He chops wood and cares for the stock.*
>
> *We are all saddened to learn that the gold mine is nowhere to be found. However, I must judge there is a reason for you to stay in Washington, for you have not indicated that you will be returning soon.*
>
> *I am surprised with you, Samuel, that you have taken up friendship with a Chinese boy. Those people are heathens and not to be trusted. You should never eat their food since they put into it all sorts of vile creatures. Refrain from allowing any into your cabin, as they are infested with vermin.*
>
> *Elizabeth and I are well; however, I fear my mother is not doing well. She does not leave her chair by the window, and her cough is worsening. If she were to see her son-in-law and her grandson, she may be invigorated sufficiently to regain her strength, but I trust your judgment, Charles.*
>
> *I anxiously await your return.*
>
> *Your devoted wife and Samuel's mother,*
> *Mary Chambers*

But the letter disturbed Samuel. The hidden message had been clear—she wished for Samuel to be home doing the work, helping Uncle Jake. Samuel was man enough he could be running the farm while his father looked for gold.

Nevertheless, Samuel wrote a cheerful letter back. He wrote glowingly of the gold his father had earned at the Ruby placer and about the ledge he had discovered. He was reticent to say much because he had learned that many of the strikes never proved to be more than a "glint in the pan" as he had so often heard. He was careful to avoid any mention of seeing the Sheepeaters. He did tell her about the Chinese opium use and how Chen avoided it, hoping it would make her think more kindly of him. He told her the story about one expressman who was bringing in the mail and how the bag was digging holes into his back because of some hard objects. Finally, the expressman could take the discomfort no longer, ripped off the pack, and beat the bag with a limb until the protruding objects had been flattened and no longer poked him. When the expressman reached Washington, he discovered the cans he had been hammering were tobacco tins full of opium. The opium leaked out and glued all the letters together. He assured her that her letter was not among them.

Carefully, he folded some small, flat nuggets into a piece of paper and included them with the letter.

CHAPTER 41

A day later, Charles and Samuel turned down the street toward the assay office and met several men clustered about, talking. Sheriff Sinclair sat his bay, his tan frock coat catching the morning sun, another man with him. One man gestured toward his father and spoke his name. Sinclair looked up.

"The Chinese pack train went out yesterday and got hit," Sinclair explained.

"Anyone hurt?"

A couple of men started talking, one nodding.

"I'll fill you in later," Sinclair said. "I just got here. I'm looking for a couple men willing to go with me and give me a hand. Right now, all I got is Ned Waxman."

Ben Morton, one of the men standing in the street, muttered, "Not many of us care that it got hit. The yellow heathens can all go to hell as far as I care. It's our gold anyhows."

Sinclair turned on him. "I already got your opinion, Ben. Whether you like it or not, we're bound by law to protect them as well."

Another man spoke, "It's not so much we don't want to give you a hand, sheriff. You know the chances of catching them are next to nothing. They hit them near the Secesh. We won't even be there for a day. They have six or so trails they can take out of there."

"Probably so, but I got an obligation to try. I'm not asking much. A couple more men, and we'll head out."

Ned interjected, "You all know if we don't do somethin', they'll be back. Next time, it could be our gold they jump."

"What gold?" someone scoffed, bringing a laugh from the group.

"I'll go," Charles offered.

Samuel looked up. "Take me with you, Pa."

Sinclair turned around. "Thanks, Samuel, but you're the one I won't take. You already had your fair share of trouble."

Sinclair addressed the group, "Anyone going meet me back here. I got a couple more folks to check with."

The men began disbanding.

"I'll be okay, Samuel," Charles said. "I'm not working right now. This camp's been good to us. You go ahead and meet with Mr. Hinley. I'll see you on my way out of town." Charles did not wait for Samuel's reply. He headed at a quick trot back toward the cabin for his gear.

*   *   *

Hinley had been watching from his shop. "I presume you know what has happened."

"The Chinese pack train got hit," Samuel confirmed.

"It was Hong King's. He owns that big saloon. The scoundrels probably surmised this pack string would be carrying gold being it was near the last of the season."

Samuel knew it was. Chen had hinted it would be.

"Who got hurt?" Samuel was concerned for the Chinese.

"One of the Celestials from Lewiston got shot in the leg. He shall survive." Hinley handed a piece of ore to Samuel along with his glass. "Have a look before it is pulverized."

Samuel took the glass and sample but hesitated. "They get anything?"

"Aye, they got the gold. That was what they were after." Hinley laid out his tools. "Your friend, that Chinese boy—what's his name again? He has been doing most of the interpreting."

"That's Chen."

"Chen," Hinley said. "Seems like a smart boy. I mean, for a Celestial. You and he get along."

"I reckon."

"They tore the pack string up quite thoroughly and then proceeded to ransack all the packs, but the Celestials nearly bested them." Hinley laughed. "The scoundrels darn near missed the gold. The Celestials had most of it sewn into pouches and hidden on themselves. Oh, there was some decoy gold in the packs but not much."

Hinley set some of the ore on the grinding plate and motioned to Samuel. "Are you going to look at that or not?"

Samuel held the glass to his eye and studied the sample. His breath caught. A smear of tiny specks of gold ran across the piece in and among numerous specks of gray. "It's rich." Samuel beamed. He handed it to Hinley. "Where'd you get it? That's a rich piece of ore."

"Aye, it is." He tossed it onto the plate. "I thought you would have recognized it. It's yours from that rich spot. You have forgotten that I told you I would get it run today."

Samuel sat down, unsure of what to do. "Pa wants to leave, you know."

"Aye, lad," Hinley replied, beginning to mull the pieces. "Would you like to do this?" He gestured at the muller. "What about you? Do you want to leave?"

"I'm not sure." Samuel began pulverizing the Sheepeater sample, watching the tiny pieces explode under the muller. "Something about finding the O'Riley and the spot where this came from … it's hard to explain. I don't just want to sell out. I want to see what's there. I want to see the gold in it."

"You can come back."

Samuel did not reply.

*　　　*　　　*

Charles returned, having packed his gear, and said good-bye. "I'm taking the rifle." He handed the pistol to Samuel.

Samuel took it, unsure of what to say or what he would do. "Guess I'll take the steel and hammer up to the O'Riley and try to break out ore on the discovery spot where it seems richest."

"That would be good." Charles turned to Hinley. "Think you can start putting out the word we have a decent strike? See if anyone has any interest in buying a mine?"

"It's not a mine yet," Hinley said, a bit unkindly.

"I reckon not," Charles said, brushing off the comment. "Samuel's been bringing out enough assays. Wouldn't you say that someone might be interested?"

"Perhaps, but not likely until spring … and most likely not until you do some drilling and blasting and have a good vein showing."

"I can see your point, but now I got to do what I can." Charles turned to go. "Thanks, Ray, for giving my son a shot at this. Don't know if he'll ever use what you taught him, but he seems to know what he's doing."

"Aye," Hinley replied.

Samuel shook his father's hand. "Be safe, Pa."

"I will, though I doubt we'll catch up to them. But if they know we're taking them seriously, they might not be back to try it again."

Samuel watched his father trot away on Buster. "I'm guessing they *will* be back again," he said quietly. "The pickings around here are too easy." He resumed working down the Sheepeater ore.

"When you get that quartered, you may prepare it for firing. I have several samples ready to go."

Samuel thought of the highwaymen. "Any idea how many bandits there were?" He figured it would take a bunch to stop a thirty-six-animal pack train.

"Someone said three, maybe four."

"And they jumped an entire pack train?"

"You know the Celestials. They would have no weapons other than knives. I'm certain they put up no fight." Hinley opened the furnace and began packing it with charcoal.

"Except that one of them got himself shot."

"That was purely by accident."

Samuel smiled; he could see that possibility.

"Unfortunately, your father and the posse shall not get close. You know this country, lad. It will swallow up a man pretty quick, particularly if he chooses not to be found." Hinley began measuring flux into the small tin cups. "In the event you're wondering, I'm adding a mite more litharge. Your samples are carrying respectable silver."

Samuel began to quarter the samples.

"You do understand there are those around who didn't mind seeing the Celestials' string get jumped. There are those talking about it not being right that they are taking our gold and sending it to China. Some have confided in me their desire to remove them from their old claims and have sought my help to do so. Ben Morton is one. To that, I say poppycock. Nevertheless, there are an increasing number who feel justified in taking the Celestials' gold."

"I caught a bit of that," Samuel replied. He finished reducing the sample to a few ounces. "Sample's ready for weighing."

"Bring it to the balance, and you shall proceed."

Samuel felt honored but uneasy. Hinley never allowed him near the balances. "You want a full assay-ton or a half?"

"I recommend two half-ton assays, Samuel, just for good measure. It will give us a check in case the numbers look crazy."

Samuel selected the half-ton weight and carefully measured out the equivalent in powdered sample until it balanced. He dumped it into a clean crucible and began weighing the second.

"You almost look like you know what you are doing," Hinley commented. He mixed in the flux and added the borax.

Together, they fit the samples into the furnace along with four other crucibles. Hinley ignited the charcoal and sealed the furnace. "I can tend these if you want to drop by later."

"Sure," Samuel said. "I have an errand I'm on."

"You know, Samuel, I don't mind saying this. When you arrived town, I did not believe you or your father had a chance in Hades to succeed. Today, I can say I never met anyone new to this country to make two strikes like you have done—three if you count your placer."

"Thanks." Samuel felt warmed but also distressed. They had found gold but nothing like they had hoped. "You gave me a lot of pointers, Mr. Hinley."

"I did, but you put the teaching to use," Hinley said and then fixed his eyes on Samuel. "I just cannot fathom why you do not follow up on this strike. From its looks, you would have a rich producer. For sure, I do not understand."

"It's hard to explain. Let's say I got a lot of figuring to do before I go."

*   *   *

Samuel left the assay shop and went to Sing Mann's to find Chen. "Do some reading?" he asked.

Chen lit up, smiling. "Sure, Sam." He led the way to the table in the back.

Samuel pulled out the book from Ma Reynolds and the stack of papers he had Chen writing on.

"I have some tea." Chen reached for the pot on the woodstove.

"I would like that," Samuel replied. "You know we're fixin' to head out?"

Chen paused in pouring the tea.

"We will take what gold we've found and return home."

"I understand. I will miss you, Sam. I have much to learn about Ahmelicah," Chen said quietly and resumed pouring.

"I will miss learning about China."

Chen smiled. "You will miss Chinese New Year. In winter, we have two weeks of celebration. We light many firecrackers every day and have parade. Have lots to eat. Even Ahmelicahns will join us. Many gifts for everyone. New year is year of monkey," Chen explained.

"Year of the monkey?"

"Now is year of goat. Twelve years, twelve animals. I was born in year of dragon." Chen addressed Samuel. "How many years are you, Sam?"

"I'm fifteen in December."

Chen laughed. "One year under me. You born in year of snake."

Samuel shivered, remembering the rattlesnake. "You know my pa went with the posse?"

"Then you will not leave for a few days. That is good. I want to read more before you go."

Samuel flipped open the book. "Did anyone know who they were? The men who held up Hong King's train?"

"They say they look like men who roped Kan Dick."

"Finney and Culler." An icy feeling flooded Samuel. "What about the others?"

"Ohnee one. Other, no one ever see him."

"I'm sorry they got the Chinese gold, Chen."

Chen shrugged. "Bandits take white man gold also."

"I suppose." Samuel spread out the papers. "Shall we?" He pointed to words, and Chen responded with what they were. Samuel had him repeat them, trying to teach him how to pronounce them correctly. Next, he had Chen write the words. Each time they had met, he went over the words Chen knew, and he added a few new ones. He had only linked a few words, such as *thank you* and *I am Sing Chen.*

Samuel was still thinking about the robbery. "They got a lot of gold, didn't they, Chen?"

Chen nodded.

"That gold was going back to China for families and for land. Some of it was yours."

"Yes. Some go to pay boss man. Some go to buy food and tools. Some go to company that helps us."

"That means some of your people will have to stay in America longer."

"Yes, must stay in land of foreign devil longer."

"What?"

"Land of foreign devil. You the devil." Chen grinned.

"I'm not the devil."

"All Ahmelicahn foreign devil. This is the land of foreign devil." Chen nodded solemnly.

Samuel was quiet for a moment. "The Chinese didn't have to come here."

"No choice, Sam. This also the land of the golden mountain. Chinese men say China is bad. Many Chinese are hunted by emperor and killed. People lose land in war. Then drought. Many people starve. Too many people. Chinese had to leave China. Come to Ahmelicah. Ahmelicah has none of these problems."

Samuel understood America meant opportunity for the Chinese. "But we do have problems. Outlaws just stole your gold. We just fought a war over slavery."

"Yes, now no slave in Ahmelicah," Chen agreed, brightening. "In China, still many slave. Some Chinese bling slave here." Chen looked away. "If saloon man find me, he own me. Same as slave."

"Slaves, Chen. Try to say the 'S.'"

"Slave-ss."

Samuel frowned. "So the Chinese come to the land of the devil because the devil is not as bad as the opportunities."

"No, he bad, but not as bad as *things in China*." Chen looked at Samuel. "Don't worry, Sam. You have ohnee little devil in you."

"Gee, thanks." Samuel grinned. "And you can all go back to China."

Chen's face became serious again. "That is what we want. We are sojourners. We go back to China. We here ohnee for short time, but we can't pay boss man, can't pay company, can't get money to send home to family. Can't go home. Ohnee a few Chinese come to land of golden mountain and go back home."

Samuel wondered if Chen would also be trapped in America, but he knew Chen was smart. If anyone could make it here, he could, but what family would he return to? He had been born in San Francisco.

"Do you hear from your uncle and grandparents?"

Chen shook his head. "Sometime, but too dangerous. Saloon man find me."

Samuel guessed the letters he wrote were at risk of being intercepted.

"Sing Mann sometime hears. Things are not good, Sam." A shadow crossed Chen's face. "I hear bad things all around my family. Maybe go home and will not have family."

Samuel felt an emptiness. Chen had never known his relatives in China and possibly never would.

They worked for a while longer until Samuel figured Hinley had finished the assays.

"I think that is enough for today, Chen. I will come by on Sunday if you wish."

"Maybe I will not be here. I go to gardens all winter to help Sang Yune build new garden."

Samuel folded the papers and handed them to Chen. "You should practice. Write the words you know. Maybe Mr. Hinley will help you. He thinks you're smart." On impulse, he handed him the book as well. "Take the book. You can look through it for words you know. Write down the words you want to learn. See Mr. Hinley."

"Cannot take book."

"Yes, take it." Samuel made him take it, pushing it into his hands much like Chen had done with the green onions when they had first met. "So long, Chen. You have been a good friend."

"No, I wait to see you before you go, Sam. Then say good-bye."

* * *

Samuel thought about the assays. Hardly able to contain himself, he almost ran to the shop.

"How'd it go?" he asked, thumping through the door.

Hinley raised his hand, pencil grasped in his fingers, causing Samuel to pause. He was in the process of weighing the final button. Samuel knew even a breath of air could cause the balance to fluctuate. Hinley finished writing some numbers.

"What? You think I should have some good news for you?"

"I think you do."

He handed the first paper across to Samuel.

It read 5.9 ounces in gold. Silver was 13.3 ounces. Samuel's heart raced.

"Here's the control." Hinley handed him the second paper. It read 6.2 ounces in gold and 14.3 ounces of silver.

"Quite simply, that is the best assay I have seen since arriving here," Hinley said quietly. "At least on a sample that has not been handpicked high-grade."

Samuel felt stunned; prickles washed his face. He wanted to sit down. As much as he wanted to scream for joy, he put his head in his hands.

"What? I thought for sure you'd be asking for help on the paperwork for a new claim. And if you ask me, I have a name for it as well ... the Samuel Chambers. It's going to be rich, Samuel."

Samuel found himself laughing. "I guess I got some figuring to do. Got to sell one in order to stake the other."

"You can drop the O'Riley."

Samuel did not know what to think. He remembered the Sheepeaters. He remembered the arrow back at the cabin. "I got some *serious* figuring to do."

A loaded pack train passed by the window.

"Another outfit heading out to winter, I surmise," Hinley observed. "I have been counting them over the past few days. I know of no placers still operating, and I expect fewer shall resume in the spring," he mused. "Now it will be the hardrock miners and the snow. It will be a quiet winter."

"What are you going to be doing?"

"Same as before. Most of my work is for the quartz mines. All four of the big mines and a couple of the smaller ones—about sixty miners—will work through the winter. I've already enough assay work to last all winter. Plus, I shall do a few runs of fines and refine a few bars of gold."

CHAPTER 42

His father with the posse, Samuel returned to the O'Riley with the steel and hammer. He searched the pits he had dug for any sign of better ore he might have missed, digging on a few spots, using the steel and hammer to break out pieces he could. He stacked the quartz to the side. The vein was well exposed where he had worked it. Samuel felt some satisfaction. Production off the entire vein should be significant.

He returned to the main discovery pit. Hinley had instructed him to go as deep as possible along the vein. If they started drilling and blasting, this would be the site where they would possibly put in a hoist shaft. The two assays had shown this was the best material.

All day he swung the hammer against the granite, pulverizing it into small pieces, but he found it difficult to remove much from around the vein. In places, he wedged the steel into the cracks, pried chunks of rock loose, and rolled them from the excavation. Whenever he managed to expose the quartz vein, he chiseled it out and stacked it, but he was recovering very little. The surrounding granite was becoming more resistant. Maybe his father and he could do better—when his father returned.

He swung with the hammer against the steel; it bounced from the rock, slamming his knuckles into the rough granite. Instinctively, he brought his injured hand to his mouth and nursed the cut. Blood oozed from three or four skinned areas. Shaking his hand, he tried to relieve the sting. Drops of blood spattered onto the broken rock. He shook it again and looked up as if to check if anyone had seen.

Samuel took another swing. The point of the steel penetrated the rock, and he pried out some fragments. More blood spattered onto the white quartz. Blood trickled down his fingers. He put the hammer down and washed his hand with water from his canteen. He walked back toward his camp for a piece of cloth to bind his wound.

Fading light on the peaks to the east caught his attention. Despite his pain, the beauty caused him to pause. A strange feeling overtook him. This was his strike. Through his sweat and blood, he was free to dig out the gold and do with it as he liked. He could make a living doing this. The work was difficult, but he was free to put in the effort. God would reward his efforts; he knew it.

For a moment, he thought of his family. He recognized the sacrifices they had made for him, and now he was on the eve of making his own way. This was work he could do. But there was still an emptiness. Something was missing. He thought of Miss Lilly but shook his head. Although the longing was there, it was more than what Miss Lilly could give, and now he had come to realize it.

Samuel reached his gear and tore apart a piece of cloth that he had wrapped food in and bound his hand. An inexplicable ache had grown within his chest.

After some dinner, he watched the stars begin to come into view. He picked out the Big Dipper and located the North Star. He tried to pick out Draco, the dragon, the constellation between the Big and Little Dippers. He recalled Chen was born in the year of the dragon.

The temperature dropped. Samuel picked up a piece of wood to add to the fire and was caught by its curved shape. It could be a dragon. He ran his hand along it, noting where it had been broken from the tree's trunk. The end was split, forming what looked remarkably like an open mouth with ragged teeth. He set it aside and tossed some other pieces of wood onto the fire. Later, he carefully placed the "dragon" into his saddlebag.

*   *   *

The following morning was bitter cold. The seep where he had been collecting water for camp was frozen. Samuel built a fire and melted ice for a short time, getting water to drink. He knew he could not work much longer, at least not without taking the animals for water.

He warmed the steel and hammer before he returned to work, but by the time he got to the pit, it had cooled. He built a second fire nearer to the pit but found himself frequently pausing to warm his fingers and the steel. Wispy clouds began filling the northwestern sky—typically ones that brought snow.

In one last effort, Samuel located the area on the vein that appeared darkest gray and worked at it until he had enough chips for another good sample. He examined a couple pieces, imagining he could see some tiny specks of gold.

The clouds had thickened, and his breath hung heavy in the still air. By the time he had struck camp and packed his gear, it had begun snowing. It was a wet snow, large flakes, penetrating cold.

Samuel could not help but look around before he headed down the hill. Could this be the last time he would ever see this spot? Spooky stamped his impatience while Samuel paused. Would this be another empty pit someone happened upon years in the future and wondered about who had dug it and why?

* * *

The snow continued the next day. Samuel pulled hay down for the stock and kept the stove hot. His father returned on the evening.

"Rain and snow turned us around near the Salmon River canyon," he explained. "Got anything hot?"

Samuel poured him some coffee.

He took a sip. "Nice to have something hot. Got downright cold in a hurry. I wouldn't doubt the snow we see on the peaks after this will stick." He began pulling his boots off, examining one. "Going to have to get a new pair," he muttered. "Yours still holding up?"

"They're good." Samuel turned them for his father to see. "Did you catch them?"

"We got close," Charles said, leaning back. "We split up, and Waxman and Bleau followed their tracks down a gulch near French Creek. I guessed they might double back and convinced the sheriff to go with me down another gulch. Waxman and Bleau jumped them, and they exchanged fire. Too far out of range to put much pressure on them though."

Samuel added more wood to the stove.

"But they did try to turn up our way, and we cut them off. They saw us and turned back down so it was a long shot. They fired a couple of rounds at us. I returned fire and came mighty close. May have nicked one of the horses. The black that one of them was riding sure went crazy, almost cartwheeled. Threw the man, but one of his partners helped him up. They skedaddled."

"Probably Finney," Samuel interjected. "Was one of the other horses a dun?"

"Another light-colored horse, maybe."

"That was Culler."

Charles studied Samuel. "You remember their horses?"

"I ran into a couple bad guys before, remember?" Samuel replied. Vivid images of Dudgin and Smith came back. When he first saw Finney and Culler, they had reminded him of Dudgin and Smith. "They—" Samuel shook his head, struggling with a new thought as a clammy fear crept over him. He remembered Chen's description. "They *look like* men who roped Kan Dick."

Charles lowered his cup. "You look like you just saw a ghost."

It took a moment before Samuel could speak.

"Pa, it might not be Finney and Culler. No one on that pack string had ever seen Finney and Culler. The packers could only describe them. You and Sheriff Sinclair were too far off to recognize their horses." Samuel found himself shaking. "I'm thinking ... it was those scum who murdered Bender, the same ones who were thinking of dry-gulching us on our way in—Dudgin and Smith."

"Those scum? I'd near forgotten about them."

"I took great care to remember them, Pa. They intended to kill me. They probably got a new partner is all."

"Could be, son," he said, shaking his head, "but I doubt it. I can't imagine them being foolhardy enough to come back here." He drained his cup. "Anyhow, it started raining on us in the canyon, and they had their pick of trails, so we called it off. Sheriff went on ahead with Waxman to spread the word. Sent me and Bleau back."

Chalres refilled his cup. "So tell me what's up with the O'Riley."

Samuel could not shake his thoughts about Dudgin and Smith. He could barely keep his thoughts focused on the samples he had collected and the digging he had done.

"Time I looked it over," Charles said. "We'll give her a try when the snow quits."

Samuel was not so sure the snow would quit and that winter had not arrived.

*   *   *

News reached Warren's camp of the Chicago fire. Men stood in the streets, talking and wondering about relatives and friends. Some commented on the fires they had lived with for two years and how fortunate none had burned through the camp. Samuel tried to imagine the destruction. If all of Washington burned, it would be but a burnt match in a forest fire in comparison.

The next several days, the weather turned pleasant, and the snow melted except for in the shadows and on the higher peaks. The aspens and willows had shed their leaves. The landscape had turned somber gray and muted green.

Father and son packed the tent and gear and headed up toward the O'Riley. Samuel's repeated trips had etched a thin trail into the earth. They camped farther down the gulch where some water still seeped through a small meadow, where the stock could get water and grass.

Samuel took his father to the O'Riley and showed him the sample sites along the vein.

Charles stood for a moment. "You did all this? From the looks, I would have figured it to be ten men." He climbed down into one of the small pits, bent down, and examined it, running his hand across the exposed quartz. "This is a good-looking vein, son. This is what miners seek. I think you've got something here."

Samuel pointed to the chipped areas where some of the gray specks showed. "You can't see it, but there's gold in this," he said. "Actually, most of the gray is galena and silver."

"It's a lot different than placer gold," Charles mused. "There's no mistaking when you see placer gold in a sluice box."

They began breaking out what quartz they could, adding it to the stacks Samuel had begun.

"We should have invested in powder and fuse. This isn't going to get us very far."

Samuel knew but did not comment.

By the end of the second day, they had what they figured to be the better part of three tons, mostly loose pieces they had collected from along the vein.

"We mill this, the results might help convince someone to buy the mine," Charles insisted. "Then we're heading home."

*　　　*　　　*

The following day, Charles visited with the mill owners, attempting to find one who would process their ore within a few days. Samuel remained behind, bringing in some more hay and doing some cooking for the upcoming week. Late afternoon, he inspected the sluice. He was surprised to see some water had collected in the catch basin, almost enough to run a few buckets of gravel. He began digging around the boulders and scraping out some gravel.

Charles rode up, noticing. "Still trying to get under those boulders?"

"The snow melted, and we got some water, so I figured I'd try a few buckets." Samuel straightened. "But somebody else is going to have to drill and shoot these boulders to get them out."

"Maybe we should. Nothing else seems to be working out."

"What do you mean?"

Charles swung down from Buster. "It's unlikely we'll be able to have any ore processed before next spring."

Samuel leaned heavily against his shovel. "That for sure?"

"Pretty much. Let's go warm up. I'll tell you about it."

Samuel stoked the fire and when the coffee had heated, poured some.

"None of the mills can run our ore. They all have contracts with the mines and can't shut down and do a cleanup to run our small amount. The earliest anyone could run our ore is the mill at the Charity, and that would be in February."

"The middle of winter."

"To them, it doesn't matter. They operate year-round." Charles sipped his coffee. "Our ore should be processed using Mr. Bradshaw's mill. That's two miles farther than the Charity. You already know they won't open till sometime in early spring. The good news is they agreed to fit us in if we can get some ore to them. Mr. Bradshaw is thinking most of the ore will come from his Summit vein." Charles ran his hand through his hair. "You know we were over there last spring—where we first started looking for O'Riley's ledge."

"Yes, I realized that when I was talking to Mr. Hinley. Those prospectors we ran into that day—that's where the Summit is."

"I wasn't going to tell you. We were probably standing on it."

Samuel nodded, remembering. "If you want, I can get a mortar and pestle," he suggested. "It might be our only chance. I could hand-select some ore. Let the buyer know it was hand-selected, and he could make his offer accordingly."

Charles pushed his hands apart. "I think we should just turn the cabin back over to Mr. Alexander and let Mr. Hinley sell the O'Riley and head home while the weather holds."

Samuel felt devastated. He was not ready. He did not want to walk away. There was still some time. He stared at the floor, a burning coming to his eyes.

"We could stay a couple weeks, even drill and blast, but I think we'd just be up to our ears in snow trying to get out of here, and we still wouldn't have a buyer. If we do stay, we'll just be burning through the rest of the gold we've saved to take home."

Samuel nodded. He realized unless the gold was crumbling free of the quartz, their chances of selling and making any decent money were pretty slim. His mine might be a good one—even a rich one—but only time would tell, and they did not have time.

*   *   *

Early morning when they rose, frost covered the meadow in a thick, white, glistening layer. It etched the needles of the conifers and outlined the branches of the shrubs. Steam floated above the creek, tracing its path through the meadow. The stock breathed heavy clouds into the still morning air. The sun rose, turning the woods into a glittering, sparkling kaleidoscope of colors.

They officially put the O'Riley up for sale. Hinley advised them it would not likely sell. "Certainly not until next summer when investors are more likely, but I shall try."

"We'll leave in a few days," Charles said. "Got some business to wrap up yet." He addressed Samuel. "If you want to say good-bye to your Chinese friend, now's a good time."

Samuel was thankful his father had guessed. He hoped Chen had not already left for the South Fork, but Chen had said he would see him before he left.

The usual two Chinese, who often sat under the overhang and smoked their long-stemmed pipes, nodded to Samuel, smiling. "Hehwoh." They no longer rose to leave when he arrived.

Sing Mann, dressed in his red tunic edged in gold, stood with his hands in his cuffs as was his custom. He bowed slightly when Samuel came in. "Hehwoh, Mistah Samyew."

Samuel bowed in return. "Hello, Mann," he replied. "It's good to see you."

Mann nodded and smiled. "Chen here."

Chen came from the back part of the store, the pungent odor of joss sticks following after.

They greeted each other. Chen's dark eyes flashed, revealing his distress. "You are going?"

"Yes, I'm heading out soon, Chen. I want you to have this." He handed Chen the dragon he had carved from the twisted piece of wood. He had drawn some black, frowning eyes and painted the body red.

Chen's eyes sparkled; he grinned broadly.

"You were born in the year of the dragon. I found the stick and thought you should have it."

Chen cast his eyes frantically around. He spoke briefly to Mann. "Thank you, Sam."

Mann stepped away and then returned, handing Samuel a small brass snake. "Mann and I would like to give you this ... for year of the snake."

"You don't have to." Samuel hated snakes. He figured the Chinese astrology had it wrong when it came to him, but he accepted the gift.

Mann spoke rapidly, smiling broadly, gesturing toward Chen.

Chen quietly interpreted, "He says man born in year of dragon is special, honest, and brave."

Mann spoke again, looking at Samuel as he spoke.

"He says man born in year of snake work very hard, bring joy, and is very wise." Chen smiled. "Mann knows these things. He is very wise as well."

Mann addressed Samuel. "All true." He bowed.

"That's Chinese astrology," Samuel said. "I confess I don't place much faith in astrology. God blesses us all and gives us all gifts. It's up to each of us to use them."

"Yes. He give you gifts of wisdom and bringing joy."

Samuel shrugged. He was not getting anywhere.

Mann spoke again, making a sweeping circle with his hands and bringing them together. He briefly bowed toward Chen and then toward Samuel.

Chen was silent until Mann addressed him questioningly.

"He says snake and dragon make good friends. Not so much with other snakes or different animals. You snake. I am dragon. He says we are good friends."

Samuel nodded. He could not argue with either claim. And now he was saying good-bye.

"He says we will see each other again. We are tied strong together."

Samuel felt shaken, wondering. Sing Mann smiled, nodding.

CHAPTER 43

Samuel made his way toward the assay shop. After the number of times he had been in town, he wondered why he had not seen Miss Lilly. Every time he came to town, he worried he would meet her. Every time, he wondered what he would do. Maybe he could just visit and talk, but then other possibilities stormed through his mind. He thought it best to avoid her.

As if she were reading his mind, she appeared.

"Hello, Miss Lilly," Samuel managed. He did not think she looked as bouncy as usual.

"I thought I might miss you," she murmured. "I seen you a couple times going to the assay shop."

"I'm still helping Mr. Hinley sometimes."

"But now you're leaving?"

"Before the winter hits," Samuel replied. He studied her face. It looked drawn.

"I thought you might have come by, and I missed seeing you. I've been ill awhile. But I'm good now." She smiled, but Samuel sensed something lacking.

"I got work right now," Samuel said, and he immediately felt miserable. "I got to go."

"I'll still see you?"

Samuel knew she would not. "I'm sorry. My pa wants us to leave. We're headin' out soon before the winter sets in."

Miss Hattie came walking toward them. "Lilly, you need to be coming in." She took her arm.

"Hi, Samuel." She beamed. "It's getting cold. Lilly and I need to be headin' in." She started to lead Lilly away. Aside, she said, "And if'n you want, my place is a lot warmer than that cabin of yours."

Lilly frowned and then quietly said, "If I don't see you before you go,

Samuel, I'll be looking for you first thing in the spring." Miss Hattie swept her away.

"Good-bye, Miss Lilly." Samuel did not have the opportunity to correct her thoughts or the heart to do so. He went into the assay shop.

*   *   *

Hinley greeted him and handed him the O'Riley sample. "You might as well get started on this. We should be able to fire it tomorrow. How much time do you have?"

"I can work for a while."

For Hinley to trust him made Samuel proud, but he also wondered if he would ever work on another assay. He dumped the pieces from the bag and began pulverizing them.

Hinley watched. "I must admit I have been dwelling on that rich sample we assayed. I cannot fathom why you would not wish to develop that ledge— unless there is a reason you have not disclosed."

"Partly there is a reason," Samuel replied, scraping the small pieces together. "It's hard to reach and will be even harder to get ore out of there. I knew we couldn't do anything with it, since we never planned on staying."

"Sell it."

Samuel shook his head. "I guess part of me says I'll be back someday." He rolled the muller across the particles.

"I can understand that."

"So if someone shows up and asks you about it, you can assume I'm not coming back. They'll be like me looking for O'Riley's ledge."

Hinley shook his head. "Personally, I shall hope to see you, Samuel. I know you have an obligation to your father, but soon, you shall be your own man."

"I reckon."

"You know you could winter on the Salmon and finish things next spring."

"Pa is set on going back," Samuel said. "We wouldn't know where to camp anyhow."

"I knew a man who started a homestead a few miles downstream from Shearer's ferry. I don't know if he got much of a cabin built, but he had a fair-paying winter placer." Hinley began measuring flux. "There's also a bar a bit farther down where you could pitch a tent. No one would run you off if you're there over winter."

*　　　*　　　*

A day later, Charles and Samuel headed into Washington to settle up with Hinley.

They entered the assay shop.

Charles asked, "Any buyers?"

"Is it spring yet?" Hinley eyed him.

"How did the assays come out?" Samuel asked.

"Actually, quite good." Hinley's tone indicated that he had not expected the results.

Samuel was not certain he had heard correctly.

He handed the papers to Charles. "Each of your assays ran just over 3.8 ounces."

Samuel grinned. "You know that's pretty much high-grade. I was breaking rock out of the best place I could find."

Hinley nodded. "Aye. However, an investor shall know that. You have been honest, for which I can vouch."

"And no one's interested." Charles tossed down the papers.

"It's nigh on winter, Charles," Hinley replied. "No one can begin to develop a mine like the O'Riley until next season. No mill is nearby, and looking at the weather, the O'Riley will likely be under snow within the week and shall not be out from underneath it until June. No one wishes to tie up his money any longer than necessary."

Charles stood quietly.

Samuel knew what his father was thinking. They would be going home pretty much empty-handed just as they had come.

"You know, Charles," Hinley began, "it's not my business, but you might say I have welcomed Samuel's help. He could be successful with this business, and although I do not need the competition, I could use an assistant."

"Thanks, Ray," Charles said. "We've pretty much been bothering you since we got here. I figure if you get an offer on the O'Riley, you can handle the details for us. I'll give you a percentage for your trouble."

"Another thing to consider, Charles," Hinley continued. "I know a place down on the Salmon you could placer for the winter until you could get back here and finish proving up the O'Riley."

"Samuel told me about the place," Charles replied. "I'm obliged."

"A fair number of men move to the Salmon for the winter, work some of the bars down there, and then return in the spring. They manage to stay alive."

"Thanks, Ray. You've always been a help."

"Sorry, Charles, not my business," Hinley said. "Just after all your hard work, it does me no pleasure watching you walk out on it."

Charles nodded and folded the papers. "What do I owe you?"

Hinley shook his head. "Drop by on your way out."

*   *   *

The next morning, his father returned to Washington, and Samuel remained behind to do some packing. On a whim, he checked the sluice a final time. He was pleasantly surprised to see a good amount of water in the catch basin. The recent rain and snows had saturated the ground. He brought up some of the last gravel he had started to dig a few days ago and released the water. He sprinkled it in, watching as the water washed it through the sluice, spreading it downward, the black sand lagging behind, catching behind the cleats, and sometimes revealing some bright specks of gold.

Samuel grabbed the last bucket and sprinkled it in. He watched as the gravel washed through, and then he froze, disbelieving. Winking in the sunlight were several small nuggets sitting in a swarm of finer gold. *Pay dirt!* Needles of joy washed across him.

He scraped more gravel from around the boulders and washed it through the sluice, dipping the last of the water from the catch basin by bucket to finish. More small nuggets showed. Samuel could hardly contain himself.

He studied the gulch and began doing some rough measurements. What he determined caused his heart to race. He reworked his figures and came up with the same conclusion.

Samuel picked out what remaining gold he could from the sluice—nearly a third of an ounce—and then brought buckets of water from the spring creek and washed the remaining fines from the sluice into a tub. He lugged the tub back to the creek where he washed the fines down, picking out the remaining larger gold particles. Finished, he piled the fines where he could find them and carried the tools back to the cabin.

Late afternoon, his father returned. "I been working out details on selling everything. I talked to Mr. Alexander about this place. I said for him to sell the cabin for what he could and send us fifty dollars."

"That won't be near enough." Samuel handed him nearly half an ounce of coarse gold.

His father looked up. "What in blazes?"

Samuel laughed. "Off the Sweet Mary, Pa. It came from deeper around the boulders."

"That's the best we've seen."

"I went for one last look at the placer and saw there was enough water so I ran as much gravel as I could." Samuel was silent for a moment. "Pa, I been thinking about it real hard, doing some ciphering. I figure based on how much gravel I've dug and run and on what I figure still remains, we could have twenty ounces." Samuel showed the paper he had done his figuring on to his father.

Charles stopped halfway to taking a drink of coffee and almost slammed the cup down, taking the paper.

"It can't be that much."

"That's just to clear out around the boulders. I've been figuring the gravel is getting richer about half again for every foot I go down. If you look at the angle the gulch makes, the gravel should go down another two to three feet before we hit bedrock. We're in a good seam of gravel that could be rich—really rich."

Charles was silent.

"You know all the gold you hit at McLane's placer when you hit bedrock? I figure we're about to do the same thing. That means we could get thirty to forty ounces in just a few days."

Charles ran his hands through his hair. "Not a thing we can do about it without water."

"There'll be plenty of water come spring."

Charles slowly shook his head. "Home's too far. We'd get there and have to turn right around and come back." He pushed his hands across his knees. "At present, we might have enough gold to get us home, but I don't think we have enough to get us back, and we certainly don't have enough to leave any for your ma or Uncle Jake."

Samuel took and folded the paper. His father was prepared to walk away from it. "Maybe Mr. Hinley can show these figures to someone who would buy it and send us the money," Samuel whispered. He felt his eyes burning. They had sacrificed so much to reach this point, their hopes, their dreams, everything they had worked for. *How could they be walking away?*

"That's a good idea. You should study on that, son."

*   *   *

That evening, snow clouds sifted into the valley. They finished a meal of leftover potatoes and venison. Their gear was packed and stood against the wall. Come morning, they would throw their bedding together, pack Molly, and leave for Iowa.

Charles suddenly shook his head. "Hell, Samuel, thanks to you, we have two really good prospects. The O'Riley could bust wide open and become a paying mine, and we might get a good run on the Sweet Mary." He studied Samuel. "What do you say we do?"

Samuel was surprised that his father asked.

"I want to see Ma and Elizabeth and Grandma and everyone, Pa, I really do—" he began.

"Then why do I keep second-guessing myself? Come morning, we'll go."

"—but I've put my very self into this. Except for winter stopping us, we can do it now. We can go home with good money like you wanted."

"I can make it without the money, Samuel. You know that."

"It's more, Pa. I want to prove it to myself as well."

Charles studied Samuel. "You're willing to stay on?"

Samuel nodded.

Slowly, Charles nodded. "Okay. We'll find that place on the river and stick out the winter. Soon as we can get in over the snow next spring, we're coming back. No second-guessing, though. Deal?" He stuck out his hand.

Samuel shook his father's hand. "Deal." A feeling of incredible joy swept over him. They were still in the game.

* * *

As he prepared for bed, Samuel noticed that snow had begun falling and was rapidly blanketing the meadow. He briefly worried they would be snowbound and unable to leave Warren's camp, but he knew the stock could push through a foot or more of snow if they had solid footing underneath. His father had said the meadow would get six feet, but he knew it would not be until midwinter. By then they would be on the river placer mining.

He glanced around their cabin. It had been home for several months. He wondered about the one they were heading to on the Salmon. He did not remember one on their trip in, and he worried that they might not find it. Then he worried there might not be enough placer gold in the river bar to see them through the winter. Already he knew the winter would take what gold they had mined just for them to stay alive and care for their stock.

* * *

Morning saw Charles and Samuel on the trail, fully packed and leading Molly, breaking the untouched snow before them, following a thin white thread that snaked through the timber toward Steamboat Summit.

Samuel turned to look back at the white emptiness of the country they had left. It was hard to fathom a town was back there, huddled in the falling snow, a town where people would somehow continue their lives through the winter and hope for summer. Samuel watched as some snow slid from the branches of a fir, showering down onto the trail behind them. Snowflakes snicked against his face.

He turned and urged Spooky forward, Molly plodding after. He warmly thought about the trail ahead and the chance they would have to visit the Shearers when they reached their ferry on the Salmon River, maybe late tomorrow. Perhaps they would stay the night. He thought of soon reaching Burgdorf's. They would probably not stay long, but Samuel knew his father would not refuse a hot swim. Maybe Jenkins would still be there, and he could tell him something more about the girl at Slate Creek. Samuel had been thinking of her. Being as they would be neighbors on the Salmon River, it might be possible to visit the town, maybe even see her. His heart quickened at the thought. But then he thought of Miss Lilly. He would see her come spring. He would see Hinley again and Scott. Only Chen did not know he would be returning. He thought of Chen, who would be down on the South Fork tending the gardens, maybe studying words from Ma Reynolds's book, hoping someday to return to China.

Inexplicably an ache crept over him. The winter ahead now seemed endless. Even if they found the cabin, how they would survive until April was a mystery.

ACKNOWLEDGMENTS

Many people have inspired and encouraged me to write, and each has had a part in this book. A special thanks goes to my family—to my wife, Susan, who has always supported my many interests, including my writing, and who offered insight on the foods of the times; to my sons, Scott and Tim, who accompanied me on numerous backpacking trips, including several to the Idaho Salmon River country; and to my daughter, Krystle, who always encouraged me to continue writing and helps with administrative support. Nothing was possible without my family.

As a boy, I grew up in McCall, Idaho, and wrote down the stories some of the pioneers of the region shared with me. Among these individuals are Sam and Jesse (Tim) Williams, Carmel Parks, Ray Beseker, and Dave Spielman. My father, William Dorris, a game warden and bush pilot, took me hunting in this country and related his stories, especially about the Sheepeater Indians. My brothers, who are also bush pilots, George, Mike, Pat, and Bill, all shared their knowledge of the Salmon River wilderness and accompanied me on my many trips as youngsters. My sister, Linda, read the manuscript, giving me valuable suggestions. Montana ranchers Jane Wertheimer and Jim Raths reviewed information on ranching. Don Chapman contributed information on the historic salmon runs and fishery.

Published sources included Johnny Carrey and Cort Conley's *River of No Return*, Sister M. Alfreda Elsensohn's two volumes, *Pioneer Days in Idaho County*, Cheryl Helmers's *Warren Times*, a compilation of news articles of the Warren region, Lawrence Kingsbury, various articles on the Chinese of Warren, and Dr. Liping Zhu's *A Chinaman's Chance*. Mining technical information was based on Leonard S. Austin's *The Fire Assay*, Frank Crampton's *Deep Enough*, and Otis E. Young's *Western Mining*.

The cover is from my oil painting titled *Warren Meadows,* and the line drawings are my pen and ink sketches.

AUTHOR'S NOTES

When I first visited Warren's camp (Warren, Idaho) as a young teenager, a longtime Warren prospector taught me how to recognize gold ore and took me to a quartz ledge that ran dozens of feet, the hanging wall showing visible gold in a rusty red quartz. The ledge, inaccessible and now reclaimed by the forest, is the basis for O'Riley's lost ledge.

In 1871, a teenage white boy and a teenage Chinese boy resided in Washington, Idaho Territory. Among historical people were Frederick, Susan, and their son, George Shearer, at their ferry (now the Howard Ranch); Fred Burgdorf at his hot springs; Warren Hunt; Charlie Bemis; Sheriff Sinclair; Doctor C. A. Sears; R. McLane; and Amasa (Pony) Smead. Historical vignettes involving these people are accurate, and readers will recognize other historical individuals used in context. How these individuals would have interacted with Samuel Chambers and Sing Chen are, of course, fictional. The life of Warren's camp is depicted as it could be based on historical accounts of the time.

All geography is described as it exists. Although some of the trails are lost, the routes described are accurate. Bare Knob Creek is known as the Left Fork of Slaughter Creek. Other place names from 1871 are used—for example, Elk Creek (now Elkhorn Creek). The mines and mills that are depicted and events surrounding them are historically correct. The Sweet Mary and the O'Riley are fictional but based on similar mines. Most of Warren's buildings have disappeared, but they included the businesses depicted, except for some names like Ma Reynolds's boarding house and Hinley's assay building. Little evidence of the Chinese structures remains. Some old Chinese cabins can be found buried under brush and timber. The Chinese cemetery remains. The Chinese terrace gardens remain, now overgrown and returning to the land.

The Chinese flooded into Idaho Territory during this novel's setting and remained at Warren, reworking old placers and peddling vegetables, bringing with them their opium and Oriental beliefs, living in their own ways, yet becoming an integral part of the community. At times, they outnumbered the whites three to one. As a result of the Chinese Exclusion Act of 1882, their numbers continued a steady decline until the last Chinese at Warren died in 1934.

This region is on the western edge of Sheepeater country, and the Sheepeater Indians depicted relate to characters in my first novel, *Sheepeater: To Cry for a Vision*. A forthcoming novel will further Samuel's life in the Warren country, and the follow-up to it will depict the Sheepeater War of 1879. The series will revolve around the same characters from *Sheepeater* and *Sojourner*.

The ghosts of this time can still be felt, and if one listens, their stories are still being told. I hope the reader grants me the leeway to weave these historical vignettes into a novel that allows me to share their stories.

CPSIA information can be obtained at www.ICGtesting.com
Printed in the USA
LVOW041923191211

260159LV00007B/68/P